PENROD
HIS COMPLETE STORY

Books By

BOOTH TARKINGTON

Alice Adams
Beasley's Christmas Party
Beauty and the Jacobin
Cherry
Claire Ambler
Conquest of Canaan
Gentle Julia
Growth
Harlequin and Columbine
His Own People
In the Arena
Looking Forward and Others
Mirthful Haven
Monsieur Beaucaire
Penrod
Penrod and Sam
Penrod, His Complete Story
Ramsey Milholland
Seventeen
The Beautiful Lady
The Fascinating Stranger and Other Stories
The Flirt
The Gentleman from Indiana
The Guest of Quesnay
The Magnificent Ambersons
The Man from Home
The Midlander
The New Penrod Book—Penrod Jashber
The Plutocrat
The Turmoil
The Two Vanrevels
The World Does Move
Women
Young Mrs. Greeley

Books By

BOOTH TARKINGTON

"*My goodness!*" *Penrod said indignantly. "Don't you know anything at all!*"

PENROD
HIS COMPLETE STORY

PENROD · PENROD AND SAM
PENROD JASHBER

BY
BOOTH TARKINGTON

Illustrated by
GORDON GRANT

DOUBLEDAY & COMPANY, INC.
Garden City, New York

A DEDICATORY WORD BY THE AUTHOR

THIS book owes its existence to a lady connected by marriage with the writer, for at the time of her consent to become thus related she made virtually the condition that he should write something about a boy. Not long afterward—that is to say some nineteen years ago—her insistence upon his living up to the letter of the contract became so pressing that with a mind much misdoubting his knowledge of a dangerous subject he projected the first of these Penrodic episodes into manuscript, and, upon reading it to its real progenitor, found that it amused her encouragingly. Naturally, then, hoping to continue Mrs. Tarkington's amusements, he went on writing something about a boy, and, a year later, published "Penrod", Part I of this present volume. Part II, "Penrod and Sam", appeared as a book in Nineteen-Sixteen; the principal substance of "Penrod Jashber", Part III, although written at about that time, was not published as a book until more than a decade later.

Throughout this period, which extends from the first appearance of "Penrod" in a magazine now perished, the writer has received from affable readers, strangers to him, encouragement to discourse further upon the subject, and, as this encouragement still amiably increases rather than diminishes his correspondence, he has come to an agreement with his publisher that a complete and slightly edited edition, containing all he knows or can know upon the subject, might in time usefully supplant the earlier more fragmentary volumes. Therefore the compilation has been made and is here displayed as the author's final word upon "a boy's doings in the days when the stable was empty but not yet rebuilt into a garage."

It seems fitting that the earlier dedications of the three
component parts be preserved in the order of previous pub-
lication: that to the three nephews, John, Donald and Booth
Jameson, to whom the writer has naturally a special gratitude for "material kindly and unconsciously supplied", that
to Mrs. Tarkington who was the rewarding progenitor of
the whole, and that to Dr. William Holland Wilmer who
has enabled the writer seeingly and gratefully to inscribe
the signature

BOOTH TARKINGTON.

CONTENTS

PART ONE

PENROD

PART TWO

PENROD AND SAM

PART THREE

PENROD JASHBER

CONTENTS.

ILLUSTRATIONS

IN COLOUR

IN BLACK AND WHITE

PART ONE

PENROD

CHAPTER I

A BOY AND HIS DOG

PENROD sat morosely upon the back fence and gazed with envy at Duke, his wistful dog.

A bitter soul dominated the various curved and angular surfaces known by a careless world as the face of Penrod Schofield. Except in solitude, that face was almost always cryptic and emotionless; for Penrod had come into his twelfth year wearing an expression carefully trained to be inscrutable. Since the world was sure to misunderstand everything, mere defensive instinct prompted him to give it as little as possible to lay hold upon. Nothing is more impenetrable than the face of a boy who has learned this, and Penrod's was habitually as fathomless as the depth of his hatred this morning for the literary activities of Mrs.

Lora Rewbush—an almost universally respected fellow-citizen, a lady of charitable and poetic inclinations, and one of his own mother's most intimate friends.

Mrs. Lora Rewbush had written something that she called "The Children's Pageant of the Table Round", and it was to be performed in public that very afternoon at the Women's Arts and Guild Hall for the benefit of the Coloured Infants' Betterment Society. And if any flavour of sweetness remained in the nature of Penrod Schofield after the dismal trials of the school-week just past, that problematic, infinitesimal remnant was made pungent acid by the imminence of his destiny to form a prominent feature of the spectacle, and to declaim the loathsome sentiments of a character named upon the programme the Child Sir Lancelot.

After each rehearsal he had plotted escape, and only ten days earlier there had been a glimmer of light: Mrs. Lora Rewbush caught a very bad cold, and it was hoped it might develop into pneumonia; but she recovered so quickly that not even a rehearsal of the Children's Pageant was postponed. Darkness closed in. Penrod had rather vaguely debated plans for a self-mutilation such as would make his appearance as the Child Sir Lancelot inexpedient on public grounds. It was a heroic and attractive thought; but the results of some extremely sketchy preliminary experiments caused him to abandon it.

There was no escape; and at last his hour was hard upon him. Therefore he brooded on the fence and gazed with envy at his wistful Duke.

The dog's name was undescriptive of his person, which was obviously the result of a singular series of mésalliances. He wore a grizzled moustache and indefinite whiskers; he was small and shabby, and looked like an old postman. Penrod envied Duke because he was sure Duke would never be compelled to be a Child Sir Lancelot. He thought a dog free and unshackled to go or come as the wind listeth. Penrod forgot the life he led Duke.

There was a long soliloquy upon the fence, a plaintive monologue without words: the boy's thoughts were adjectives, but they were expressed by a running film of pictures in his mind's eye, morbidly prophetic of the hideosities before him. Finally he spoke aloud, with such spleen that Duke rose from his haunches and lifted one ear in keen anxiety.

> " 'I hight Sir Lancelot du Lake, the Child,
> Gentul-hearted, meek, and mild.
> What though I'm *but* a littul child,
> Gentul-hearted, meek, and——' *Oof!*"

All of this except "oof" was a quotation from the Child Sir Lancelot, as conceived by Mrs. Lora Rewbush. Choking upon it, Penrod slid down from the fence, and with slow and thoughtful steps entered a one-storied wing of the stable, consisting of a single apartment, floored with cement and used as a storeroom for broken bric-à-brac, old paint-buckets, decayed garden-hose, worn-out carpets, dead furniture, and other condemned odds and ends not yet considered hopeless enough to be given away.

In one corner stood a large box, a part of the building itself; it was eight feet high and open at the top, and it had been constructed as a sawdust magazine from which was drawn material for the horse's bed in a stall on the other side of the partition. The big box, so high and towerlike, so commodious, so suggestive, had ceased to fulfil its legitimate function, though, providentially, it had been at least half full of sawdust when the horse died. Two years had gone by since that passing; an interregnum in transportation during which Penrod's father was "thinking" (he explained sometimes) of an automobile. Meanwhile, the gifted and generous sawdust-box had served brilliantly in war and peace: it was Penrod's stronghold.

There was a partially defaced sign upon the front wall

of the box; the donjon-keep had known mercantile impulses:

The O. K. RaBiT Co.
PENROD ScHoFiELD AND CO.
iNQuiRE FOR PRicEs

This was a venture of the preceding vacation, and had netted, at one time, an accrued and owed profit of $1.38. Prospects had been brightest on the very eve of cataclysm. The storeroom was locked and guarded; but twenty-seven rabbits and Belgian hares, old and young, had perished here on a single night—through no human agency, but in a foray of cats, the besiegers treacherously tunnelling up through the sawdust from the small aperture that opened into the stall beyond the partition. Commerce has its martyrs.

Penrod climbed upon a barrel, stood on tiptoe, grasped the rim of the box; then, using a knot-hole as a stirrup, threw one leg over the top, drew himself up, and dropped within. Standing upon the packed sawdust, he was just tall enough to see over the top.

Duke had not followed him into the storeroom, but remained near the open doorway in a concave and pessimistic attitude. Penrod felt in a dark corner of the box and laid hands upon a simple apparatus consisting of an old bushel-basket with a few yards of clothes-line tied to each of its handles. He passed the ends of the lines over a big spool, which revolved upon an axle of wire suspended from a beam overhead, and, with the aid of this improvised pulley, lowered the empty basket until it came to rest in an upright position upon the floor of the storeroom at the foot of the sawdust-box.

"Elevay-ter!" shouted Penrod. "Ting-ting!"

Duke, old and intelligently apprehensive, approached slowly, in a semicircular manner, deprecatingly, but with courtesy. He pawed the basket delicately; then, as if that were all his master had expected of him, uttered one bright

"Elevay-ter!" shouted Penrod. "Ting-ting!"

bark, sat down and looked up triumphantly. His hypocrisy was shallow: many a horrible quarter of an hour had taught him his duty in this matter.

"El-e-*vay*-ter!" shouted Penrod sternly. "You want me to come down there *to* you?"

Duke looked suddenly haggard. He pawed the basket feebly again and, upon another outburst from on high, prostrated himself flat. Again threatened, he gave a superb impersonation of a worm.

"You get in that el-e-vAy-ter!"

Reckless with despair, Duke jumped into the basket, landing in a dishevelled posture, which he did not alter until he had been drawn up and poured out upon the floor of sawdust within the box. There, shuddering, he lay in doughnut shape and presently slumbered.

It was dark in the box, a condition that might have been remedied by sliding back a small wooden panel on runners, which would have let in ample light from the alley; but Penrod Schofield had more interesting means of illumination. He knelt, and from a former soap-box, in a corner, took a lantern without a chimney, and a large oil-can, the leak in the latter being so nearly imperceptible that its banishment from household use had seemed to Penrod as inexplicable as it was providential.

He shook the lantern near his ear: nothing splashed; there was no sound but a dry clinking. But there was plenty of kerosene in the can; and he filled the lantern, striking a match to illumine the operation. Then he lit the lantern and hung it upon a nail against the wall. The sawdust floor was slightly impregnated with oil, and the open flame quivered in suggestive proximity to the side of the box; however, some rather deep charrings of the plank against which the lantern hung offered evidence that the arrangement was by no means a new one, and indicated at least a possibility of no fatality occurring this time.

Next, Penrod turned up the surface of the sawdust in another corner of the floor, and drew forth a cigar-box in which were half a dozen cigarettes, made of hayseed and thick brown wrapping paper, a lead-pencil, an eraser, and a small note-book, the cover of which was labelled in his own handwriting:

"English Grammar. Penrod Schofield. Room 6, Ward School Nomber Seventh."

The first page of this book was purely academic; but the study of English undefiled terminated with a slight jar at the top of the second: "Nor must an adverb be used to modif——"

Immediately followed:

"HARoLD RAMoREZ THE RoADAGENT
OR WiLD LiFE AMoNG THE
ROCKY MTS."

And the subsequent entries in the book appeared to have little concern with Room 6, Ward School Nomber Seventh.

MR WILSON

CHAPTER II

ROMANCE

THE author of "Harold Ramorez", etc., lit one of the hayseed cigarettes, seated himself comfortably, with his back against the wall and his right shoulder just under the lantern, elevated his knees to support the note-book, turned to a blank page, and wrote, slowly and earnestly:

"CHAPITER THE SIXTH"

He took a knife from his pocket, and, broodingly, his eyes upon the inward embryos of vision, sharpened his pencil. After that, he extended a foot and meditatively rubbed Duke's back with the side of his shoe. Creation, with Pen-

11

rod, did not leap, full-armed, from the brain; but finally he began to produce. He wrote very slowly at first, and then with increasing rapidity; faster and faster, gathering momentum and growing more and more fevered as he sped, till at last the true fire came, without which no lamp of real literature may be made to burn.

Mr. Wilson reched for his gun but our hero had him covred and soon said Well I guess you don't come any of that on me my freind.

Well what makes you so sure about it sneered the other bitting his lip so savageley that the blood ran. You are nothing but a common Roadagent any way and I do not propose to be bafled by such, Ramorez laughed at this and kep Mr. Wilson covred by his ottomatick

Soon the two men were struggling together in the deathroes but soon Mr Wilson got him bound and gaged his mouth and went away for awhile leavin our hero, it was dark and he writhd at his bonds writhing on the floor wile the rats came out of their holes and bit him and vernim got all over him from the floor of that helish spot but soon he manged to push the gag out of his mouth with the end of his toungeu and got all his bonds off

Soon Mr Wilson came back to tant him with his helpless condition flowed by his gang of detectives and they said Oh look at Ramorez sneering at his plight and tanted him with his helpless condition because Ramorez had put the bonds back sos he would look the same but could throw them off him when he wanted to Just look at him now sneered they. To hear him talk you would thought he was hot stuff and they said Look at him now, him that was going to do so much, Oh I would not like to be in his fix

Soon Harold got mad at this and jumped up with blasing eyes throwin off his bonds like they were air   Ha Ha sneered he I guess you better not talk so much next time. Soon there flowed another awful struggle and siezin his ottomatick back from Mr Wilson he shot two of the detectives through the heart Bing Bing went the ottomatick and two more went to meet their Maker only two detectives left now and so he stabbed one and the scondrel went to meet his Maker for now our hero was fighting for his very life. It was dark in there now for night had falen and a terrible view met the eye Blood was just all over everything and the rats were eatin the dead men.

Soon our hero manged to get his back to the wall for he was fighting for his very life now and shot Mr Wilson through the abodmen   Oh said Mr Wilson you —— —— —— (*The dashes are Penrod's.*)

Mr Wilson stagerd back vile oaths soilin his lips for he was in pain Why you—— ——you sneered he I will get you yet —— ——you Harold Ramorez

The remanin scondrel had an ax which he came near our heros head with but missed him and ramand stuck in the wall Our heros amunition was exhausted what was he to do, the remanin scondrel would soon get his ax lose so our hero sprung forward and bit him till his teeth met in the flech for now our hero was fighting for his very life. At this the remanin scondrel also cursed and swore vile oaths. Oh sneered he—— —— ——you Harold Ramorez what did you bite me for Yes sneered Mr Wilson also and he has shot me in the abodmen too the——

Soon they were both cursin and reviln him together Why you —— —— —— —— ——sneered they what did you want to injure us for——you Harold Ramorez you have not got any sence and you think you are so much but you are no better than anybody else and you are a—— —— —— —— —— ——

Soon our hero could stand this no longer. If you could learn to act like gentlmen said he I would not do any more to you now and your low vile exppresions have not got any effect on me only to injure your own self when you go to meet your Maker Oh I guess you have had enogh for one day and I think you have learned a lesson and will not soon atemp to beard Harold Ramorez again so with a tantig laugh he cooly lit a cigarrete and takin the keys of the cell from Mr Wilson poket went on out

Soon Mr Wilson and the wonded detective manged to bind up their wonds and got up off the floor—— ——it I will have that dasstads life now sneered they if we have to swing for it —— —— —— ——him he shall not eccape us again the low down —— —— —— —— ——

Chapter seventh

A mule train of heavily laden burros laden with gold from the mines was to be seen wondering among the highest clifts and

gorgs of the Rocky Mts and a tall man with a long silken mus-
tash and a cartigde belt could be heard cursin vile oaths because
he well knew this was the lair of Harold Ramorez Why—— ——
——you you—— —— —— ——mules you sneered he because the
poor mules were not able to go any quicker——you I will show
you Why —— —— —— —— —— ——it sneered he his oaths
growing viler and viler I will whip you—— —— —— —— ——
—— ——you sos you will not be able to walk for a week——
——you you mean old—— —— —— —— —— —— —— ——
——mules you

Scarcly had the vile words left his lips when——

"Penrod!"

It was his mother's voice, calling from the back porch.
Simultaneously, the noon whistles began to blow, far and
near; and the romancer in the sawdust-box, summoned
prosaically from steep mountain passes above the clouds,
paused with stubby pencil half-way from lip to knee. His
eyes were shining; there was a rapt sweetness in his gaze.
As he wrote, his burden had grown lighter; thoughts of
Mrs. Lora Rewbush had almost left him; and in particular
as he recounted (even by the chaste dash) the annoyed expressions of Mr. Wilson, the wounded detective, and the
silken moustached mule-driver, he had felt mysteriously relieved concerning the Child Sir Lancelot. Altogether he
looked a better and a brighter boy.

"Pen-*rod!*"

The rapt look faded slowly. He sighed but moved not.

"Penrod! We're having lunch early just on your account,
so you'll have plenty of time to be dressed for the
pageant. Hurry!"

There was silence in Penrod's eyry.

"*Pen*-rod!"

Mrs. Schofield's voice sounded nearer, indicating a threatened approach. Penrod bestirred himself: he blew out the
lantern, and shouted plaintively:

"Well, ain't I coming fast's I can?"

"Do hurry," the voice returned, withdrawing; and the kitchen door could be heard to close.

Languidly, Penrod proceeded to set his house in order.

Replacing his manuscript and pencil in the cigar-box, he carefully buried the box in the sawdust, put the lantern and oil-can back in the soap-box, adjusted the elevator for the reception of Duke, and, in no uncertain tone, invited the devoted animal to enter.

Duke stretched himself amiably, affecting not to hear; and, when this pretence became so obvious that even a dog could keep it up no longer, sat down in a corner, facing it, his back to his master and his head perpendicular, nose upward, supported by the convergence of the two walls. This, from a dog, is the last word, the *comble* of the immutable. Penrod commanded, stormed, tried gentleness; persuaded with honeyed words and pictured rewards. Duke's eyes looked backward; otherwise he moved not. Time elapsed. Penrod stooped to flattery—finally to insincere caresses; then, losing patience, spouted sudden threats. Duke remained immovable, frozen fast to his great gesture of implacable despair.

A footstep sounded on the threshold of the storeroom.

"Penrod, come down from that box this instant!"

"Ma'am?"

"Are you up in that sawdust-box again?" As Mrs. Schofield had just heard her son's voice issue from the box, and also, as she knew he was there anyhow, her question must have been put for oratorical purposes only. "Because if you are," she continued promptly, "I'm going to ask your papa not to let you play there any——"

Penrod's forehead, his eyes, the tops of his ears and most of his hair, became visible to her at the top of the box. "I ain't 'playing'!" he said indignantly.

"Well, what *are* you doing?"

"Just coming down," he replied, in a grieved but patient tone.

"Then why don't you *come?*"

"I got Duke here. I got to get him *down*, haven't I? You don't suppose I want to leave a poor dog in here to starve, do you?"

"Well, hand him down over the side to me. Let me——"

"I'll get him down all right," said Penrod. "I got him up here, and I guess I can get him down!"

"Well then, *do* it!"

"I will if you'll let me alone. If you'll go on back to the house I promise to be there inside of two minutes. Honest!"

He put extreme urgency into this, and his mother turned toward the house. "If you're not there in two minutes——"

"I will be!"

After her departure, Penrod expended some finalities of eloquence upon Duke, then disgustedly gathered him up in his arms, dumped him into the basket and, shouting sternly, "All in for the ground floor—step back there, madam—all ready, Jim!" lowered dog and basket to the floor of the store-room. Duke sprang out in tumultuous relief and bestowed frantic affection upon his master as the latter slid down from the box.

Penrod dusted himself sketchily, experiencing a sense of satisfaction, dulled by the overhanging afternoon, perhaps, but perceptible; he had the feeling of one who has been true to a cause. The operation of the elevator was unsinful and, save for the shock to Duke's nervous system, it was harmless; but Penrod could not possibly have brought himself to exhibit it in the presence of his mother or any other grown person in the world. The reasons for secrecy were undefined; at least, Penrod did not define them.

CHAPTER III

THE COSTUME

AFTER lunch his mother and his sister Margaret, a pretty girl of nineteen, dressed him for the sacrifice. They stood him near his mother's bedroom window and did what they would to him.

During the earlier anguishes of the process he was mute, exceeding the pathos of the stricken calf in the shambles; but a student of eyes might have perceived in his soul the premonitory symptoms of a sinister uprising. At a rehearsal (in citizens' clothes) attended by mothers and grown-up sisters, Mrs. Lora Rewbush had announced that she wished the costuming to be "as mediæval and artistic as possible". Otherwise, and as to details, she said, she would leave the costumes entirely to the good taste of the children's parents.

17

Mrs. Schofield and Margaret were no archæologists, but they knew that their taste was as good as that of other mothers and sisters concerned; so with perfect confidence they had planned and executed a costume for Penrod, and the only misgiving they felt was connected with the tractability of the Child Sir Lancelot himself.

Stripped to his underwear, he had been made to wash himself vehemently; then they began by shrouding his legs in a pair of silk stockings, once blue but now mostly whitish. Upon Penrod they visibly surpassed mere ampleness; but they were long, and it required only a rather loose imagination to assume that they were tights.

The upper part of his body was next concealed from view by a garment so peculiar that its description becomes difficult. In 1886, Mrs. Schofield, then unmarried, had worn at her "coming-out party" a dress of vivid salmon silk that had been remodelled after her marriage to accord with various epochs of fashion until a final, unskilful campaign at a dye-house had left it in a condition certain to attract much attention to the wearer. Mrs. Schofield had considered giving it to Della, the cook; but had decided not to do so, because you never could tell how Della was going to take things, and cooks were scarce.

It may have been the word "mediæval" (in Mrs. Lora Rewbush's rich phrase) that had inspired the idea for a last conspicuous usefulness; at all events, the bodice of that once salmon dress, somewhat modified and moderated, now took a position, for its farewell appearance in society, upon the back, breast and arms of the Child Sir Lancelot.

The area thus costumed ceased at the waist, leaving a Jaeger-like and unmediæval gap thence to the tops of the stockings. The inventive genius of woman triumphantly bridged it, but in a manner that imposes upon history almost insuperable delicacies of narration. Penrod's father was an old-fashioned man: the twentieth century had failed to shake his faith in red flannel for cold weather; and it was while Mrs. Schofield was putting away her husband's winter

"Oh, that's all right," said Margaret. "They always powdered their hair in Colonial times."

underwear that she perceived how hopelessly one of the elder specimens had dwindled; and simultaneously she received the inspiration that resulted in a pair of trunks for the Child Sir Lancelot, and added an earnest bit of colour, as well as a genuine touch of the Middle Ages, to his costume. Reversed, fore to aft, with the greater part of the legs cut off, and strips of silver braid covering the seams, this garment, she felt, was not traceable to its original source.

When it had been placed upon Penrod, the stockings were attached to it by a system of safety-pins, not very perceptible at a distance. Next, after being severely warned against stooping, Penrod got his feet into the slippers he wore to dancing-school—"patent-leather pumps" now decorated with large pink rosettes.

"If I can't stoop," he began, smolderingly, "I'd like to know how'm I goin' to kneel in the pag——"

"You must *manage!*" This, uttered through pins, was evidently thought to be sufficient.

They fastened some ruching about his slender neck, pinned ribbons at random all over him, and then Margaret thickly powdered his hair.

"Oh, yes, that's all right," she said, replying to a question put by her mother. "They always powdered their hair in Colonial times."

"It doesn't seem right to me—exactly," Mrs. Schofield objected gently. "Sir Lancelot must have been ever so long before Colonial times."

"That doesn't matter," Margaret reassured her. "Nobody'll know the difference—Mrs. Lora Rewbush least of all. I don't think she knows a thing about it, though, of course, she does write splendidly and the words of the pageant are just beautiful. Stand still, Penrod!" (The author of "Harold Ramorez" had moved convulsively.) "Besides, powdered hair's always becoming. Look at him. You'd hardly know it was Penrod!"

The pride and admiration with which she pronounced this undeniable truth might have been thought tactless;

but Penrod, not analytical, found his spirits somewhat
elevated. No mirror was in his range of vision and, though
he had submitted to cursory measurements of his person a
week earlier, he had no previous acquaintance with the
costume. He began to form a not unpleasing mental picture
of his appearance, something somewhere between the portraits of George Washington and a vivid memory of Miss
Julia Marlowe at a matinée of "Twelfth Night".

He was additionally cheered by a sword that had been
borrowed from a neighbour who was a Knight of Pythias.
Finally there was a mantle, an old golf cape of Margaret's.
Fluffy polka-dots of white cotton had been sewed to it
generously; also it was ornamented with a large cross of red
flannel, suggested by the picture of a Crusader in a newspaper advertisement. The mantle was fastened to Penrod's
shoulder (that is, to the shoulder of Mrs. Schofield's ex-
bodice) by means of large safety-pins, and arranged to
hang down behind him, touching his heels, but obscuring
nowise the glory of his façade. Then, at last, he was allowed
to step before a mirror.

It was a full-length glass, and the worst immediately
happened. It might have been a little less violent, perhaps,
if Penrod's expectations had not been so richly and poeti-
cally idealized; but, as things were, the revolt was volcanic.

Victor Hugo's account of the fight with the devilfish in
"Toilers of the Sea" encourages a belief that, had Hugo
lived and increased in power, he might have been equal to
a proper recital of the half hour that followed Penrod's
first sight of himself as the Child Sir Lancelot. But Mr.
Wilson himself, dastard but eloquent foe of Harold Ramorez, could not have expressed, with all the vile dashes at
his command, the sentiments that animated Penrod's bosom
when the instantaneous and unalterable conviction descended
upon him that he was intended by his loved ones to make a
public spectacle of himself in his sister's stockings and part
of an old dress of his mother's.

To him these familiar things were not disguised at all;

there seemed no possibility that the whole world would not know them at a glance. The stockings were worse than the bodice. He had been assured that these could not be recognized; but, seeing them in the mirror, he was certain that no human eye could fail at first glance to detect the difference between himself and the former purposes of these stockings. Fold, wrinkle and void shrieked their history with a hundred tongues, invoking earthquake, eclipse and blue ruin. The frantic youth's final submission was obtained only after a painful telephonic conversation between himself and his father, the latter having been called up and upon, by the exhausted Mrs. Schofield, to subjugate his offspring by wire.

The two ladies made all possible haste, after this, to deliver Penrod into the hands of Mrs. Lora Rewbush; nevertheless, they found opportunity to exchange earnest congratulations upon his not having recognized the humble but serviceable paternal garment now brilliant about the Lancelotish middle. Altogether, they felt that the costume was a success. Penrod looked like nothing ever remotely imagined by Sir Thomas Malory or Alfred Tennyson;— for that matter, he looked like nothing ever before seen on earth; but, as Mrs. Schofield and Margaret took their places in the audience at the Women's Arts and Guild Hall, the anxiety they felt concerning Penrod's elocutionary and gesticular powers, so soon to be put to public test, was pleasantly tempered by their satisfaction that, owing to their efforts, his outward appearance would be a credit to the family.

CHAPTER IV

DESPERATION

THE Child Sir Lancelot found himself in a large anteroom behind the stage—a room crowded with excited children, all about equally mediæval and artistic. Penrod was less conspicuous than he thought himself; but he was so preoccupied with his own shame, steeling his nerves to meet the first inevitable taunting reference to his sister's stockings, that he failed to perceive there were others present in much of his own unmanned condition. Retiring to a corner immediately upon his entrance, he managed to unfasten the mantle at the shoulders, and, drawing it round him, pinned it again at his throat so that it concealed the rest of his costume. This permitted a temporary relief but increased his horror of the moment when,

In pursuance of the action of the "pageant", the sheltering garment must be cast aside.

Some of the other child knights were also keeping their mantles close about them. A few of the envied opulent swung brilliant fabrics from their shoulders airily, showing off hired splendours from a professional costumer's stock, while one or two were insulting examples of parental indulgence, particularly little Maurice Levy, the Child Sir Galahad. This shrinking person went clamorously about, making it known everywhere that the best tailor in town had been dazzled by a great sum into constructing his costume. It consisted of blue velvet knickerbockers, a white satin waistcoat, and a beautifully cut little swallow-tailed coat with pearl buttons. The mediæval and artistic triumph was completed by a mantle of yellow velvet and little white boots, sporting gold tassels.

All this radiance paused in a brilliant career and addressed the Child Sir Lancelot, gathering an immediately formed semicircular audience of little girls. Woman was ever the trailer of magnificence.

"What *you* got on?" inquired Mr. Levy, after dispensing information. "What you got on under that ole golf cape?"

Penrod looked upon him coldly. At other times his questioner would have approached him with deference, even with apprehension. But to-day the Child Sir Galahad was somewhat intoxicated with the power of his own beauty.

"What *you* got on?" he repeated.

"Oh, nothin'," said Penrod, with an indifference assumed at great cost to his nervous system.

The elate Maurice was inspired to set up as a wit. "Then you're nakid!" he shouted exultantly. "Penrod Schofield says he hasn't got nothin' on under that ole golf cape! He's nakid! He's nakid."

The indelicate little girls giggled delightedly, and a javelin pierced the inwards of Penrod when he saw that the Child Elaine, amber-curled and beautiful Marjorie Jones, lifted golden laughter to the horrid jest.

Other boys and girls came flocking to the uproar. "He's nakid, he's nakid!" shrieked the Child Sir Galahad. "Penrod Schofield's nakid! He's *na-a-a-kid!*"

"Hush, hush!" Mrs. Lora Rewbush cried, pushing her way into the group. "Remember, we are all little knights and ladies to-day. Little knights and ladies of the Table Round would not make so much noise. Now, children, we must begin to take our places on the stage. Is everybody here?"

Penrod made his escape under cover of this diversion; he slid behind Mrs. Lora Rewbush, and, being near a door, opened it unnoticed and went out quickly, closing it behind him. He found himself in a narrow and vacant hallway that led to a door marked "Janitor's Room".

Burning with outrage, heart-sick at the sweet, cold-blooded laughter of Marjorie Jones, Penrod rested his elbows upon a window-sill and speculated upon the effects of a leap from the second story. One of the reasons he gave it up was his desire to live on Maurice Levy's account: already he was forming educational plans for the Child Sir Galahad.

A stout man in blue overalls passed through the hallway, muttering to himself petulantly. "I reckon they'll find that hall hot enough *now!*" he said, conveying to Penrod an impression that some too feminine women had sent him upon an unreasonable errand to the furnace. He went into the Janitor's Room and, emerging a moment later, minus the overalls, passed Penrod again with a bass rumble— "Dern 'em!" it seemed he said—and made a gloomy exit by the door at the upper end of the hallway.

The conglomerate and delicate rustle of a large, mannerly audience was heard as the janitor opened and closed the door; and stage-fright seized the boy. The orchestra began an overture, and, at that, Penrod, trembling violently, tip-toed down the hall into the Janitor's Room. It was a cul-de-sac: there was no outlet save by the way he had come.

Despairingly he doffed his mantle and looked down upon

himself for a last sickening assurance that the stockings were as obviously and disgracefully Margaret's as they had seemed in the mirror at home. For a moment he was encouraged: perhaps he was no worse than some of the other boys. Then he noticed that a safety-pin had opened; one of those connecting the stockings with his trunks. He sat down to fasten it and his eye fell for the first time with particular attention upon the trunks. Until this instant he had been preoccupied with the stockings.

Slowly recognition dawned in his eyes.

The Schofields' house stood on a corner at the intersection of two main-travelled streets; the fence was low, and the publicity obtained by the washable portion of the family apparel, on Mondays, had often been painful to Penrod; for boys have a peculiar sensitiveness in these matters. A plain, matter-of-fact washerwoman, employed by Mrs. Schofield, never left anything to the imagination of the passer-by; and of all her calm display the scarlet flaunting of his father's winter wear had most abashed Penrod. One day Marjorie Jones, all gold and starch, had passed when the dreadful things were on the line; Penrod had hidden himself, shuddering. The whole town, he was convinced, knew these garments intimately and derisively.

And now, as he sat in the janitor's chair, the horrible and paralyzing recognition came. He had not an instant's doubt that every fellow-actor, as well as every soul in the audience, would recognize what his mother and sister had put upon him. For as the awful truth became plain to himself it seemed blazoned to the world; and far, far louder than the stockings, the trunks did fairly bellow the grisly secret: *whose* they were and WHAT they were!

Most people have suffered in a dream the experience of finding themselves very inadequately clad in the midst of a crowd of well-dressed people, and such dreamers' sensations are comparable to Penrod's, though faintly, because Penrod was awake and in much too full possession of the most active capacities for anguish.

A human male whose dress has been damaged, or reveals some vital lack, suffers from a hideous and shameful loneliness that makes every second absolutely unbearable until he is again as others of his sex and species; and there is no act or sin whatever too desperate for him in his struggle to attain that condition. Also, there is absolutely no embarrassment possible to a woman which is comparable to that of a man under corresponding circumstances; and in this a boy is a man. Gazing upon the ghastly trunks, the stricken Penrod felt that he was a degree worse than nude; and a great horror of himself filled his soul.

"Penrod Schofield!"

The door into the hallway opened, and a voice demanded him. He could not be seen from the hallway; but the hue and the cry was up, and he knew he must be taken. It was only a question of seconds. He huddled in his chair.

"Penrod Schofield!" Mrs. Lora Rewbush cried angrily. The distracted boy rose and, as he did so, a long pin sank deep into his back. He extracted it frenziedly, which brought to his ears a protracted and sonorous ripping too easily located by a final gesture of horror.

"Penrod Schofield!" Mrs. Lora Rewbush had come out into the hallway.

And now, in this extremity, when all seemed lost indeed, particularly including honour, the dilating eye of the outlaw fell upon the blue overalls that the janitor had left hanging upon a peg.

Inspiration and action were almost simultaneous.

CHAPTER V

THE PAGEANT OF THE TABLE ROUND

PENROD!" Mrs. Lora Rewbush stood in the doorway, indignantly gazing upon a Child Sir Lancelot mantled to the heels. "Do you know that you have kept an audience of five hundred people waiting for ten minutes?" She, also, detained the five hundred while she spake further.

"Well," Penrod said contentedly, as he followed her toward the buzzing stage, "I was just sitting there thinking."

Two minutes later the curtain rose on a mediæval castle hall richly done in the new stage-craft made in Germany and consisting of pink and blue cheesecloth. The Child King Arthur and the Child Queen Guinevere were disclosed upon thrones, with the Child Elaine and many other celebrities in attendance; while about fifteen Child Knights were seated at a dining-room table round that was covered with a large Oriental rug and displayed (for the knights' refreshment) a banquet service of silver loving-cups and trophies borrowed from the Country Club and some local automobile manufacturers.

In addition to this splendour, potted plants and palms have seldom been more lavishly used in any castle on the stage or off. The footlights were aided by a "spot-light" from the rear of the hall; and the children were revealed in a blaze of glory.

A hushed, multitudinous "O-*oh*" of admiration came from the decorous and delighted audience. Then the children sang feebly:

> "Chuldrun of the Tabul Round,
>   Lit-tul knights and ladies we.
> Let our voy-siz all resound
>   Faith and hope and charitee!"

The Child King Arthur rose, extended his sceptre with the decisive gesture of a semaphore, and spake:

> "Each littul knight and lady born
> Has noble deeds *to* perform
> In *thee* child-world of shivullree,
> No matter how small his share may be.
> Let each advance and tell in turn
> What claim has each to knighthood earn."

The Child Sir Mordred, the villain of this piece, rose in his place at the table round, and piped the only lines ever written by Mrs. Lora Rewbush that Penrod Schofield could have pronounced without loathing. Georgie Bassett, a really angelic boy, had been selected for the rôle of Mordred. His perfect conduct had earned for him the sardonic sobriquet, "The Little Gentleman", among his boy acquaintances. (Naturally he had no friends.) Hence the other boys supposed that he had been selected for the wicked Mordred as a reward of virtue. He declaimed serenely:

> "I hight Sir Mordred the Child, and I teach
> Lessons of selfishest evil, and reach
> Out into darkness. Thoughtless, unkind,
> And ruthless is Mordred, and unrefined."

The Child Mordred was properly rebuked and denied the accolade, though, like the others, he seemed to have assumed the title already. He made a plotter's exit. Whereupon Maurice Levy rose, bowed, announced that he highted the Child Sir Galahad, and continued with perfect *sang-froid:*

> "I am the purest of the pure.
> I have but kindest thoughts each day.
> I give my riches to the poor,
> And follow in the Master's way."

This elicited tokens of approval from the Child King Arthur, and he bade Maurice "stand forth" and come near the throne, a command obeyed with the easy grace of conscious merit.

It was Penrod's turn. He stepped back from his chair, the table between him and the audience, and began in a high, breathless monotone:

> "I hight Sir Lancelot du Lake, the Child,
> Gentul-hearted, meek, and mild.
> What though I'm *but a* littul child,
> Gentul-heartud, meek, and mild,
> I do my share though but—though but——"

Penrod paused and gulped. The voice of Mrs. Lora Rewbush was heard from the wings, prompting irritably, and the Child Sir Lancelot repeated:

> "I do my share though but—though but a tot,
> I pray you knight Sir Lancelot!"

This also met the royal favour, and Penrod was bidden to join Sir Galahad at the throne. As he crossed the stage,

Mrs. Schofield whispered to Margaret: "That boy! He's unpinned his mantle and fixed it to cover his whole costume. After we worked so hard to make it becoming!"

"Never mind; he'll have to take the cape off in a minute," Margaret returned. She leaned forward suddenly, narrowing her eyes to see better. "What *is* that thing hanging about his left ankle?" she whispered uneasily. "How queer! He must have got tangled in something."

"Where?" Mrs. Schofield asked in alarm.

"His left foot. It makes him stumble. Don't you see? It looks—it looks like an elephant's foot!"

The Child Sir Lancelot and the Child Sir Galahad clasped hands before their Child King. Penrod was conscious of a great uplift. In a moment he would have to throw aside his mantle; but even so he was protected and sheltered in the human garment of a man. His stage-fright had passed, for the audience was but an indistinguishable blur of darkness beyond the dazzling lights. His most repulsive speech (that in which he proclaimed himself a "tot") was over and done with; and now at last the small, moist hand of the Child Sir Galahad lay within his own. Craftily his brown fingers stole from Maurice's palm to the wrist. The two boys declaimed in concert:

> "We are two chuldrun of the Tabul Round
>   Strewing kindness all a-round.
> With love and good deeds striving ever for the best,
>   May our littul efforts e'er be blest.
> Two littul hearts we offer. See
> United in love, faith, hope, and char—*Ow!*"

The conclusion of the duet was marred. The Child Sir Galahad suddenly stiffened, and, uttering an irrepressible shriek of anguish, gave a brief exhibition of the contortionist's art. (*"He's twistin' my wrist! Dern you, leggo!"*)

The voice of Mrs. Lora Rewbush was again heard from the wings; it sounded bloodthirsty. Penrod released his victim, and the Child King Arthur, somewhat disconcerted, extended his sceptre and, with the assistance of the enraged prompter, said:

"Sweet child-friends of the Tabul Round,
In brotherly love and kindness abound,
Sir Lancelot, you have spoken well,
Sir Galahad, too, as clear as bell.
So now pray doff your mantles gay.
You shall be knighted this very day."

And Penrod doffed his mantle.

Simultaneously, a thick and vasty gasp came from the audience, as from five hundred bathers in a wholly unexpected surf. This gasp was punctuated irregularly over the auditorium by imperfectly subdued screams both of dismay and incredulous joy, and by two dismal shrieks. Altogether it was an extraordinary sound, a sound never to be forgotten by anyone who heard it. It was almost as unforgettable as the sight that caused it; the word "sight" being here used in its vernacular sense, for Penrod, standing unmantled and revealed in all the mediæval and artistic glory of the janitor's blue overalls, falls within its meaning.

The janitor was a heavy man, and his overalls, upon Penrod, were merely oceanic. The boy was at once swaddled and lost within their blue gulfs and vast saggings; and the left leg, too hastily rolled up, had descended with a distinctively elephantine effect, as Margaret had observed. Certainly, the Child Sir Lancelot was at least a sight.

It is probable that a great many in that hall must have had, even then, a consciousness that they were looking on at History in the Making. A supreme act is recognizable at sight: it bears the birthmark of immortality. But Penrod, that marvellous boy, had begun to declaim, even with the gesture of flinging off his mantle for the accolade:

"I first, the Child Sir Lancelot du Lake,
Will volunteer to knighthood take,
And kneeling here before your throne
I vow to——"

He finished his speech unheard. The audience had recovered breath but had lost self-control, and there ensued something later described by a participant as a sort of cultured riot.

The actors in the "pageant" were not so dumfounded by Penrod's costume as might have been expected. A few precocious geniuses perceived that the overalls were the Child Lancelot's own comment on maternal intentions; and these were profoundly impressed: they regarded him with the grisly admiration of young and ambitious criminals for a jail-mate about to be distinguished by hanging. But most of the children simply took it to be the case (a little strange but not startling) that Penrod's mother had dressed him like that—which is pathetic. They tried to go on with the "pageant".

They made a brief, manful effort. But the irrepressible outbursts from the audience bewildered them; every time Sir Lancelot du Lake the Child opened his mouth, the great, shadowy house fell into an uproar, and the children into confusion. Strong women and brave girls in the audience went out into the lobby, shrieking and clinging to one another. Others remained, rocking in their seats, helpless and spent. The neighbourhood of Mrs. Schofield and Margaret became, tactfully, a desert. Friends of the author went behind the scenes and encountered a hitherto unknown phase of Mrs. Lora Rewbush; they said, afterward, that she hardly seemed to know what she was doing. She begged to be left alone somewhere with Penrod Schofield, for just a little while.

They led her away.

CHAPTER VI

EVENING

THE sun was setting behind the back fence (though at a considerable distance) as Penrod Schofield approached that fence and looked thoughtfully up at the top of it, apparently having in mind some purpose to climb up and sit there. Debating this, he passed his fingers gently up and down the backs of his legs; and then something seemed to decide him not to sit anywhere. He leaned against the fence, sighed profoundly and gazed at Duke, his wistful dog.

The sigh was reminiscent: episodes of simple pathos were passing before his inward eye. About the most painful was the vision of lovely Marjorie Jones, weeping with rage as the Child Sir Lancelot was dragged, insatiate, from the

35

prostrate and howling Child Sir Galahad, after an on-
slaught delivered the precise instant the curtain began to
fall upon the demoralized "pageant". And then—oh, pangs!
oh, woman!—she slapped at the ruffian's cheek as he was
led past her by a resentful janitor, and, turning, flung her
arms round the Child Sir Galahad's neck.

*"Penrod Schofield, don't you dare ever speak to me again
as long as you live!"* Maurice's little white boots and gold
tassels had done their work.

At home the late Child Sir Lancelot was consigned to a
locked clothes-closet pending the arrival of his father. Mr.
Schofield came and, shortly after, there was put into practice
an old patriarchal custom. It is a custom of inconceivable
antiquity: probably primordial, certainly prehistoric, but
still in vogue in some remaining citadels of the ancient
simplicities of the Republic.

And now, therefore, in the dusk, Penrod leaned against
the fence and sighed.

His case is comparable to that of an adult who could have
survived a similar experience. Looking back to the sawdust-
box, fancy pictures this comparable adult a serious and
inventive writer engaged in congenial literary activities in
a private retreat. We see this period marked by the creation
of some of the most virile passages of a Work dealing exclusively in red corpuscles and huge primal impulses. We
see this thoughtful man dragged from his calm seclusion
to a horrifying publicity; forced to adopt the stage and,
himself a writer, compelled to exploit the repulsive sentiments of an author not only personally distasteful to him
but whose whole method and school in *belles lettres* he
despises.

We see him reduced by desperation and modesty to stealing a pair of overalls. We conceive him to have ruined, then,
his own reputation, and to have utterly disgraced his
family; next, to have engaged in the *duello* and to have
been spurned by his lady-love, thus lost to him (according
to her own declaration) forever. Finally, we must behold:

imprisonment by the authorities; the third degree—and flagellation.

We conceive our man deciding that his career had been perhaps too eventful. Yet Penrod had condensed all of it into eight hours.

It appears that he had at least some shadowy perception of a recent fulness of life, for, as he leaned against the fence, gazing upon his wistful Duke, he sighed again and murmured aloud:

"Well, hasn't this been a day!"

But in a little while a star came out, freshly lighted, from the highest part of the sky, and Penrod, looking up, noticed it casually and a little drowsily. He yawned. Then he sighed once more, but not reminiscently: evening had come; the day was over.

It was a sigh of pure *ennui*.

CHAPTER VII

EVILS OF DRINK

NEXT day Penrod acquired a dime by a simple and antique process that was without doubt sometimes practised by the boys of Babylon. When the teacher of his class in Sunday-school requested the weekly contribution, Penrod, fumbling honestly (at first) in the wrong pockets, managed to look so embarrassed that the gentle lady told him not to mind, and said she was often forgetful herself. She was so sweet about it that, looking into the future, Penrod began to feel confident of a small but regular income.

At the close of the afternoon services he did not go home but proceeded to squander the funds just withheld from China upon an orgy of the most pungently forbidden description. In a Drug Emporium near the church he purchased a five-cent sack of candy consisting for the most part of the heavily flavoured hoofs of horned cattle, but undeniably substantial and so generously capable of resisting solution that the purchaser must needs be avaricious beyond reason who did not realize his money's worth.

Equipped with this collation, Penrod contributed his remaining nickel to a picture show, countenanced upon the seventh day by the legal but not the moral authorities. Here, in cozy darkness, he placidly insulted his liver with jaw-breaker upon jaw-breaker from the paper sack, and in a surfeit of content watched the silent actors on the screen.

One film made a lasting impression upon him. It depicted with relentless pathos the drunkard's progress; beginning with his conversion to beer in the company of loose travelling men; pursuing him through an inexplicable lapse into evening clothes and the society of some remarkably painful ladies, next, exhibiting the effects of alcohol on the victim's domestic disposition, the unfortunate man was seen in the act of striking his wife and, subsequently, his pleading baby daughter with an abnormally heavy walking-stick. Their flight—through the snow—to seek the protection of a relative was shown, and finally, the drunkard's picturesque behaviour at the portals of a madhouse.

So fascinated was Penrod that he postponed his departure until this film came round again, by which time he had finished his unnatural repast and almost, but not quite, decided against following the profession of a drunkard when he grew up.

Emerging, satiated, from the theatre, a public timepiece before a jeweller's shop confronted him with an unexpected dial and imminent perplexities. How was he to explain at home these hours of dalliance? There was a steadfast rule that he return direct from Sunday-school; and Sunday rules were important, because on that day there was his father, always at home and at hand, perilously ready for action. One of the hardest conditions of boyhood is the almost continuous strain put upon the powers of invention by the constant and harassing necessity for explanations of every natural act.

Proceeding homeward through the deepening twilight as rapidly as possible, at a gait half skip and half canter, Penrod made up his mind in what manner he would account for his long delay, and, as he drew nearer, rehearsed in words the opening passage of his defence.

"Now see here," he determined to begin; "I do not wish to be blamed for things I couldn't help, nor any other boy. I was going along the street by a cottage and a lady put her head out of the window and said her husband was drunk and whipping her and her little girl, and she asked me wouldn't I come in and help hold him. So I went in and tried to get hold of this drunken lady's husband where he was whipping their baby daughter, but he wouldn't pay any attention, and I *told* her I ought to be getting home, but she kep' on askin' me to stay——"

At this point he reached the corner of his own yard, where a coincidence not only checked the rehearsal of his eloquence but happily obviated all occasion for it. A cab from the station drew up in front of the gate, and there descended a troubled lady in black and a fragile little girl about three. Mrs. Schofield rushed from the house and enfolded both in hospitable arms.

They were Penrod's Aunt Clara and cousin, also Clara, from Dayton, Illinois, and in the flurry of their arrival everybody forgot to put Penrod to the question. It is doubtful, however, if he felt any relief; there may have been even a slight, unconscious disappointment not altogether dissimilar to that of an actor deprived of a good part.

In the course of some really necessary preparations for dinner he stepped from the bathroom into the pink-and-white bedchamber of his sister, and addressed her rather thickly through a towel.

"When'd Mamma find out Aunt Clara and Cousin Clara were coming?"

"Not till she saw them from the window. She just happened to look out as they drove up. Aunt Clara telegraphed this morning, but it wasn't delivered."

"How long they goin' to stay?"

"I don't know."

Penrod ceased to rub his shining face, and thoughtfully tossed the towel through the bathroom door. "Uncle John won't try to make 'em come back home, I guess, will he?" (Uncle John was Aunt Clara's husband, a successful manufacturer of stoves, and his lifelong regret was that he had not entered the Baptist ministry.) "He'll let 'em stay here quietly, won't he?"

"What *are* you talking about?" Margaret demanded, turning from her mirror. "Uncle John sent them here. Why shouldn't he let them stay?"

Penrod looked crestfallen. "Then he hasn't taken to drink?"

"Certainly not!" She emphasized the denial with a pretty peal of soprano laughter.

"Then why," asked her brother gloomily, "why did Aunt Clara look so worried when she got here?"

"Good gracious! Don't people worry about anything except somebody's drinking? Where did you get such an idea?"

"Well," he persisted, "you don't *know* it ain't that."

She laughed again, whole-heartedly. "Poor Uncle John! He won't even allow grape juice or ginger ale in his house. They came because they were afraid little Clara might catch the measles. She's very delicate, and there's such an epidemic of measles among the children over in Dayton the schools had to be closed. Uncle John got so worried that last night he dreamed about it; and this morning he couldn't stand it any longer and packed them off over here, though he thinks it's wicked to travel on Sunday. And Aunt Clara was worried when she got here because they'd forgotten to check her trunk and it will have to be sent by express. Now what in the name of the common sense put it into your head that Uncle John had taken to——"

"Oh, nothing." He turned lifelessly away and went downstairs, a new-born hope dying in his bosom. Life seemed needlessly dull sometimes.

CHAPTER VIII

SCHOOL

NEXT morning, when he had once more resumed the dreadful burden of education, it seemed infinitely duller. And yet what pleasanter sight is there than a schoolroom well filled with children of those sprouting years just before the 'teens? The casual visitor, gazing from the teacher's platform upon these busy little heads, needs only a blunted memory to experience the most agreeable and exhilarating sensations. Still, for the greater part, the children are unconscious of the happiness of their condition; for nothing is more pathetically true than that we "never know when we are well off." The boys in a public school are less aware of their happy state than are the girls; and, of all the boys in his room, probably Penrod himself had the least appreciation of his felicity.

He sat staring at an open page of a textbook, but not studying; not even reading; not even thinking. Nor was he lost in a reverie: his mind's eye was shut, as his physical eye might well have been, for the optic nerve, flaccid with *ennui*, conveyed nothing whatever of the printed page upon which the orb of vision was partially focused. Penrod was doing something very unusual and rare, something almost never accomplished except by coloured people or by a boy in school on a spring day: he was doing really nothing at all. He was merely a state of being.

From the street a sound stole in through the open window, and abhorring Nature began to fill the vacuum called Penrod Schofield; for the sound was the spring song of a mouth-organ, coming down the sidewalk. The windows were intentionally above the level of the eyes of the seated pupils; but the picture of the musician was plain to Penrod, painted for him by a quality in the runs and trills, partaking of the oboe, of the calliope and of cats in anguish; an excruciating sweetness obtained only by the wallowing, walloping yellow-pink palm of a hand whose back was Congo black and shiny. The music came down the street and passed beneath the window, accompanied by the care-free shuffling of a pair of old shoes scuffing syncopations on the cement sidewalk. It passed into the distance; became faint and blurred; was gone. Emotion stirred in Penrod a great and poignant desire; but (perhaps fortunately) no fairy godmother made her appearance. Otherwise Penrod would have gone down the street in a black skin, playing the mouth-organ, and an unprepared coloured youth would have found himself enjoying educational advantages for which he had no ambition whatever.

Roused from perfect apathy, the boy cast about the schoolroom an eye wearied to nausea by the perpetual vision of the neat teacher upon the platform, the backs of the heads of the pupils in front of him, and the monotonous

stretches of blackboard threateningly defaced by arith-
metical formulæ and other insignia of torture. Above the
blackboard, the walls of the high room were of white plaster
—white with the qualified whiteness of old snow in a soft
coal town. This dismal expanse was broken by four litho-
graphic portraits, votive offerings of a thoughtful publisher.
The portraits were of good and great men, kind men, men
who loved children. Their faces were noble and benevolent.
But the lithographs offered the only rest for the eyes of
children fatigued by the everlasting sameness of the schoolroom. Long day after long day, interminable week in and
interminable week out, vast month on vast month, the pupils
sat with those four portraits beaming kindness down upon
them. The faces became permanent in the consciousness of
the children; they became an obsession—in and out of
school the children were never free of them. The four faces
haunted the minds of children falling asleep; they hung
upon the minds of children waking at night; they rose fore-
bodingly in the minds of children waking in the morning;
they became monstrously alive in the minds of children lying
sick of fever. Never, while the children of that schoolroom
lived, would they be able to forget one detail of the four
lithographs: the hand of Longfellow was fixed, for them,
forever, in his beard. And by a simple and unconscious
association of ideas, Penrod Schofield was accumulating an
antipathy for the gentle Longfellow and for James Russell
Lowell and for Oliver Wendell Holmes and for John Green-
leaf Whittier that would never permit him to peruse a
work of one of those great New Englanders without a
feeling of personal resentment.

His eyes fell slowly and inimically from the brow of
Whittier to the braid of reddish hair belonging to Victorine
Riordan, the little octoroon girl who sat directly in front
of him. Victorine's back was as familiar to Penrod as the
necktie of Oliver Wendell Holmes. So was her gayly
coloured plaid waist. He hated the waist as he hated Victorine herself, without knowing why. Enforced companion-

ship in large quantities and on an equal basis between the sexes appears to sterilize the affections, and schoolroom romances are few.

Victorine's hair was thick, and the brickish glints in it were beautiful; but Penrod was very tired of it. A tiny knot of green ribbon finished off the braid and kept it from unravelling; and beneath the ribbon there was a final wisp of hair that was just long enough to repose upon Penrod's desk when Victorine leaned back in her seat. It was there now. Thoughtfully, he took the braid between thumb and forefinger, and, without disturbing Victorine, dipped the end of it and the green ribbon into the ink-well of his desk. He brought hair and ribbon forth dripping purple ink, and partially dried them on a blotter, though, a moment later when Victorine leaned forward, they were still able to add a few picturesque touches to the plaid waist.

Rudolph Krauss, across the aisle from Penrod, watched the operation with protuberant eyes, fascinated. Inspired to imitation, he took a piece of chalk from his pocket and wrote "RATS" across the shoulder-blades of the boy in front of him, then looked across appealingly to Penrod for tokens of congratulation. Penrod yawned. It may not be denied that at times he appeared to be a very self-centred boy.

CHAPTER IX

SOARING

HALF the members of the class passed out to a recitation-room, the empurpled Victorine among them, and Miss Spence started the remaining half through the ordeal of trial by mathematics. Several boys and girls were sent to the blackboard, and Penrod, spared for the moment, followed their operations a little while with his eyes but not with his mind; then, sinking deeper in his seat, limply abandoned the effort. His eyes remained open but saw nothing; the routine of the arithmetic lesson reached his ears in familiar, meaningless sounds but he heard nothing; and yet, this time, he was profoundly occupied. He had drifted away from the painful land of facts, and floated now in a new sea of fancy that he had just discovered.

47

Maturity forgets the marvellous realness of a boy's day-dreams, how colourful they glow, rosy and living, and how opaque the curtain closing down between the dreamer and the actual world. That curtain is almost sound-proof, too, and causes more throat-trouble among parents than is suspected.

The nervous monotony of the schoolroom inspires a some-times unbearable longing for something astonishing to happen, and, as every boy's fundamental desire is to do something astonishing himself, so as to be the centre of all human interest and awe, it was natural that Penrod should discover in fancy the delightful secret of self-levitation. He found, in this curious series of imaginings, during the lesson in arithmetic, that the atmosphere may be navigated as by a swimmer under water, but with infinitely greater ease and with perfect comfort in breathing. In his mind he extended his arms gracefully, at a level with his shoulders, and delicately paddled the air with his hands, which at once caused him to be drawn up out of his seat and elevated gently to a position about midway between the floor and the ceiling, where he came to an equilibrium and floated; a sensation not the less exquisite because of the screams of his fellow pupils, appalled by the miracle. Miss Spence her-self was amazed and frightened; but he only smiled down carelessly upon her when she commanded him to return to earth; and then, when she climbed upon a desk to pull him down, he quietly paddled himself a little higher, leaving his toes just out of her reach. Next, he swam through a few slow somersaults to show his mastery of the new art, and, with the shouting of the dumfounded scholars ringing in his ears, turned on his side and floated swiftly out of the window, immediately rising above the housetops, while people in the street below him shrieked, and a trolley car stopped dead in wonder.

With almost no exertion he paddled himself, many yards at a stroke, to the girls' private school where Marjorie Jones was a pupil—Marjorie Jones of the amber curls and the golden voice! Long before the "Pageant of the Table Round" she had offered Penrod a hundred proofs that she considered him wholly undesirable and ineligible. At the Friday Afternoon Dancing Class she consistently incited and led the laughter at him whenever Professor Bartet singled him out for admonition in matters of feet and decorum. And but yesterday she had chid him for his slavish lack of memory in daring to offer her a greeting on the way to Sunday-school. "Well! I expect you must forgot I told you never to speak to me again! If I was a boy, I'd be too proud to come hanging around people that don't speak to me, even if I *was* the Worst Boy in Town!" So she flouted him. But now, as he floated in through the window of her classroom and swam gently along the ceiling like an escaped toy balloon, she fell upon her knees beside her little desk, and, lifting up her arms toward him, cried with love and admiration:

"Oh, *Pen*rod!"

He negligently kicked a globe from the high chandelier, and, smiling coldly, floated out through the hall to the front steps of the school, while Marjorie followed, imploring him to grant her one kind look.

In the street an enormous crowd had gathered, headed by Miss Spence and a brass band; and a cheer from a hundred thousand throats shook the very ground as Penrod swam overhead. Marjorie knelt upon the steps and watched adoringly while Penrod took the drum-major's baton and, performing sinuous evolutions above the crowd, led the band. Then he threw the baton so high that it disappeared from sight; but he went swiftly after it, a double delight, for he had not only the delicious sensation of rocketing safely up and up into the blue sky but also that of standing in the crowd below, watching and admiring himself as he dwindled to a speck, disappeared and then, emerging from a cloud, came speeding down, with the baton in his hand, to the level of the treetops, where he beat time for the band and the vast throng and Marjorie Jones, who all united in the "Star-spangled Banner" in honour of his aerial achievements. It was a great moment.

It was a great moment; but something seemed to threaten it. The face of Miss Spence looking up from the crowd grew too vivid—unpleasantly vivid. She was beckoning him and shouting, "Come down, Penrod Schofield! Penrod Schofield, come down here!" He could hear her above the band and the singing of the multitude; she seemed intent on spoiling everything. Marjorie Jones was weeping to show how sorry she was that she had formerly slighted him, and throwing kisses to prove that she loved him; but Miss Spence kept jumping between him and Marjorie, incessantly calling his name.

He grew more and more irritated with her; he was the most important person in the world and was engaged in proving it to Marjorie Jones and the whole city, and yet Miss Spence seemed to feel she still had the right to order him about as she did in the old days when he was an ordinary schoolboy. He was furious; he was sure she wanted him to do something disagreeable. It seemed to him that she had screamed "Penrod Schofield!" thousands of times.

From the beginning of his aerial experiments in his own schoolroom, he had not opened his lips, knowing somehow that one of the requirements for air floating is perfect silence on the part of the floater; but, finally, irritated beyond measure by Miss Spence's clamorous insistence, he was unable to restrain an indignant rebuke—and immediately came to earth with a frightful bump.

Miss Spence—in the flesh—had directed toward the physical body of the absent Penrod an inquiry as to the fractional consequences of dividing seventeen apples, fairly, among three boys, and she was surprised and displeased to receive no answer, although to the best of her knowledge and belief he was looking fixedly at her. She repeated her question crisply, without visible effect; then summoned him by name with increasing asperity. Twice she called him, while all his fellow pupils turned to stare at the gazing boy. She advanced a step from the platform.

"Penrod Schofield!"

"Oh, my goodness!" he shouted suddenly. "Can't you keep still a *minute?*"

CHAPTER X

UNCLE JOHN

MISS SPENCE gasped. So did the pupils. The whole room filled with a swelling conglomerate *"O-o-o-o-h!"*

As for Penrod himself, the walls reeled with the shock. He sat with his mouth open, a mere lump of stupefaction. For the appalling words that he had hurled at the teacher were as inexplicable to him as to any other who heard them.

Nothing is more treacherous than the human mind; nothing else so loves to play the Iscariot. Even when patiently bullied into a semblance of order and training, it may prove but a base and shifty servant. And Penrod's mind was not his servant; it was a master, with the April wind's whims; and it had just played him a diabolical trick. The very jolt with

which he came back to the schoolroom in the midst of his
fancied flight jarred his day-dream utterly out of him;
and he sat, open-mouthed in horror at what he had said.

The unanimous gasp of awe was protracted. Miss Spence,
however, finally recovered her breath, and, returning deliberately to the platform, faced the school. "And then, for
a little while", as pathetic stories sometimes recount,
"everything was very still." It was so still, in fact, that
Penrod's new-born notoriety could almost be heard growing. This grisly silence was at last broken by the teacher.

"Penrod Schofield, stand up!"

The miserable child obeyed.

"What did you mean by speaking to me in that way?"

He hung his head, raked the floor with the side of his
shoe, swayed, swallowed, looked suddenly at his hands with
the air of never having seen them before, then clasped
them behind him. The school shivered in ecstatic horror,
every fascinated eye upon him; yet there was not a soul
in the room but was profoundly grateful to him for the
sensation—including the offended teacher herself. Unhappily, all this gratitude was unconscious and altogether
different from the kind that results in testimonials and
loving-cups. On the contrary!

"Penrod Schofield!"

He gulped.

"Answer me at once! Why did you speak to me like
that?"

"I was——" He choked, unable to continue.

"Speak out!"

"I was just—thinking," he managed to stammer.

"That will not do," she returned sharply. "I wish to
know immediately why you spoke as you did."

The stricken Penrod answered helplessly: "Because I was
just thinking." Upon the very rack he could have offered
no ampler truthful explanation. It was all he knew about it.

"Thinking what?"

"Just thinking."

Miss Spence's expression gave evidence that her power of self-restraint was undergoing a remarkable test. However, after taking counsel with herself, she commanded: "Come here!"

He shuffled forward, and she placed a chair upon the platform near her own.

"Sit there!"

Then (but not at all as if nothing had happened) she continued the lesson in arithmetic. Spiritually the children may have learned a lesson in very small fractions indeed as they gazed at the fragment of sin before them on the stool of penitence. They all stared at him attentively with hard and passionately interested eyes, in which there was never one trace of pity. It cannot be said with precision that he writhed; his movement was more a slow, continuous squirm effected with a ghastly assumption of languid indifference; while his gaze, in the effort to escape the marble-hearted glare of his schoolmates, affixed itself with apparent permanence to the waistcoat button of James Russell Lowell just above the "U" in "Russell".

Classes came and classes went, grilling him with eyes. Newcomers received the story of the crime in darkling whispers; and the outcast sat and sat and sat, and squirmed and squirmed and squirmed. (He did one or two things with his spine that a professional contortionist would have observed with real interest.) And all this while of freezing suspense was but the criminal's detention awaiting trial. A known punishment may be anticipated with some measure of equanimity; at least, the prisoner may prepare himself to undergo it; but the unknown looms more monstrous for every attempt to guess it. Penrod's crime was unique; there were no rules to aid him in estimating the vengeance to fall upon him for it. What seemed most probable was that he would be expelled from the school in the presence of his family, the mayor and council, and afterward whipped by his father upon the State House steps, with the entire city as audience by invitation of the authorities.

The outcast sat and sat and sat, and squirmed and squirmed and squirmed.

Noon came. The rows of children filed out, every head turning for a last unpleasingly speculative look at the outlaw. Then Miss Spence closed the door into the cloakroom and that into the big hall, and came and sat at her desk, near Penrod. The tramping of feet outside, the shrill calls and shouting and the changing voices of the older boys ceased to be heard—and there was silence. Penrod, still affecting to be occupied with Lowell, was conscious that Miss Spence looked at him intently.

"Penrod," she said gravely, "what excuse have you to offer before I report your case to the principal?"

The word "principal" struck him to the vitals. Grand Inquisitor, Grand Khan, Sultan, Emperor, Tsar, Cæsar Augustus—these are comparable. He stopped squirming instantly, and sat rigid.

"I want an answer. Why did you shout those words at me?"

"Well," he murmured, "I was just—thinking."

"Thinking what?" she asked sharply.

"I don't know."

"That won't do!"

He took his left ankle in his right hand and regarded it helplessly.

"That won't do, Penrod Schofield," she repeated severely. "If that is all the excuse you have to offer I shall report your case this instant!"

And she rose with fatal intent.

But Penrod was one of those whom the precipice inspires. "Well, I *have* got an excuse."

"Well"—she paused impatiently—"what is it?"

He had not an idea; but he felt one coming, and replied automatically, in a plaintive tone: "I guess anybody that had been through what *I* had to go through last night would think they had an excuse."

Miss Spence resumed her seat, though with the air of being ready to leap from it instantly. "What has last night to do with your insolence to me this morning?"

"Well, I guess you'd see," he returned, emphasizing the plaintive note, "if you knew what *I* know."

"Now, Penrod," she said, in a kinder voice, "I have a high regard for your mother and father, and it would hurt me to distress them; but you must either tell me what was the matter with you or I'll have to take you to Mrs. Houston."

"Well, ain't I going to?" he cried, spurred by the dread name. "It's because I didn't sleep last night."

"Were you ill?" The question was put with some dryness. He felt the dryness. "No'm; *I* wasn't."

"Then if someone in your family was so ill that even you were kept up all night, how does it happen they let you come to school this morning?"

"It wasn't illness," he returned, shaking his head mournfully. "It was lots worse'n anybody's being sick. It was—it was—well, it was jest awful."

"*What* was?" He remarked with anxiety the incredulity in her tone.

"It was about Aunt Clara," he said.

"Your Aunt Clara!" she repeated. "Do you mean your mother's sister who married Mr. Farry of Dayton, Illinois?"

"Yes—Uncle John," returned Penrod sorrowfully. "The trouble was about him."

Miss Spence frowned a frown that he rightly interpreted as one of continued suspicion. "She and I were in school together," she said. "I used to know her very well, and I've always heard her married life was entirely happy. I don't——"

"Yes, it was," he interrupted, "until last year when Uncle John took to running with travelling men——"

"What?"

"Yes'm." He nodded solemnly. "That was what started it. At first he was a good, kind husband; but these travelling men would coax him into a saloon on his way from work, and they got him to drinking beer and then ales, wines, liquors and cigars——"

"Penrod!"

"Ma'am?"

"I'm not inquiring into your Aunt Clara's private affairs; I'm asking you if you have anything to say which would palliate——"

"That's what I'm tryin' to *tell* you about, Miss Spence," he pleaded,—"if you'd jest only let me. When Aunt Clara and her little baby daughter got to our house last night——"

"You say Mrs. Farry is visiting your mother?"

"Yes'm—not just visiting—you see, she *had* to come. Well, of course, little baby Clara, she was so bruised up and mauled, where he'd been hittin' her with his cane——"

"You mean that your uncle had done such a thing as *that!*" Miss Spence exclaimed, suddenly disarmed by this scandal.

"Yes'm, and Mamma and Margaret had to sit up all night nursin' little Clara—and *Aunt* Clara was in such a state *somebody* had to keep talkin' to *her*, and there wasn't anybody but me to do it, so I——"

"But where was your father?" she cried.

"Ma'am?"

"Where was your father while——"

"Oh—Papa?" Penrod paused, reflected; then brightened. "Why, he was down at the train, waitin' to see if Uncle John would try to follow 'em and make 'em come home so's he could persecute 'em some more. I wanted to do that; but they said if he did come I mightn't be strong enough to hold him, and——" The brave lad paused again, modestly. Miss Spence's expression was encouraging. Her eyes were wide with astonishment, and there may have been in them, also, the mingled beginnings of admiration and self-reproach. Penrod, warming to his work, felt safer every moment.

"And so," he continued, "I had to sit up with Aunt Clara. She had some pretty big bruises, too, and I had to——"

"But why didn't they send for a doctor?" However, this question was only a flicker of dying incredulity.

"Oh, they didn't want any *doctor*," exclaimed the inspired realist promptly. "They don't want anybody to *hear* about it because Uncle John might reform—and then where'd he be if everybody knew he'd been a drunkard and whipped his wife and baby daughter?"

"Oh!" said Miss Spence.

"You see, he used to be upright as anybody," he went on explanatively. "It all begun——"

"Began, Penrod."

"Yes'm. It all commenced from the first day he let those travelling men coax him into the saloon."

Penrod narrated the downfall of his Uncle John at length. In detail he was nothing short of plethoric; and incident followed incident, sketched with such vividness, such abundance of colour, and such verisimilitude to a drunkard's life as a drunkard's life should be, that had Miss Spence possessed the rather chilling attributes of William J. Burns himself, the last trace of skepticism must have vanished from her mind. Besides, there are two things that will be believed of any man whatsoever, and one of them is that he has taken to drink. And in every sense it was a moving picture that, with simple but eloquent words, the virtuous Penrod set before his teacher.

His eloquence increased with what it fed on; and as with the eloquence so with self-reproach in the gentle bosom of the teacher. She cleared her throat with difficulty once or twice during his description of his ministering night with Aunt Clara. "And I said to her, 'Why, Aunt Clara, what's the use of takin' on so about it?' And I said, 'Now, Aunt Clara, all the crying in the world can't make things any better.' And then she'd just keep catchin' hold of me, and sob and kind of holler, and I'd say, '*Don't* cry, Aunt Clara —*please* don't cry.'"

Then, under the influence of some fragmentary survivals of the respectable portion of his Sunday adventures, his theme became more exalted; and, only partially misquoting a phrase from a psalm, he related how he had made it of comfort to Aunt Clara, and how he had besought her to seek Higher guidance in her trouble.

The surprising thing about a structure such as Penrod was erecting is that the taller it becomes the more ornamentation it will stand. Gifted boys have this faculty of building magnificence upon cobwebs—and Penrod was gifted. Under the spell of his really great performance, Miss Spence gazed more and more sweetly upon the prodigy of spiritual beauty and goodness before her, until at last, when Penrod came to the explanation of his "just thinking", she was forced to turn her head away.

"You mean, dear," she said gently, "that you were all worn out and hardly knew what you were saying?"

"Yes'm."

"And you were thinking about all those dreadful things so hard that you forgot where you were?"

"I was thinking," he said simply, "how to save Uncle John."

And the end of it for this mighty boy was that the teacher kissed him!

CHAPTER XI

FIDELITY OF A LITTLE DOG

THE returning students, that afternoon, observed that Penrod's desk was vacant—and nothing could have been more impressive than that sinister mere emptiness. The accepted theory was that Penrod had been arrested. How breathtaking, then, the sensation when, at the beginning of the second hour, he strolled in with inimitable carelessness and, rubbing his eyes, somewhat noticeably in the manner of one who has snatched an hour of much needed sleep, took his place as if nothing in particular had happened. This, at first supposed to be a superhuman exhibition of sheer audacity, became but the more dumfounding when Miss Spence—looking up from her desk—greeted him with a pleasant little nod. Even after school, Penrod gave numerous maddened investigators no relief. All he would consent to say was:

"Oh, I just *talked* to her."

A mystification not entirely unconnected with the one thus produced was manifested at his own family dinner-table the following evening. Aunt Clara had been out rather late, and came to the table after the rest were seated. She wore a puzzled expression.

"Do you ever see Mary Spence nowadays?" she inquired, as she unfolded her napkin, addressing Mrs. Schofield. Penrod abruptly set down his soupspoon and gazed at his aunt with flattering attention.

"Yes; sometimes," Mrs. Schofield said. "She's Penrod's teacher."

"Is she?" Mrs. Farry said. "Do you—" She paused. "Do people think her a little—queer, these days?"

"Why, no," her sister returned. "What makes you say that?"

"She has acquired a very odd manner," Mrs. Farry said decidedly. "At least, she seemed odd to *me*. I met her at the corner just before I got to the house, a few minutes ago, and after we'd said howdy-do to each other she kept hold of my hand and looked as though she was going to cry. She seemed to be trying to say something, and choking——"

"But I don't think that's so very queer, Clara. She knew you in school, didn't she?"

"Yes, but——"

"And she hadn't seen you for so many years, I think it's perfectly natural she——"

"Wait! She stood there squeezing my hand and struggling to get her voice—and I got really embarrassed—and then finally she said, in a kind of tearful whisper, 'Be of good cheer—this trial will pass!'"

"How queer!" Margaret exclaimed.

Penrod sighed, and returned somewhat absently to his soup.

"Well, I don't know," Mrs. Schofield said thoughtfully.

"Of course she's heard about the outbreak of measles in Dayton, since they had to close the schools, and she knows you live there——"

"But doesn't it seem a *very* exaggerated way," Margaret suggested, "to talk about measles?"

"Wait!" Aunt Clara begged. "After she said that, she said something even queerer, and then put her handkerchief to her eyes and hurried away."

Penrod laid down his spoon again and moved his chair slightly back from the table. A spirit of prophecy was upon him: he knew that someone was going to ask a question that he felt might better remain unspoken.

"What *was* the other thing she said?" Mr. Schofield inquired, thus immediately fulfilling his son's premonition.

"She said," Mrs. Farry returned slowly, looking about the table, "she said, 'I know that Penrod is a great, great comfort to you!' "

There was a general exclamation of surprise. It was a singular thing, and in no manner may it be considered complimentary to Penrod that this speech of Miss Spence's should have immediately confirmed Mrs. Farry's doubts about her in the minds of all his family.

Mr. Schofield shook his head pityingly. "I'm afraid she's a goner," he went so far as to say.

"Of all the weird ideas!" Margaret cried.

"I never heard anything like it in my life!" Mrs. Schofield exclaimed. "Was that *all* she said?"

"Every word!"

Penrod again resumed attention to his soup. His mother looked at him curiously, and then, struck by a sudden thought, gathered the glances of the adults of the table by a significant movement of the head, and, by another, conveyed an admonition to drop the subject until later. Miss Spence was Penrod's teacher: it was better, for many reasons, not to discuss the subject of her queerness before him. This was Mrs. Schofield's thought at the time. Later she had another, and it kept her awake.

The next afternoon, Mr. Schofield, returning at five o'clock from the cares of the day, found the house deserted, and sat down to read his evening paper in what appeared to be an uninhabited apartment known to its own world as the "drawing-room". A sneeze, unexpected both to him and the owner, informed him of the presence of another person.

"Where are you, Penrod?" the parent asked, looking about.

"Here," said Penrod meekly.

Stooping, Mr. Schofield discovered his son squatting under the piano, near an open window—his wistful Duke lying beside him.

"What are you doing there?"

"Me?"

"Why under the piano?"

"Well," the boy returned, with grave sweetness, "I was just kind of sitting here—thinking."

"All right." Mr. Schofield, rather touched, returned to the digestion of a murder, his back once more to the piano; and Penrod silently drew from beneath his jacket (where he had slipped it simultaneously with the sneeze) a paper-backed volume entitled: "Slimsy, the Sioux City Squealer, or, 'Not Guilty, Your Honor.' "

In this manner the reading-club continued in peace, absorbed, contented, the world well forgot—until a sudden, violently irritated slam-bang of the front door startled the members; and Mrs. Schofield burst into the room and threw herself into a chair, moaning.

"What's the matter, Mamma?" her husband asked, laying aside his paper.

"Henry Passloe Schofield," returned the lady, "I don't know what *is* to be done with that boy; I do *not!*"

"You mean Penrod?"

"Who else could I mean?" She sat up, exasperated, to stare at him. "Henry Passloe Schofield, you've got to take this matter in your hands—it's beyond me!"

"Well, what has he——"

"Last night I got to thinking," she began rapidly, "about what Clara told us—thank Heaven she and Margaret and little Clara have gone to tea at Cousin Charlotte's!—but they'll be home soon—about what she said about Miss Spence——"

"You mean about Penrod's being a comfort?"

"Yes, and I kept thinking and thinking and thinking about it till I couldn't stand it any——"

"By *George!*" Mr. Schofield shouted startlingly, stooping to look under the piano. A statement that he had suddenly remembered his son's presence would be lacking in accuracy, for the highly sensitized Penrod was, in fact, no longer present. No more was Duke, his faithful dog.

"What's the matter?"

"Nothing," he returned, striding to the open window and looking out. "Go on."

"Oh," she moaned, "it must be kept from Clara—and I'll never hold up my head again if John Farry ever hears of it!"

"Hears of *what?*"

"Well, I just couldn't stand it, I got so curious; and I thought of course if Miss Spence *had* become a little unbalanced it was my duty to know it, as Penrod's mother and she his teacher; so I thought I would just call on her at her apartment after school and have a chat and see—and I did and—oh——"

"Well?"

"I've just come from there, and she told me—she told me! Oh, I've *never* known anything like this!"

"*What* did she tell you?"

Mrs. Schofield, making a great effort, managed to assume a temporary appearance of calm. "Henry," she said solemnly, "bear this in mind: whatever you do to Penrod, it must be done in some place when Clara won't hear it. But the first thing to do is to find him."

Within view of the window from which Mr. Schofield

was gazing was the closed door of the storeroom in the stable, and just outside this door Duke was performing a most engaging trick.

His young master had taught Duke to "sit up and beg" when he wanted anything, and, if that didn't get it, to "speak". Duke was facing the closed door and sitting up and begging, and now he also spoke—in a loud, clear bark.

There was an open transom over the door, and from this descended—hurled by an unseen agency—a can half filled with old paint.

It caught the small besieger of the door on his thoroughly surprised right ear, encouraged him to some remarkable acrobatics, and turned large portions of him a dull blue. Allowing only a moment to perplexity, and deciding, after a single and evidently unappetizing experiment, not to cleanse himself of paint, the loyal animal resumed his quaint, upright posture.

Mr. Schofield seated himself on the window-sill, whence he could keep in view that pathetic picture of unrequited love. "Go on with your story, Mamma," he said. "I think I can find Penrod when we want him." And a few minutes later he added, "And I think I know the place to do it in."

Again the faithful voice of Duke was heard, pleading outside the bolted door.

CHAPTER XII

MISS RENNSDALE ACCEPTS

"ONE-TWO-THREE; one-two-three—glide!" said Professor Bartet, emphasizing his instructions by a brisk collision of his palms at "glide". "One-two-three; one-two-three—glide!"

The school week was over, at last; but Penrod's troubles were not.

Round and round the ballroom went the seventeen struggling little couples of the Friday Afternoon Dancing Class. Round and round went their reflections with them, swimming rhythmically in the polished, dark floor—white and blue and pink for the girls; black, with dabs of white, for the white-collared, white-gloved boys; and sparks and slivers of high light everywhere as the glistening pumps flickered along the surface like a school of flying fish. Every small pink face—with one exception—was painstaking and set for duty. It was a conscientious little merry-go-round.

"One-two-three; one-two-three—glide! One-two-three; one-two-three—glide! One-two-th—Ha! Mister Penrod Schofield, you lose the step. Your left foot! No, no! This is the left! See—like me! Now again! One-two-three; one-two-three—glide! Better! Much better! Again! One-two-three; one-two-three—gl—Stop! Mr. Penrod Schofield, this dancing class is provided by the kind parents of the pupilses as much to learn the mannerss of good societies as to dance. You think you shall ever see a gentleman in good societies to tickle his partner in the dance till she say Ouch? Never! I assure you it is not done. Again! Now then! Piano, please! One-two-three; one-two-three—glide! Mr. Penrod Schofield, your right foot—your right foot! No, no! Stop!"

The merry-go-round came to a standstill.

"Mr. Penrod Schofield and partner"—Professor Bartet wiped his brow—"will you kindly observe me? One-two-three—glide! So! Now then—no; you will please keep your places, ladies and gentlemen. Mr. Penrod Schofield, I would puttickly like your attention; this is for you!"

"Pickin' on me again!" the smouldering Penrod murmured to his small, unsympathetic partner. "Can't let me alone a minute!"

"Mister Georgie Bassett, please step to the centre," said the professor.

Mr. Bassett complied with modest alacrity.

"Teacher's pet!" Penrod whispered hoarsely. He had nothing but contempt for Georgie Bassett. The parents, guardians, aunts, uncles, cousins, governesses, housemaids, cooks, chauffeurs and coachmen, appertaining to the members of the dancing class, all dwelt in the same part of town and shared certain communal theories; and among the most firmly established was that which maintained Georgie Bassett to be the Best Boy in Town. Contrariwise, the unfortunate Penrod, largely because of his recent dazzling but disastrous attempts to control forces far beyond him, had been given a clear title as the Worst Boy in Town. (Population, 135,000.) To precisely what degree his reputation was the product of his own energies cannot be calculated. It was Marjorie Jones who first applied the description, in its definite simplicity, the day after the "pageant", and, possibly, her frequent and effusive repetitions of it, even upon wholly irrelevant occasions, had something to do with its prompt and quite perfect acceptance by the community.

"Miss Rennsdale will please do me the fafer to be Mr. Georgie Bassett's partner for one moment," said Professor Bartet. "Mr. Penrod Schofield will please give his attention. Miss Rennsdale and Mister Bassett, obliche me, if you please. Others please watch. Piano, please! Now then!"

Miss Rennsdale, aged eight—the youngest lady in the class—and Mr. Georgie Bassett one-two-three-glided with consummate technique for the better education of Penrod Schofield. It is possible that amber-curled, beautiful Marjorie felt that she, rather than Miss Rennsdale, might have been selected as the example of perfection—or perhaps her remark was only woman.

"Stopping everybody for that boy!" Marjorie said.

Penrod, across the circle from her, heard distinctly— nay, he was obviously intended to hear; but over a scorched heart he preserved a stoic front. Whereupon Marjorie whispered derisively in the ear of her partner, Maurice Levy, who wore a pearl pin in his tie.

"Again, please, everybody—ladies and gentlemen!" cried Professor Bartet. "Mister Penrod Schofield, if you please, pay puttickly attention! Piano, please! Now then!"

The lesson proceeded. At the close of the hour Professor Bartet stepped to the centre of the room and clapped his hands for attention.

"Ladies and gentlemen, if you please to seat yourselves quietly," he said; "I speak to you now about to-morrow. As you all know—Mister Penrod Schofield, I am not sticking up in a tree outside that window! If you do me the fafer

to examine I am here, insides of the room. Now then! Piano,
pl—no, I do not wish the piano! As you all know, this is the
last lesson of the season until next October. To-morrow is
our special afternoon; beginning three o'clock, we dance
the cotillon. But this afternoon comes the test of mannerss.
You must see if each know how to make a little formal call
like a grown-up people in good societies. You have had
good, perfect instruction; let us see if we know how to perform like societies ladies and gentlemen twenty-six years
of age. Now, when you are dismissed each lady will go to
her home and prepare to receive a call. The gentlemen
will allow the ladies time to reach their houses and to prepare to receive callers; then each gentleman will call upon
a lady and beg the pleasure to engage her for a partner
in the cotillon to-morrow. You all know the correct, proper
form for these calls, because didn't I work teaching you last
lesson till I thought I would drop dead? Yes! Now each
gentleman, if he reach a lady's house behind some other
gentleman, then he must go somewhere else to a lady's
house, and keep calling until he secures a partner; so, as
there are the same number of both, everybody shall have a
partner. Now please all remember that if in case—Mister
Penrod Schofield, when you make your call on a lady I beg
you to please remember that gentlemen in good societies do
not scratch the back in societies as you appear to attempt;
so please allow the hands to rest carelessly in the lap. Now
please all remember that if in case—Mister Penrod Schofield, if you please! Gentlemen in societies do not scratch
the back by causing frictions between it and the back of
your chair, either! Nobody else is itching here! *I* do not
itch! I cannot talk if you must itch! In the name of Heaven,
why must you always itch? What was I saying? Where—
ah! the cotillon—yes! For the cotillon it is important nobody shall fail to be here to-morrow; but if anyone should
be so very ill he cannot possible come he must write a very
polite note of regrets in the form of good societies to his
engaged partner to excuse himself—and he must give the

reason. I do not think anybody is going to be that sick to-morrow—no; and I will find out and report to parents if anybody would try it and not be. But it is important for the cotillon that we have an even number of so many couples, and if it should happen that someone comes and her partner has sent her a polite note that he has genuine reasons why he cannot come, the note must be handed at once to me, so that I arrange some other partner. Is all understood? Yes. The gentlemen will remember now to allow the ladies plenty of time to reach their houses and prepare to receive calls. Ladies and gentlemen, I thank you for your polite attention."

It was nine blocks to the house of Marjorie Jones; but Penrod did it in less than seven minutes from a flying start—such was his haste to lay himself and his hand for the cotillon at the feet of one who had so recently spoken unamiably of him in public. He had not yet learned that the only safe male rebuke to a scornful female is to stay away from her—especially if that is what she desires. However, he did not wish to rebuke her; simply and ardently he wished to dance the cotillon with her. Resentment was swallowed up in hope.

The fact that Miss Jones's feeling for him bore a striking resemblance to that of Simon Legree for Uncle Tom, deterred him not at all. Naturally, he was not wholly unconscious that when he should lay his hand for the cotillon at her feet it would be her inward desire to step on it; but he believed that if he were first in the field Marjorie would have to accept. These things are governed by law.

It was his fond intention to reach her house even in advance of herself, and with grave misgiving he beheld a large automobile at rest before the sainted gate. Forthwith, a sinking feeling became a portent inside him as little Maurice Levy emerged from the front door of the house.

" 'Lo, Penrod!" said Maurice airily.

"What you doin' in there?" Penrod inquired.

"In where?"

"In Marjorie's."

"Well, what shouldn't I be doin' in Marjorie's?" Mr. Levy returned indignantly. "I was inviting her for my partner in the cotillon—what you s'pose?"

"You haven't got any right to!" Penrod protested hotly. "You can't do it yet."

"I did do it yet!" said Maurice.

"You can't!" Penrod insisted. "You got to allow them time first. He said the ladies had to be allowed time to prepare."

"Well, ain't she had time to prepare?"

"When?" Penrod demanded, stepping close to his rival threateningly. "I'd like to know when——"

"When?" the other echoed, with shrill triumph. "When? Why, in Mamma's sixty-horse powder limousine automobile, what Marjorie came home with me in! I guess that's when!"

An impulse in the direction of violence became visible upon the countenance of Penrod.

"I expect you need some wiping down," he began dangerously. "I'll give you sumpthing to remem——"

"Oh, you will!" Maurice cried with astonishing truculence, contorting himself into what he may have considered a posture of defense. "Let's see you try it, you—you itcher!"

For the moment, defiance from such a source was dumfounding. Then, luckily, Penrod recollected something and glanced at the automobile.

Perceiving therein not only the alert chauffeur but the magnificent outlines of Mrs. Levy, his enemy's mother, he manœuvred his lifted hand so that it seemed he had but meant to scratch his ear.

"Well, I guess I better be goin'," he said casually. "See you t'-morrow!"

Maurice mounted to the lap of luxury, and Penrod strolled away with an assumption of careless ease that was put to a severe strain when, from the rear window of the car, a sudden protuberance in the nature of a small, dark, curly head shrieked scornfully:

"Go on—you big stiff!"

The cotillon loomed dismally before Penrod now; but it was his duty to secure a partner and he set about it with a dreary heart. The delay occasioned by his fruitless attempt on Marjorie and the altercation with his enemy at her gate had allowed other ladies ample time to prepare for callers —and to receive them. Sadly he went from house to house, finding that he had been preceded in one after the other. Altogether his hand for the cotillon was declined eleven times that afternoon on the legitimate ground of previous engagement. This, with Marjorie, scored off all except five of the seventeen possible partners; and four of the five were also sealed away from him, as he learned in chance encounters with other boys upon the street.

One lady alone remained; he bowed to the inevitable and entered this lorn damsel's gate at twilight with an air of great discouragement. The lorn damsel was Miss Rennsdale, aged eight.

We are apt to forget that there are actually times of life when too much youth is a handicap. Miss Rennsdale was beautiful; she danced like a première; she had every charm but age. On that account alone had she been allowed so much time to prepare to receive callers that it was only by the most manful efforts she could keep her lip from trembling.

A decorous maid conducted the long-belated applicant to her where she sat upon a sofa beside a nursery governess. The decorous maid announced him composedly as he made his entrance.

"Mr. Penrod Schofield!"

Miss Rennsdale suddenly burst into loud sobs.

"Oh!" she wailed. "I just knew it would be him!"

The decorous maid's composure vanished at once—likewise her decorum. She clapped her hand over her mouth and fled, uttering sounds. The governess, however, set herself

*Following the form prescribed by Professor Bartet,
he advanced several paces toward the stricken lady
and bowed formally*

to comfort her heartbroken charge, and presently succeeded in restoring Miss Rennsdale to a semblance of that poise with which a lady receives callers and accepts invitations to dance cotillons. But she continued to sob at intervals.

Feeling himself at perhaps a disadvantage, Penrod made offer of his hand for the morrow with a little embarrassment. Following the form prescribed by Professor Bartet, he advanced several paces toward the stricken lady and bowed formally.

"I hope," he said by rote, "you're well, and your parents also in good health. May I have the pleasure of dancing the cotillon as your partner t'-morrow afternoon?"

The wet eyes of Miss Rennsdale searched his countenance without pleasure, and a shudder wrung her small shoulders; but the governess whispered to her instructively, and she made a great effort.

"I thu-thank you fu-for your polite invu-invu-invutation; and I ac——" Thus far she progressed when emotion overcame her again. She beat frantically upon the sofa with fists and heels. "Oh, I *did* want it to be Georgie Bassett!"

"No, no, no!" said the governess, and whispered urgently, whereupon Miss Rennsdale was able to complete her acceptance.

"And I ac-accept wu-with pu-pleasure!" she moaned, and immediately, uttering a loud yell, flung herself face downward upon the sofa, clutching her governess convulsively.

Somewhat disconcerted, Penrod bowed again.

"I thank you for your polite acceptance," he murmured hurriedly; "and I trust—I trust—I forget. Oh, yes—I trust we shall have a most enjoyable occasion. Pray present my compliments to your parents; and I must now wish you a very good afternoon."

Concluding these courtly demonstrations with another bow he withdrew in fair order, though thrown into partial confusion in the hall by a final wail from his crushed hostess:

"Oh! Why couldn't it be anybody but *him!*"

CHAPTER XIII

THE SMALLPOX MEDICINE

NEXT morning Penrod woke in profound depression of spirit, the cotillon ominous before him. He pictured Marjorie Jones and Maurice, graceful and light-hearted, flitting by him fairylike, loosing silvery laughter upon him as he engaged in the struggle to keep step with a partner about four years and two feet his junior. It was hard enough for Penrod to keep step with a girl of his size.

The foreboding vision remained with him, increasing in vividness, throughout the forenoon. He found himself unable to fix his mind upon anything else, and, having bent his gloomy footsteps toward the sawdust-box, after breakfast, presently descended therefrom, abandoning Harold

Ramorez where he had left him the preceding Saturday. Then, as he sat communing silently with wistful Duke, in the storeroom, coquettish fortune looked his way.

It was the habit of Penrod's mother not to throw away anything whatsoever until years of storage conclusively proved there would never be a use for it; but a recent house-cleaning had ejected upon the back porch a great quantity of bottles and other paraphernalia of medicine, left over from illnesses in the family during a period of several years. This débris Della, the cook, had collected in a large market basket, adding to it some bottles of flavouring extracts that had proved unpopular in the household; also, old catsup bottles; a jar or two of preserves gone bad; various rejected dental liquids—and other things. And she carried the basket out to the storeroom in the stable.

Penrod was at first unaware of what lay before him. Chin on palms, he sat upon the iron rim of a former aquarium and stared morbidly through the open door at the checkered departing back of Della. It was another who saw treasure in the basket she had left.

Mr. Samuel Williams, aged eleven, and congenial to Penrod in years, sex and disposition, appeared in the doorway, shaking into foam a black liquid within a pint bottle, stoppered by a thumb.

"Yay, Penrod!" the visitor gave greeting.

"Yay," said Penrod with slight enthusiasm. "What you got?"

"Lickrish water."

"Drinkin's!" Penrod demanded promptly. This is equivalent to the cry of "Biters" when an apple is shown, and establishes unquestionable title.

"Down to there!" Sam stipulated, removing his thumb to affix it firmly as a mark upon the side of the bottle—a check upon gormandizing that remained carefully in place while Penrod drank. This rite concluded, the visitor's eye fell upon the basket deposited by Della. He emitted tokens of pleasure.

"Looky! Looky! Looky there! That ain't any good pile o' stuff—oh, no!"

"What for?"

"Drug store!" Sam shouted. "We'll be partners——"

"Or else," Penrod suggested, "I'll run the drug store and you be a customer——"

"No! Partners!" Sam insisted, with such conviction that his host yielded; and within ten minutes the drug store was doing a heavy business with imaginary patrons. Improvising counters with boards and boxes, and setting forth a very druggish-looking stock from the basket, each of the partners found occupation to his taste—Penrod as salesman and Sam as prescription clerk.

"Here you are, madam!" Penrod said briskly, offering a vial of Sam's mixing to an invisible matron. "This will cure your husband in a few minutes. Here's the camphor, mister. Call again! Fifty cents' worth of pills? Yes, madam. There you are! Hurry up with that dose for the nigger lady, Bill!"

"I'll 'tend to it soon's I get time, Jim," the prescription clerk replied. "I'm busy fixin' the smallpox medicine for the sick policeman downtown."

Penrod stopped sales to watch this operation. Sam had found an empty pint bottle and, with the pursed lips and measuring eye of a great chemist, was engaged in filling it from other bottles. First, he poured into it some of the syrup from the condemned preserves, and a quantity of extinct hair oil; next, the remaining contents of a dozen small vials cryptically labelled with physicians' prescriptions; then some remnants of catsup and essence of beef and what was left in several bottles of mouthwash; after that, a quantity of rejected flavouring extract—topping off by shaking into the mouth of the bottle various powders from small pink papers, relics of Mr. Schofield's influenza of the preceding winter.

Sam examined the combination with concern, appearing unsatisfied. "We got to make that smallpox medicine good

Penrod stopped sales to watch this operation

and strong!" he remarked; and, his artistic sense growing more powerful than his appetite, he poured about a
quarter of the licorice water into the smallpox medicine.

"What you doin'?" protested Penrod. "What you want
to waste that lickrish water for? We ought to keep it to
drink when we're tired."

"I guess I got a right to use my own lickrish water any
way I want to," the prescription clerk replied. "I tell you,
you can't get smallpox medicine too strong. Look at her
now!" He held the bottle up admiringly. "She's as black as
lickrish. I bet you she's strong all right!"

"I wonder how she tastes?" said Penrod thoughtfully.

"Don't smell so awful much," Sam observed, sniffing the
bottle—"a good deal, though!"

"I wonder if it'd make us sick to drink it?" said Penrod.

Sam looked at the bottle thoughtfully; then his eye,
wandering, fell upon Duke, placidly curled up near the
door, and lighted with the advent of an idea new to him, but
old, old in the world—older than Egypt!

"Let's give Duke some!" he cried.

That was the spark. They acted immediately; and a
minute later Duke, released from custody with a competent
potion of the smallpox medicine inside him, settled conclusively their doubts concerning its effect. The patient
animal, accustomed to expect the worst at all times, walked
out of the door, shaking his head with an air of considerable
annoyance, opening and closing his mouth with singular
energy—and so repeatedly that they began to count the
number of times he did it. Sam thought it was thirty-nine
times; but Penrod had counted forty-one before other and
more striking symptoms appeared.

All things come from Mother Earth and must return—
Duke restored much at this time. Afterward, he ate heartily
of grass; and then, over his shoulder, he bent upon his
master one inscrutable look and departed feebly to the
front yard.

The two boys had watched the process with warm interest. "I told you she was strong!" said Mr. Williams proudly.

"Yes, sir—she is!" Penrod was generous enough to admit. "I expect she's strong enough——" He paused in thought, and added: "We haven't got a horse any more."

"I bet you she'd fix him if you had!" said Sam. And it may be that this was no idle boast.

The pharmaceutical game was not resumed; the experiment upon Duke had made the drug store commonplace and stimulated the appetite for stronger meat. Lounging in the doorway, the near-vivisectionists sipped licorice water alternately and conversed.

"I bet some of our smallpox medicine would fix ole P'fessor Bartet all right!" quoth Penrod. "I wish he'd come along and ask us for some."

"We could tell him it was lickrish water," added Sam, liking the idea. "The two bottles look almost the same."

"Then we wouldn't have to go to his ole cotillon this afternoon," Penrod sighed. "There wouldn't be any!"

"Who's your partner, Pen?"

"Who's yours?"

"Who's yours? I just ast you."

"Oh, she's all right!" And Penrod smiled boastfully.

"I bet you wanted to dance with Marjorie!" said his friend.

"Me? I wouldn't dance with that girl if she begged me to! I wouldn't dance with her to save her from drowning! I wouldn't da——"

"Oh, no—you wouldn't!" interrupted Mr. Williams skeptically.

Penrod changed his tone and became persuasive.

"Looky here, Sam," he said confidentially. "I've got a mighty nice partner; but my mother don't like her mother, and so I've been thinking I better not dance with her. I'll tell you what I'll do; I've got a mighty good sling in the house, and I'll give it to you if you'll change partners."

"You want to change and you don't even know who mine is!" Sam said, and he made the simple though precocious deduction: "Yours must be a lala! Well, I invited Mabel Rorebeck, and she wouldn't let me change if I wanted to. Mabel Rorebeck'd rather dance with me," he continued serenely, "than anybody; and she said she was awful afraid you'd ast her. But I ain't goin' to dance with Mabel after all, because this morning she sent me a note about her uncle died last night—and P'fessor Bartet'll have to find me a partner after I get there. Anyway I bet you haven't got any sling—and I bet your partner's Baby Rennsdale!"

"What if she is?" said Penrod. "She's good enough for *me!*" This speech held not so much modesty in solution as intended praise of the lady. Taken literally, however, it was an understatement of the facts and wholly insincere.

"Yay!" jeered Mr. Williams, upon whom his friend's hypocrisy was quite wasted. "How can your mother not like her mother? Baby Rennsdale hasn't got any mother! You and her'll be a sight!"

That was Penrod's own conviction; and with this corroboration of it he grew so spiritless that he could offer no retort. He slid to a despondent sitting posture upon the doorsill and gazed wretchedly upon the ground, while his companion went to replenish the licorice water at the hydrant—enfeebling the potency of the liquor no doubt, but making up for that in quantity.

"Your mother goin' with you to the cotillon?" Sam asked, when he returned.

"No. She's goin' to meet me there. She's goin' somewhere first."

"So's mine," said Sam. "I'll come by for you."

"All right."

"I better go before long. Noon whistles been blowin'."

"All right," Penrod repeated dully.

Sam turned to go; but paused. A new straw hat was peregrinating along the fence near the two boys. This hat belonged to someone passing upon the sidewalk of the cross-street; and the someone was Maurice Levy. Even as they stared, he halted and regarded them over the fence with two small, dark eyes.

Fate had brought about this moment and this confrontation.

CHAPTER XIV

MAURICE LEVY'S CONSTITUTION

"'L O, SAM!" Maurice said cautiously. "What you doin'?"
Penrod at that instant had a singular experience
—an intellectual shock like a flash of fire in the
brain. Sitting in darkness, a great light flooded him with
wild brilliance. He gasped.

"What you doin'?" Mr. Levy repeated.

Penrod sprang to his feet, seized the licorice bottle, shook
it with stoppering thumb, and took a long drink with histrionic unction.

"What you doin'?" Maurice asked for the third time, Sam
Williams not having decided upon a reply.

It was Penrod who answered. "Drinkin' lickrish water,"
he said simply, and wiped his mouth with such delicious

enjoyment that Sam's jaded thirst was instantly stimulated. He took the bottle eagerly from Penrod.

"A-a-h!" exclaimed Penrod, smacking his lips. "That was a good un!"

The eyes above the fence glistened.

"Ask him if he don't want some," Penrod whispered urgently. "Quit drinkin' it! It's no good any more. Ask him!"

"What for?" the practical Sam demanded.

"Go on and ask him!" Penrod whispered fiercely.

"Say, M'rice!" Sam called, waving the bottle. "Want some?"

"Bring it here!" Mr. Levy requested.

"Come on over and get some," returned Sam, being prompted.

"I can't. Penrod Schofield's after me."

"No, I'm not," Penrod said reassuringly. "I won't touch you, M'rice. I made up with you yesterday afternoon—don't you remember? You're all right with me, M'rice."

Maurice looked undecided. But Penrod had the delectable bottle again, and, tilting it above his lips, affected to let the cool liquid purl enrichingly into him, while with his right hand he stroked his middle façade ineffably. Maurice's mouth watered.

"Here!" cried Sam, stirred again by the superb manifestations of his friend. "Gimme that!"

Penrod brought the bottle down, surprisingly full after so much gusto, but withheld it from Sam; and the two scuffled for its possession. Nothing in the world could have so worked upon the desire of the yearning observer beyond the fence.

"Honest, Penrod—you ain't goin' to touch me if I come in your yard?" he called. "Honest?"

"Cross my heart!" answered Penrod, holding the bottle away from Sam. "And we'll let you drink all you want."

Maurice hastily climbed the fence, and while he was thus occupied Mr. Samuel Williams received a great enlightenment. With startling rapidity Penrod, standing just outside the storeroom door, extended his arm within the room, deposited the licorice water upon the counter of the drug store, seized in its stead the bottle of smallpox medicine, and extended it cordially toward the advancing Maurice.

Genius is like that—great, simple, broad strokes!

Dazzled, Mr. Samuel Williams leaned against the wall. He had the sensations of one who comes suddenly into the presence of a chef-d'œuvre. Perhaps his first coherent thought was that almost universal one on such huge occasions: "Why couldn't *I* have done that!"

Sam might have been even more dazzled had he guessed that he figured not altogether as a spectator in the sweeping and magnificent conception of the new Talleyrand. Sam had no partner for the cotillon. If Maurice was to be absent from that festivity—as it began to seem he might be—Penrod needed a male friend to take care of Miss Rennsdale; and he believed he saw his way to compel Mr. Williams to be that male friend. For this he relied largely upon the prospective conduct of Miss Rennsdale when he should get the matter before her—he was inclined to believe she would favour the exchange. As for Talleyrand Penrod himself, he was going to dance that cotillon with Marjorie Jones!

"You can have all you can drink at one pull, M'rice," Penrod said kindly.

"You said I could have all I want!" protested Maurice, reaching for the bottle.

"No, I didn't," Penrod returned quickly, holding it away from the eager hand.

"He did, too! Didn't he, Sam?"

Sam could not reply; his eyes, fixed upon the bottle, protruded strangely.

"You heard him—didn't you, Sam?"

"Well, if I did say it I didn't mean it!" Penrod said hastily, quoting from one of the authorities. "Looky here,

M'rice," he continued, assuming a more placative and reasoning tone, "that wouldn't be fair to us. I guess we want some of our own lickrish water, don't we? The bottle ain't much over two-thirds full anyway. What I meant was, you can have all you can drink at one pull."

"How do you mean?"

"Why, this way: you can gulp all you want, so long as you keep swallering; but you can't take the bottle out of your mouth and commence again. Soon's you quit swaller- ing it's Sam's turn."

"No; you can have next, Penrod," Sam said.

"Well, anyway, I mean M'rice has to give the bottle up the minute he stops swallering."

Craft appeared upon the face of Maurice, like a poster pasted on a wall. "I can drink so long I don't stop swaller- ing?"

"Yes; that's it."

"All right!" he cried. "Gimme the bottle!"

And Penrod placed it in his hand.

"You promise to let me drink until I quit swallering?" Maurice insisted.

"Yes!" said both boys together.

With that, Maurice placed the bottle to his lips and be- gan to drink. Penrod and Sam leaned forward in breathless excitement. They had feared Maurice might smell the con- tents of the bottle; but that danger was past—this was the crucial moment. Their fondest hope was that he would make his first swallow a voracious one—it was impossible to imagine a second. They expected one big, gulping swal- low and then an explosion, with fountain effects.

Little they knew the mettle of their man! Maurice swal- lowed once; he swallowed twice—and thrice—and he con- tinued to swallow! No Adam's apple was sculptured on that juvenile throat; but the internal progress of the liquid was not a whit the less visible. His eyes gleamed with cunning and malicious triumph, sidewise, at the stunned conspirators; he was fulfilling the conditions of the draught, not once breaking the thread of that marvellous swallering.

His audience stood petrified. Already Maurice had swallowed more than they had given Duke—and still the liquor receded in the uplifted bottle! And now the clear glass gleamed above the dark contents full half the vessel's length —and Maurice went on drinking! Slowly the clear glass increased in its dimensions—slowly the dark diminished.

Sam Williams made a horrified movement to check him— but Maurice protested passionately with his disengaged arm and made vehement vocal noises remindful of the contract; whereupon Sam desisted and watched the continuing performance in a state of grisly fascination.

Maurice drank it all! He drained the last drop and threw the bottle in the air, uttering loud ejaculations of triumph and satisfaction.

"Hah!" he cried, blowing out his cheeks, inflating his chest, squaring his shoulders, patting his stomach and wiping his mouth contentedly. "Hah! Aha! Waha! Wafwah! But that was good!"

The two boys stood looking at him in stupor.

"Well, I gotta say this," said Maurice graciously: "You stuck to your bargain all right and treated me fair."

Stricken with a sudden horrible suspicion, Penrod entered the storeroom in one stride and lifted the bottle of licorice water to his nose—then to his lips. It was weak but good; he had made no mistake. And Maurice had really drained —to the dregs—the bottle of old hair tonics, dead catsups, syrups of undesirable preserves, condemned extracts of vanilla and lemon, decayed chocolate, ex-essence of beef, mixed dental preparations, aromatic spirits of ammonia, spirits of nitre, alcohol, arnica, quinine, ipecac, sal volatile, nux vomica and licorice water—with traces of arsenic, belladonna and strychnine.

Penrod put the licorice water out of sight and turned to face the others. Maurice was seating himself on a box just outside the door and had taken a package of cigarettes from his pocket.

"Nobody can see me from here, can they?" he said, striking a match. "You fellers smoke?"

"No," said Sam, staring at him haggardly.

"No," said Penrod in a whisper.

Maurice lit his cigarette and puffed showily.

"Well, sir," he remarked, "you fellers are certainly square —I gotta say that much. Honest, Penrod, I thought you was after me! I did think so," he added sunnily; "but now I guess you like me, or else you wouldn't of stuck to it about lettin' me drink it all if I kept on swallering."

He chatted on with complete geniality, smoking his cigarette in content. And as he ran from one topic to another his hearers stared at him in a kind of torpor. Never once did they exchange a glance with each other; their eyes were frozen to Maurice. The cheerful conversationalist made it evident that he was not without gratitude.

"Well," he said, as he finished his cigarette and rose to go, "you fellers have treated me nice—and some day you come over to my yard; I'd like to run with you fellers. You're the kind of fellers I like."

Penrod's jaw fell; Sam's mouth had been open all the time. Neither spoke.

"I gotta go," Maurice observed, consulting a handsome watch. "Gotta get dressed for the cotillon right after lunch. Come on, Sam. Don't you have to go, too?"

Sam nodded dazedly.

"Well, good-bye, Penrod," said Maurice cordially. "I'm glad you like me all right. Come on, Sam."

Penrod leaned against the doorpost and with fixed and glazing eyes watched the departure of his two visitors. Maurice was talking volubly, with much gesticulation, as they went; but Sam walked mechanically and in silence, staring at his brisk companion and keeping at a little distance from him.

They passed from sight, Maurice still conversing gayly

—and Penrod slowly betook himself into the house, his head bowed upon his chest.

Some three hours later, Mr. Samuel Williams, waxen clean and in sweet raiment, made his reappearance in Penrod's yard, yodelling a code-signal to summon forth his friend. He yodelled loud, long and frequently, finally securing a faint response from the upper air.

"Where are you?" Mr. Williams shouted, his roving glance searching ambient heights. Another low-spirited yodel reaching his ear, he perceived the head and shoulders of his friend projecting above the roofridge of the stable. The rest of Penrod's body was concealed from view, reposing upon the opposite slant of the gable and precariously secured by the crooking of his elbows over the ridge.

"Yay! What you doin' up there?"

"Nothin'."

"You better be careful!" Sam called. "You'll slide off and fall down in the alley if you don't look out. I come pert' near it last time we was up there. Come on down! Ain't you goin' to the cotillon?"

Penrod made no reply. Sam came nearer.

"Say," he called up in a guarded voice, "I went to our telephone a while ago and ast him how he was feelin', and he said he felt fine!"

"So did I," said Penrod. "He told me he felt bully!"

Sam thrust his hands in his pockets and brooded. The opening of the kitchen door caused a diversion. It was Della.

"Musther Penrod," she bellowed forthwith, "come ahn down fr'm up there! Y'r mamma's at the dancin' class waitin' fer ye, an' she's telephoned me they're goin' to begin —an' what's the matter with ye? Come ahn down fr'm up there!"

"Come on!" Sam urged. "We'll be late. There go Maurice and Marjorie now."

A glittering car spun by, disclosing briefly a genre picture of Marjorie Jones in pink, supporting a monstrous sheaf of American Beauty roses. Maurice, sitting shining and joyous beside her, saw both boys and waved them a hearty greeting as the car turned the corner.

Penrod uttered some muffled words and then waved both arms—either in response or as an expression of his condition of mind; it may have been a gesture of despair. How much intention there was in this act—obviously so rash, considering the position he occupied—it is impossible to say. Undeniably there must remain a suspicion of deliberate purpose.

Della screamed and Sam shouted. Penrod had disappeared from view.

The delayed dance was about to begin a most uneven cotillon under the direction of its slightly frenzied instructor, when Samuel Williams arrived.

Mrs. Schofield hurriedly left the ballroom; while Miss Rennsdale, flushing with sudden happiness, curtsied profoundly to Professor Bartet and obtained his attention.

"I have told you fifty times," he informed her passionately ere she spoke, "I cannot make no such changes. If your partner comes you have to dance with him. You are going to drive me crazy, sure! What is it? What now? What you want?"

The damsel curtsied again and handed him the following communication, addressed to herself:

"Dear madam Please excuse me from dancing the cotilon with you this afternoon as I have fell off the barn

"Sincerely yours
"PENROD SCHOFIELD."

CHAPTER XV

THE TWO FAMILIES

PENROD entered the schoolroom, Monday morning, picturesquely leaning upon a man's cane shortened to support a cripple approaching the age of twelve. He arrived about twenty minutes late, limping deeply, his brave young mouth drawn with pain, and the sensation he created must have been a solace to him; the only possible criticism of this entrance being that it was just a shade too heroic. Perhaps for that reason it failed to stagger Miss Spence, a woman so saturated with suspicion that she penalized Penrod for tardiness as promptly and as coldly as if he had been a mere, ordinary, unmutilated boy. Nor would she entertain any discussion of the justice of her ruling. It seemed, almost, that she feared to argue with him.

However, the distinction of cane and limp remained to him, consolations that he protracted far into the week— until Thursday evening, in fact, when Mr. Schofield, observing from a window his son's pursuit of Duke round and round the backyard, confiscated the cane, with the promise that it should not remain idle if he saw Penrod limping again. Thus, succeeding a depressing Friday, another Saturday brought the necessity for new inventions.

It was a scented morning in apple-blossom time. At about ten of the clock Penrod emerged hastily from the kitchen door. His pockets bulged abnormally; so did his cheeks, and he swallowed with difficulty. A threatening mop, wielded by a cooklike arm in a checkered sleeve, followed him through the doorway, and he was preceded by a small, hurried, wistful dog with a warm doughnut in his mouth. The kitchen door slammed petulantly, enclosing the sore voice of Della, whereupon Penrod and Duke seated themselves upon the pleasant sward and immediately consumed the spoils of their raid.

From the cross-street that formed the side boundary of the Schofields' ample yard came a jingle of harness and the cadenced clatter of a pair of trotting horses, and Penrod, looking up, beheld the passing of a fat acquaintance, torpid amid the conservative splendours of a rather old-fashioned victoria. This was Roderick Magsworth Bitts, Junior, a fellow sufferer at the Friday Afternoon Dancing Class, but otherwise not often a companion; a home-sheltered lad, tutored privately and preserved against the coarsening influences of rude comradeship and miscellaneous information. Heavily overgrown in all physical dimensions, virtuous, and placid, this cloistered mutton was wholly uninteresting to Penrod Schofield. Nevertheless, Roderick Magsworth Bitts, Junior, was a personage on account of the importance of the Magsworth Bitts family; and it was Penrod's destiny to increase Roderick's celebrity far, far beyond its present aristocratic limitations.

The Magsworth Bittses were important because they

At about ten of the clock Penrod emerged hastily from the kitchen door

were impressive; there was no other reason. And they were impressive because they believed themselves important. The adults of the family were impregnably formal; they dressed with reticent elegance, and wore the same nose and the same expression—an expression which indicated that they knew something exquisite and sacred that other people could never know. Other people, in their presence, were apt to feel mysteriously ignoble and to become secretly uneasy about ancestors, gloves and pronunciation. The Magsworth Bitts manner was withholding and reserved, though sometimes gracious, granting small smiles as great favours and giving off a chilling kind of preciousness. Naturally, when any citizen of the community did anything unconventional or improper, or made a mistake, or had a relative who went wrong, that citizen's first and worst fear was that the Magsworth Bittses would hear of it. In fact, this painful family had for years terrorized the community, though the community had never realized that it was terrorized, and invariably spoke of the family as the "most charming circle in town." By common consent, Mrs. Roderick Magsworth Bitts officiated as the supreme model as well as critic-in-chief of morals and deportment for all the unlucky people prosperous enough to be elevated to her acquaintance.

Magsworth was the important part of the name. Mrs. Roderick Magsworth Bitts was a Magsworth born, herself, and the Magsworth crest decorated not only Mrs. Magsworth Bitts's note-paper but was on the china, on the table linen, on the chimney-pieces, on the opaque glass of the front door, on the victoria, and on the harness, though omitted from the garden-hose and the lawn-mower.

Naturally, no sensible person dreamed of connecting that illustrious crest with the unfortunate and notorious Rena Magsworth whose name had grown week by week into larger and larger type upon the front pages of newspapers, owing to the gradually increasing public, and official belief that she had poisoned a family of eight. However, the statement that no sensible person could have connected the Magsworth Bitts family with the arsenical Rena takes no account of Penrod Schofield.

Penrod never missed a murder, a hanging or an electrocution in the newspapers; he knew almost as much about Rena Magsworth as her jurymen did, though they sat in a court-room two hundred miles away, and he had it in mind—so frank he was—to ask Roderick Magsworth Bitts, Junior, if the murderess happened to be a relative.

The present encounter, being merely one of apathetic greeting, did not afford the opportunity. Penrod took off his cap, and Roderick, seated between his mother and one of his grown-up sisters, nodded sluggishly; but neither Mrs. Magsworth Bitts nor her daughter acknowledged the salutation of the boy in the yard. They disapproved of him as a person of little consequence, and that little, bad. Snubbed, Penrod thoughtfully restored his cap to his head. A boy can be cut as effectually as a man, and this one was chilled to a low temperature. He wondered if they despised him because they had seen a last fragment of doughnut in his hand; then he thought that perhaps it was Duke who had disgraced him. Duke was certainly no fashionable looking dog.

The resilient spirits of youth, however, presently revived, and, discovering a spider upon one knee and a beetle simultaneously upon the other, Penrod forgot Mrs. Roderick Magsworth Bitts in the course of some experiments infringing upon the domain of Doctor Carrel. Penrod's efforts—with the aid of a pin—to effect a transference of living organism were unsuccessful; but he convinced himself forever that a spider cannot walk with a beetle's legs. Della then enhanced zoölogical interest by depositing upon the back porch a large rat-trap from the cellar, the prison of four live rats awaiting execution.

Penrod at once took possession, retiring to the empty stable, where he installed the rats in a small wooden box with a sheet of broken window-glass—held down by a brickbat—over the top. Thus the symptoms of their agitation, when the box was shaken or hammered upon, could be studied at leisure. Altogether this Saturday was starting splendidly.

After a time, the student's attention was withdrawn from his specimens by a peculiar smell, that, being followed up by a system of selective sniffing, proved to be an emanation leaking into the stable from the alley. He opened the back door.

Across the alley was a cottage that a thrifty neighbour had built on the rear line of his lot and rented to negroes; and the fact that a negro family was now in process of "moving in" was manifested by the presence of a thin mule and a ramshackle wagon, the latter laden with the semblance of a stove and a few other unpretentious household articles.

A very small dark boy stood near the mule. In his hand was a rusty chain, and at the end of the chain the delighted Penrod perceived the source of the special smell he was tracing—a large raccoon. Duke, who had shown not the slightest interest in the rats, set up a frantic barking and simulated a ravening assault upon the strange animal. It was only a bit of acting, however, for Duke was an old dog, had suffered much and desired no unnecessary sorrow, wherefore he confined his demonstrations to alarums and excursions, and presently sat down at a distance and expressed himself by intermittent threatenings in a quavering falsetto.

"What's that 'coon's name?" Penrod asked, intending no discourtesy.

"Aim gommo mame," said the small darky.

"What?"

"Aim gommo mame."

"*What?*"

The small darky looked annoyed. "Aim *gommo* mame, I hell you," he said impatiently.

Penrod conceived that insult was intended. "What's the

matter of you?" he demanded advancing. "You get fresh with *me*, and I'll——"

"Hyuh, white boy!" A coloured youth of Penrod's own age appeared in the doorway of the cottage. "You let 'at brothuh mine alone. He ain' do nothin' to you."

"Well, why can't he answer?"

"He can't. He can't talk no better'n what he *was* talkin'. He tongue-tie'."

"Oh," Penrod said mollified. Then, obeying an impulse so universally aroused in the human breast under like circumstances that it has become a quip, he turned to the afflicted one.

"Talk some more," he begged eagerly.

"I hoe you ackoom aim gommo mame," was the prompt response, in which a slight ostentation was manifest. Unmistakable tokens of vanity had appeared upon the small, swart countenance.

"What's he mean?" Penrod asked, enchanted.

"He say he tole you 'at 'coon ain' got no name."

"What's *your* name?"

"I'm name Herman."

"What's his name?" Penrod pointed to the tongue-tied boy.

"Verman."

"What!"

"Verman. Was three us boys in ow fam'ly. Ol'est one name Sherman. 'N'en come me; I'm Herman. 'N'en come him; he Verman. Sherman dead. Verman, he de littles' one."

"You goin' to live here?"

"Umhuh. Done move in f'm way outen on a fahm."

He pointed to the north with his right hand, and Penrod's eyes opened wide as they followed the gesture. Herman had no forefinger on that hand.

"Look there!" Penrod exclaimed. "You haven't got any finger!"

"*I* mum map," said Verman, with egregious pride.

"*He* done 'at," Herman interpreted, chuckling. "Yessuh;

done chop 'er spang off, long 'go. He's a playin' wif a ax an' I lay my finguh on de do'-sill an' I say, 'Verman, chop 'er off!' So Verman he chop 'er right spang off up to de roots! Yessuh."

"What *for?*"

"Jes' fo' nothin'."

"He hoe me hoo," said Verman.

"Yessuh, I tole him to," said Herman, "an' he chop 'er off, an' ey ain't airy oth' one evuh grown on wheres de ole one use to grow. Nosuh!"

"But what'd you tell him to do it for?"

"Nothin'. I jes' said it 'at way—an' he jes' chop 'er off!"

Both brothers looked pleased and proud. Penrod's profound interest was flatteringly visible, a tribute to their unusualness.

"Hem bow goy," suggested Verman eagerly.

"Aw ri'," Herman said. "Ow sistuh Queenie, she a growed-up woman; she got a goituh."

"Got a what?"

"Goituh. Swellin' on her neck—grea' big swellin'. She heppin' Mammy move in now. You look in de front-room winduh wheres she sweepin'; you kin see it on her."

Penrod looked in the window and was rewarded by a fine view of Queenie's goitre. He had never before seen one, and only the lure of further conversation on the part of Verman brought him from the window.

"Verman say tell you 'bout Pappy," explained Herman. "Mammy an' Queenie move in town an' go' git de house all fix up befo' Pappy git out."

"Out of where?"

"Jail. Pappy cut a man, an' de police done kep' him in jail evuh sense Chris'mus-time; but dey go' tuhn him loose ag'in nex' week."

"What'd he cut the other man with?"

"Wif a pitchfawk."

Penrod began to feel that a lifetime spent with this fascinating family were all too short. The brothers, glowing

with amiability, were as enraptured as he. For the first
time in their lives they moved in the rich glamour of sen-
sationalism. Herman was prodigal of gesture with his right
hand; and Verman, chuckling with delight, talked fluently,
though somewhat consciously. They cheerfully agreed to
keep the raccoon—already beginning to be mentioned as
"our 'coon" by Penrod—in Mr. Schofield's empty stable,
and, when the animal had been chained to the wall near the
box of rats and supplied with a pan of fair water, they
assented to their new friend's suggestion (inspired by a fine
sense of the artistic harmonies) that the heretofore name-
less pet be christened Sherman, in honour of their deceased
relative.

At this juncture was heard from the front yard the
sound of that yodelling that is the peculiar accomplishment of those whose voices have not "changed". Penrod
yodelled a response; and Mr. Samuel Williams appeared, a
large bundle under his arm.

"Yay, Penrod!" was his greeting, casual enough from
without; but, having entered, he stopped short and emitted
a prodigious whistle. "*Ya-a-ay!*" he then shouted. "Look at
the 'coon!"

"I guess you better say, 'Look at the 'coon!'" Penrod
returned proudly. "They's a good deal more'n him to look
at, too. Talk some, Verman."

Verman complied.

Sam was warmly interested. "What'd you say his name
was?" he asked.

"Verman."

"How d'you spell it?"

"V-e-r-m-a-n," Penrod replied, having previously received
this information from Herman.

"Oh!" said Sam.

"Point to sumpthing, Herman," Penrod commanded, and
Sam's excitement, when Herman pointed, was sufficient to
the occasion.

Penrod, the discoverer, continued his exploitation of the manifold wonders of the Sherman, Herman and Verman collection. With the air of a proprietor he escorted Sam into the alley for a good look at Queenie (who seemed not to care for her increasing celebrity) and proceeded to a dramatic climax—the recital of the episode of the pitchfork and its consequences.

The cumulative effect was enormous, and could have but one possible result. The normal boy is always at least one half Barnum.

"Let's get up a SHOW!"

Penrod and Sam both claimed to have said it first, a question left unsettled in the ecstasies of hurried preparation. The bundle under Sam's arm, brought with no definite purpose, proved to have been an inspiration. It consisted of broad sheets of light yellow wrapping-paper, discarded by Sam's mother in her spring house-cleaning. There were half-filled cans and buckets of paint in the storeroom adjoining the carriage-house, and presently the side wall of the stable flamed information upon the passer-by from a great and spreading poster.

"Publicity", primal requisite of all theatrical and amphitheatrical enterprise thus provided, subsequent arrangements proceeded with a fury of energy that transformed the empty hay-loft. True, it is impossible to say just what the hay-loft was transformed into; but history warrantably clings to the statement that it was transformed. Duke and Sherman were secured to the rear wall at a considerable distance from each other, after an exhibition of reluctance on the part of Duke, during which he displayed a nervous energy and agility almost miraculous in so small and middle-aged a dog. Benches were improvised for spectators; the rats were brought up; finally the rafters, corn-crib and hay-chute were ornamented with flags and strips of bunting from Sam Williams's attic, Sam returning from the excursion wearing an old silk hat, and accompanied (on account of a rope) by a fine dachshund encountered on the highway. In the matter of personal decoration paint was generously used: an interpretation of the spiral, inclining to whites and greens, becoming brilliantly effective upon the dark facial backgrounds of Herman and Verman; while the countenances of Sam and Penrod were each supplied with the black moustache and imperial, lacking which no professional showman can be esteemed conscientious.

It was regretfully decided, in council, that no attempt be made to add Queenie to the list of exhibits, her brothers warmly declining to act as ambassadors in that cause. They were certain Queenie would not like the idea, they said, and Herman picturesquely described her activity on occasions when she had been annoyed by too much attention to her appearance. However, Penrod's disappointment was alleviated by an inspiration that came to him in a moment of pondering upon the dachshund, and the entire party went forth to add an enriching line to the poster.

They found a group of seven, including two adults, already gathered in the street to read and admire this work.

SCHoFiELD & WiLLiAMS
BiG SHOW
ADMiSSioN 1 CENT oR 20 PiNS
MUSUEM oF CURioSiTES
Now GoiNG oN
SHERMAN HERMAN & VERMAN
THiER FATHERS iN JAiL STABED A
MAN WiTH A
PiTCHFORK
SHERMAN THE WiLD ANIMAL
CAPTURED iN AFRiCA
HERMAN THE ONE FiNGERED TATOOD
WILD MAN VERMAN THE SAVAGE TATOOD
WILD BoY TALKS ONLY iN HiS NAiTiVE
LANGUAGS. Do NoT FAIL TO SEE DUKE
THE INDiAN DOG ALSO THE MiCHiGAN
TRAiNED RATS

A heated argument took place between Sam and Penrod, the point at issue being settled, finally, by the drawing of straws; whereupon Penrod, with pardonable self-importance —in the presence of an audience now increased to nine— slowly painted the words inspired by the dachshund:

IMPoRTENT Do NoT MISS THE SoUTH AMERiCAN DoG PART ALLIGATOR.

CHAPTER XVI

THE NEW STAR

SAM, Penrod, Herman and Verman withdrew in considerable state from non-paying view, and, repairing to the hay-loft, declared the exhibition open to the public. Oral proclamation was made by Sam, and then the loitering multitude was enticed by the seductive strains of a band; the two partners performing upon combs and paper, Herman and Verman upon tin pans with sticks.

The effect was immediate. Visitors appeared upon the stairway and sought admission. Herman and Verman took position among the exhibits, near the wall; Sam stood at the entrance, officiating as barker and ticket-seller; while Penrod, with debonair suavity, acted as curator, master of ceremonies and lecturer. He greeted the first to enter with a courtly bow. They consisted of Miss Rennsdale and her nursery governess, and they paid spot cash for their admission.

"Walk in, lay-deeze, walk right in—pray do not obstruck the passageway," said Penrod, in a remarkable voice. "Pray be seated; there is room for each and all."

Miss Rennsdale and governess were followed by Mr. Georgie Bassett and baby sister (which proves the perfection of Georgie's character) and six or seven other neighbourhood children—a most satisfactory audience, although, subsequent to Miss Rennsdale and governess, admission was wholly by pin.

"*Gen*-til-mun and *lay*-deeze," Penrod shouted, "I will first call your at-tain-shon to our genuine South American dog, part alligator!" He pointed to the dachshund, and added, in his ordinary tone, "That's him." Straightway reassuming the character of showman, he bellowed: "*Next*, you see Duke, the genuine, full-blooded Indian dog from the far Western Plains and Rocky Mountains. *Next*, the trained Michigan rats, captured 'way up there and trained to jump and run all around the box at the—at the—at the slightest *pre*-text!" He paused, partly to take breath and partly to enjoy his own surprised discovery that this phrase was in his vocabulary.

"At the slightest *pre*-text!" he repeated, and continued, suiting the action to the word: "I will now hammer upon the box and each and all may see these genuine full-blooded Michigan rats perform at the slightest *pre*-text! There! (That's all they do now; but I and Sam are goin' to train 'em lots more before this afternoon.) *Gen*-til-mun and *lay*-deeze, I will kindly now call your at-tain-shon to Sherman, the wild animal from Africa, costing the lives of the wild trapper and many of his companions. *Next*, let me kindly interodoos Herman and Verman. Their father got mad and stuck his pitchfork right inside of another man, exactly as promised upon the advertisements outside the big tent, and got put in jail. Look at them well, gen-til-mun and lay-deeze, there is no extra charge, and *re-mem-bur* you are each and all now looking at two wild, tattooed men which the father of is in jail. Point, Herman. Each and all will have a chance to see. Point to sumpthing else, Herman. This is the only genuine one-fingered tattooed wild man. Last on the programme, gen-til-mun and lay-deeze, we have Verman, the savage tattooed wild boy that can't speak only his native foreign languages. Talk some, Verman."

Verman obliged and made an instantaneous hit. He was encored rapturously, again and again; and, thrilling with the unique pleasure of being appreciated and misunderstood at the same time, would have talked all day but too gladly. Sam Williams, however, with a true showman's foresight, whispered to Penrod, who rang down on the monologue.

"*Gen*-til-mun and *lay*-deeze, this closes our pufformance. Pray pass out quietly and with as little jostling as possible. As soon as you are all out, there's goin' to be a new pufformance, and each and all are welcome at the same and simple price of admission. Pray pass out quietly and with as little jostling as possible. *Re-mem-bur* the price is only one cent, the tenth part of a dime, or twenty pins, no bent ones taken. Pray pass out quietly and with as little jostling as possible. The Schofield and Williams Military Band will play before each pufformance, and each and all are welcome for the same and simple price of admission. Pray pass out quietly and with as little jostling as possible.

Forthwith, the Schofield and Williams Military Band began a second overture, in which something vaguely like a tune was at times distinguishable; and all of the first audience returned, most of them having occupied the interval in hasty excursions for more pins; Miss Rennsdale and governess, however, again paying coin of the Republic and receiving deference and the best seats accordingly. And when a third performance found all of the same inveterate patrons once more crowding the auditorium, and seven recruits added, the pleasurable excitement of the partners in their venture will be understood by any one who has seen a metropolitan manager strolling about the foyer of his theatre some evening during the earlier stages of an assured "phenomenal run".

From the first, there was no question which feature of the entertainment was the attraction extraordinary: Verman— Verman, the savage tattooed wild boy, speaking only his native foreign languages—Verman was a triumph! Beaming, wreathed in smiles, melodious, incredibly fluent, he had but to open his lips and a dead hush fell upon the audience. Breathless, they leaned forward, hanging upon his every semi-syllable, and, when Penrod checked the flow, burst into thunders of applause, that Verman received with happy laughter.

Alas! he delayed not o'er long to display all the egregiousness of a new star; but for a time there was no caprice of his too eccentric to be forgiven. During Penrod's lecture upon the other curios, the tattooed wild boy continually stamped his foot, grinned and gesticulated, tapping his tiny chest, and pointing to himself as it were to say: "Wait for Me! I am the Big Show." So soon they learn; so soon they learn! And (again alas!) this spoiled darling of public favour, like many another, was fated to know, in good time, the fickleness of that favour.

But during all the morning performances he was the idol of his audience and looked it! The climax of his popularity came during the fifth overture of the Schofield and Williams Military Band, when the music was quite drowned in the agitated clamours of Miss Rennsdale, who was endeavouring to ascend the stairs in spite of the physical dissuasion of her governess.

"I *won't* go home to lunch!" screamed Miss Rennsdale, her voice accompanied by a sound of ripping. "I *will* hear the tattooed wild boy talk some more! It's lovely—I *will* hear him talk! I *will! I will!* I want to listen to Verman— I *want* to— I WANT to——"

Wailing, she was borne away—of her sex not the first to be fascinated by obscurity, nor the last to champion its eloquence.

Verman was almost unendurable after this; but, like many, many other managers, Schofield and Williams restrained their choler, and even laughed fulsomely when their principal attraction essayed the rôle of a comedian in private, and capered and squawked in sheer, fatuous vanity.

The first performance of the afternoon rivalled the successes of the morning, and, although Miss Rennsdale was detained at home, thus drying up the single source of cash income developed before lunch, Maurice Levy appeared, escorting Marjorie Jones, and paid coin for two admissions, dropping the money into Sam's hand with a careless—nay, a contemptuous—gesture. At sight of Marjorie, Penrod Schofield flushed under his new moustache (repainted since noon) and lectured as he had never lectured before. A new grace invested his every gesture; a new sonorousness rang in his voice; a simple and manly pomposity marked his very walk as he passed from curio to curio. And when he fearlessly handled the box of rats and hammered upon it with cool *insouciance,* he beheld—for the first time in his life—a purl of admiration eddying in Marjorie's lovely eye, a certain softening of that eye. And then Verman spake—and Penrod was forgotten. Marjorie's eye rested upon him no more.

A heavily equipped chauffeur ascended the stairway, bearing the message that Mrs. Levy awaited her son and his lady. Thereupon, having devoured the last sound permitted (by the managers) to issue from Verman, Mr. Levy and Miss Jones departed to a real matinée at a real theatre, the limpid eyes of Marjorie looking back softly over her shoulder—but only at the tattooed wild boy. Nearly always it is woman who puts the irony into life.

After this, perhaps because of sated curiosity, perhaps on account of a pin famine, the attendance began to languish. Only four responded to the next call of the band:

Maurice Levy appeared, escorting Marjorie Jones,
and paid coin for two admissions

the four dwindled to three; finally the entertainment was given for one *blasé* auditor, and Schofield and Williams looked depressed. Then followed an interval when the band played in vain.

About three o'clock Schofield and Williams were gloomily discussing various unpromising devices for startling the public into a renewal of interest, when another patron unexpectedly appeared and paid a cent for his admission. News of the Big Show and Museum of Curiosities had at last penetrated the far, cold spaces of interstellar niceness, for this new patron consisted of no less than Roderick Magsworth Bitts, Junior, escaped in a white "sailor suit" from the Manor during a period of severe maternal and tutorial preoccupation.

He seated himself without parley, and the pufformance was offered for his entertainment with admirable conscientiousness. True to the Lady Clara caste and training, Roderick's pale, fat face expressed nothing except an impervious superiority and, as he sat, cold and unimpressed upon the front bench, like a large, white lump, it must be said that he made a discouraging audience "to play to". He was not, however, unresponsive—far from it. He offered comment very chilling to the warm grandiloquence of the orator.

"That's my uncle Ethelbert's dachshund," he remarked, at the beginning of the lecture. "You better take him back if you don't want to get arrested." And when Penrod, rather uneasily ignoring the interruption, proceeded to the exploitation of the genuine, full-blooded Indian dog, Duke, "Why don't you try to give that old dog away?" Roderick asked. "You couldn't sell him."

"My Papa would buy me a lots better 'coon than that," was the information volunteered a little later, "only I wouldn't want the nasty old thing."

Herman of the missing finger obtained no greater indulgence. "Pooh!" said Roderick. "We have two fox-terriers in our stables that took prizes at the kennel show, and their tails were *bit* off. There's a man that always bites fox-terriers' tails off."

"Oh, my gosh, what a lie!" exclaimed Sam Williams ignorantly. "Go on with the show whether he likes it or not, Penrod. He's paid his money."

Verman, confident in his own singular powers, chuckled openly at the failure of the other attractions to charm the frosty visitor, and, when his turn came, poured forth a torrent of conversation that was straightway dammed.

"Rotten," said Mr. Bitts languidly. "Anybody could talk like that. *I* could do it if I wanted to."

Verman paused suddenly.

"*Yes*, you could!" Penrod exclaimed, stung. "Let's hear you do it, then."

"Yessir!" the other partner shouted. "Let's just hear you *do* it!"

"I said I could if I wanted to," responded Roderick. "I didn't say I *would*."

"Yay! Knows he can't!" sneered Sam.

"I can, too, if I try."

"Well, let's hear you try."

So challenged, the visitor did try; but, in the absence of an impartial jury, his effort was considered so pronounced a failure that he was howled down, derided and mocked with great clamours.

"Anyway," said Roderick, when things had quieted down, "if I couldn't get up a better show than this I'd sell out and leave town."

Not having enough presence of mind to inquire what he would sell out, his adversaries replied with mere formless yells of scorn.

"I could get up a better show than this with my left hand," Roderick asserted.

"Well, what would you have in your ole show?" Penrod asked, condescending to language.

"That's all right, what I'd *have*. I'd have enough!"

"You couldn't get Herman and Verman in *your* ole show."

"No, and I wouldn't want 'em, either!"

"Well, what *would* you have?" Penrod insisted derisively. "You'd have to have *sumpthing*—you couldn't be a show yourself!"

"How do *you* know?" This was but meandering while waiting for ideas, and evoked another yell.

"You think you could be a show all by yourself?" Penrod demanded.

"How do *you* know I couldn't?"

Two white boys and two black boys shrieked their scorn of the boaster.

"I could, too!" Roderick raised his voice to a sudden howl, obtaining a hearing.

"Well, why don't you tell us how?"

"Well, *I* know *how*, all right," said Roderick. "If anybody asks you, you can just tell him I know *how*, all right."

"Why, you can't *do* anything," Sam began argumentatively. "You talk about being a show all by yourself; what could you try to do? Show us sumpthing you can do."

"I didn't say I was going to *do* anything," returned the badgered one, still evading.

"Well, then, how'd you *be* a show?" Penrod demanded. "*We* got a show here, even if Herman didn't point or Verman didn't talk. Their father stabbed a man with a pitchfork, I guess, didn't he?"

"How do *I* know?"

"Well, I guess he's in jail, ain't he?"

"Well, what if their father is in jail? I didn't say he wasn't, did I?"

"Well, *your* father ain't in jail, is he?"

"Well, I never said he was, did I?"

"Well, then," continued Penrod, "how could you be a——" He stopped abruptly, staring at Roderick, the birth of an idea plainly visible in his altered expression. He had suddenly remembered his intention to ask Roderick Magsworth Bitts, Junior, about Rena Magsworth, and this recollection collided in his mind with the irritation produced by Roderick's claiming some mysterious attainment that would warrant his setting up as a show in his single person. Penrod's whole manner changed instantly.

"Roddy," he asked, almost overwhelmed by a prescience of something vast and magnificent, "Roddy, are you any relation of Rena Magsworth?"

Roderick had never heard of Rena Magsworth, although a concentration of the sentence yesterday pronounced upon her had burned, black and horrific, upon the face of every newspaper in the country. He was not allowed to read the journals of the day and his family's indignation over the sacrilegious coincidence of the name had not been expressed in his presence. But he saw that it was an awesome name to Penrod Schofield and Samuel Williams. Even Herman and Verman, though lacking many educational advantages on account of a long residence in the country, were informed on the subject of Rena Magsworth through hearsay, and they joined in the portentous silence.

"Roddy," Penrod repeated, "honest, is Rena Magsworth some relation of yours?"

There is no obsession more dangerous to its victims than a conviction—especially an inherited one—of superiority: this world is so full of Missourians. And from his earliest years Roderick Magsworth Bitts, Junior, had been trained to believe in the importance of the Magsworth family. At every meal he absorbed a sense of Magsworth greatness, and yet, in his infrequent meetings with persons of his own age and sex, he was treated as negligible. Now, dimly, he perceived that there was a Magsworth claim of some sort that was impressive, even to boys. Magsworth blood was the essential of all true distinction in the world, he knew. Consequently, having been driven into a *cul-de-sac*, as a result of flagrant and unfounded boasting, he was ready to take advantage of what appeared to be a triumphal way out.

"Roddy," Penrod said again, with solemnity, "is Rena Magsworth some relation of yours?"

"*Is* she, Roddy?" Sam asked, almost hoarsely.

"She's my aunt!" shouted Roddy.

Silence followed. Sam and Penrod, spellbound, gazed upon Roderick Magsworth Bitts, Junior. So did Herman and Verman. Roddy's staggering lie had changed the face of things utterly. No one questioned it; no one realized that it was much too good to be true.

"Roddy," Penrod said, in a voice tremulous with hope, "Roddy, will you join our show?"

Roddy joined.

Even he could see that the offer implied his being starred as the paramount attraction of a new order of things. It was obvious that he had swelled out suddenly, in the estimation of the other boys, to the importance he had been taught to believe his native gift and natural right. The sensation was pleasant. He had often been treated with effusion by grown-up callers and by acquaintances of his mother and sisters; he had heard ladies speak of him as "charming" and "that delightful child", and little girls had sometimes shown him deference; but until this moment no boy had ever allowed him, for one moment, to presume even to equality. Now, in a trice, he was not only admitted to comradeship but patently valued as something rare and sacred to be acclaimed and pedestalled. In fact, the very first thing that Schofield and Williams did was to find a box for him to stand upon.

The misgivings roused in Roderick's bosom by the subsequent activities of the firm were not bothersome enough to make him forego his prominence as Exhibit A. He was not a "quick-minded" boy, and it was long (and much happened) before he thoroughly comprehended the causes of his new celebrity. He had a shadowy feeling that if the affair came to be heard of at home it might not be liked; but, intoxicated by the glamour and bustle that surround a public character, he made no protest. On the contrary, he entered whole-heartedly into the preparations for the new show. Assuming, with Sam's assistance, a blue moustache and "sideburns", he helped in the painting of a new poster, which, supplanting the old one on the wall of the stable facing the cross-street, screamed bloody murder at the passers in that rather populous thoroughfare.

SCHoFiELD & WiLLiAMS
NEW BIG SHoW
RoDERiCK MAGSWoRTH BiTTS JR
ONLY LiViNG NEPHEW
oF
RENA MAGSWORTH
THE FAMOS
MUDERESS GoiNG To BE HUNG
NEXT JULY KiLED EiGHT PEOPLE
PUT ARSiNECK iN THiER MiLK ALSO
SHERMAN HERMAN AND VERMAN
THE MiCHiGAN RATS DOG PART
ALLiGATOR DUKE THE GENUiNE
InDiAN DoG ADMiSSioN 1 CENT oR
20 PiNS SAME AS BEFORE Do NoT
MiSS THiS CHANSE TO SEE RoDERiCK
ONLY LiViNG NEPHEW oF RENA
MAGSWORTH THE GREAT FAMOS
MUDERESS
GoiNG To BE

HUNG

CHAPTER XVII

RETIRING FROM THE SHOW BUSINESS

MEGAPHONES were constructed out of heavy wrapping-paper, and Penrod, Sam and Herman set out in different directions, delivering vocally the inflammatory proclamation of the poster to a large section of the residential quarter, and leaving Roderick Magsworth Bitts, Junior, with Verman in the loft, shielded from all deadhead eyes. Upon the return of the heralds, the Schofield and Williams Military Band played deafeningly, and an awakened public once more thronged to fill the coffers of the firm.

Prosperity smiled again. The very first audience after the acquisition of Roderick was larger than the largest of the morning. Master Bitts—the only exhibit placed upon a box—was a supercurio. All eyes fastened upon him and remained, hungrily feasting, throughout Penrod's luminous oration.

But the glory of one light must ever be the dimming of another. We dwell in a vale of seesaws—and cobwebs spin fastest upon laurel. Verman, the tattooed wild boy, speaking only in his native foreign languages, Verman the gay, Verman the caperer, capered no more; he chuckled no more, he beckoned no more, nor tapped his chest, nor wreathed his idolatrous face in smiles. Gone, all gone, were his little artifices for attracting the general attention to himself; gone was every engaging mannerism that had endeared him to the mercurial public. He squatted against the wall and glowered at the new sensation. It was the old story—the old, old story of too much temperament: Verman was suffering from artistic jealousy.

The second audience contained a cash-paying adult, a spectacled young man whose poignant attention was very flattering. He remained after the lecture and put a few questions to Roddy that were answered rather confusedly upon promptings from Penrod. The young man went away without having stated the object of his interrogations; but it became quite plain, later in the day. This same object caused the spectacled young man to make several brief but stimulating calls directly after leaving the Schofield and Williams Big Show, and the consequences thereof loitered not by the wayside.

The Big Show was at high tide. Not only was the auditorium filled and throbbing; there was an indubitable line —by no means wholly juvenile—waiting for admission to the next pufformance. A group stood in the street examining the poster earnestly as it glowed in the long, slanting rays of the westward sun, and people in automobiles and other vehicles had halted wheel in the street to read the message so piquantly given to the world. These were the conditions when a crested victoria arrived at a gallop, and a large, chastely magnificent and highly flushed woman descended and progressed across the yard with an air of violence.

At sight of her, the adults of the waiting line hastily disappeared, and most of the pausing vehicles moved instantly on their way. She was followed by a stricken man in livery.

The stairs to the auditorium were narrow and steep; Mrs. Roderick Magsworth Bitts was of a stout favour; and the voice of Penrod was audible during the ascent.

"*Re-mem-bur*, gentilmun and lay-deeze, each and all are now gazing upon Roderick Magsworth Bitts, Junior, the only living nephew of the great Rena Magsworth. She stuck ars'nic in the milk of eight separate and distinck people to put in their coffee and each and all of 'em died. The great ars'nic murderess, Rena Magsworth, gentilmun and lay-deeze, and Roddy's her only living nephew. She's a relation of all the Bitts family; but he's her one and only living nephew. Re-*mem*-bur! Next July she's goin' to be hung, and, each and all, you now see before you———"

Penrod paused abruptly, seeing something before himself—the august and awful presence that filled the entryway. And his words (it should be related) froze upon his lips.

Before *her*self, Mrs. Roderick Magsworth Bitts saw her son—her scion—wearing a moustache and sideburns of blue, and perched upon a box flanked by Sherman and Verman, the Michigan rats, the Indian dog Duke, Herman and the dog part alligator.

Roddy, also, saw something before himself. It needed no prophet to read the countenance of the dread apparition in the entryway. His mouth opened—remained open—then filled to capacity with a calamitous sound of grief not unmingled with apprehension.

Penrod's reason staggered under the crisis. For a horrible moment he saw Mrs. Roderick Magsworth Bitts approaching like some fatal mountain in avalanche. She seemed to grow larger and redder; lightnings played about her head; he had a vague consciousness of the audience spraying out in flight, of the squealings, tramplings and dispersals of a stricken field. The mountain was close upon him———

He stood by the open mouth of the hay-chute that went through the floor to the manger below. Penrod also went through the floor. He propelled himself into the chute and shot down; but not quite to the manger, for Mr. Samuel Williams had thoughtfully stepped into the chute a moment in advance of his partner. Penrod lit upon Sam.

Catastrophic noises resounded in the loft; volcanoes seemed to romp upon the stairway.

There ensued a period when only a shrill keening marked the passing of Roderick as he was borne to the tumbril. Then all was silence.

. . . Sunset, striking through a western window, rouged the walls of the Schofields' library, where gathered a joint family council and court martial of four—Mrs. Schofield, Mr. Schofield, and Mr. and Mrs. Williams, parents of Samuel of that ilk. Mr. Williams read aloud a conspicuous passage from the last edition of the evening paper:

"Prominent people here believed close relations of woman sentenced to hang. Angry denial by Mrs. R. Magsworth Bitts. Relationship admitted by younger member of family. His statement confirmed by boy-friends——"

"Don't!" Mrs. Williams said, addressing her husband vehemently. "We've all read it a dozen times. We've got plenty of trouble on our hands without hearing *that* again!"

Singularly enough, Mrs. Williams did not look troubled; she looked as if she were trying to look troubled. Mrs. Schofield wore a similar expression. So did Mr. Schofield. So did Mr. Williams.

"What did she say when she called *you* up?" Mrs. Schofield inquired breathlessly of Mrs. Williams.

"She could hardly speak at first, and then when she did talk, she talked so fast I couldn't understand most of it, and——"

"It was just the same when she tried to talk to me," Mrs. Schofield said, nodding.

"I never did hear any one in such a state before," Mrs. Williams continued. "So furious——"

"Quite justly, of course," Mrs. Schofield said.

"Of course. And she said Penrod and Sam had enticed Roderick away from home—usually he's not allowed to go outside the yard except with his tutor or a servant—and had told him to say that horrible creature was his aunt——"

"How in the world do you suppose Sam and Penrod ever thought of such a thing as *that!*" Mrs. Schofield exclaimed. "It must have been made up just for their 'show'. Della says there were just *streams* going in and out all day. Of course it wouldn't have happened; but this was the day Margaret and I spend every month in the country with Aunt Sarah, and I didn't *dream*——"

"She said one thing I thought rather tactless," Mrs. Williams interrupted. "Of course we must allow for her being dreadfully excited and wrought up; but I do think it wasn't quite delicate in her, and she's usually the very soul of delicacy. She said that Roderick had *never* been allowed to associate with—common boys——"

"Meaning Sam and Penrod," Mrs. Schofield said. "Yes, she said that to me, too."

"She said that the most awful thing about it," Mrs. Williams went on, "was that, though she's going to prosecute the newspapers, many people would always believe the story, and——"

"Yes, I imagine they will," Mrs. Schofield said musingly. "Of course you and I and everybody who really know the Bitts and Magsworth families understand the perfect absurdity of it; but I suppose there are ever so many who'll believe it, no matter what the Bittses and Magsworths say."

"Hundreds and hundreds!" Mrs. Williams said. "I'm afraid it will be a great come-down for them."

"I'm afraid so," Mrs. Schofield said gently. "A very great one—yes, a very, very great one."

"Well," Mrs. Williams observed, after a thoughtful pause, "there's only one thing to be done, and I suppose it had better be done right away." She glanced toward the two gentlemen.

"Certainly," Mr. Schofield agreed. "But where *are* they?"

"Have you looked in the stable?" his wife asked.

"I searched it. They've probably started for the West."

"Did you look in the sawdust-box?"

"No, I didn't."

"Then that's where they are."

Thus, in the early twilight, the now historic stable was approached by two fathers charged to do the only thing to be done. They entered the storeroom.

"Penrod!" said Mr. Schofield.

"Sam!" said Mr. Williams.

Nothing disturbed the twilight hush.

But by means of a ladder, brought from the carriage-house, Mr. Schofield mounted to the top of the sawdust-box. He looked within and discerned the dim outlines of three quiet figures, the third being that of a small dog.

The two boys rose, upon command, descended the ladder after Mr. Schofield, bringing Duke with them, and stood before the authors of their being, who bent upon them sinister and threatening brows. With hanging heads and despondent countenances, each still ornamented with a moustache and an imperial, Penrod and Sam awaited sentence.

This is a boy's lot: anything he does, anything whatever, may afterward turn out to have been a crime—he never knows.

And punishment and clemency are alike inexplicable.

Mr. Williams took his son by the ear.

"You march home!" he commanded.

Sam marched, not looking back, and his father followed the small figure implacably.

"You goin' to whip me?" Penrod quavered, alone with Justice.

"Wash your face at that hydrant," his father said sternly.

*Mr. Schofield looked within and discerned the out-
lines of three quiet figures.*

About fifteen minutes later, Penrod, hurriedly entering the corner drug store, two blocks distant, was astonished to perceive a familiar form at the soda counter.

"Yay, Penrod," said Sam Williams. "Want some sody? Come on. He didn't lick me. He didn't do anything to me at all. He gave me a quarter."

"So'd mine," said Penrod.

CHAPTER XVIII

MUSIC

BOYHOOD is the longest time in life—for a boy. The last term of the school-year is made of decades, not of weeks, and living through them is like waiting for the millennium. But they do pass, somehow, and at last there came a day when Penrod was one of a group that capered out from the gravelled yard of "Ward School, Nomber Seventh", carolling a leave-taking of the institution, of their instructress, and not even forgetting Mr. Capps, the janitor.

> "Good-bye, teacher! Good-bye, school!
> Good-bye, Cappsie, dern ole fool!"

Penrod sang the loudest. For every boy, there is an age when he "finds his voice". Penrod's had not "changed";

but he had found it. Inevitably that thing had come upon his family and the neighbours; and his father, a somewhat dyspeptic man, quoted frequently the expressive words of the "Lady of Shalott"; but there were others whose sufferings were as poignant.

Vacation-time warmed the young of the world to pleasant languor; and a morning came that was like a brightly coloured picture in a child's fairy story. Miss Margaret Schofield, reclining in a hammock upon the front porch, was beautiful in the eyes of a newly made senior, well favoured and in fair raiment, beside her. A guitar rested lightly upon his knee, and he was trying to play—a matter of some difficulty, as the floor of the porch also seemed inclined to be musical. From directly under his feet came a voice of song, shrill, loud, incredibly piercing and incredibly flat, dwelling upon each syllable with incomprehensible reluctance to leave it.

> "I have lands and earthly pow-wur.
> I'd give all for a now-wur,
> Whi-ilst setting at *my-y-y* dear old mother's knee-ee,
> So-o-o rem-mem-bur whilst you're young——"

Miss Schofield stamped heartily upon the musical floor. "It's Penrod," she explained. "The lattice at the end of the porch is loose, and he crawls under and comes out all bugs. He's been having a dreadful singing fit lately—running away to picture shows and vaudeville, I suppose."

Mr. Robert Williams looked upon her yearningly. He touched a thrilling chord on his guitar and leaned nearer. "But you said you *have* missed me," he began. "I——"

The voice of Penrod drowned all other sounds.

> "So-o-o rem-mem-bur, whi-i-ilst you're young,
> That the day-a-ys to you will come,
> When you're o-o-old and only in the way,
> Do not scoff at them *bee*-cause——"

"Penrod!" Miss Schofield stamped again.

"You *did* say you'd missed me," said Mr. Robert Williams, seizing hurriedly upon the silence. "Didn't you say——"

A livelier tune rose upward.

> "Oh, you talk about your fascinating beauties,
>   Of your dem-*o*-zells, your belles,
> But the littil dame I met, while in the city,
>   She's par excellaws the queen of all the swells.
> She's sweeter far——"

Margaret rose and jumped up and down repeatedly in a well-calculated area, whereupon the voice of Penrod cried chokedly, *"Quit* that!" and there were subterranean coughings and sneezings.

"You want to choke a person to death?" he inquired severely, appearing at the end of the porch, a cobweb upon his brow. And, continuing, he put into practice a newly acquired phrase, "You better learn to be more considerick of other people's comfort."

Slowly and grievedly he withdrew, passed to the sunny side of the house, reclined in the warm grass beside his wistful Duke, and presently sang again.

> "She's sweeter far than the flower I named her after,
>   And the memery of her smile it haunts me YET!
> When in after years the moon is sofly beamun'
>   And at eve I smell the smell of mignonette
> I will re-CALL that——"

"Pen-*rod!*"

Mr. Schofield appeared at an open window upstairs, a book in his hand.

"Stop it!" he commanded. "Can't I stay home with a headache *one* morning from the office without having to listen to—I never *did* hear such squawking!" He retired from the window, having too impulsively called upon his Maker. Penrod, shocked and injured, entered the house;

but presently his voice was again audible as far as the front porch. He was holding converse with his mother, somewhere in the interior.

"Well, what of it? Sam Williams told me his mother said if Bob ever did think of getting married to Margaret, his mother said she'd like to know what in the name o' goodness they expect to——"

Bang! Margaret thought it better to close the front door. The next minute Penrod opened it. "I suppose you want the whole family to get a sunstroke," he said reprovingly. "Keepin' every breath of air out o' the house on a day like this!"

And he sat down implacably in the doorway.

The serious poetry of all languages has omitted the little brother; and yet he is one of the great trials of love—the immemorial burden of courtship. Tragedy should have found place for him; but he has been left to the haphazard vignettist of Grub Street. He is the grave and real menace of lovers; his head is sacred and terrible, his power illimitable. There is one way—only one—to deal with him; but Robert Williams, having a brother of Penrod's age, understood that way.

Robert had one dollar in the world. He gave it to Penrod immediately.

Enslaved forever, the new Rockefeller rose and went forth upon the highway, an overflowing heart bursting the floodgates of song.

"In her eyes the light of love was soffly gleamun',
    So sweetlay,
    So neatlay.
On the banks the moon's soff light was brightly streamun',
    Words of love I then spoke *to* her,
    She was purest of the *pew*-er.
'Littil sweetheart, do not sigh,
Do not weep and do not cry.
I will build a littil cottige just for yew-*ew*-EW and I.' "

In fairness, it must be called to mind that boys older than Penrod have these wellings of pent melody; a wife can never tell when she is to undergo a musical morning, and even the golden wedding brings her no security, a man of ninety is liable to bust-loose in song, any time.

Invalids murmured pitifully as Penrod came within hearing; and people trying to think cursed the day that they were born, when he went shrilling by. His hands in his pockets, his shining face uplifted to the sky of June, he passed down the street, singing his way into the heart's deepest hatred of all who heard him.

> "One evuning I was sturow-ling
>   Midst the city of the *Dead,*
> I viewed where all a-round me
>   Their *peace*-full graves was SPREAD.
> But that which touched me mostlay——"

He had reached his journey's end, a junk-dealer's shop wherein lay the long-desired treasure of his soul—an accordion that might have possessed a high quality of interest for an antiquarian, being unquestionably a ruin, beautiful in decay and quite beyond the sacrilegious reach of the restorer. But it was still able to disgorge sounds—loud, strange, compelling sounds that could be heard for a remarkable distance in all directions; and it had one rich calf-like tone that had gone to Penrod's heart. He obtained the instrument for twenty-two cents, a price long since agreed upon with the junk-dealer, who falsely claimed a loss of profit, Shylock that he was! He had found the wreck in an alley.

With this purchase suspended from his shoulder by a faded green cord, Penrod set out in a somewhat homeward direction, but not by the route he had just travelled, though his motive for the change was not humanitarian. It was his desire to display himself thus troubadouring to the gaze of Marjorie Jones. Heralding his advance by continuous ex-

periments in the music of the future, he pranced upon his
blithesome way, the faithful Duke at his heels. (It was easier
for Duke than it would have been for a younger dog, because, with advancing age, he had begun to grow a little
deaf.)

Turning the corner nearest to the glamoured mansion of
the Joneses, the boy jongleur came suddenly face to face
with Marjorie, and, in the delicious surprise of the encounter, ceased to play, his hands, in agitation, falling
from the instrument.

Bareheaded, the sunshine glorious upon her amber curls,
Marjorie was strolling hand-in-hand with her baby brother,
Mitchell, four years old. She wore pink that day—unforgettable pink, with a broad, black patent-leather belt, shimmering reflections dancing upon its surface. How beautiful she
was! How sacred the sweet little baby brother, whose
privilege it was to cling to that small hand, delicately powdered with freckles.

"Hello, Marjorie," said Penrod, affecting carelessness.

"Hello!" said Marjorie, with unexpected cordiality. She
bent over her baby brother with motherly affections. "Say
'howdy' to the gentymuns, Mitchy-Mitch," she urged
sweetly, turning him to face Penrod.

"*Won't!*" said Mitchy-Mitch, and, to emphasize his
refusal, kicked the gentymuns upon the shin.

Penrod's feelings underwent instant change, and, in the
sole occupation of disliking Mitchy-Mitch, he wasted
precious seconds that might have been better employed in
philosophic consideration of the startling example, just
afforded, of how a given law operates throughout the universe in precisely the same manner perpetually. Mr. Robert
Williams would have understood this easily.

"Oh, oh!" Marjorie cried, and put Mitchy-Mitch behind
her with too much sweetness. "Maurice Levy's gone to
Atlantic City with his mamma," she remarked conversation-
ally, as if the kicking incident were quite closed.

"That's nothin'," Penrod returned, keeping his eye uneasily upon Mitchy-Mitch. "I know plenty people been better places than that—Chicago and everywhere."

There was unconscious ingratitude in his low rating of Atlantic City, for it was largely to the attractions of that resort he owed Miss Jones's present attitude of friendliness. Of course, too, she was curious about the accordion. It would be dastardly to hint that she had noticed a paper bag that bulged the pocket of Penrod's coat, and yet this bag was undeniably conspicuous—"and children are very like grown people sometimes!"

Penrod brought forth the bag, purchased on the way at a drug store, and till this moment *unopened*, which expresses in a word the depth of his sentiment for Marjorie. It contained an abundant fifteen-cents' worth of lemon drops, jaw-breakers, licorice sticks, cinnamon drops and shopworn chocolate creams.

"Take all you want," he said, with off-hand generosity.

"Why, Penrod Schofield," exclaimed the wholly thawed damsel, "you nice boy!"

"Oh, that's nothin'," he returned airily. "I got a good deal of money, nowadays."

"Where from?"

"Oh—just around." With a cautious gesture he offered a jaw-breaker to Mitchy-Mitch, who snatched it indignantly and set about its absorption without delay.

"Can you play on that?" Marjorie asked, with some difficulty, her cheeks being rather too hilly for conversation. "Want to hear me?"

She nodded, her eyes sweet with anticipation.

This was what he had come for. He threw back his head, lifted his eyes dreamily, as he had seen real musicians lift theirs, and distended the accordion preparing to produce the wonderful calf-like noise that was the instrument's great charm. But the distention evoked a long wail that was at once drowned in another one.

"Ow! Owowaoh! Wowohah! Waow*wow!*" shrieked Mitchy-Mitch and the accordion together.

Never had he so won upon her; never had she let him feel so close to her before

Mitchy-Mitch, to emphasize his disapproval of the accordion, opening his mouth still wider, lost therefrom the jaw-breaker, which rolled in the dust. Weeping, he stooped to retrieve it, and Marjorie, to prevent him, hastily set her foot upon it. Penrod offered another jaw-breaker; but Mitchy-Mitch struck it from his hand, desiring the former, which had convinced him of its sweetness.

Marjorie moved inadvertently; whereupon Mitchy-Mitch pounced upon the remains of his jaw-breaker and restored them, with accretions, to his mouth. His sister, uttering a cry of horror, sprang to the rescue, assisted by Penrod, whom she prevailed upon to hold Mitchy-Mitch's mouth open while she excavated. This operation being completed, and Penrod's right thumb severely bitten, Mitchy-Mitch closed his eyes tightly, stamped, squealed, bellowed, wrung his hands, and then, unexpectedly, kicked Penrod again.

Penrod put a hand in his pocket and drew forth a copper two-cent piece, large, round and fairly bright.

He gave it to Mitchy-Mitch.

Mitchy-Mitch immediately stopped crying and gazed upon his benefactor with the eyes of a dog.

This world!

Thereafter did Penrod—with complete approval from Mitchy-Mitch—play the accordion for his lady to his heart's content, and hers. Never had he so won upon her; never had she let him feel so close to her before. They strolled up and down upon the sidewalk, eating, one thought between them, and soon she had learned to play the accordion almost as well as he. So passed a happy hour, which the Good King René of Anjou would have envied them, while Mitchy-Mitch made friends with Duke, romped about his sister and her swain, and clung to the hand of the latter, at intervals, with fondest affection and trust.

The noon whistles failed to disturb this little Arcady; only the sound of Mrs. Jones's voice—for the third time summoning Marjorie and Mitchy-Mitch to lunch—sent Penrod on his way.

"I could come back this afternoon, I guess," he said, in parting.

"I'm not goin' to be here. I'm goin' to Baby Rennsdale's party."

Penrod looked blank, as she intended he should. Having thus satisfied herself, she added: "There aren't goin' to be any boys there."

He was instantly radiant again. "Marjorie——"

"Hum?"

"Do you wish I was goin' to be there?"

She looked shy, and turned away her head.

"*Marjorie Jones!*" (This was a voice from home.) "*How many more times shall I have to call you?*"

Marjorie moved away, her face still hidden from Penrod. "Do you?" he urged.

At the gate, she turned quickly toward him, and said over her shoulder, all in a breath: "Yes! Come again to-morrow morning and I'll be on the corner. Bring your 'cordion!"

And she ran into the house, Mitchy-Mitch waving a loving hand to the boy on the sidewalk until the front door closed.

CHAPTER XIX

THE INNER BOY

PENROD went home in splendour, pretending that he and Duke were a long procession; and he made enough noise to render the auricular part of the illusion perfect. His own family were already at the lunch-table when he arrived, and the parade halted only at the door of the dining-room.

"Oh *Something!*" shouted Mr. Schofield, clasping his bilious brow with both hands. "Stop that noise! Isn't it awful enough for you to *sing?* Sit *down!* Not with that thing on! Take that green rope off your shoulder! Now take that thing out of the dining-room and throw it in the ash-can! Where did you get it?"

"Where did I get what, Papa?" Penrod asked meekly,

depositing the accordion in the hall just outside the dining-room door.

"That da—that third-hand concertina."

"It's a 'cordion," Penrod said, taking his place at the table and noticing that both Margaret and Mr. Robert Williams (who happened to be a guest) were growing red.

"I don't care what you call it," Mr. Schofield said irritably. "I want to know where you got it."

Penrod's eyes met Margaret's; hers had a strained expression. She very slightly shook her head. Penrod sent Mr. Williams a grateful look, and might have been startled if he could have seen himself in a mirror at that moment; for he regarded Mitchy-Mitch with concealed but vigorous aversion, and the resemblance would have horrified him.

"A man gave it to me," he answered gently, and was rewarded by the visibly regained ease of his patron's manner, while Margaret leaned back in her chair and looked at her brother with real devotion.

"I should think he'd have been glad to," said Mr. Schofield. "Who was he?"

"Sir?" In spite of the candy that he had consumed in company with Marjorie and Mitchy-Mitch, Penrod had begun to eat lobster croquettes earnestly.

"Who *was* he?"

"Who do you mean, Papa?"

"The man who gave you that ghastly Thing!"

"Yessir. A man gave it to me."

"I say, Who *was* he?" Mr. Schofield shouted.

"Well, I was just walking along, and the man came up to me—it was right down in front of Colgates', where most of the paint's rubbed off the fence——"

"Penrod!" The father used his most dangerous tone.

"Sir?"

"Who was the man who gave you the concertina?"

"I don't know. I was walking along——"

"You never saw him before?"

"No, sir. I was just walk——"

"That will do," Mr. Schofield said, rising. "I suppose every family has its secret enemies and this was one of ours. I must ask to be excused!"

With that, he went out crossly, stopping in the hall a moment before passing beyond hearing. And, after lunch, Penrod sought in vain for his accordion; he even searched the library where his father sat reading, though, upon inquiry, Penrod explained that he was looking for a misplaced school-book. He thought he ought to study a little every day, he said, even during vacation-time. Much pleased, Mr. Schofield rose and joined the search, finding the missing work on mathematics with singular ease—which cost him precisely the price of the book the following September.

Penrod departed to study in the backyard. There, after a cautious survey of the neighbourhood, he managed to dislodge the iron cover of the cistern, and dropped the arithmetic within. A fine splash rewarded his listening ear. Thus assured that when he looked for that book again no one would find it for him, he replaced the cover and betook himself pensively to the highway, discouraging Duke from following by repeated volleys of stones, some imaginary and others all too real.

Distant strains of brazen horns and the throbbing of drums were borne to him upon the kind breeze, reminding him that the world was made for joy, and that the Barzee and Potter Dog and Pony Show was exhibiting in a banlieue not far away. So, thither he bent his steps—the plentiful funds in his pocket burning hot holes all the way. He had paid twenty-two cents for the accordion, and fifteen for candy; he had bought the mercenary heart of Mitchy-Mitch for two: it certainly follows that there remained to him of his dollar, sixty-one cents—a fair fortune, and most unusual.

Arrived upon the populous and festive scene of the Dog and Pony Show, he first turned his attention to the brightly decorated booths that surrounded the tent. The cries of the peanut vendors, of the popcorn men, of the toy-balloon sellers, the stirring music of the band, playing before the performance to attract a crowd, the shouting of excited children and the barking of the dogs within the tent, all sounded exhilaratingly in Penrod's ears and set his blood a-tingle. Nevertheless, he did not squander his money or fling it to the winds in one grand splurge. Instead, he began cautiously with the purchase of an extraordinarily large pickle, which he obtained from an aged negress for his odd cent, too obvious a bargain to be missed. At an adjacent stand he bought a glass of raspberry lemonade (so alleged) and sipped it as he ate the pickle. He left nothing of either.

Next, he entered a small restaurant-tent and for a modest nickel was supplied with a fork and a box of sardines, previously opened, it is true, but more than half full. He consumed the sardines utterly, but left the tin box and the fork, after which he indulged in an inexpensive half-pint of lukewarm cider at one of the open booths. Mug in hand, a gentle glow radiating toward his surface from various centres of activity deep inside him, he paused for breath— and the cool, sweet cadences of the watermelon man fell delectably upon his ear:

"Ice-cole *water*-melon; ice-cole water-*melon;* the biggest slice of *ice*-cold, ripe, red, *ice*-cole, rich an' rare; the biggest slice of ice-cole watermelon ever cut by the hand of man! *Buy* our *ice*-cole watermelon?"

Penrod, having drained the last drop of cider, complied with the watermelon man's luscious entreaty, and received a round slice of the fruit, magnificent in circumference and something over an inch in thickness. Leaving only the really dangerous part of the rind behind him, he wandered away from the vicinity of the watermelon man and supplied himself with a bag of peanuts, which, with the expenditure of a dime for admission, left a quarter still warm in his pocket. However, he managed to "break" the coin at a stand inside the tent, where a large, oblong paper box of popcorn was handed him, with twenty cents change. The box was too

The first bite convinced him that he had made a mis-
take

large to go into his pocket; but, having seated himself
among some wistful Polack children, he placed it in his lap
and devoured the contents at leisure during the performance. The popcorn was heavily larded with partially boiled
molasses, and Penrod sandwiched mouthfuls of peanuts with
gobs of this mass until the peanuts were all gone. After
that, he ate with less avidity, a sense almost of satiety beginning to manifest itself to him; and it was not until the
close of the performance that he disposed of the last morsel.

He descended a little heavily to the outflowing crowd in
the arena, and bought a caterwauling toy balloon, but
showed no great enthusiasm in manipulating it. Near the
exit, as he came out, was a hot-waffle stand that he had
overlooked, and a sense of duty obliged him to consume the
three waffles that the waffle man cooked for him upon command, and thickly powdered with sugar.

They left a hottish taste in his mouth; they had not been
quite up to his anticipation, indeed, and it was with a sense
of relief that he turned to the "hokey-pokey" cart that stood
close at hand, laden with square slabs of "Neapolitan ice-
cream" wrapped in paper. He thought the ice-cream would
be cooling; but somehow it fell short of the desired effect and
left a peculiar savour in his throat.

He walked away, too languid to blow his balloon, and
passed a fresh-taffy booth with strange indifference. A bare-
armed man was manipulating the taffy over a hook, pulling
a great white mass to the desired stage of "candying"; but
Penrod did not pause to watch the operation. In fact, he
averted his eyes (which were slightly glazed) in passing.
He did not analyze his motives: simply, he was conscious that
he preferred not to look at the mass of taffy.

For some reason, he put a considerable distance between
himself and the taffy-stand; but before long halted in the
presence of a red-faced man who flourished a long fork over
a small cooking apparatus and shouted jovially: "Winnies!
Here's your hot winnies! Hot winny-*wurst!* Food for the

over-worked brain, nourishing for the weak stummick, entertaining for the tired business man! *Here's* your hot winnies, three for a nickel, a half-a-dime, the twentieth-pot-of-a-dollah!"

This, above all nectar and ambrosia, was the favourite dish of Penrod Schofield. Nothing inside him now craved it —on the contrary! But memory is the great hypnotist; his mind argued against his inwards that opportunity knocked at his door: "winny-wurst" was rigidly forbidden by the home authorities. Besides, there was a last nickel in his pocket; and nature protested against its survival. Also, the red-faced man had himself proclaimed his wares nourishing for the weak stummick.

Penrod placed the nickel in the red hand of the red-faced man.

He ate two of the three greasy, cigarlike shapes cordially pressed upon him in return. The first bite convinced him. that he had made a mistake; these winnies seemed of a very inferior flavour, almost unpleasant, in fact. But he felt obliged to conceal his poor opinion of them for fear of offending the red-faced man. He ate without haste or eagerness—so slowly, indeed, that he began to think the red-faced man might dislike him, as a deterrent of trade. Perhaps Penrod's mind was not working well, for he failed to remember that no law compelled him to remain under the eye of the red-faced man; but the virulent repulsion excited by his attempt to take a bite of the third sausage inspired him with at least an excuse for postponement.

"Mighty good," he murmured feebly, placing the sausage in the pocket of his jacket with a shaking hand. "Guess I'll save this one to eat at home, after—after dinner."

He moved sluggishly away, wishing he had not thought of dinner. A side-show, undiscovered until now, failed to arouse his interest, not even exciting a wish that he had known of its existence when he had money. For a time he stared without comprehension at a huge canvas poster depicting the chief attraction, the weather-worn colours conveying no meaning to his torpid eye. Then, little by little, the poster became more vivid to his consciousness. There was a greenish-tinted person in the tent, it seemed, who thrived upon a reptilian diet.

Suddenly, Penrod decided that it was time to go home.

CHAPTER XX

BROTHERS OF ANGELS

INDEED, doctor," said Mrs. Schofield, with agitation and profound conviction, just after eight o'clock that evening, "I shall *always* believe in mustard plasters— mustard plasters and hot-water bags. If it hadn't been for them I don't believe he'd have *lived* till you got here— I do *not!*"

"Margaret," Mr. Schofield called from the open door of a bedroom, "Margaret, where did you put that aromatic ammonia? Where's Margaret?"

But he had to find the aromatic spirits of ammonia himself, for Margaret was not in the house. She stood in the shadow beneath a maple tree near the street corner, a guitar-case in her hand; and she scanned with anxiety a briskly

148

approaching figure. The arc light, swinging above, revealed
this figure as that of him she awaited. He was passing toward
the gate without seeing her, when she arrested him with a
fateful whisper.

"*Bob!*"

Mr. Robert Williams swung about hastily. "Why,
Margaret!"

"Here, take your guitar," she whispered hurriedly. "I
was afraid if Father happened to find it he'd break it all to
pieces!"

"What for?" asked the startled Robert.

"Because I'm sure he knows it's yours."

"But what——"

"Oh, Bob," she moaned, "I was waiting here to tell you.
I was so afraid you'd try to come in——"

"*Try!*" the unfortunate young man exclaimed, quite
dumfounded. "*Try* to come——"

"Yes, before I warned you. I've been waiting here to tell
you, Bob, you mustn't come near the house—if I were you
I'd stay away from even this neighbourhood—far away!
For a while I don't think it would be actually *safe* for——"

"Margaret, will you please——"

"It's all on account of that dollar you gave Penrod this
morning," she wailed. "First, he bought that horrible concertina that made Papa so furious——"

"But Penrod didn't tell that I——"

"Oh, wait!" she cried lamentably. "Listen! He didn't tell
at lunch; but he got home about dinner-time in the most—
well! I've seen pale people before, but nothing like Penrod.
Nobody could *imagine* it—not unless they'd seen him! And
he looked so *strange*, and kept making such unnatural faces,
and at first all he would say was that he'd eaten a little piece
of apple and thought it must have some microbes on it.
But he got sicker and sicker, and we put him to bed—and
then we all thought he was going to die—and, of *course*,
no little piece of apple would have—well, and he kept getting
worse—and then he said he'd had a dollar. He said he'd

spent it for the concertina, and watermelon, and chocolate-creams, and licorice sticks, and lemon-drops, and peanuts, and jaw-breakers, and sardines, and raspberry lemonade, and pickles, and popcorn, and ice-cream, and cider, and sausage—there was sausage in his pocket, and Mamma says his jacket is ruined—and cinnamon drops—and waffles—and he ate four or five lobster croquettes at lunch—and Papa said, 'Who gave you that dollar?' Only he didn't say *'who'* —he said something horrible, Bob! And Penrod thought he was going to die, and he said *you* gave it to him, and oh! it was just pitiful to hear the poor child, Bob, because he thought he was dying, you see, and he blamed you for the whole thing. He said if you'd only let him alone and not given it to him, he'd have grown up to be a good man—and now he couldn't! I never heard anything so heart-rending—he was so weak he could hardly whisper; but he kept trying to talk, telling us over and over it was all your fault."

In the darkness Mr. Williams's facial expression could not be seen; but his voice sounded hopeful.

"Is he—is he still in a great deal of pain?"

"They say the crisis is past," Margaret said; "but the doctor's still up there. He said it was the acutest case of indigestion he had ever treated in the whole course of his professional practice."

"Of course *I* didn't know what he'd do with the dollar," Robert said.

She did not reply.

He began plaintively, "Margaret, you don't——"

"I've never seen Papa and Mamma so upset about anything," she said, rather primly.

"You mean they're upset about *me?*"

"We are *all* very much upset," Margaret returned, more starch in her tone as she remembered not only Penrod's sufferings but a duty she had vowed herself to perform.

"Margaret! *You* don't——"

"Robert," she said firmly and, also, with a rhetorical complexity that breeds a suspicion of pre-rehearsed—"Robert, for the present I can only look at it in one way: when you gave that money to Penrod you put into the hands of an unthinking little child a weapon which might be, and, indeed was, the means of his undoing. Boys are not respon——"

"But you saw me give him the dollar, and you didn't——"

"Robert!" she checked him with increasing severity. "I am only a woman and not accustomed to thinking everything out on the spur of the moment; but I cannot change my mind. Not now, at least."

"And you think I'd better not come in to-night?"

"To-night!" she gasped. "Not for *weeks!* Papa would——"

"But Margaret," he urged plaintively, "how can you blame me for——"

"I have not used the word 'blame'," she interrupted. "But I must insist that for your carelessness to—to wreak such havoc—cannot fail to—to lessen my confidence in your powers of judgment. I cannot change my convictions in this matter—not to-night—and I cannot remain here another instant. The poor child may need me. Robert, good-night."

With chill dignity she withdrew, entered the house and returned to the sick-room, leaving the young man in outer darkness to brood upon his crime—and upon Penrod.

That sincere invalid became convalescent upon the third day; and a week elapsed, then, before he found an opportunity to leave the house unaccompanied—save by Duke. But at last he set forth and approached the Jones neighbourhood in high spirits, pleasantly conscious of his pallor, hollow cheeks and other perquisites of illness provocative of interest.

One thought troubled him a little because it gave him a sense of inferiority to a rival. He believed, against his will, that Maurice Levy could have successfully eaten chocolate-creams, licorice sticks, lemon-drops, jaw-breakers, peanuts, waffles, lobster croquettes, sardines, cinnamon-drops, water-melon, pickles, popcorn, ice-cream and sausage with raspberry lemonade and cider. Penrod had admitted to himself that Maurice could do it and afterward attend to business, or pleasure, without the slightest discomfort; and this was probably no more than a fair estimate of one of the great constitutions of all time. As a digester, Maurice Levy would have disappointed a Borgia.

Fortunately, Maurice was still at Atlantic City—and now the convalescent's heart leaped. In the distance he saw Marjorie coming—in pink again, with a ravishing little parasol over her head. And alone! No Mitchy-Mitch was to mar this meeting.

Penrod increased the feebleness of his steps, now and then leaning upon the fence as if for support.

"How do you do, Marjorie?" he said, in his best sick-room voice, as she came near.

To his pained amazement, she proceeded on her way, her nose at a celebrated elevation—an icy nose.

She cut him dead.

He threw his invalid's airs to the winds and hastened after her.

"Marjorie," he pleaded, "what's the matter? Are you mad? Honest, that day you said to come back next morning, and you'd be on the corner, I was sick. Honest, I was *awful* sick, Marjorie! I had to have the doctor——"

"*Doctor!*" She whirled upon him, her lovely eyes blazing. "I guess *we've* had to have the doctor enough at *our* house, thanks to *you*, Mister Penrod Schofield. Papa says you haven't got *near* sense enough to come in out of the rain, after what you did to poor little Mitchy-Mitch——"

"What?"

"Yes, and he's sick in bed *yet!*" Marjorie went on, with unabated fury. "And Papa says if he ever catches you in this part of town——"

"*What'd* I do to Mitchy-Mitch?" Penrod gasped.

"You know well enough what you did to Mitchy-Mitch!" she cried. "You gave him that great, big, nasty two-cent piece!"

"Well, what of it?"

"Mitchy-Mitch swallowed it!"

"What!"

"And Papa says if he ever just lays eyes on you, once, in this neighbourhood——"

But Penrod had started for home.

In his embittered heart there was increasing a critical disapproval of the Creator's methods. When He made pretty girls, thought Penrod, why couldn't He have left out their little brothers?

CHAPTER XXI

RUPE COLLINS

FOR several days after this, Penrod thought of growing up to be a monk, and engaged in good works so far as to carry some kittens (that otherwise would have been drowned) and a pair of Margaret's outworn dancing-slippers to a poor, ungrateful old man sojourning in a shed up the alley. And although Mr. Robert Williams, after a very short interval, began to leave his guitar on the front porch again, exactly as if he thought nothing had happened, Penrod, with his younger vision of a father's mood, remained coldly distant from the Jones neighbourhood. With his own family his manner was gentle, proud and sad; but not for long enough to frighten them. The change came with mystifying abruptness at the end of the week.

It was Duke who brought it about.

Duke could chase a much bigger dog out of the Scho-fields' yard and far down the street. This might be thought to indicate unusual valour on the part of Duke and cow-ardice on that of the bigger dogs whom he undoubtedly put to rout. On the contrary, all such flights were founded in mere superstition, for dogs are even more superstitious than boys and coloured people; and the most firmly estab-lished of all dog superstitions is that any dog—be he the smallest and feeblest in the world—can whip any trespasser whatsoever.

A rat-terrier believes that on his home grounds he can whip an elephant. It follows, of course, that a big dog, away from his own home, will run from a little dog in the little dog's neighbourhood. Otherwise, the big dog must face a charge of inconsistency, and dogs are as consistent as they are superstitious. A dog believes in war; but he is con-vinced that there are times when it is moral to run; and the thoughtful physiognomist, seeing a big dog fleeing out of a little dog's yard, must observe that the expression of the big dog's face is more conscientious than alarmed: it is the expression of a person performing a duty to himself.

Penrod understood these matters perfectly; he knew that the gaunt brown hound Duke chased up the alley had fled only out of deference to a custom, yet Penrod could not refrain from bragging of Duke to the hound's owner, a fat-faced stranger of twelve or thirteen, who had wandered into the neighbourhood.

"You better keep that ole yellow dog o' yours back," Penrod said ominously, as he climbed the fence. "You bet-ter catch him and hold him till I get mine inside the yard again. Duke's chewed up some pretty bad bulldogs around here."

The fat-faced boy gave Penrod a fishy stare. "You'd oughta learn him not to do that," he said. "It'll make him sick."

"What will?"

The stranger laughed raspingly and gazed up the alley, where the hound, having come to a halt, now coolly sat down, and, with an expression of roguish benevolence, patronizingly watched the tempered fury of Duke, whose assaults and barkings were becoming perfunctory.

"What'll make Duke sick?" Penrod demanded.

"Eatin' dead bulldogs people leave around here."

This was not improvisation but formula, adapted from other occasions to the present encounter; nevertheless, it was new to Penrod, and he was so taken with it that resentment lost itself in admiration. Hastily committing the gem to memory for use upon a dog-owning friend, he inquired in a sociable tone:

"What's your dog's name?"

"Dan. You better call your ole pup, 'cause Dan eats *live* dogs."

Dan's actions poorly supported his master's assertion, for, upon Duke's ceasing to bark, Dan rose and showed the most courteous interest in making the little, old dog's acquaintance. Dan had a great deal of manner, and it became plain that Duke was impressed favourably in spite of former prejudice, so that presently the two trotted amicably back to their masters and sat down with the harmonious but indifferent air of having known each other intimately for years.

They were received without comment, though both boys looked at them reflectively for a time. It was Penrod who spoke first.

"What number you go to?" (In an "oral lesson in English", Penrod had been instructed to put this question in another form: "May I ask which of our public schools you attend?")

"Me? What number do I go to?" said the stranger, contemptuously. "I don't go to *no* number in vacation!"

"I mean when it ain't."

"Third," the fat-faced boy returned. "I got 'em *all* scared in *that* school."

"What of?" innocently asked Penrod, to whom "the Third"—in a distant part of town—was undiscovered country.

"What of? I guess you'd soon see what of, if you ever was in that school about one day. You'd be lucky if you got out alive!"

"Are the teachers mean?"

The other boy frowned with bitter scorn. "Teachers! Teachers don't order *me* around, I can tell you! They're mighty careful how they try to run over Rupe Collins."

"Who's Rupe Collins?"

"Who is he?" the fat-faced boy echoed incredulously. "Say, ain't you got *any* sense?"

"What?"

"Say, wouldn't you be just as happy if you had *some* sense?"

"Ye-es." Penrod's answer, like the look he lifted to the impressive stranger, was meek and placative. "Rupe Collins is the principal at your school, I guess."

The other yelled with jeering laughter, and mocked Penrod's manner and voice. " 'Rupe Collins is the principal at your school, I guess!' " He laughed harshly again, then suddenly showed truculence. "Say, 'bo, whyn't you learn enough to go in the house when it rains? What's the matter of you, anyhow?"

"Well," Penrod urged timidly, "nobody ever *told* me who Rupe Collins is: I got a *right* to think he's the principal, haven't I?"

The fat-faced boy shook his head disgustedly. "Honest, you make me sick!"

Penrod's expression became one of despair. "Well, who *is* he?" he cried.

" 'Who *is* he?' " mocked the other, with a scorn that withered. " 'Who *is* he?' ME!"

"Oh!" Penrod was humiliated but relieved: he felt that he had proved himself criminally ignorant, yet a peril seemed to have passed. "Rupe Collins is *your* name, then, I guess. I kind of thought it was, all the time."

The fat-faced boy still appeared embittered, burlesquing this speech in a hateful falsetto. "'Rupe Collins is *your* name, then, I guess!' Oh, you 'kind of thought it was, all the time,' did you?" Suddenly concentrating his brow into a histrionic scowl he thrust his face within an inch of Penrod's. "Yes, sonny, Rupe Collins is my name, and you better look out what you say when he's around or you'll get in big trouble! *You understan' that, 'bo?"*

Penrod was cowed but fascinated; he felt that there was something dangerous and dashing about this newcomer.

"Yes," he said, feebly, drawing back. "My name's Penrod Schofield."

"Then I reckon your father and mother ain't got good sense," said Mr. Collins promptly, this also being formula.

"Why?"

"'Cause if they had they'd of give you a good name!" And the agreeable youth instantly rewarded himself for the wit with another yell of rasping laughter, after which he pointed suddenly at Penrod's right hand.

"Where'd you get that wart on your finger?" he demanded severely.

"Which finger?" asked the mystified Penrod, extending his hand.

"The middle one."

"Where?"

"There!" Rupe Collins exclaimed, seizing and vigorously twisting the wartless finger naïvely offered for his inspection.

"Quit!" Penrod shouted in agony. "*Quee*-yut!"

"Say your prayers!" Rupe commanded, and continued to twist the luckless finger until Penrod writhed to his knees.

"*Ow!*" The victim, released, looked grievously upon the still painful finger.

At this Rupe's scornful expression altered to one of

"*Yes, sonny, Rupe Collins is my name, and you better look out what you say when he's around!*"

contrition. "Well, I declare!" he exclaimed remorsefully. "I didn't s'pose it would hurt. Turn about's fair play; so now you do that to me."

He extended the middle finger of his left hand and Penrod promptly seized it, but did not twist it, for he was instantly swung round with his back to his amiable new acquaintance; Rupe's right hand operated upon the back of Penrod's slender neck; Rupe's knee tortured the small of Penrod's back.

"*Ow!*" Penrod bent far forward involuntarily and went to his knees again.

"Lick dirt," Rupe commanded, forcing the captive's face to the sidewalk; and the suffering Penrod completed this ceremony.

Mr. Collins evinced satisfaction by means of his horse laugh. "You'd last jest about one day up at the Third!" he said. "You'd come runnin' home yellin' '*Mom-muh, mom-muh*' before recess was over!"

"No, I wouldn't," Penrod protested rather weakly, dusting his knees.

"You would, too!"

"No, I w——"

"Looky here," said the fat-faced boy, darkly, "what you mean, counterdicking me?"

He advanced a step and Penrod hastily qualified his contradiction. "I mean, I don't *think* I would. I——"

"You better look out!" Rupe moved closer, and unexpectedly grasped the back of Penrod's neck again. "Say, 'I *would* run home yellin' '*Mom*-muh!'' "

"Ow! I *would* run home yellin' 'Mom-muh'."

"There!" said Rupe, giving the helpless nape a final squeeze. "That's the way we do up at the Third."

Penrod rubbed his neck and asked meekly: "Can you do that to any boy up at the Third?"

"See here now," Rupe said, in the tone of one goaded beyond all endurance, "*you* say if I can! You better say it quick, or——"

"I knew you could," Penrod interposed hastily, with the pathetic semblance of a laugh. "I only said that in fun."

"In 'fun'!" Rupe repeated stormily. "You better look out how you——"

"Well, I *said* I wasn't in earnest!" Penrod retreated a few steps. "*I* knew you could, all the time. I expect *I* could do it to some of the boys up at the Third, myself. Couldn't I?"

"No, you couldn't."

"Well, there must be *some* boy up there that I could——"

"No, they ain't! You better——"

"I expect not, then," Penrod said, quickly.

"You *better* 'expect not'. Didn't I tell you once you'd never get back alive if you ever tried to come up around the Third? You want me to *show* you how we do up there, 'bo?"

He began a slow and deadly advance, whereupon Penrod timidly offered a diversion: "Say, Rupe, I got a box of rats in our stable under a glass cover, so you can watch 'em jump around when you hammer on the box. Come on and look at 'em."

"All right," said the fat-faced boy, slightly mollified. "We'll let Dan kill 'em."

"No, *sir!* I'm goin' to keep 'em. They're kind of pets; I've had 'em all summer—I got names for 'em, and——"

"Looky here, 'bo. Did you hear me say we'll let Dan kill 'em?"

"Yes, but I won't——"

"*What* won't you?" Rupe became sinister immediately. "It seems to me you're gettin' pretty fresh around here."

"Well, I don't want——"

Mr. Collins once more brought into play the dreadful eye-to-eye scowl as practised "up at the Third", and, sometimes, also by young leading men upon the stage. Frowning appallingly, and thrusting forward his underlip, he placed his nose almost in contact with the nose of Penrod, whose eyes naturally became crossed.

"Dan kills the rats. See?" hissed the fat-faced boy, maintaining the horrible juxtaposition.

"Well, all right," Penrod said, swallowing. "*I* don't want 'em much." And when the pose had been relaxed, he stared at his new friend for a moment, almost with reverence. Then he brightened. "Come on, Rupe!" he cried enthusiastically, as he climbed the fence. "We'll give our dogs a little live meat—'bo!'"

CHAPTER XXII

THE IMITATOR

AT THE dinner-table, that evening, Penrod surprised his family by remarking, in a voice they had never heard him attempt—a law-giving voice of intentional gruffness: "Any man that's makin' a hunderd dollars a month is makin' good money."

"What?" Mr. Schofield asked, staring, for the previous conversation had concerned the illness of an infant relative in Council Bluffs.

"Any man that's makin' a hunderd dollars a month is makin' good money."

"What *is* he talking about!" Margaret appealed to the invisible.

"Well," Penrod said, frowning, "that's what foremen at the ladder works get."

164

"How in the world do you know?" his mother asked.

"Well, I *know* it! A hunderd dollars a month is good money, I tell you!"

"Well, what of it?" the father said, impatiently.

"Nothin'. I only said it was good money."

Mr. Schofield shook his head, dismissing the subject, and here he made a mistake; he should have followed up his son's singular contribution to the conversation. That would have revealed the fact that there was a certain Rupe Collins whose father was a foreman at the ladder works. All clues are important when a boy makes his first remark in a new key.

" 'Good money'?" Margaret repeated, curiously. "What is 'good' money?"

Penrod turned upon her a stern glance. "Say, wouldn't you be just as happy if you had *some* sense?"

"Penrod!" his father shouted. But Penrod's mother gazed with dismay at her son; he had never before spoken like that to his sister.

Mrs. Schofield might have been more dismayed than she was, if she had realized that it was the beginning of an epoch. After dinner, Penrod was slightly scalded in the back as the result of telling Della, the cook, that there was a wart on the middle finger of her right hand. Della thus proving poor material for his new manner to work upon, he approached Duke, in the backyard, and, bending double, seized the lowly animal by the forepaws.

"I let you know my name's Penrod Schofield," hissed the boy. He protruded his underlip ferociously, scowled and thrust forward his head until his nose touched the dog's. "And you better look out when Penrod Schofield's around, or you'll get in big trouble! *You understan'* that, 'bo?"

The next day, and the next, the increasing change in Penrod puzzled and distressed his family, who had no idea of its source. How might they guess that hero-worship takes such forms? They were vaguely conscious that a rather shabby boy, not of the neighbourhood, came to "play" with

Penrod several times; but they failed to connect this circumstance with the peculiar behaviour of the son of the house, whose ideals (his father remarked) seemed to have suddenly become identical with those of Gyp the Blood.

Meanwhile, for Penrod himself, "life had taken on new meaning, new richness." He had become a fighting man—in conversation at least. "Do you want to know how I do when they try to slip up on me from behind?" he asked Della. And he enacted for her unappreciative eye a scene of fistic manœuvres wherein he held an imaginary antagonist helpless in a net of stratagems.

Frequently, when he was alone, he would outwit and pummel this same enemy, and, after a cunning feint, land a dolorous stroke full upon a face of air. "There! I guess you'll know better next time. That's the way we do up at the Third!"

Sometimes, in solitary pantomime, he encountered more than one opponent at a time, for numbers were apt to come upon him treacherously, especially at a little after his rising hour, when he might be caught at a disadvantage—perhaps standing on one leg to encase the other in his knickerbockers. Like lightning, he would hurl the trapping garment from him, and, ducking and pivoting, deal great sweeping blows among the circle of sneaking devils. (That was how he broke the clock in his bedroom.) And while these battles were occupying his attention, it was a waste of voice to call him to breakfast, though if his mother, losing patience, came to his room, she would find him seated on the bed pulling at a stocking. "Well, ain't I coming fast as I *can?*"

At the table and about the house generally he was bumptious, loud with fatuous misinformation, and assumed a domineering tone that neither satire nor reproof seemed able to reduce; but it was among his own intimates that his new superiority was most outrageous. He twisted the fingers and squeezed the necks of all the boys of the neighbourhood, meeting their indignation with a hoarse and rasping laugh he had acquired after short practice in the stable, where he jeered and taunted the lawn-mower, the garden-scythe and the wheelbarrow quite out of countenance.

Likewise he bragged to the other boys by the hour, Rupe Collins being the chief subject of encomium—next to Penrod himself. "That's the way we do up at the Third" became staple explanation of violence, for Penrod, like Tartarin, was plastic in the hands of his own imagination, and at times convinced himself that he really was one of those dark and murderous spirits exclusively of whom "the Third" was composed—according to Rupe Collins.

Then, when Penrod had exhausted himself repeating to nausea accounts of the prowess of himself and his great friend, he would turn to two other subjects for vainglory. These were his father and Duke.

Mothers must accept the fact that between babyhood and manhood their sons do not boast of them. The boy, with boys, is a Choctaw; and either the influence or the protection of women is shameful. "Your mother won't let you" is an insult. But "My father won't let me" is a dignified explanation and cannot be hooted. A boy is ruined among his fellows if he talks much of his mother or sisters; and he must recognize it as his duty to offer at least the appearance of persecution to all things ranked as female, such as cats and every species of fowl. But he must champion his father and his dog, and, ever ready to pit either against any challenger, must picture both as ravening for battle and absolutely unconquerable.

Penrod, of course, had always talked by the code; but, under the new stimulus, Duke was represented virtually as a cross between Bob, Son of Battle, and a South American vampire; and this in spite of the fact that Duke himself often sat close by, a living lie, with the hope of peace in his heart. As for Penrod's father, that gladiator was painted as of sentiments and dimensions suitable to a superdemon composed of equal parts of Goliath, Jack Johnson and the Emperor Nero.

Even Penrod's walk was affected; he adopted a gait that was a kind of taunting swagger; and, when he passed other children on the street, he practised the habit of feinting a blow; then, as the victim dodged, he rasped the triumphant horse laugh that he gradually mastered to horrible perfection. He did this to Marjorie Jones—ay! this was their next meeting, and such is Eros, young! What was even worse, in Marjorie's opinion, he went on his way without explanation, and left her standing on the corner talking about it, long after he was out of hearing.

Within five days from his first encounter with Rupe Collins, Penrod had become unbearable. He even almost alienated Sam Williams, who for a time submitted to finger twisting and neck squeezing and the new style of conversation, but finally declared that Penrod made him "sick". He made the statement with fervour, one sultry afternoon, in Mr. Schofield's stable, in the presence of Herman and Verman.

"You better look out, 'bo," said Penrod, threateningly. "I'll show you a little how we do up at the Third."

"Up at the Third!" Sam repeated with scorn. "You haven't ever been up there."

"I haven't?" Penrod cried. "I *haven't?*"

"No, you haven't!"

"Looky here!" Penrod, darkly argumentative, prepared to perform the eye-to-eye business. "When haven't I been up there?"

"You haven't *never* been up there!" In spite of Penrod's closely approaching nose, Sam maintained his ground and appealed for confirmation. "Has he, Herman?"

"I don' reckon so," Herman said, laughing.

"*What!*" Penrod transferred his nose to the immediate vicinity of Herman's nose. "You don't reckon so, 'bo, don't you? You better look out how you reckon around here! *You understan' that, 'bo?*"

Herman bore the eye-to-eye very well; indeed, it seemed

to please him, for he continued to laugh, while Verman chuckled delightedly. The brothers had been in the country picking berries for a week, and it happened that this was their first experience of the new manifestation of Penrod.

"*Haven't* I been up at Third?" the sinister Penrod demanded.

"I don't reckon so. How come you ast *me?*"

"Didn't you just hear me *say* I been up there?"

"Well," Herman said mischievously, "hearin' ain't believin'!"

Penrod clutched him by the back of the neck; but Herman, laughing loudly, ducked and released himself at once, retreating to the wall.

"You take that back!" Penrod shouted, striking out wildly.

"Don't git mad," the small darky begged, while a number of blows falling upon his warding arms failed to abate his amusement, and a sound one upon the cheek only made him laugh the more unrestrainedly. He behaved exactly as if Penrod were tickling him, and his brother, Verman, rolled with joy in a wheelbarrow. Penrod pummelled till he was tired, and produced no greater effect.

"There!" he panted, desisting finally. "*Now* I reckon you know whether I been up there or not!"

Herman rubbed his smitten cheek. "Pow!" he exclaimed. "Pow-ee! You cert'ny did lan' me good one *nat* time! Oo-ee! she *hurt!*"

"You'll get hurt worse'n that," Penrod assured him, "if you stay around here much. Rupe Collins is comin' this afternoon, he said. We're goin' to make some policemen's billies out of the rake handle."

"You go' spoil new rake you' pa bought?"

"What do *we* care? I and Rupe got to have billies, haven't we?"

"How you make 'em?"

"Melt lead and pour in a hole we're goin' to make in the

end of 'em. Then we're goin' to carry 'em in our pockets, and if anybody says anything to us—*oh*, oh! look out! They won't get a crack on the head—*oh*, no!"

"When's Rupe Collins coming?" Sam Williams inquired rather uneasily. He had heard a great deal too much of this personage; but as yet the pleasure of actual acquaintance had been denied him.

"He's liable to be here any time," Penrod answered. "You better look out. You'll be lucky if you get home alive, if you stay till *he* comes."

"I ain't afraid of him," Sam returned, conventionally.

"You are, too!" (There was some truth in the retort.) "There ain't any boy in this part of town but me that wouldn't be afraid of him. You'd be afraid to talk to him. You wouldn't get a word out of your mouth before old Rupie'd have you where you'd wished you never come around *him*, lettin' on like you was so much! *You* wouldn't run home yellin' 'Mom-muh' or nothin'! *Oh*, no!"

"Who Rupe Collins?" asked Herman.

"'Who Rupe Collins?'" Penrod mocked, and used his rasping laugh; but, instead of showing fright, Herman appeared to think he was meant to laugh, too. So he did, echoed by Verman. "You just hang around here a little while longer," Penrod added grimly, "and you'll find out who Rupe Collins is, and I pity *you* when you do!"

"What he go' do?"

"You'll see; that's all! You just wait and——"

At this moment a brown hound ran into the stable through the alley door, wagged a greeting to Penrod, and fraternized with Duke. The fat-faced boy appeared upon the threshold and gazed coldly about the little company in the carriage-house, whereupon the coloured brethren, ceasing from merriment, were instantly impassive, and Sam Williams moved a little nearer the door leading into the yard.

Obviously, Sam regarded the newcomer as a redoubtable if not ominous figure. He was a head taller than either Sam or Penrod; head and shoulders taller than Herman, who was short for his age; and Verman could hardly be used for purposes of comparison at all, being a mere squat brown spot, not yet quite nine years on this planet. And to Sam's mind, the aspect of Mr. Collins realized Penrod's portentous foreshadowings. Upon the fat face there was an expression of truculent intolerance that had been cultivated by careful habit to such perfection that Sam's heart sank at sight of it. A somewhat enfeebled twin to this expression had of late often decorated the visage of Penrod, and appeared upon that ingenuous surface now, as he advanced to welcome the eminent visitor.

The host swaggered toward the door with a great deal of shoulder movement, carelessly feinting a slap at Verman in passing, and creating by various means the atmosphere of a man who has contemptuously amused himself with underlings while awaiting an equal.

"Hello, 'bo!" Penrod said in the deepest voice possible to him.

"Who you callin' 'bo?" was the ungracious response, accompanied by immediate action of a similar nature. Rupe held Penrod's head in the crook of an elbow and massaged his temples with a hard-pressing knuckle.

"I was only in fun, Rupie," pleaded the sufferer, and then, being set free, "Come here, Sam," he said.

"What for?"

Penrod laughed pityingly. "Pshaw, I ain't goin' to hurt you. Come on." Sam, maintaining his position near the other door, Penrod went to him and caught him round the neck.

"Watch me, Rupie!" Penrod called, and performed upon Sam the knuckle operation that he had himself just undergone, Sam submitting mechanically, his eyes fixed with increasing uneasiness upon Rupe Collins. Sam had a premonition that something even more painful than Penrod's knuckle was going to be inflicted upon him.

"*That* don't hurt," said Penrod, pushing him away.

"Yes, it does, too!" Sam rubbed his temple.

"Puh! It didn't hurt me, did it, Rupie? Come on in, Rupe: show this baby where he's got a wart on his finger."

"*You* showed me that trick," Sam objected. "You already did that to me. You tried it twice this afternoon and I don't know how many times before, only you weren't strong enough after the first time. Anyway, I know what it is, and I don't——"

"Come on, Rupe," said Penrod. "Make the baby lick dirt."

At this bidding, Rupe approached, while Sam, still protesting, moved to the threshold of the outer door; but Penrod seized him by the shoulders and swung him indoors with a shout.

"Little baby wants to run home to its Mom-muh! Here he is, Rupie."

Thereupon was Penrod's treachery to an old comrade properly rewarded, for as the two struggled, Rupe caught each by the back of the neck, simultaneously, and, with creditable impartiality, forced both boys to their knees.

"Lick dirt!" he commanded, forcing them still forward, until their faces were close to the stable floor.

At this moment he received a real surprise. With a loud whack something struck the back of his head, and, turning, he beheld Verman in the act of lifting a piece of lath to strike again.

"Em moys ome!" said Verman, the Giant Killer.

"He tongue-tie'," Herman explained. "He say, let 'em boys alone."

Rupe addressed his host briefly: "Chase them nigs out o' here!"

"Don' call me nig," said Herman. "I mine my own biznuss. You let 'em boys alone."

Rupe strode across the still prostrate Sam, stepped upon Penrod, and, equipping his countenance with the terrifying scowl and protruded jaw, lowered his head to the level of Herman's.

"Nig, you'll be lucky if you leave here alive!" And he

leaned forward till his nose was within less than an inch of Herman's nose.

It could be felt that something awful was about to happen, and Penrod, as he rose from the floor, suffered an unexpected twinge of apprehension and remorse: he hoped that Rupe wouldn't *really* hurt Herman. A sudden dislike of Rupe and Rupe's ways rose within him, as he looked at the big boy overwhelming the little darky with that ferocious scowl. Penrod, all at once, felt sorry about something indefinable; and, with equal vagueness, he felt foolish. "Come on, Rupe," he suggested, feebly, "let Herman go, and let's us make our billies out of the rake handle."

The rake handle, however, was not available, if Rupe had inclined to favour the suggestion. Verman had discarded his lath for the rake, which he was at this moment lifting in the air.

"You ole black nigger," the fat-faced boy said venomously to Herman, "I'm agoin' to——"

But he had allowed his nose to remain too long near Herman's. Penrod's familiar nose had been as close with only a ticklish spinal effect upon the not very remote descendant of Congo man-eaters. The result produced by the glare of Rupe's unfamiliar eyes, and by the dreadfully suggestive proximity of Rupe's unfamiliar nose, was altogether different. Herman's and Verman's Bangala great-grandfathers never considered people of their own jungle neighbourhood proper material for a meal; but they looked upon strangers—especially truculent strangers—as distinctly edible.

Penrod and Sam heard Rupe suddenly squawk and bellow; saw him writhe and twist and fling out his arms like flails, though without removing his face from its juxtaposition; indeed, for a moment, the two heads seemed even closer.

Then they separated—and battle was on!

CHAPTER XXIII

COLOURED TROOPS IN ACTION

HOW neat and pure is the task of the chronicler who has the tale to tell of a "good rousing fight" between boys or men who fight in the "good old English way", according to a model set for fights in books long before Tom Brown went to Rugby. There are seconds and rounds and rules of fair-play, and always there is great good feeling in the end—though sometimes, to vary the model, "the Butcher" defeats the hero—and the chronicler who stencils this fine old pattern on his page is certain of applause as the stirrer of "red blood". There is no surer recipe.

But, when Herman and Verman set to, the record must be no more than a few fragments left by the expurgator. It has been perhaps sufficiently suggested that the altercation

in Mr. Schofield's stable opened with mayhem in respect to
the aggressor's nose. Expressing vocally his indignation
and the extremity of his pained surprise, Mr. Collins
stepped backward, holding his left hand over his nose, and
striking at Herman with his right. Then Verman hit him
with the rake.

Verman struck from behind. He struck as hard as he
could. And he struck with the tines down. For, in his simple,
direct African way he wished to kill his enemy, and he
wished to kill him as soon as possible. That was his single,
earnest purpose.

On this account, Rupe Collins was peculiarly unfortunate. He was plucky and he enjoyed conflict; but neither
his ambitions nor his anticipations had ever included murder. He had not learned that an habitually aggressive person runs the danger of colliding with beings in one of those
lower stages of evolution wherein theories about "hitting
below the belt" have not yet made their appearance.

The rake glanced from the back of Rupe's head to his
shoulder; but it felled him. Both darkies jumped full upon
him instantly, and the three rolled and twisted upon the
stable floor, unloosing upon the air sincere maledictions
closely connected with complaints of cruel and unusual
treatment; while certain expressions of feeling presently
emanating from Herman and Verman indicated that Rupe
Collins, in this extremity, was proving himself not too slav-
ishly addicted to fighting by rule. Dan and Duke, mistaking all for mirth, barked gayly.

From the panting, pounding, yelling heap issued words
and phrases hitherto quite unknown to Penrod and Sam;
also, a hoarse repetition in the voice of Rupe concerning
his ear left it not to be doubted that additional mayhem
was taking place. Appalled, the two spectators retreated
to the doorway nearest the yard, where they stood dumbly
watching the cataclysm.

The struggle increased in primitive simplicity: time and
again the howling Rupe got to his knees only to go down

again as the earnest brothers, in their own way, assisted him to a more reclining position. Primal forces operated here, and the two blanched, slightly higher products of evolution, Sam and Penrod, no more thought of interfering than they would have thought of interfering with an earthquake.

At last, out of the ruck rose Verman, disfigured and maniacal. With a wild eye he looked about him for his trusty rake; but Penrod, in horror, had long since thrown the rake out into the yard. Naturally, it had not seemed necessary to remove the lawn-mower.

The frantic eye of Verman fell upon the lawn-mower, and instantly he leaped to its handle. Shrilling a wordless war-cry, he charged, propelling the whirling, deafening knives straight upon the prone legs of Rupe Collins. The lawn-mower was sincerely intended to pass longitudinally over the body of Mr. Collins from heel to head; and it was the time for a death-song. Black Valkyrie hovered in the shrieking air.

"Cut his gizzud out!" shrieked Herman, urging on the whirling knives.

They touched and lacerated the shin of Rupe, as, with the supreme agony of effort a creature in mortal peril puts forth before succumbing, he tore himself free of Herman and got upon his feet.

Herman was up as quickly. He leaped to the wall and seized the garden-scythe that hung there.

"I'm go' to cut you' gizzud out," he announced definitely, "an' eat it!"

Rupe Collins had never run from anybody (except his father) in his life; he was not a coward; but the present situation was very, very unusual. He was already in a badly dismantled condition, and yet Herman and Verman seemed discontented with their work: Verman was swinging the grass-cutter about for a new charge, apparently still wishing to mow him, and Herman had made a quite plausible statement about what he intended to do with the scythe.

Rupe paused but for an extremely condensed survey of
the horrible advance of the brothers, and then, uttering a
blood-curdled scream of fear, ran out of the stable and up
the alley at a speed he had never before attained, so that
even Dan had hard work to keep within barking distance.
And a 'cross-shoulder glance, at the corner, revealing Verman and Herman in pursuit, the latter waving his scythe
overhead, Mr. Collins slackened not his gait, but, rather,
out of great anguish, increased it, the while a rapidly developing purpose became firm in his mind—and ever after
so remained—not only to refrain from visiting that neighbourhood again but never by any chance to come within
a mile of it.

From the alley door, Penrod and Sam watched the flight,
and were without words. When the pursuit rounded the corner, the two looked wanly at each other; but neither spoke
until the return of the brothers from the chase.

Herman and Verman came back, laughing and chuckling.

"Hiyi!" cackled Herman to Verman, as they came. "See
'at ole boy run!"

"Who-ee!" Verman shouted in ecstasy.

"Nev' did see boy run so fas'!" Herman continued, tossing the scythe into the wheelbarrow. "I bet he home in bed
by viss time!"

Verman roared with delight, appearing to be wholly unconscious that the lids of his right eye were swollen shut
and that his attire, not too finical before the struggle,
now entitled him to unquestioned rank as a *sansculotte*.
Herman was a similar ruin, and gave as little heed to his
condition.

Penrod looked dazedly from Herman to Verman and back
again. So did Sam Williams.

"Herman," said Penrod, in a weak voice, "you wouldn't
honest of cut his gizzard out, would you?"

"Who? Me? I don' know. He mighty mean ole boy!"
Herman shook his head gravely, and then, observing that
Verman was again convulsed with unctuous merriment,

joined laughter with his brother. "Sho! I guess I uz dess *talkin'* whens I said 'at! Reckon he thought I meant it, f'm de way he tuck an' run. Hiyi! Reckon he thought ole Herman bad man! No, suh, I uz dess talkin', 'cause I nev' would cut *no*body! I ain' tryin' git in no jail—*no*, suh!"

Penrod looked at the scythe; he looked at Herman. He looked at the lawn-mower and he looked at Verman. Then he looked out in the yard at the rake. So did Sam Williams.

"Come on, Verman," said Herman. "We ain' got 'at stove-wood f' supper yit."

Giggling reminiscently, the brothers disappeared, leaving silence behind them in the carriage-house. Penrod and Sam retired slowly into the shadowy interior, each glancing, now and then, with a preoccupied air, at the open, empty doorway where the late afternoon sunshine was growing ruddy. At intervals one or the other scraped the floor reflectively with the side of his shoe. Finally, still without either having made any effort at conversation, they went out into the yard and stood, continuing their silence.

"Well," said Sam, at last, "I guess it's time I better be gettin' home. So long, Penrod!"

"So long, Sam," said Penrod, feebly.

With a solemn gaze he watched his friend out of sight. Then he went slowly into the house, and after an interval occupied in a unique manner, appeared in the library, holding a pair of brilliantly gleaming shoes in his hand.

Mr. Schofield, reading the evening paper, glanced frowningly over it at his offspring.

"Look, Papa," Penrod said. "I found your shoes where you'd taken 'em off in your room, to put on your slippers, and they were all dusty. So I took 'em out on the back porch and gave 'em a good blacking. They shine up fine, don't they?"

"Well, I'll be d-dud-dummed!" the startled Mr. Schofield said.

Penrod was zigzagging back to normal.

CHAPTER XXIV

"LITTLE GENTLEMAN"

THE midsummer sun was stinging hot outside the little barber-shop next to the corner drug store and Penrod, undergoing a coifing, was adhesive enough to retain upon his face much hair as it fell from the shears. There is a mystery here: the tonsorial processes are not unagreeable to manhood; in truth, they are soothing; but the hairs detached from a boy's head get into his eyes, his ears, his nose, his mouth and down his neck, and he does everywhere itch excruciatingly. Wherefore he blinks, winks, weeps, twitches, condenses his countenance, and squirms; and perchance the barber's scissors clip more than intended —belike an outlying flange of ear.

"Um—muh—*ow!*" Penrod said, this thing having happened.

"D' I touch y' up a little?" the barber inquired, smiling falsely.

"Ooh—*uh!*" The boy in the chair offered inarticulate protest, as the wound was rubbed with alum.

"*That* don't hurt!" the barber said. "You *will* get it, though, if you don't sit stiller," he continued, nipping in the bud any attempt on the part of his patient to think that he already had "it".

"Pfuff!" Penrod said, meaning no disrespect, but endeavouring to dislodge a temporary moustache from his lip.

"You ought to see how still that little Georgie Bassett sits," the barber went on, reprovingly. "I hear everybody says he's the best boy in town."

"Pfuff! *Phirr!*" There was a touch of intentional contempt in this.

"I haven't heard nobody around the neighbourhood makin' no such remarks," the barber added, "about nobody of the name of Penrod Schofield."

"Well," said Penrod, clearing his mouth after a struggle, "who wants 'em to? Ouch!"

"I hear they call Georgie Bassett the 'little gentleman'," the barber ventured provocatively, meeting with instant success.

"They better not call *me* that," Penrod returned truculently. "I'd like to hear anybody try. Just once, that's all! I bet they'd never try it ag—— *Ouch!*"

"Why? What'd you do to 'em?"

"It's all right what I'd *do!* I bet they wouldn't want to call me that again long as they lived!"

"What'd you do if it was a little girl? You wouldn't hit her, would you?"

"Well, I'd—— Ouch!"

"You wouldn't hit a little girl, would you?" the barber persisted, gathering into his powerful fingers a mop of hair from the top of Penrod's head and pulling that suffering head into an unnatural position. "Doesn't the Bible say it ain't never right to hit the weak sex?"

"Ow! *Say,* look *out!*"

"So you'd go and punch a pore, weak, little girl, would you?" the barber said reprovingly.

"Well, who said I'd hit her?" demanded the chivalrous Penrod. "I bet I'd *fix* her though, all right. She'd see!"

"You wouldn't call her names, would you?"

"No, I wouldn't! What hurt is it to call anybody names?"

"Is that *so!*" the barber exclaimed. "Then you was intending what I heard you hollering at Fisher's grocery delivery wagon driver fer a favour, the other day when I was goin' by your house, was you? I reckon I better tell him, because he says to me after*werds* if he ever lays eyes on you when you ain't in your own yard, he's goin' to do a whole lot o' things you ain't goin' to like! Yessir, that's what he says to *me!*"

"He better catch me first, I guess, before he talks so much."

"Well," the barber resumed, "that ain't sayin' what you'd do if a young lady ever walked up and called you a little gentleman. *I* want to hear what you'd do to her. I guess I know, though—come to think of it."

"What?" Penrod demanded.

"You'd sick that pore ole dog of yours on her cat, if she had one, I expect," the barber guessed derisively.

"No, I would not!"

"Well, what *would* you do?"

"I'd do enough. Don't worry about that!"

"Well, suppose it was a boy, then. What'd you do if a boy come up to you and says, 'Hello, little gentleman'?"

"He'd be lucky," said Penrod, with a sinister frown, "if he got home alive."

"Suppose it was a boy twice your size?"

"Just let him try," said Penrod ominously. "You just let him try. He'd never see daylight again; that's all!"

The barber dug ten active fingers into the helpless scalp before him and did his best to displace it, while the anguished Penrod, becoming instantly a seething crucible

of emotion, misdirected his natural resentment into maddened brooding upon what he would do to a boy "twice his
size" who should dare to call him "little gentleman". The
barber shook him as his father had never shaken him; the
barber buffeted him, rocked him frantically to and fro;
the barber seemed to be trying to wring his neck; and Penrod saw himself in staggering zigzag pictures, destroying
large, screaming, fragmentary boys who had insulted him.

The torture stopped suddenly; and clenched, weeping
eyes began to see again, while the barber applied cooling
lotions that made Penrod smell like a coloured housemaid's
ideal.

"Now what," asked the barber, combing the reeking locks
gently, "what would it make you so mad fer, to have somebody call you a little gentleman? It's a kind of compliment,
as it were, you might say. What would you want to hit
anybody fer *that* fer?"

To the mind of Penrod, this question was without meaning or reasonableness. It was within neither his power nor
his desire to analyze the process by which the phrase had
become offensive to him, and was now rapidly assuming the
proportions of an outrage. He knew only that his gorge
rose at the thought of it.

"You just let 'em try it!" he said threateningly, as he
slid down from the chair. And as he went out of the door,
after further conversation on the same subject, he called
back those warning words once more: "Just let 'em try it!
Just once—that's all *I* ask 'em to. They'll find out what
they *get!*"

The barber chuckled. Then a fly lit on the barber's nose
and he slapped at it, and the slap missed the fly but did
not miss the nose. The barber was irritated. At this moment
his birdlike eye gleamed a gleam as it fell upon customers
approaching: the prettiest little girl in the world, leading
by the hand her baby brother, Mitchy-Mitch, coming to
have Mitchy-Mitch's hair clipped, against the heat.

It was a hot day and idle, with little to feed the mind—and the barber was a mischievous man with an irritated nose. He did his worst.

Meanwhile, the brooding Penrod pursued his homeward way; no great distance but long enough for several one-sided conflicts with malign insulters made of thin air. "You better *not* call me that!" he muttered. "You just try it, and you'll get what other people got when *they* tried it. You better not ack fresh with *me!* Oh, you *will*, will you?" He delivered a vicious kick full upon the shins of an iron fence-post, which suffered little, though Penrod instantly regretted his indiscretion. "Oof!" he grunted, hopping; and went on after bestowing a look of awful hostility upon the fence-post. "I guess you'll know better next time," he said, in parting, to this antagonist. "You just let me catch you around here again and I'll——" His voice sank to inarticulate but ominous murmurings. He was in a dangerous mood.

Nearing home, however, his belligerent spirit was diverted to happier interests by the discovery that some workmen had left a caldron of tar in the cross-street, close by his father's stable. He tested it but found it inedible. Also, as a substitute for professional chewing-gum it was unsatisfactory, being insufficiently boiled down and too thin, though of a pleasant, lukewarm temperature. But it had an excess of one quality—it was sticky. It was the stickiest tar Penrod had ever used for any purposes whatsoever, and nothing upon which he wiped his hands served to rid them of it; neither his polka-dotted shirt waist nor his knicker-bockers; neither the fence, nor even Duke, who came unthinkingly wagging out to greet him, and retired wiser.

Nevertheless, tar is tar. Much can be done with it, no matter what its condition; so Penrod lingered by the caldron, though from a neighbouring yard could be heard the voices of comrades, including that of Sam Williams. On the ground about the caldron were scattered chips and sticks and bits of wood to the number of a great multitude. Penrod mixed quantities of this refuse into the tar, and interested himself in seeing how much of it he could keep moving in slow swirls upon the ebon surface.

Other surprises were arranged for the absent workmen. The caldron was almost full, and the surface of the tar near the rim. Penrod endeavoured to ascertain how many pebbles and brickbats, dropped in, would cause an overflow. Labouring heartily to this end, he had almost accomplished it, when he received the suggestion for an experiment on a much larger scale. Embedded at the corner of a grass-plot across the street was a whitewashed stone, the size of a small watermelon and serving no purpose whatever save the questionable one of decoration. It was easily pried up with a stick, though getting it to the caldron tested the full strength of the ardent labourer. Instructed to perform such a task, he would have sincerely maintained its impossibility; but now, as it was unbidden, and promised rather destructive results, he set about it with unconquerable energy, feeling certain that he would be rewarded with a mighty splash. Perspiring, grunting vehemently, his back aching and all muscles strained, he progressed in short stages until the big stone lay at the base of the caldron. He rested a moment, panting, then lifted the stone, and was bending his shoulders for the heave that would lift it over the rim, when a sweet, taunting voice, close behind him, startled him cruelly.

"How do you do, *little gentleman!*"

Penrod squawked, dropped the stone, and shouted, "Shut up, you dern fool!" purely from instinct, even before his about-face made him aware who had so spitefully addressed him.

It was Marjorie Jones. Always dainty, and prettily dressed, she was in speckless and starchy white to-day, and a refreshing picture she made, with the new-shorn and powerfully scented Mitchy-Mitch clinging to her hand. They had stolen up behind the toiler, and now stood laughing together in sweet merriment. Since the passing of Penrod's Rupe Collins period, he had experienced some severe qualms at the recollection of his last meeting with Marjorie and his Apache behaviour; in truth, his heart instantly became as wax at sight of her, and he would have offered her fair speech; but, alas! in Marjorie's wonderful eyes there shone a consciousness of new powers for his undoing, and she denied him opportunity.

"Oh, oh!" she cried, mocking his pained outcry. "What a way for a *little gentleman* to talk! Little gentlemen don't say wicked——"

"Marjorie!" Penrod, enraged and dismayed, felt himself stung beyond all endurance. Insult from her was bitterer to endure than from any other. "Don't you call me that again!"

"Why not, *little gentleman?*"

He stamped his foot. "You better stop!"

Marjorie sent into his furious face her lovely, spiteful laughter.

"Little gentleman, little gentleman, little gentleman!" she said deliberately. "How's the little gentleman, this afternoon? Hello, little gentleman!"

Penrod, quite beside himself, danced eccentrically. "Dry up!" he howled. "Dry up, dry up, dry up, dry *up!*"

Mitchy-Mitch shouted with delight and applied a finger to the side of the caldron—a finger immediately snatched away and wiped upon a handkerchief by his fastidious sister.

" 'Ittle gellamun!" said Mitchy-Mitch.

"You better look out!" Penrod whirled upon this small offender with grim satisfaction. Here was at least something male that could without dishonour be held responsible. "You say that again, and I'll give you the worst——"

"You will *not!*" snapped Marjorie, instantly vitriolic. "He'll say just whatever he wants to, and he'll say it just as *much* as he wants to. Say it again, Mitchy-Mitch!"

" 'Ittle gellamun!" said Mitchy-Mitch promptly.

"Ow-*yah!*" Penrod's tone-production was becoming

affected by his mental condition. "You say that again, and I'll——"

"Go on, Mitchy-Mitch," Marjorie cried. "He can't do a thing. He don't *dare!* Say it some more, Mitchy-Mitch—say it a whole lot!"

Mitchy-Mitch, his small, fat face shining with confidence in his immunity, complied.

" 'Ittle gellamun!" he squeaked malevolently. " 'Ittle gellamun! 'Ittle gellamun! 'Ittle gellamun!"

The desperate Penrod bent over the whitewashed rock, lifted it, and then—outdoing Porthos, John Ridd and Ursus in one miraculous burst of strength—heaved it into the air.

Marjorie screamed.

But it was too late. The big stone descended into the precise midst of the caldron and Penrod got his mighty splash. It was far, far beyond his expectations.

Spontaneously there were grand and awful effects—volcanic spectacles of nightmare and eruption. A black sheet of eccentric shape rose out of the caldron and descended upon the three children, who had no time to evade it.

After it fell, Mitchy-Mitch, who stood nearest the caldron, was the thickest, though there was enough for all. Br'er Rabbit would have fled from any of them.

CHAPTER XXV

TAR

WHEN Marjorie and Mitchy-Mitch got their breath they used it vocally; and seldom have more penetrating sounds issued from human throats. Coincidentally, Marjorie, quite baresark, laid hands upon the largest stick within reach and fell upon Penrod with blind fury. He had the presence of mind to flee, and they went round and round the caldron, while Mitchy-Mitch feebly endeavoured to follow—his appearance, in this pursuit, being pathetically like that of a bug fished out of an inkwell, alive but discouraged.

Attracted by the riot, Samuel Williams made his appearance, vaulting a fence, and was immediately followed by Maurice Levy and Georgie Bassett. They stared incredulously at the extraordinary spectacle before them.

"Little GEN-TIL-MUN!" shrieked Marjorie, with a wild stroke that landed full upon Penrod's tarry cap.

"*Oooch!*" bleated Penrod.

"It's Penrod!" Sam Williams shouted, recognizing him by the voice. For an instant he had been in some doubt.

"Penrod Schofield!" Georgie Bassett exclaimed. "*What* does this mean?" That was Georgie's style and had helped to win him his title.

Marjorie leaned, panting, upon her stick. "I cu-called—uh—him—oh!" she sobbed—"I called him a lul-little—oh—gentleman! And oh—lul-look!—oh! lul-look at my du-dress! Lul-look at Mu-mitchy—oh—Mitch—oh!"

Unexpectedly, she smote again—with results—and then, seizing the indistinguishable hand of Mitchy-Mitch, she ran wailing homeward down the street.

"'Little gentleman'?" said Georgie Bassett, with some evidences of disturbed complacency. "Why, that's what they call *me!*"

"Yes, and you *are* one, too!" the maddened Penrod shouted. "But you better not let anybody call *me* that! I've stood enough around here for one day, and you can't run over *me*, Georgie Bassett. Just you put that in your gizzard and smoke it!"

"Anybody has a perfect right," Georgie said with dignity, "to call a person a little gentleman. There's lots of names nobody ought to call; but this one's a *nice*——"

"You better look out!"

Unavenged bruises were distributed all over Penrod, both upon his body and upon his spirit. Driven by subtle forces, he had dipped his hands in catastrophe and disaster: it was not for a Georgie Bassett to beard him. Penrod was about to run amuck.

"I haven't called you a little gentleman, yet," said Georgie. "I only said it. Anybody's got a right to *say* it."

"Not around *me!* You just try it again and——"

"I shall say it," Georgie returned, "all I please. Anybody in this town has a right to *say* 'little gentleman'——"

Bellowing insanely, Penrod plunged his right hand into the caldron, rushed upon Georgie and made awful work of his hair and features.

Alas, it was but the beginning! Sam Williams and Maurice Levy screamed with delight, and, simultaneously infected, danced about the struggling pair, shouting frantically:

"Little gentleman! Little gentleman! Sick him, Georgie! Sick him, little gentleman! Little gentleman! Little gentleman!"

The infuriated outlaw turned upon them with blows and more tar, which gave Georgie Bassett his opportunity and later seriously impaired the purity of his fame. Feeling himself hopelessly tarred, he dipped both hands repeatedly into the caldron and applied his gatherings to Penrod. It was bringing coals to Newcastle, but it helped to assuage the just wrath of Georgie.

The four boys gave a fine imitation of the Laocoön group complicated by an extra figure—frantic splutterings and chokings, strange cries and stranger words issued from this tangle; hands dipped lavishly into the inexhaustible reservoir of tar, with more and more picturesque results. The caldron had been elevated upon bricks and was not perfectly balanced; under a heavy impact of the struggling group it lurched and went partly over, pouring forth a Stygian tide that formed a deep pool in the gutter.

It was the fate of Master Roderick Bitts, that exclusive and immaculate person, to make his appearance upon the chaotic scene at this juncture. All in the cool of a white "sailor suit", he turned aside from the path of duty—which led straight to the house of a maiden aunt—and paused to hop with joy upon the sidewalk. A repeated epithet continuously half panted, half squawked, somewhere in the nest of gladiators, caught his ear, and he took it up excitedly, not knowing why.

"Little gentleman!" shouted Roderick, jumping up and

down in childish glee. "Little gentleman! Little gentleman! Lit——"

A frightful figure tore itself free from the group, encircled this innocent bystander with a black arm, and hurled him headlong. Full length and flat on his face went Roderick into the Stygian pool. The frightful figure was Penrod. Instantly, the pack flung themselves upon him again, and, carrying them with him, he went over upon Roderick, who from that instant was as active a belligerent as any there.

Thus began the Great Tar Fight, the origin of which proved, afterward, so difficult for parents to trace, owing to the opposing accounts of the combatants. Marjorie said Penrod began it; Penrod said Mitchy-Mitch began it; Sam Williams said Georgie Bassett began it; Georgie and Maurice Levy said Penrod began it; Roderick Bitts, who had not recognized his first assailant, said Sam Williams began it.

Nobody thought of accusing the barber. But the barber did not begin it; it was the fly on the barber's nose that began it—though, of course, something else began the fly. Somehow, we never manage to hang the real offender.

The end came only with the arrival of Penrod's mother, who had been having a painful conversation by telephone with Mrs. Jones, the mother of Marjorie, and came forth to seek an errant son. It is a mystery how she was able to pick out her own, for by the time she got there his voice was too hoarse to be recognizable.

Mr. Schofield's version of things was that Penrod was insane. "He's a stark, raving lunatic!" the father declared, descending to the library from a before-dinner interview with the outlaw, that evening. "I'd send him to military school; but I don't believe they'd take him. Do you know *why* he says all that awfulness happened?"

"When Margaret and I were trying to scrub him," Mrs. Schofield responded wearily, "he said 'everybody' had been calling him names."

Thus began the Great Tar Fight

"This is not the Gracie I'm Fighting"

" 'Names!' " her husband snorted. " 'Little gentleman!' *That's* the vile epithet they called him! And because of it he wrecks the peace of six homes!"

"*Sh!* Yes; he told us about it," Mrs. Schofield said, moaning. "He told us several hundred times, I should guess, though I didn't count. He's got it fixed in his head, and we couldn't get it out. All we could do was to put him in the closet. He'd have gone out again after those boys if we hadn't. I don't know *what* to make of him!"

"He's a mystery to *me!*" her husband said. "And he refuses to explain why he objects to being called 'little gentleman'. Says he'd do the same thing—and worse—if anybody dared to call him that again. He said if the President of the United States called him that he'd try to whip him. How long did you have him locked up in the closet?"

"*Sh!*" Mrs. Schofield said warningly. "About two hours; but I don't think it softened his spirit at all, because when I took him to the barber's to get his hair clipped again, on account of the tar in it, Sammy Williams and Maurice Levy were there for the same reason, and they just *whispered* 'little gentleman', so low you could hardly hear them— and Penrod began fighting with them right before me, and it was really all the barber and I could do to drag him away from them. The barber was very kind about it; but Penrod——"

"I tell you he's a lunatic!" Mr. Schofield would have said the same thing of a Frenchman infuriated by the epithet "camel". The philosophy of insult needs expounding.

"*Sh!*" Mrs. Schofield said. "It does seem a kind of frenzy."

"Why on earth should any sane person mind being called——"

"*Sh!*" Mrs. Schofield said. "It's beyond *me!*"

"What are you *sh*-ing m⸗ for?" Mr. Schofield demanded explosively.

"*Sh!*" Mrs. Schofield said. "It's Mr. Kinosling, the new rector of Saint Joseph's."

"Where?"

"*Sh!* On the front porch with Margaret; he's going to stay for dinner. I do hope——"

"Bachelor, isn't he?"

"Yes."

"*Our* old minister was speaking of him the other day," Mr. Schofield said, "and he didn't seem so terribly impressed."

"*Sh!* Yes; about thirty, and of course *so* superior to most of Margaret's friends—boys home from college. She thinks she likes young Robert Williams, I know—but he laughs so much! Of course there isn't any comparison. Mr. Kinosling talks so intellectually; it's a good thing for Margaret to hear that kind of thing, for a change—and, of course, he's very spiritual. He seems very much interested in her." She paused to muse. "I think Margaret likes him; he's so different, too. It's the third time he's dropped in this week, and I——"

"Well," said Mr. Schofield grimly, "if you and Margaret want him to come again, you'd better not let him see Penrod."

"But he's asked to see him; he seems interested in meeting all the family. And Penrod nearly always behaves fairly well at table." She paused, and then put to her husband a question referring to his interview with Penrod upstairs. "Did you—did you—do it?"

"No," he answered gloomily. "No, I didn't, but——" He was interrupted by a violent crash of china and metal in the kitchen, a shriek from Della, and the outrageous voice of Penrod. The well-informed Della, ill-inspired to set up for a wit, had ventured to address the scion of the house roguishly as "little gentleman", and Penrod, by means of the rapid elevation of his right foot, had removed from her supporting hands a laden tray. Both parents started for the kitchen, Mr. Schofield completing his interrupted sentence on the way.

"But I will, now!"

The rite thus promised was hastily but accurately performed in that apartment most distant from the front porch; and, twenty minutes later, Penrod descended to dinner. The Rev. Mr. Kinosling had asked for the pleasure of meeting him, and it had been decided that the only course possible was to cover up the scandal for the present, and to offer an undisturbed and smiling family surface to the gaze of the visitor.

Scorched but not bowed, the smouldering Penrod was led forward for the social formulæ simultaneously with the somewhat bleak departure of Robert Williams, who took his guitar with him, this time, and went in forlorn unconsciousness of the powerful forces already set in secret motion to be his allies.

The punishment just undergone had but made the haughty and unyielding soul of Penrod more stalwart in revolt; he was unconquered. Every time the one intolerable insult had been offered him, his resentment had become the hotter, his vengeance the more instant and furious. And, still burning with outrage, but upheld by the conviction of right, he was determined to continue to the last drop of his blood the defense of his honour, whenever it should be assailed, no matter how mighty or august the powers that attacked it. In all ways, he was a very sore boy.

During the brief ceremony of presentation, his usually inscrutable countenance wore an expression interpreted by his father as one of insane obstinacy, while Mrs. Schofield found it an incentive to inward prayer. The fine graciousness of Mr. Kinosling, however, was unimpaired by the glare of virulent suspicion given him by this little brother: Mr. Kinosling mistook it for a natural curiosity concerning one who might possibly become, in time, a member of the family. He patted Penrod upon the head, which was, for many reasons, in no condition to be patted with any pleasure to the patter. Penrod felt himself in the presence of a new enemy.

"How do you do, my little lad," said Mr. Kinosling. "I trust we shall become fast friends."

To the ear of his little lad, it seemed he said, "A trost we shall bick-home fawst frainds." Mr. Kinosling's pronunciation was, in fact, slightly precious; and the little lad, simply mistaking it for some cryptic form of mockery of himself, assumed a manner and expression arguing so ill for the proposed friendship that Mrs. Schofield hastily interposed the suggestion of dinner, and the small procession went in to the dining-room.

"It has been a delicious day," said Mr. Kinosling, presently; "warm but balmy." With a benevolent smile he addressed Penrod, who sat opposite him. "I suppose, little gentleman, you have been indulging in the usual outdoor sports of vacation?"

Penrod laid down his fork and glared, open-mouthed at Mr. Kinosling.

"You'll have another slice of breast of the chicken?" Mr. Schofield inquired, loudly and quickly.

"A lovely day!" Margaret exclaimed, with equal promptitude and emphasis. "Lovely, oh, lovely! Lovely!"

"Beautiful, beautiful, beautiful!" Mrs. Schofield said, and, after a glance at Penrod, which confirmed her impression that he intended to say something, she continued, "Yes, beautiful, beautiful, beautiful, beautiful, beautiful, beautiful!"

Penrod closed his mouth and sank back in his chair—and his relatives took breath.

Mr. Kinosling looked pleased. This responsive family, with its ready enthusiasm, made the kind of audience he liked. He passed a delicate white hand gracefully over his tall, pale forehead, and smiled indulgently.

"Youth relaxes in summer," he said. "Boyhood is the age of relaxation; one is playful, light, free, unfettered. One runs and leaps and enjoys one's self with one's companions. It is good for the little lads to play with their friends; they jostle, push and wrestle, and simulate little, happy struggles with one another in harmless conflict. The young muscles are toughening. It is good. Boyish chivalry develops, enlarges, expands. The young learn quickly, intuitively, spontaneously. They perceive the obligations of *noblesse oblige*. They begin to comprehend the necessity of caste and its requirements. They learn what birth means—ah,—that is, they learn what it means to be well born. They learn courtesy in their games; they learn politeness, consideration for one another in their pastimes, amusements, lighter occupations. I make it my pleasure to join them often, for I sympathize with them in all their wholesome joys as well as in their little bothers and perplexities. I understand them, you see; and let me tell you it is no easy matter to understand the little lads and lassies." He sent to each listener his beaming glance, and, permitting it to come to rest upon Penrod, inquired:

"And what do you say to that, little gentleman?"

Mr. Schofield uttered a stentorian cough. "More? You'd better have some more chicken! More! Do!"

"More chicken!" urged Margaret simultaneously. "Do please! Please! More! Do! More!"

"Beautiful, beautiful," Mrs. Schofield began. "Beautiful, beautiful, beautiful, beautiful——"

It is not known in what light Mr. Kinosling viewed the expression of Penrod's face. Perhaps he mistook it for awe; perhaps he received no impression at all of its extraordinary quality. He was a rather self-engrossed young man, just then engaged in a double occupation, for he not only talked but supplied from his own consciousness a critical though favourable auditor as well, which of course kept him quite busy. Besides, it is oftener than is suspected the case that extremely peculiar expressions upon the countenances of boys are entirely overlooked, and suggest nothing to the minds of people staring straight at them. Certainly Penrod's expression—which, to the perception of his family, was perfectly horrible—caused not the faintest perturbation in the breast of Mr. Kinosling.

Mr. Kinosling waived the chicken, and continued to talk. "Yes, I think I may claim to understand boys," he said, smiling thoughtfully. "One has been a boy one's self. Ah, it is not all playtime! I hope our young scholar here does not overwork himself at his Latin, at his classics, as I did, so that at the age of eight years I was compelled to wear glasses. He must be careful not to strain the little eyes at his scholar's tasks, not to let the little shoulders grow round over his scholar's desk. Youth is golden; we should keep it golden, bright, glistening. Youth should frolic, should be sprightly; it should play its cricket, its tennis, its handball. It should run and leap; it should laugh, should sing madrigals and glees, carol with the lark, ring out in chanties, folk-songs, ballads, roundelays——"

He talked on. At any instant Mr. Schofield held himself ready to cough vehemently and shout, "More chicken!" to drown out Penrod in case the fatal words again fell from those eloquent lips; and Mrs. Schofield and Margaret kept themselves prepared at all times to assist him. So passed a threatening meal, which Mrs. Schofield hurried, by every means with decency, to its conclusion. She felt that somehow they would all be safer out in the dark of the front porch, and led the way thither as soon as possible.

"No cigar, I thank you." Mr. Kinosling, establishing himself in a wicker chair beside Margaret, waved away her father's proffer. "I do not smoke. I have never tasted tobacco in any form." Mrs. Schofield was confirmed in her opinion that this would be an ideal son-in-law. Mr. Schofield was not so sure.

"No," said Mr. Kinosling. "No tobacco for me. No cigar, no pipe, no cigarette, no cheroot. For me, a book—a volume of poems, perhaps. Verses, rhymes, lines metrical and cadenced—those are my dissipation. Tennyson by preference: 'Maud', or 'Idylls of the King'—poetry of the sound

Victorian days; there is none later. Or Longfellow will rest me in a tired hour. Yes; for me, a book, a volume in the hand, held lightly between the fingers."

Mr. Kinosling looked pleasantly at his fingers as he spoke, waving his hand in a curving gesture that brought it into the light of a window faintly illumined from the interior of the house. Then he passed those graceful fingers over his hair, and turned toward Penrod, who was perched upon the railing in a dark corner.

"The evening is touched with a slight coolness," said Mr. Kinosling. "Perhaps I may request the little gentleman——"

"B'gr-r-*ruff!*" Mr. Schofield coughed. "You'd better change your mind about a cigar."

"No, I thank you. I was about to request the lit——"

"*Do* try one," Margaret urged. "I'm sure Papa's are nice ones. Do try——"

"No, I thank you. I remarked a slight coolness in the air, and my hat is in the hallway. I was about to request——"

"I'll get it for you," Penrod said suddenly.

"If you will be so good," Mr. Kinosling said. "It is a black bowler hat, little gentleman, and placed upon a table in the hall."

"I know where it is." Penrod entered the door, and a feeling of relief, mutually experienced, carried from one to another of his three relatives their interchanged congratulations that he had recovered his sanity.

"'The day is done, and the darkness,'" began Mr. Kinosling—and recited that poem entire. He followed it with "The Children's Hour", and, after a pause at the close, to allow his listeners time for a little reflection upon his rendition, he passed his hand again over his head, and called, in the direction of the doorway:

"I believe I will take my hat now, little gentleman."

"Here it is," said Penrod, unexpectedly climbing over the porch railing, in the other direction. His mother and father and Margaret had supposed him to be standing in the hallway out of deference, and because he thought it tactful not to interrupt the recitations. All of them remembered, later, that this supposed thoughtfulness on his part struck them as unnatural.

"Very good, little gentleman!" Mr. Kinosling said, and being somewhat chilled, placed the hat firmly upon his head, pulling it down as far as it would go. It had a pleasant warmth, which he noticed at once. The next instant, he noticed something else, a peculiar sensation of the scalp— a sensation that he was quite unable to define. He lifted his hand to take the hat off, and entered upon a strange experience: his hat seemed to have decided to remain where it was.

"Do you like Tennyson as much as Longfellow, Mr. Kinosling?" Margaret inquired.

"I—ah—I cannot say," he returned absently. "I—ah— each has his own—flavour and savour, each his—ah— ah——"

Struck by a strangeness in his tone, she peered at him curiously through the dusk. His outlines were indistinct; but she made out that his arms were uplifted in a singular gesture. He seemed to be wrenching at his head.

"Is—is anything the matter?" she asked anxiously. "Mr. Kinosling, are you ill?"

"Not at—all," he replied, in the same odd tone. "I—ah —I believe——"

He dropped his hands from his hat, and rose. His manner was slightly agitated. "I fear I may have taken a trifling— ah—cold. I should—ah—perhaps be—ah—better at home. I will—ah—say good-night."

At the steps, he instinctively lifted his hand to remove his hat, but did not do so, and, saying "Good-night" again in a frigid voice, departed with visible stiffness from that house, to return no more.

"Well, of all——!" Mrs. Schofield cried, astounded. "What was the matter? He just went—like that!" She made a flurried gesture. "In heaven's name, Margaret, what *did* you say to him?"

"*I!*" Margaret exclaimed indignantly. "Nothing! He just *went!*"

"Why, he didn't even take off his hat when he said goodnight!" Mrs. Schofield said.

Margaret, who had crossed to the doorway, caught the ghost of a whisper behind her, where stood Penrod.

"*You bet he didn't!*"

He knew not that he was overheard.

A frightful suspicion flashed through Margaret's mind —a suspicion that Mr. Kinosling's hat would have to be either boiled off or shaved off. With growing horror she recalled Penrod's long absence when he went to bring the hat.

"Penrod," she cried, "let me see your hands!"

She had toiled at those hands herself late that afternoon, nearly scalding her own, but at last achieving a lily purity.

"Let me see your hands!"

She seized them.

Again they were tarred!

PART TWO

PENROD AND SAM

CHAPTER XXVI

PENROD AND SAM

URING the daylight hours of several autumn
Saturdays there had been severe outbreaks of
cavalry in the Schofield neighbourhood. The sabres
were of wood; the steeds were imaginary, and both were
employed in a game called "bonded pris'ner" by its in-
ventors, Masters Penrod Schofield and Samuel Williams.
The pastime was not intricate. When two enemies met, they
fenced spectacularly until the person of one or the other
was touched by the opposing weapon; then, when the ensu-
ing claims of foul play had been disallowed and the subsequent argument settled, the combatant touched was
considered to be a prisoner until such time as he might
be touched by the hilt of a sword belonging to one of his

205

own party, which effected his release and restored to him the full enjoyment of hostile activity. Pending such rescue, however, he was obliged to accompany the forces of his captor whithersoever their strategical necessities led them, which included many strange places. For the game was exciting, and, at its highest pitch, would sweep out of an alley into a stable, out of that stable and into a yard, out of that yard and into a house, and through that house with the sound (and effect upon furniture) of trampling herds. In fact, this very similarity must have been in the mind of the distressed coloured woman in Mrs. Williams's kitchen, when she declared that she might "jes' as well try to cook right spang in the middle o' the stock-yards."

All up and down the neighbourhood the campaigns were waged, accompanied by the martial clashing of wood upon wood and by many clamorous arguments.

"You're a pris'ner, Roddy Bitts!"

"I am not!"

"You are, too! I touched you."

"Where, I'd like to know!"

"On the sleeve."

"You did not! I never felt it. I guess I'd 'a' felt it, wouldn't I?"

"What if you didn't? I touched you, and you're bonded. I leave it to Sam Williams."

"Yah! Course you would! He's on your side! *I* leave it to Herman."

"No, you won't! If you can't show any *sense* about it, we'll do it over, and I guess you'll *see* whether you feel it or not! There! *Now,* I guess you——"

"Aw, squash!"

Strangely enough, the undoubted champion proved to be the youngest and darkest of all the combatants. Verman was valiant beyond all others, and, in spite of every handicap, he became at once the chief support of his own party and the despair of the opposition.

On the third Saturday this opposition had been worn

down by the successive captures of Maurice Levy and
Georgie Bassett until it consisted of only Sam Williams and
Penrod. Hence, it behooved these two to be wary, lest they
be wiped out altogether; and Sam was dismayed indeed,
upon cautiously scouting round a corner of his own stable, to
find himself face to face with the valorous and skilful Verman, who was acting as an outpost, or picket, of the enemy.

Verman immediately fell upon Sam, horse and foot, and
Sam would have fled but dared not, for fear he might be
touched from the rear. Therefore, he defended himself as
best he could, and there followed a lusty whacking, in the
course of which Verman's hat, a relic and too large, fell
from his head, touching Sam's weapon in falling.

"There!" panted Sam, desisting immediately. "That
counts! You're bonded, Verman."

"Aim meewer!" Verman protested.

Interpreting this as "Ain't neither", Sam invented a law
to suit the occasion. "Yes, you are; that's the rule, Verman. I touched your hat with my sword, and your hat's
just the same as you."

"Imm mop!" Verman insisted.

"Yes, it is," said Sam, already warmly convinced (by his
own statement) that he was in the right. "Listen here! If
I hit you on the shoe, it would be the same as hitting *you*,
wouldn't it? I guess it'd count if I hit you on the shoe,
wouldn't it? Well, a hat's just the same as shoes. Honest,
that's the rule, Verman, and you're a pris'ner."

Now, in the arguing part of the game, Verman's impediment coöperated with a native amiability to render him
far less effective than in the actual combat. He chuckled,
and ceded the point.

"Aw wi," he said, and cheerfully followed his captor to
a hidden place among some bushes in the front yard, where
Penrod lurked.

"Looky what *I* got!" Sam said importantly, pushing
his captive into this retreat. "*Now*, I guess you won't say
I'm not so much use any more! Squat down, Verman, so's

they can't see you if they're huntin' for us. That's one o' the rules—honest. You got to squat when we tell you to."

Verman was agreeable. He squatted, and then began to laugh uproariously.

"Stop that noise!" Penrod commanded. "You want to bekray us? What you laughin' at?"

"Ep mack im mimmup," Verman giggled.

"What's he mean?" Sam asked.

Penrod was more familiar with Verman's utterance, and he interpreted.

"He says they'll get him back in a minute."

"No, they won't. I'd just like to see——"

"Yes, they will, too," Penrod said. "They'll get him back for the main and simple reason we can't stay here all day, can we? And they'd find us anyhow, if we tried to. There's so many of 'em against just us two, they can run in and touch him soon as they get up to us—and then *he'll* be after us again and——"

"Listen here!" Sam interrupted. "Why can't we put some *real* bonds on him? We could put bonds on his wrists and around his legs—we could put 'em all over him, easy as nothin'. Then we could gag him——"

"No, we can't," said Penrod. "We can't, for the main and simple reason we haven't got any rope or anything to make the bonds with, have we? I wish we had some o' that stuff they give sick people. *Then*, I bet they wouldn't get him back so soon!"

"Sick people?" Sam repeated, not comprehending.

"It makes 'em go to sleep, no matter what you do to 'em," Penrod explained. "That's the main and simple reason they can't wake up, and you can cut off their ole legs—or their arms, or anything you want to."

"Hoy!" exclaimed Verman, in a serious tone. His laughter ceased instantly, and he began to utter a protest sufficiently intelligible.

"You needn't worry," Penrod said gloomily. "We haven't got any o' that stuff; so we can't do it."

"Well, we got to do sumpthing," Sam said.

His comrade agreed, and there was a thoughtful silence; but presently Penrod's countenance brightened.

"I know!" he exclaimed. "*I* know what we'll do with him. Why, I thought of it just as *easy!* I can most always think of things like that, for the main and simple reason—well, I thought of it just as soon——"

"Well, what is it?" Sam demanded crossly. Penrod's reiteration of his new-found phrase, "for the main and simple reason", had been growing more and more irksome to his friend all day, though Sam was not definitely aware that the phrase was the cause of his annoyance. "*What* are we goin' to do with him, you know so much?"

Penrod rose and peered over the tops of the bushes, shading his eyes with his hand, a gesture that was unnecessary but had a good appearance. He looked all round about him in this manner, finally vouchsafing a report to the impatient Sam.

"No enemies in sight—just for the main and simple reason I expect they're all in the alley and in Georgie Bassett's backyard."

"I bet they're not!" Sam said scornfully, his irritation much increased. "How do *you* know so much about it?"

"Just for the main and simple reason," Penrod replied, with dignified finality.

And at that, Sam felt a powerful impulse to do violence upon the person of his comrade-in-arms. The emotion that prompted this impulse was so primitive and straightforward that it almost resulted in action; but Sam had a vague sense that he must control it as long as he could.

"Bugs!" he said.

Penrod was sensitive, and this cold word hurt him. However, he was under the domination of his strategic idea, and he subordinated private grievance to the common weal. "Get up!" he commanded. "You get up, too, Verman. You got to—it's the rule. Now here—I'll *show* you what we're goin' to do. Stoop over, and both o' you do just exackly like

I do. You watch *me*, because this biz'nuss has got to be done *right!*"

Sam muttered something; he was becoming more insurgent every moment, but he obeyed. Likewise, Verman rose to his feet, ducked his head between his shoulders, and trotted out to the sidewalk at Sam's heels, both following Penrod and assuming a stooping position in imitation of him. Verman was delighted with this phase of the game, and, also, he was profoundly amused by Penrod's pomposity. Something dim and deep within him perceived it to be cause for such merriment that he had ado to master himself, and was forced to bottle and cork his laughter with both hands. They proved insufficient; sputterings burst forth between his fingers.

"You stop that!" Penrod said, looking back darkly upon the prisoner.

Verman endeavoured to oblige, though giggles continued to leak from him at intervals, and the three boys stole along the fence in single file, proceeding in this fashion until they reached Penrod's own front gate. Here the leader ascertained, by a reconnaissance as far as the corner, that the hostile forces were still looking for them in another direction. He returned in a stealthy but important manner to his disgruntled follower and the hilarious captive.

"Well," said Sam impatiently, "I guess I'm not goin' to stand around here all day, I guess! You got anything you want to do, why'n't you go on and *do* it?"

Penrod's brow was already contorted to present the appearance of detached and lofty concentration—a histrionic failure, since it did not deceive the audience. He raised a hushing hand.

"*Sh!*" he murmured. "I got to think."

"Bugs!" the impolite Mr. Williams said again.

Verman bent double, squealing and sputtering; indeed, he was ultimately forced to sit upon the ground, so exhausting was the mirth to which he now gave way. Penrod's composure was somewhat affected and he showed annoyance.

"Oh, I guess you won't laugh quite so much about a minute from now, ole Mister Verman!" he said severely. "You get up from there and do like I tell you."

"Well, why'n't you *tell* him why he won't laugh so much, then?" Sam demanded, as Verman rose. "Why'n't you do sumpthing and quit talkin' so much about it?"

Penrod haughtily led the way into the yard.

"You follow me," he said, "and I guess you'll learn a little sense!"

Then, abandoning his *hauteur* for an air of mystery, equally irritating to Sam, he stole up the steps of the porch, and, after a moment's manipulation of the knob of the big front door, contrived to operate the fastenings, and pushed the door open.

"Come on," he whispered, beckoning. And the three boys mounted the stairs to the floor above in silence—save for a belated giggle on the part of Verman that was restrained upon a terrible gesture from Penrod. Verman buried his mouth as deeply as possible in a ragged sleeve, and confined his demonstrations to a heaving of the stomach and diaphragm.

Penrod led the way into Margaret's dainty room, and closed the door.

"There," he said, in a low and husky voice, "I expect you'll see what I'm goin' to do now!"

"Well, what?" the skeptical Sam asked. "If we stay here very long your mother'll come and send us downstairs. What's the good of——"

"*Wait*, can't you?" Penrod wailed, in a whisper. "My goodness!" And going to an inner door, he threw it open, disclosing a clothes-closet hung with pretty garments of many kinds, while upon its floor were two rows of shoes and slippers of great variety and charm.

A significant thing is to be remarked concerning the door

of this somewhat intimate treasury: there was no knob or latch upon the inner side, so that, when the door was closed, it could be opened only from the outside.

"There!" said Penrod. "You get in there, Verman, and I'll bet they won't get to touch you back out o' bein' our pris'ner very soon, *now!* Oh, I guess not!"

"Pshaw!" said Sam. "Is that all you were goin' to do? Why, your mother'll come and make him get out the first——"

"No, she won't. She and Margaret have gone to my aunt's in the country, and aren't goin' to be back till dark. And even if he made a lot o' noise, it's kind of hard to hear anything from in there, anyway, when the door's shut. Besides, he's got to keep quiet—that's the rule, Verman. You're a pris'ner, and it's the rule you can't holler or nothin'. You unnerstand that, Verman?"

"Aw wi," said Verman.

"Then go on in there. Hurry!"

The obedient Verman marched into the closet and sat down among the shoes and slippers, where he presented an interesting effect of contrast. He was still subject to hilarity—though endeavouring to suppress it by means of a patent-leather slipper—when Penrod closed the door.

"There!" said Penrod, leading the way from the room. "I guess *now* you see!"

Sam said nothing, and they came out to the open air and reached their retreat in the Williams' yard again, without his having acknowledged Penrod's service to their mutual cause.

"I thought of that just as easy!" Penrod remarked, probably prompted to this odious bit of complacency by Sam's withholding the praise that might naturally have been expected. And he was moved to add, "I guess it'd of been a pretty long while if we'd had to wait for you to think of something as good as that, Sam."

"Why would it?" Sam asked. "Why would it of been such a long while?"

"Oh," Penrod responded airily, "just for the main and simple reason!"

Sam could bear it no longer. "Oh, hush up!" he shouted.

Penrod was stung. "Do you mean *me?*" he demanded.

"Yes, I do!" the goaded Sam replied.

"Did you tell *me* to hush up?"

"Yes, I did!"

"I guess you don't know who you're talkin' to," Penrod said ominously. "I guess I just better show you who you're talkin' to like that. I guess you need a little sumpthing, for the main and simple——"

Sam uttered an uncontrollable howl and sprang upon Penrod, catching him round the waist. Simultaneously with this impact, the wooden swords spun through the air and were presently trodden underfoot as the two boys wrestled to and fro.

Penrod was not altogether surprised by the onset of his friend. He had been aware of Sam's increasing irritation (though neither boy could have clearly stated its cause) and that very irritation produced a corresponding emotion in the bosom of the irritator. Mentally, Penrod was quite ready for the conflict—nay, he welcomed it—though, for the first few moments, Sam had the physical advantage.

However, it is proper that a neat distinction be drawn here. This was a conflict; but neither technically nor in the intention of the contestants was it a fight. Penrod and Sam were both in a state of high exasperation, and there was great bitterness; but no blows fell and no tears. They strained, they wrenched, they twisted, and they panted and muttered: "Oh, no, you don't!" "Oh, I guess I do!" "Oh, you will, will you?" "You'll see what you get in about a minute!" "I guess you'll learn some sense this time!"

Streaks and blotches began to appear upon the two faces, where colour had been heightened by the ardent application of a cloth sleeve or shoulder, while ankles and insteps were scraped and toes were trampled. Turf and shrubberies suffered, also, as the struggle went on, until finally the wrestlers pitched headlong into a young lilac bush, and came to earth together, among its crushed and sprawling branches.

"*Ooch!*" and "*Wuf!*" were the two exclamations that marked this episode, and then, with no further comment, the struggle was energetically continued upon a horizontal plane. Now Penrod was on top, now Sam; they rolled, they squirmed, they suffered. And this contest endured. It went on and on, and it was impossible to imagine its coming to a definite termination. It went on so long that to both the participants it seemed to be a permanent thing, a condition that had always existed and that must always exist perpetually.

And thus they were discovered by a foray of the hostile party, headed by Roddy Bitts and Herman and followed by the bonded prisoners, Maurice Levy and Georgie Bassett. These and others caught sight of the writhing figures, and charged down upon them with loud cries of triumph.

"Pris'ner! Pris'ner! Bonded pris'ner!" shrieked Roddy Bitts, and touched Penrod and Sam, each in turn, with his sabre. Then, seeing that they paid no attention and that they were at his mercy, he recalled the fact that several times, during earlier stages of the game, both of them had been unnecessarily vigorous in "touching" his own rather plump person. Therefore, the opportunity being excellent, he raised his weapon again, and, repeating the words "bonded pris'ner" as ample explanation of his deed, brought into play the full strength of his good right arm. He used the flat of the sabre.

Whack! Whack! Roddy was perfectly impartial. It was a cold-blooded performance and even more effective than he anticipated. For one thing, it ended the civil war instantly. Sam and Penrod leaped to their feet, shrieking and bloodthirsty, while Maurice Levy capered with joy, Herman was so overcome that he rolled upon the ground, and Georgie Bassett remarked virtuously:

"It serves them right for fighting."

But Roddy Bitts foresaw that something not within the rules of the game was about to happen.

"Here! You keep away from me!" he quavered, retreating. "I was just takin' you pris'ners. I guess I had a right to *touch* you, didn't I?"

Alas! Neither Sam nor Penrod was able to see the matter in that light. They had retrieved their own weapons, and they advanced upon Roddy with a purposefulness that seemed horrible to him.

"Here! You keep away from me!" he said, in great alarm. "I'm goin' home."

He did go home—but only subsequently. What took place before his departure had the singular solidity and completeness of systematic violence; also, it bore the moral beauty of all actions that lead to peace and friendship, for, when it was over, and the final vocalizations of Roderick Magsworth Bitts, Junior, were growing faint with increasing distance, Sam and Penrod had forgotten their differences and felt well disposed toward each other once more. All their animosity was exhausted, and they were in a glow of good feeling, though probably they were not conscious of any direct gratitude to Roddy, whose thoughtful opportunism was really the cause of this happy result.

CHAPTER XXVII

THE BONDED PRISONER

AFTER such rigorous events, every one comprehended that the game of bonded prisoner was over, and there was no suggestion that it should or might be resumed. The fashion of its conclusion had been so consummately enjoyed by all parties (with the natural exception of Roddy Bitts) that a renewal would have been tame; hence, the various minds of the company turned to other matters and became restless. Georgie Bassett withdrew first, remembering that if he expected to be as wonderful as usual, to-morrow in Sunday-school, it was time to prepare himself, though this was not included in the statement he made alleging the cause of his departure. Being detained bodily

216

and pressed for explanation, he desperately said that he had
to go home to tease the cook—which had the rakehelly air
he thought would insure his release, but was not considered
plausible. However, he was finally allowed to go, and, as
first hints of evening were already cooling and darkening
the air, the party broke up, its members setting forth,
whistling, toward their several homes, though Penrod
lingered with Sam. Herman was the last to go from them.

"Well, I got git 'at stove-wood f' suppuh," he said, rising
and stretching himself. "I got git 'at lil' soap-box wagon,
an' go on ovuh wheres 'at new house buil'in' on Secon' Street;
pick up few shingles an' blocks layin' roun'."

He went through the yard toward the alley, and, at the
alley gate, remembering something, he paused and called to
them. The lot was a deep one, and they were too far away
to catch his meaning. Sam shouted, "Can't *hear* you!" and
Herman replied, but still unintelligibly; then, upon Sam's
repetition of "Can't *hear* you!" Herman waved his arm in
farewell, implying that the matter was of little significance,
and vanished. But if they had understood him, Penrod and
Sam might have considered his inquiry of instant importance, for Herman's last shout was to ask if either of
them had noticed "where Verman went."

Verman and Verman's whereabouts were, at this hour, of
no more concern to Sam and Penrod than was the other side
of the moon. That unfortunate bonded prisoner had been
long since utterly effaced from their fields of consciousness,
and the dark secret of their Bastille troubled them not—
for the main and simple reason that they had forgotten it.

They drifted indoors, and found Sam's mother's white cat
drowsing on a desk in the library, the which coincidence
obviously inspired the experiment of ascertaining how successfully ink could be used in making a clean white cat look
like a coach-dog. There was neither malice nor mischief in
their idea; simply, a problem presented itself to the biological
and artistic questionings beginning to stir within them. They
did not mean to do the cat the slightest injury or to cause

her any pain. They were above teasing cats, and they merely detained this one and made her feel a little wet—at considerable cost to themselves from both the ink and the cat. However, at the conclusion of their efforts, it was thought safer to drop the cat out of the window before anybody came, and, after some hasty work with blotters, the desk was moved to cover certain sections of the rug, and the two boys repaired to the bathroom for hot water and soap. They knew they had done nothing wrong; but they felt easier when the only traces remaining upon them were the less prominent ones upon their garments.

These precautions taken, it was time for them to make their appearance at Penrod's house for dinner, for it had been arranged, upon petition earlier in the day, that Sam should be his friend's guest for the evening meal. Clean to the elbows and with light hearts, they set forth. They marched, whistling—though not producing a distinctly musical effect, since neither had any particular air in mind—and they found nothing wrong with the world; they had not a care. Arrived at their adjacent destination, they found Miss Margaret Schofield just entering the front door.

"Hurry, boys!" she said. "Mamma came home long before I did, and I'm sure dinner is waiting. Run on out to the dining-room and tell them I'll be right down."

And, as they obeyed, she mounted the stairs, humming a little tune and unfastening the clasp of the long, light-blue military cape she wore. She went to her own quiet room, lit the gas, removed her hat and placed it and the cape upon the bed; after which she gave her hair a push, subsequent to her scrutiny of a mirror; then, turning out the light, she went as far as the door. Being an orderly girl, she returned to the bed and took the cape and the hat to her clothes-closet. She opened the door of this sanctuary, and, in the dark, hung her cape upon a hook and placed her hat upon the shelf. Then she closed the door again, having noted nothing unusual, though she had an impression that the place needed airing. She descended to the dinner table.

The other members of the family were already occupied with the meal, and the visitor was replying politely, in his non-masticatory intervals, to inquiries concerning the health of his relatives. So sweet and assured was the condition of Sam and Penrod that Margaret's arrival from her room meant nothing to them. Their memories were not stirred, and they continued eating, their expressions brightly placid.

But from out of doors there came the sound of a calling and questing voice, at first in the distance, then growing louder—coming nearer.

"Oh, Ver-er-man! O-o-o-oh, Ver-er-ma-a-an!"

It was the voice of Herman.

"*Oo-o-o-o-oh, Ver-er-er-ma-a-an!*"

And then two boys sat stricken at that cheerful table and ceased to eat. Recollection awoke with a bang!

"Oh, my!" Sam gasped.

"What's the matter?" Mr. Schofield said. "Swallow something the wrong way, Sam?"

"Ye-es, sir."

"*Oo-o-o-oh, Ver-er-er-ma-a-an!*"

And now the voice was near the windows of the dining-room.

Penrod, very pale, pushed back his chair and jumped up.

"What's the matter with *you?*" his father demanded. "Sit down!"

"It's Herman—that coloured boy lives in the alley," Penrod said hoarsely. "I—expect—I think——"

"Well, what's the matter?"

"I think his little brother's maybe got lost, and Sam and I better go help look——"

"You'll do nothing of the kind," Mr. Schofield said sharply. "Sit down and eat your dinner."

In a palsy, the miserable boy resumed his seat. He and Sam exchanged a single dumb glance; then the eyes of both swung fearfully to Margaret. Her appearance was one of sprightly content, and, from a certain point of view, nothing could have been more alarming. If she had opened her closet door without discovering Verman, that must have been because Verman was dead and Margaret had failed to notice the body. (Such were the thoughts of Penrod and Sam.) But she might not have opened the closet door. And whether she had or not, Verman must still be there, alive or dead, for if he had escaped he would have gone home, and their ears would not be ringing with the sinister and melancholy cry that now came from the distance, "*Oo-o-oh, Ver-er-ma-an!*"

Verman, in his seclusion, did not hear that appeal from his brother; there were too many walls between them. But he was becoming impatient for release, though, all in all, he had not found the confinement intolerable or even very irksome. His character was philosophic, his imagination calm; no bugaboos came to trouble him. When the boys closed the door upon him, he made himself comfortable upon the floor and, for a time, thoughtfully chewed a patent-leather slipper that had come under his hand. He found the patent leather not unpleasant to his palate, though he swallowed only a portion of what he detached, not being hungry at that time. The soul-fabric of Verman was of a fortunate weave; he was not a seeker and questioner. When it happened to him that he was at rest in a shady corner, he did not even think about a place in the sun. Verman took life as it came.

Naturally, he fell asleep. And toward the conclusion of his slumbers, he had this singular adventure: a lady set her foot down within less than half an inch of his nose—and neither of them knew it. Verman slept on, without being wakened by either the closing or the opening of the door. What did rouse him was something ample and soft falling upon him—Margaret's cape, which slid from the hook after she had gone.

Enveloped in its folds, Verman sat up, corkscrewing his knuckles into the corners of his eyes. Slowly he became aware of two important vacuums—one in time and one in his stomach. Hours had vanished strangely into nowhere; the game of bonded prisoner was something cloudy and remote of the long, long ago, and, although Verman knew where he was, he had partially forgotten how he came there. He perceived, however, that something had gone wrong, for he was certain that he ought not to be where he found himself.

White-Folks' House! The fact that Verman could not have pronounced these words rendered them no less clear in his mind; they began to stir his apprehension, and nothing becomes more rapidly tumultuous than apprehension once it is stirred. That he might possibly obtain release by making a noise was too daring a thought and not even conceived, much less entertained, by the little and humble Verman. For, with the bewildering gap of his slumber between him and previous events, he did not place the responsibility for his being in White-Folks' House upon the white folks who had put him there. His state of mind was that of the stable-puppy who knows he *must* not be found in the parlour. Not thrice in his life had Verman been within the doors of White-Folks' House, and, above all things, he felt that it was in some undefined way vital to him to get out of White-Folks' House unobserved and unknown. It was in his very blood to be sure of that.

Further than this point, the processes of Verman's mind become mysterious to the observer. It appears, however, that he had a definite (though somewhat primitive) conception of the usefulness of disguise; and he must have begun his preparations before he heard footsteps in the room outside his closed door.

These footsteps were Margaret's. Just as Mr. Schofield's coffee was brought, and just after Penrod had been baffled in another attempt to leave the table, Margaret rose and patted her father impertinently upon the head.

"You can't bully *me* that way!" she said. "I got home too late to dress, and I'm going to a dance. 'Scuse!"

And she began her dancing on the spot, pirouetting herself swiftly out of the room, and was immediately heard running up the stairs.

"Penrod!" Mr. Schofield shouted. "Sit down! How many

times am I going to tell you? What *is* the matter with you
to-night?"

"I *got* to go," Penrod gasped. "I got to tell Margaret
sumpthing."

"What have you 'got' to tell her?"

"It's—it's sumpthing I forgot to tell her."

"Well, it will keep till she comes downstairs," Mr. Schofield said grimly. "You sit down till this meal is finished."

Penrod was becoming frantic.

"I got to tell her—it's sumpthing Sam's mother told me to
tell her," he babbled. "Didn't she, Sam? You heard her tel'
me to tell her; didn't you, Sam?"

Sam offered prompt corroboration.

"Yes, sir; she did. She said for us both to tell her. I better
go, too, I guess, because she said——"

He was interrupted. Startlingly upon their ears rang
shriek on shriek. Mrs. Schofield, recognizing Margaret's
voice, likewise shrieked, and Mr. Schofield uttered various
sounds; but Penrod and Sam were incapable of doing anything vocally. All rushed from the table.

Margaret continued to shriek, and it is not to be denied
that there was some cause for her agitation. When she opened
the closet door, her light-blue military cape, instead of hanging on the hook where she had left it, came out into the room
in a manner that she afterward described as "a kind of horrible creep, but faster than a creep." Nothing was to be seen
except the creeping cape, she said, but, of course, she could
tell there was some awful thing inside of it. It was too large
to be a cat, and too small to be a boy; it was too large to be
Duke, Penrod's little old dog, and, besides, Duke wouldn't
act like that. It crept rapidly out into the upper hall, and
then, as she recovered the use of her voice and began to
scream, the animated cape abandoned its creeping for a
quicker gait—"a weird, heaving flop", she defined it.

The Thing then decided upon a third style of locomotion,
evidently, for when Sam and Penrod reached the front hall,

a few steps in advance of Mr. and Mrs. Schofield, it was rolling grandly down the stairs.

Mr. Schofield had only a hurried glimpse of it as it reached the bottom, close by the front door.

"Grab that thing!" he shouted, dashing forward. "Stop it! Hit it!"

It was at this moment that Sam Williams displayed the presence of mind that was his most eminent characteristic. Sam's wonderful instinct for the right action almost never failed him in a crisis, and it did not fail him now. Leaping to the door, at the very instant when the rolling cape touched it, Sam flung the door open—and the cape rolled on. With incredible rapidity and intelligence, it rolled, indeed, out into the night.

Penrod jumped after it, and the next second reappeared in the doorway holding the cape. He shook out its folds, breathing hard but acquiring confidence. In fact, he was able to look up in his father's face and say, with bright ingenuousness:

"It was just laying there. Do you know what I think? Well, it couldn't have acted that way itself. *I* think there must have been sumpthing kind of inside of it!"

Mr. Schofield shook his head slowly, in marvelling admiration. "Brilliant—oh, brilliant!" he murmured, while Mrs. Schofield ran to support the enfeebled form of Margaret at the top of the stairs.

. . . In the library, after Margaret's departure to her dance, Mr. and Mrs. Schofield were still discussing the visitation, Penrod having accompanied his homeward-bound guest as far as the front gate.

"No; you're wrong," Mrs. Schofield said, upholding a theory, earlier developed by Margaret, that the animated behaviour of the cape could be satisfactorily explained on no other ground than the supernatural. "You see, the boys saying they couldn't remember what Mrs. Williams wanted them to tell Margaret, and that probably she hadn't told them anything to tell her, because most likely they'd misunderstood something she said—well, of course, all that does sound mixed-up and peculiar; but they sound that way about half the time, anyhow. No; it couldn't possibly have had a thing to do with it. They were right there at the table with us all the time, and they came straight to the table the minute they entered the house. Before that, they'd been over at Sam's all afternoon. So, it *couldn't* have been the boys." Mrs. Schofield paused to ruminate with a little air of pride; then added: "Margaret has often thought—oh, long before this!—that she was a medium. I mean—if she would let herself. So it wasn't anything the boys did."

Mr. Schofield grunted. "I'll admit this much," he said. "I'll admit it wasn't anything we'll ever get out of 'em."

And the remarks of Sam and Penrod, taking leave of each other, one on each side of the gate, appeared to corroborate Mr. Schofield's opinion.

"Well, g'-night, Penrod," Sam said. "It was a pretty good Saturday, wasn't it?"

"Fine!" said Penrod casually. "G'-night, Sam."

CHAPTER XXVIII

THE IN-OR-IN

GEORGIE BASSETT was a boy set apart. Not only that; Georgie knew that he was a boy set apart. He would think about it for ten or twenty minutes at a time, and he could not look at himself in a mirror and remain wholly without emotion. What that emotion was, he would have been unable to put into words; but it helped him to understand that there was a certain noble something about him that other boys did not possess.

Georgie's mother had been the first to discover that Georgie was a boy set apart. In fact, Georgie did not know it until one day when he happened to overhear his mother telling two of his aunts about it. True, he had always understood that he was the best boy in town and he intended to be a minister when he grew up; but he had never before comprehended the full extent of his sanctity, and, from that fraught moment onward, he had an almost theatrical sense of his set-apartness.

Penrod Schofield and Sam Williams and the other boys of the neighbourhood all were conscious that there was something different and spiritual about Georgie, and, though this consciousness of theirs may have been a little obscure, it was none the less actual. That is to say, they knew that Georgie Bassett was a boy set apart; but they did not know that they knew it. Georgie's air and manner at all times demonstrated to them that the thing was so, and, moreover, their mothers absorbed appreciation of Georgie's wonderfulness from the very fount of it, for Mrs. Bassett's conversation was of little else. Thus, the radiance of his character became the topic of envious parental comment during moments of strained patience in many homes, so that altogether the most remarkable fact to be stated of Georgie Bassett is that he escaped the consequences as long as he did.

Strange as it may seem, no actual violence was done him, except upon the incidental occasion of a tar-fight into which he was drawn by an obvious eccentricity on the part of destiny. Naturally, he was not popular with his comrades; in all games he was pushed aside, and disregarded, being invariably the tail-ender in every pastime in which leaders "chose sides"; his counsels were slighted as worse than weightless, and all his opinions instantly hooted. Still, considering the circumstances fairly and thoughtfully, it is difficult to deny that his boy companions showed creditable moderation in their treatment of him. That is, they were moderate up to a certain date, and even then they did not directly attack him—there was nothing cold-blooded about it at all. The thing was forced upon them, and, though they all felt pleased and uplifted—while it was happening—they did not understand precisely why. Nothing could more clearly prove their innocence of heart than this very ignorance, and yet none of the grown people who later felt themselves concerned in the matter was able to look at it in that light. Now, here was a characteristic working of those reactions that produce what is sometimes called "the injustice of life", because the grown people were responsible for the whole affair and were really the guilty parties. It was from grown people that Georgie Bassett learned he was a boy set apart, and the effect upon him was what alienated his friends. Then these alienated friends were brought (by odious comparisons on the part of grown people) to a condition of mind wherein they suffered dumb annoyance, like a low fever, whenever they heard Georgie's name mentioned, while association with his actual person became every day more and more irritating. And yet, having laid this fuse and having kept it constantly glowing, the grown people expected nothing to happen to Georgie.

The catastrophe befell as a consequence of Sam Williams deciding to have a shack in his backyard. Sam had somehow obtained a vasty piano-box and a quantity of lumber, and, summoning Penrod Schofield and the coloured brethren, Herman and Verman, he expounded to them his building-plans and offered them shares and benefits in the institution he proposed to found. Acceptance was enthusiastic; straightway the assembly became a union of carpenters all of one mind, and ten days saw the shack not completed but comprehensible. Anybody could tell, by that time, that it was intended for a shack.

There was a door on leather hinges; it drooped, perhaps, but it was a door. There was a window—not a glass one, but, at least, it could be "looked out of", as Sam said. There was a chimney made of stovepipe, though that was merely decorative, because the cooking was done out of doors in an underground "furnace" that the boys excavated. There were pictures pasted on the interior walls, and, hanging from a nail, there was a crayon portrait of Sam's grandfather, which he had brought down from the attic quietly, though, as he said, it "wasn't any use on earth up there." There were two lame chairs from Penrod's attic; and along one wall ran a low and feeble structure intended to serve as a bench or divan. This would come in handy, Sam said, if any of the party "had to lay down or anything", and at a pinch (such as a meeting of the association) it would serve to seat all the members in a row.

For, coincidentally with the development of the shack, the builders became something more than partners. Later, no one could remember who first suggested the founding of a secret order, or society, as a measure of exclusiveness and to keep the shack sacred to members only; but it was an idea that presently began to be more absorbing and satisfactory than even the shack itself. The outward manifestations of it might have been observed in the increased solemnity and preoccupation of the Caucasian members and in a few ceremonial observances exposed to the public eye. As an instance of these latter, Mrs. Williams, happening to glance from a rearward window, about four o'clock one afternoon, found her attention arrested by what seemed to be a flag-raising before the door of the shack. Sam and Herman and Verman stood in attitudes of rigid attention, shoulder to shoulder, while Penrod Schofield, facing them, was apparently delivering some sort of exhortation, which he read from a scribbled sheet of foolscap. Concluding this, he lifted from the ground a long and somewhat warped clothes-prop, from one end of which hung a whitish flag, or pennon, bearing an inscription. Sam and Herman and Verman lifted their right hands, while Penrod placed the other end of the clothes-prop in a hole in the ground, with the pennon fluttering high above the shack. He then raised his own right hand, and the four boys repeated something in concert. It was inaudible to Mrs. Williams; but she was able to make out the inscription upon the pennon. It consisted of the peculiar phrase "In-Or-In" done in black paint upon a muslin ground, and consequently seeming to be in need of a blotter.

It recurred to her mind, later that evening, when she

happened to find herself alone with Sam in the library, and, in merest idle curiosity, she asked: "Sam, what does 'In-Or-In' mean?"

Sam, bending over an arithmetic, uncreased his brow till it became of a blank and marble smoothness.

"Ma'am?"

"What are those words on your flag?"

Sam gave her a long, cold, mystic look, rose to his feet and left the room with emphasis and dignity. For a moment she was puzzled. But Sam's older brother was this year completing his education at a university, and Mrs. Williams was not altogether ignorant of the obligations of secrecy imposed upon some brotherhoods; so she was able to comprehend Sam's silent withdrawal, and, instead of summoning him back for further questions, she waited until he was out of hearing and then began to laugh.

Sam's action was in obedience to one of the rules adopted, at his own suggestion, as a law of the order. Penrod advocated it warmly. From Margaret he had heard accounts of her friends in college and thus had learned much that ought to be done. On the other hand, Herman subscribed to it with reluctance, expressing a decided opinion that if he and Verman were questioned upon the matter at home and adopted the line of conduct required by the new rule, it would be well for them to depart not only from the room in which the questioning took place but from the house, and hurriedly at that. "An' *stay* away!" he concluded.

Verman, being tongue-tied—not without advantage in this case, and surely an ideal qualification for membership —was not so apprehensive. He voted with Sam and Penrod, carrying the day.

New rules were adopted at every meeting (though it cannot be said that all of them were practicable) for, in addition to the information possessed by Sam and Penrod, Herman and Verman had many ideas of their own, founded upon remarks overheard at home. Both their parents belonged to secret orders, their father to the Innapenent

'Nevolent Lodge (so stated by Herman) and their mother to the Order of White Doves.

From these and other sources, Penrod found no diffi- culty in compiling material for what came to be known as the "rixual"; and it was the rixual he was reading to the members when Mrs. Williams happened to observe the cere- monial raising of the emblem of the order.

The rixual contained the oath, a key to the secret lan- guage, or code (devised by Penrod for use in uncertain emergencies) and passwords for admission to the shack, also instructions for recognizing a brother member in the dark, and a rather alarming sketch of the things to be done dur- ing the initiation of a candidate.

This last was employed for the benefit of Master Rod- erick Magsworth Bitts, Junior, on the Saturday following the flag-raising. He presented himself in Sam's yard, not for initiation, indeed—having no previous knowledge of the Society of the In-Or-In—but for general purposes of sport and pastime. At first sight of the shack he expressed an- ticipations of pleasure, adding some suggestions for im- proving the architectural effect. Being prevented, however, from entering, and even from standing in the vicinity of the sacred building, he plaintively demanded an explana- tion; whereupon he was commanded to withdraw to the front yard for a time, and the members held meeting in the shack. Roddy was elected, and consented to undergo the initiation.

He was not the only new member that day. A short time after Roddy had been taken into the shack for the reading of the rixual and other ceremonies, little Maurice Levy entered the Williams' gate and strolled round to the back- yard, looking for Sam. He was surprised and delighted to behold the promising shack, and, like Roddy, entertained fair hopes for the future.

The door of the shack was closed; a board covered the window, but a murmur of voices came from within. Maurice stole close and listened. Through a crack he could see the flicker of a candle-flame, and he heard the voice of Penrod Schofield:

"Roddy Bitts, do you solemnly swear?"

"Well, all right," said the voice of Roddy, somewhat breathless.

"How many fingers you see before your eyes?"

"Can't see any," Roddy returned. "How could I, with this thing over my eyes, and laying down on my stummick, anyway?"

"Then the time has come," Penrod announced in solemn tones. "The time has come."

Whack!

Evidently a broad and flat implement was thereupon applied to Roddy.

"*Ow!*" complained the candidate.

"No noise!" said Penrod sternly, and added: "Roddy Bitts must now say the oath. Say exackly what I say, Roddy, and if you don't—well, you better, because you'll see! Now, say 'I solemnly swear——' "

"I solemnly swear——" Roddy said.

"To keep the secrets——"

"To keep the secrets——" Roddy repeated.

"To keep the secrets in infadelaty and violate and sanctuary."

"What?" Roddy naturally inquired.

Whack!

"*Ow!*" cried Roddy. "That's no fair!"

"You got to say just what *I* say," Penrod was heard informing him. "That's the rixual, and anyway, even if you do get it right, Verman's got to hit you every now and then, because that's part of the rixual, too. Now go on and say it. 'I solemnly swear to keep the secrets in infadelaty and violate and sanctuary.' "

"I solemnly swear——" Roddy began.

But Maurice Levy was tired of being no party to such fascinating proceedings, and he began to hammer upon the door.

"Sam! Sam Williams!" he shouted. "Lemme in there! I know lots about 'nishiatin'. Lemme in!"

The door was flung open, revealing Roddy Bitts, blindfolded and bound, lying face down upon the floor of the shack; but Maurice had only a fugitive glimpse of this pathetic figure before he, too, was recumbent. Four boys flung themselves indignantly upon him and bore him to earth.

"Hi!" he squealed. "What you doin'? Haven't you got any *sense?*"

And, from within the shack, Roddy added his own protest.

"Let me up, can't you?" he cried. "I got to see what's goin' on out there, haven't I? I guess I'm not goin' to lay here all *day!* What you think I'm made of?"

"You hush up!" Penrod commanded. "This is a nice biznuss!" he continued, deeply aggrieved. "What kind of a 'nishiation do you expect this is, anyhow?"

"Well, here's Maurice Levy gone and seen part of the secrets," said Sam, in a voice of equal plaintiveness. "Yes; and I bet he was listenin' out here, too!"

"Lemme up!" begged Maurice, half stifled. "I didn't do any harm to your old secrets, did I? Anyways, I just as soon be 'nishiated myself. I ain't afraid. So if you 'nishiate me, what difference will it make if I did hear a little?"

Struck with this idea, which seemed reasonable, Penrod obtained silence from every one except Roddy, and it was decided to allow Maurice to rise and retire to the front yard. The brother members then withdrew within the shack, elected Maurice to the fellowship, and completed the initiation of Mr. Bitts. After that, Maurice was summoned and underwent the ordeal with fortitude, though the newest brother—still tingling with his own experiences—helped to make certain parts of the rixual unprecedentedly severe.

Once endowed with full membership, Maurice and Roddy accepted the obligations and privileges of the order with enthusiasm. Both interested themselves immediately in im-

provements for the shack, and made excursions to their
homes to obtain materials. Roddy returned with a pair of
lensless mother-of-pearl opera-glasses, a contribution that
led to the creation of a new office, called the "warner". It
was his duty to climb upon the back fence once every fifteen minutes and search the horizon for intruders or "anybody that hasn't got any biznuss around here." This post
proved so popular, at first, that it was found necessary to
provide for rotation in office, and to shorten the interval
from fifteen minutes to an indefinite but much briefer
period, determined principally by argument between the
incumbent and his successor.

And Maurice Levy contributed a device so pleasant, and
so necessary to the prevention of interruption during meetings, that Penrod and Sam wondered why they had not
thought of it themselves long before. It consisted of about
twenty-five feet of garden hose in fair condition. One end
of it was introduced into the shack through a knothole, and
the other was secured by wire round the faucet of hydrant
in the stable. Thus, if members of the order were assailed
by thirst during an important session, or in the course of
an initiation, it would not be necessary for them all to leave
the shack. One could go, instead, and when he had turned
on the water at the hydrant, the members in the shack could
drink without leaving their places. It was discovered, also,
that the section of hose could be used as a speaking-tube;
and though it did prove necessary to explain by shouting
outside the tube what one had said into it, still there was a
general feeling that it provided another means of secrecy
and an additional safeguard against intrusion. It is true
that during the half-hour immediately following the instal-
lation of this convenience, there was a little violence among
the brothers concerning a question of policy. Sam, Roddy
and Verman—Verman especially—wished to use the tube
"to talk through" and Maurice, Penrod and Herman
wished to use it "to drink through." As a consequence of
the success of the latter party, the shack became too damp

for habitation until another day, and several members, as they went home at dusk, might easily have been mistaken for survivors of some marine catastrophe.

Still, not every shack is equipped with running water, and exuberance befitted the occasion. Everybody agreed that the afternoon had been one of the most successful and important in many weeks. The Order of the In-Or-In was doing splendidly, and yet every brother felt, in his heart, that there was one thing that could spoil it. Against that fatality, all were united to protect themselves, the shack, the rixual, the opera-glasses and the water-and-speaking tube. Sam spoke not only for himself but for the entire order when he declared, in speeding the last parting guest:

"Well, we got to stick to one thing or we might as well quit! *Georgie Bassett* better not come pokin' around!"

"No, *sir!*" said Penrod.

CHAPTER XXIX

GEORGIE BECOMES A MEMBER

BUT Georgie did. It is difficult to imagine how cause and effect could be more closely and patently related. Inevitably, Georgie did come poking around. How was he to refrain when daily, up and down the neighbourhood, the brothers strutted with mystic and important airs, when they whispered together and uttered words of strange import in his presence? Thus did they defeat their own object. They desired to keep Georgie at a distance, yet they could not refrain from posing before him. They wished to impress upon him the fact that he was an outsider, and they but succeeded in rousing his desire to be an insider, a desire that soon became a determination. For few were the days until he not only knew of the shack but had actually paid it a visit. That was upon a morning when the other boys were in school, Georgie having found himself indisposed until about ten o'clock, when he was able to take nourishment and subsequently to interest himself in this rather private errand. He climbed the Williams' alley fence, and, having made a modest investigation of the exterior of the shack, which was padlocked, retired without having disturbed anything except his own peace of mind. His curiosity, merely piqued before, now became ravenous and painful. It was not allayed by the mystic manners of the members or by the unnecessary emphasis they laid upon their coldness toward himself; and when a committee informed him darkly that there were "secret orders" to prevent his coming within "a hundred and sixteen feet"—such was Penrod's arbitrary language—of the Williams' yard, "in any direction", Georgie could bear it no longer, but entered his own house, and, in burning words, laid the case before a woman higher up. Here the responsibility for things is directly traceable to grown people. Within that hour, Mrs. Bassett sat in Mrs. Williams's library to address her hostess upon the subject of Georgie's grievance.

"Of course, it isn't Sam's fault," she said, concluding her interpretation of the affair. "Georgie likes Sam, and didn't blame him at all. No; we both felt that Sam would always be a polite, nice boy—Georgie used those very words—but Penrod seems to have a *very* bad influence. Georgie felt that Sam would *want* him to come and play in the shack if Penrod didn't make Sam do everything *he* wants. What hurt Georgie most is that it's *Sam's* shack, and he felt for another boy to come and tell him that he mustn't even go *near* it—well, of course, it was very trying. And he's very much hurt with little Maurice Levy, too. He said that he was sure that even Penrod would be glad to have him for a member of their little club if it weren't for Maurice—and I think he spoke of Roddy Bitts, too."

The fact that the two remaining members were coloured

was omitted from this discourse—which leads to the deduction that Georgie had not mentioned it.

"Georgie said all the other boys liked him very much," Mrs. Bassett continued, "and that he felt it his duty to join the club, because most of them were so anxious to have him, and he is sure he would have a good influence over them. He really did speak of it in quite a touching way, Mrs. Williams. Of course, we mothers mustn't brag of our sons too much, but Georgie *really* isn't like other boys. He is so sensitive, you can't think how this little affair has hurt him, and I felt that it might even make him ill. You see, I *had* to respect his reason for wanting to join the club. And if I *am* his mother"—she gave a deprecating little laugh—"I must say that it seems noble to want to join not really for his own sake but for the good that he felt his influence would have over the other boys. Don't you think so, Mrs. Williams?"

Mrs. Williams said that she did, indeed. And the result of this interview was another, which took place between Sam and his father that evening, for Mrs. Williams, after talking to Sam herself, felt that the matter needed a man to deal with it. The man did it man-fashion.

"You either invite Georgie Bassett to play in the shack all he wants to," the man said, "or the shack comes down."

"But——"

"Take your choice. I'm not going to have neighbourhood quarrels over such——"

"But, Papa——"

"That's enough! You said yourself you haven't anything against Georgie."

"I said——"

"You said you didn't like him, but you couldn't tell why. You couldn't state a single instance of bad behaviour against him. You couldn't mention anything he ever did which wasn't what a gentleman should have done. It's no use, I tell you. Either you invite Georgie to play in the shack as much as he likes next Saturday, or the shack comes down."

"But, *Papa*——"

"I'm not going to talk any more about it. If you want the shack pulled down and hauled away, you and your friends continue to tantalize this inoffensive little boy the way you have been. If you want to keep it, be polite and invite him in."

"But——"

"That's *ALL*, I said!"

Sam was crushed.

Next day he communicated the bitter substance of the edict to the other members, and gloom became unanimous. So serious an aspect did the affair present that it was felt necessary to call a special meeting of the order after school. The entire membership was in attendance; the door was closed, the window covered with a board, and the candle lighted. Then all of the brothers—expect one—began to express their sorrowful apprehensions. The whole thing was spoiled, they agreed, if Georgie Bassett had to be taken in. On the other hand, if they didn't take him in, "there wouldn't be anything left." The one brother who failed to express any opinion was little Verman. He was otherwise occupied.

Verman had been the official paddler during the initiations of Roddy Bitts and Maurice Levy; his work had been conscientious, and it seemed to be taken by consent that he was to continue in office. An old shingle from the woodshed roof had been used for the exercise of his function in the cases of Roddy and Maurice; but this afternoon he had brought with him a new one that he had picked up somewhere. It was broader and thicker than the old one, and, during the melancholy prophecies of his fellows, he whittled the lesser end of it to the likeness of a handle. Thus engaged, he bore no appearance of despondency; on the contrary, his eyes, shining brightly in the candlelight, indicated that eager thoughts possessed him, while from time to time the sound of a chuckle issued from his simple African throat. Gradually the other brothers began to notice his preoccupation, and one by one they fell silent, regarding him thoughtfully. Slowly the darkness of their countenances lifted a little; something happier and brighter began to glimmer from each boyish face. All eyes remained fascinated upon Verman.

"Well, anyway," said Penrod, in a tone that was almost cheerful, "this is only Tuesday. We got pretty near all week to fix up the 'nishiation for Saturday."

And Saturday brought sunshine to make the occasion more tolerable for both the candidate and the society. Mrs. Williams, going to the window to watch Sam when he left the house after lunch, marked with pleasure that his look and manner were sprightly as he skipped down the walk to the front gate. There he paused and yodelled for a time. An answering yodel came presently; Penrod Schofield appeared, and by his side walked Georgie Bassett. Georgie was always neat; but Mrs. Williams noticed that he exhibited unusual gloss and polish to-day. As for his expression, it was a shade too complacent under the circumstances, though, for that matter, perfect tact avoids an air of triumph under any circumstances. Mrs. Williams was pleased to observe that Sam and Penrod betrayed no resentment whatever; they seemed to have accepted defeat in a good spirit and to be inclined to make the best of Georgie. Indeed, they appeared to be genuinely excited about him— it was evident that their cordiality was eager and wholehearted.

The three boys conferred for a few moments; then Sam disappeared round the house and returned, waving his hand and nodding. Upon that, Penrod took Georgie's left arm, Sam took his right, and the three marched off to the backyard in a companionable way that made Mrs. Williams feel it had been an excellent thing to interfere a little in Georgie's interest.

Experiencing the benevolent warmth that comes of assisting in a good action, she ascended to an apartment up-stairs, and, for a couple of hours, employed herself with needle and thread in sartorial repairs on behalf of her husband and Sam. Then she was interrupted by the advent of a coloured serving-maid.

"Miz Williams, I reckon the house goin' fall down!" this pessimist said, arriving out of breath. "That s'iety o' Mist' Sam's suttenly tryin' to pull the roof down on ow haids!"

"The roof?" Mrs. Williams inquired mildly. "They aren't in the attic, are they?"

"No'm; they in the celluh; but they *reachin'* fer the roof! I nev' did hear no sech a rumpus an' squawkin' an' squawl-in' an' fallin' an' whcopin' an' whackin' an' bangin'! They troop down by the outside celluh do', n'en—bang!—they bus' loose, an' been goin' on ev' since, wuss'n Bedlun! Ef they anything down celluh ain' broke by this time, it cain' be only jes' the foundashum, an' I bet *that* ain' goin' stan' much longer! I'd gone down an' stop 'em, but I'm 'fraid to. Hones', Miz Williams, I'm 'fraid o' my life go down there, all that Bedlun goin' on. I thought I come see what you say."

Mrs. Williams laughed.

"We have to stand a little noise in the house sometimes, Fanny, when there are boys. They're just playing, and a lot of noise is usually a pretty safe sign."

"Yes'm," Fanny said. "It's yo' house, Miz Williams, not mine. You want 'em tear it down, I'm willin'.""

She departed, and Mrs. Williams continued to sew. The days were growing short, and at five o'clock she was obliged to put the work aside, as her eyes did not permit her to continue it by artificial light. Descending to the lower floor, she found the house silent, and when she opened the front door to see if the evening paper had come, she beheld Sam, Penrod and Maurice Levy standing near the gate engaged in quiet conversation. Penrod and Maurice departed while she was looking for the paper, and Sam came thoughtfully up the walk.

"Well, Sam," she said, "it wasn't such a bad thing, after all, to show a little politeness to Georgie Bassett, was it?"

Sam gave her a non-committal look—expression of every kind had been wiped from his countenance. He presented a blank surface.

"No'm," he said meekly.

"Everything was just a little pleasanter because you'd been friendly, wasn't it?"

"Yes'm."

"Has Georgie gone home?"

"Yes'm."

"I hear you made enough noise in the cellar—— Did Georgie have a good time?"

"Ma'am?"

"Did Georgie Bassett have a good time?"

"Well"—Sam now had the air of a person trying to remember details with absolute accuracy—"well, he didn't say he did, and he didn't say he didn't."

"Didn't he thank the boys?"

"No'm."

"Didn't he even thank you?"

"No'm."

"Why, that's queer," she said. "He's always so polite. He *seemed* to be having a good time, didn't he, Sam?"

"Ma'am?"

"Didn't Georgie seem to be enjoying himself?"

This question, apparently so simple, was not answered with promptness. Sam looked at his mother in a puzzled way, and then he found it necessary to rub each of his shins in turn with the palm of his right hand.

"I stumbled," he said apologetically. "I stumbled on the cellar steps."

"Did you hurt yourself?" she asked quickly.

"No'm; but I guess maybe I better rub some arnica——"

"I'll get it," she said. "Come up to your father's bathroom, Sam. Does it hurt much?"

"No'm," he answered truthfully, "it hardly hurts at all."

And having followed her to the bathroom, he insisted, with unusual gentleness, that he be left to apply the arnica to the alleged injuries himself. He was so persuasive that she yielded, and descended to the library, where she found her husband once more at home after his day's work.

"Well?" he said. "Did Georgie show up, and were they decent to him?"

"Oh, yes; it's all right. Sam and Penrod were good as gold. I saw them being actually cordial to him."

"That's well," Mr. Williams said, settling into a chair with his paper. "I was a little apprehensive, but I suppose I was mistaken. I walked home, and just now, as I passed Mrs. Bassett's, I saw Doctor Venny's car in front, and that barber from the corner shop on Second Street was going in the door. I couldn't think what a widow would need a barber and a doctor for—especially at the same time. I couldn't think what Georgie'd need such a combination for either, and then I got afraid that maybe——"

Mrs. Williams laughed. "Oh, no; it hasn't anything to do with his having been over here. I'm sure they were very nice to him."

"Well, I'm glad of that."

"Yes, indeed——" Mrs. Williams began, when Fanny appeared, summoning her to the telephone.

It is pathetically true that Mrs. Williams went to the telephone humming a little song. She was detained at the instrument not more than five minutes; then she made a plunging return into the library, a blanched and stricken woman. She made strange, sinister gestures at her husband.

He sprang up, miserably prophetic. "Mrs. Bassett?"

"Go to the telephone," Mrs. Williams said hoarsely. "She wants to talk to you, too. She *can't* talk much—she's hysterical. She says they lured Georgie into the cellar and had him beaten by negroes! That's not all——"

Mr. Williams was already on his way. "You find Sam!" he commanded, over his shoulder.

Mrs. Williams stepped into the front hall. "Sam!" she

called, addressing the upper reaches of the stairway.
"Sam!"

Not even echo answered.

"*Sam!*"

A faint clearing of somebody's throat was heard behind
her, a sound so modest and unobtrusive it was no more than
just audible, and, turning, the mother beheld her son sitting upon the floor in the shadow of the stairs and gazing
meditatively at the hatrack. His manner indicated that he
wished to produce the impression that he had been sitting
there, in this somewhat unusual place and occupation, for
a considerable time, but without overhearing anything that
went on in the library so close by.

"Sam," she cried, "what have you *done?*"

"Well—I guess my legs are all right," he said gently.
"I got the arnica on, so probably they won't hurt any
m——"

"Stand up!" she said.

"Ma'am?"

"March into the library!"

Sam marched—slow-time. In fact, no funeral march has
been composed in a time so slow as to suit this march of
Sam's. One might have suspected that he was in a state of
apprehension.

Mr. Williams entered at one door as his son crossed the
threshold of the other, and this encounter was a piteous
sight. After one glance at his father's face, Sam turned desperately, as if to flee outright. But Mrs. Williams stood
in the doorway behind him.

"You come here!" And the father's voice was as terrible
as his face. "*What did you do to Georgie Bassett?*"

"Nothin'," Sam gulped; "nothin' at all."

"What!"

"We just—we just 'nishiated him."

Mr. Williams turned abruptly, walked to the fireplace,
and there turned again, facing the wretched Sam. "That's
all you did?"

"Yes, sir."

"Georgie Bassett's mother has just told me over the telephone," Mr. Williams said, deliberately, "that you and Penrod Schofield and Roderick Bitts and Maurice Levy *lured Georgie into the cellar and had him beaten by negroes!*"

At this, Sam was able to hold up his head a little and to summon a rather feeble indignation.

"It ain't so," he declared. "We didn't any such thing lower him into the cellar. We weren't goin' *near* the cellar with him. We never *thought* of goin' down cellar. He went down there himself, first."

"So! I suppose he was running away from you, poor thing! Trying to escape from you, wasn't he?"

"He wasn't," Sam said doggedly. "We weren't chasin' him—or anything at all."

"Then why did he go in the cellar?"

"Well, he didn't exactly *go* in the cellar," Sam said reluctantly.

"Well, how did he *get* in the cellar, then?"

"He—he fell in," said Sam.

"*How* did he fall in?"

"Well, the door was open, and—well, he kept walkin' around there, and we hollered at him to keep away, but just then he kind of—well, the first *I* noticed was I couldn't *see* him, and so we went and looked down the steps, and he was sitting down there on the bottom step and kind of shouting, and——"

"See here!" Mr. Williams interrupted. "You're going to make a clean breast of this whole affair and take the consequences. You're going to tell it and tell it *all*. Do you understand that?"

"Yes, sir."

"Then you tell me how Georgie Bassett fell down the cellar steps—and tell me quick!"

"He—he was blindfolded."

"Aha! *Now* we're getting at it. You begin at the beginning and tell me just what you did to him from the time he got here. Understand?"

"Yes, sir."

"Go on, then!"

"Well, I'm goin' to," Sam protested. "We never hurt him at all. He wasn't even hurt when he fell down cellar. There's a lot of mud down there, because the cellar door leaks, and——"

"Sam!" Mr. Williams's tone was deadly. "Did you hear me tell you to begin at the beginning?"

Sam made a great effort and was able to obey.

"Well, we had everything ready for the 'nishiation before lunch," he said. "We wanted it all to be nice, because you said we had to have him, Papa, and after lunch Penrod went to guard him—that's a new part in the rixual—and he brought him over, and we took him out to the shack and blindfolded him, and—well, he got kind of mad because we wanted him to lay down on his stummick and be tied up, and he said he wouldn't, because the floor was ⌐ little bit wet in there and he could feel it sort of squashy under his shoes, and he said his mother didn't want him ever to get dirty and he just wouldn't do it; and we all kept telling him he had to, or else how could there be any 'nishiation; and he kept gettin' madder and said he wanted to have the 'nishiation outdoors where it wasn't wet and he wasn't goin' to lay down on his stummick, anyway." Sam paused for wind, then got under way again. "Well, some of the boys were tryin' to get him to lay down on his stummick, and he kind of fell up against the door and it came open and he ran out in the yard. He was tryin' to get the blindfold off his eyes, but he couldn't because it was a towel in a pretty hard knot; and he went tearin' all around the backyard, and we didn't chase him, or anything. All we did was just watch him—and that's when he fell in the cellar. Well, it didn't hurt him any. It didn't hurt him at all; but he was muddier than what he would of been if he'd just had sense enough to lay down in the shack. Well, so we thought, long as he was down in the cellar anyway, we might as well have the rest of the 'nishiation down there. So we brought the things down and—and 'nishiated him—and that's all. That's every bit we did to him."

"Yes," Mr. Williams said sardonically; "I see. What were the details of the initiation?"

"Sir?"

"I want to know what else you did to him? What was the initiation?"

"It's—it's secret," Sam murmured piteously.

"Not any longer, I assure you! The society is a thing of the past and you'll find your friend Penrod's parents agree with me in that. Mrs. Bassett had already telephoned them when she called us up. You go on with your story!"

Sam sighed deeply, and yet it may have been a consolation to know that his present misery was not altogether without its counterpart. Through the falling dusk his spirit may have crossed the intervening distance to catch a glimpse of his friend suffering simultaneously and standing within the same peril. And if Sam's spirit did thus behold Penrod in jeopardy, it was a true vision.

"Go on!" Mr. Williams said.

"Well, there wasn't any fire in the furnace because it's too warm yet, and we weren't goin' to do anything'd *hurt* him, so we put him in there——"

"In the *furnace?*"

"It was cold," Sam protested. "There hadn't been any fire there since last spring. Course we told him there was fire in it. We *had* to do that," he continued earnestly, "because that was part of the 'nishiation. We only kept him in it a little while and kind of hammered on the outside a little and then we took him out and got him to lay down on his stummick, because he was all muddy anyway, where he fell down the cellar; and how could it matter to anybody that had any sense at all? Well, then we had the rixual, and—and—why, the teeny little paddlin' he got wouldn't hurt a flea! It was that little coloured boy lives in the alley did it

—he isn't anyways near *half* Georgie's size—but Georgie got mad and said he didn't want any ole nigger to paddle him. That's what he said, and it was his own foolishness, because Verman won't let *anybody* call him 'nigger', and if Georgie was goin' to call him that he ought to had sense enough not to do it when he was layin' down that way and Verman all ready to be the paddler. And he needn't of been so mad at the rest of us, either, because it took us about twenty minutes to get the paddle away from Verman after that, and we had to lock Verman up in the laundry-room and not let him out till it was all over. Well, and then things were kind of spoiled, anyway; so we didn't do but just a little more—and that's all."

"Go on! What was the 'just a little more'?"

"Well—we got him to swaller a little teeny bit of asafidity. It wasn't enough to even make a person sneeze—it wasn't much more'n a half a spoonful—it wasn't hardly a *quarter* of a spoonf——"

"Ha!" said Mr. Williams. "That accounts for the doctor. What else?"

"Well—we—we had some paint left over from our flag, and we put just a little teeny bit of it on his hair and——"

"Ha!" said Mr. Williams. "That accounts for the barber. What else?"

"That's all," Sam said, swallowing. "Then he got mad and went home."

Mr. Williams walked to the door, and sternly motioned to the culprit to precede him through it. But just before the pair passed from her sight, Mrs. Williams gave way to an uncontrollable impulse.

"Sam," she asked, "what does 'In-Or-In' stand for?"

The unfortunate boy had begun to sniffle.

"It—it means—Innapenent Order of Infadelaty," he moaned—and plodded onward to his doom.

Not his alone: at that very moment Master Roderick Magsworth Bitts, Junior, was suffering also, consequent upon telephoning on the part of Mrs. Bassett, though Roderick's punishment was administered less on the ground of Georgie's troubles and more on that of Roddy's having affiliated with an order consisting so largely of Herman and Verman. As for Maurice Levy, he was no whit less unhappy. He fared as ill.

Simultaneously, two ex-members of the In-Or-In were finding their lot fortunate. Something had prompted them to linger in the alley in the vicinity of the shack, and it was to this fated edifice that Mr. Williams, with demoniac justice, brought Sam for the deed he had in mind.

Herman and Verman listened—awe-stricken—to what went on within the shack. Then, before it was over, they crept away and down the alley toward their own home. This was directly across the alley from the Schofields' stable, and they were horrified at the sounds that issued from the interior of the stable store-room. It was the St. Bartholomew's Eve of that neighbourhood.

"Man, man!" said Herman, shaking his head. "Glad I ain' no white boy!"

Verman seemed gloomily to assent.

CHAPTER XXX

WHITEY

PENROD and Sam made a gloomy discovery one morning in mid-October. All the week had seen amiable breezes and fair skies until Saturday, when, about breakfast-time, the dome of heaven filled solidly with gray vapour and began to drip. The boys' discovery was that there is no justice about the weather.

They sat in the carriage-house of the Schofields' empty stable; the doors upon the alley were open, and Sam and Penrod stared torpidly at the thin but implacable drizzle that was the more irritating because there was barely enough of it to interfere with a number of things they had planned to do.

"Yes; this is *nice!*" Sam said, in a tone of plaintive sarcasm. "This is a *perty* way to do!" (He was alluding to the personal spitefulness of the elements.) "I'd like to know what's the sense of it—ole sun pourin' down every day in the week when nobody needs it, then cloud up and rain all Saturday! My father said it's goin' to be a three days' rain."

"Well, nobody with any sense cares if it rains Sunday and Monday," Penrod said. "I wouldn't care if it rained every Sunday as long I lived; but I just like to know what's the reason it had to go and rain to-day. Got all the days o' the week to choose from and goes and picks on Saturday. That's a fine biz'nuss!"

"Well, in vacation——" Sam began; but at a sound from a source invisible to him he paused. "What's that?" he said, somewhat startled.

It was a curious sound, loud and hollow and unhuman, yet it seemed to be a cough. Both boys rose, and Penrod asked uneasily: "Where'd that noise come from?"

"It's in the alley," said Sam.

Perhaps if the day had been bright, both of them would have stepped immediately to the alley doors to investigate; but their actual procedure was to move a little distance in the opposite direction. The strange cough sounded again.

"*Say!*" Penrod quavered. "What *is* that?"

Then both boys uttered smothered exclamations and jumped, for the long, gaunt head that appeared in the doorway was entirely unexpected. It was the cavernous and melancholy head of an incredibly thin, old, whitish horse. This head waggled slowly from side to side; the nostrils vibrated; the mouth opened, and the hollow cough sounded again.

Recovering themselves, Penrod and Sam underwent the customary human reaction from alarm to indignation.

"What you want, you ole horse, you?" Penrod shouted. "Don't you come coughin' around *me!*"

And Sam, seizing a stick, hurled it at the intruder.

"Get out o' here!" he roared.

The aged horse nervously withdrew his head, turned tail, and made a rickety flight up the alley, while Sam and Penrod, perfectly obedient to inherited impulse, ran out into the drizzle and uproariously pursued. They were but automatons of instinct, meaning no evil. Certainly they did not know the singular and pathetic history of the old horse who wandered into the alley and ventured to look through the open door.

This horse, about twice the age of either Penrod or Sam, had lived to find himself in a unique position. He was nude, possessing neither harness nor halter; all he had was a name, Whitey, and he would have answered to it by a slight change of expression if any one had thus properly addressed him. So forlorn was Whitey's case, he was actually an independent horse; he had not even an owner. For two days and a half he had been his own master.

Previous to that period he had been the property of one Abalene Morris, a person of colour, who would have explained himself as engaged in the hauling business. On the contrary, the hauling business was an insignificant side line with Mr. Morris, for he had long ago given himself, as utterly as fortune permitted, to the talent that early in youth he had recognized as the greatest of all those surging in his bosom. In his waking thoughts and in his dreams, in health and in sickness, Abalene Morris was the dashing and emotional practitioner of an art probably more than Roman in antiquity. Abalene was a crap-shooter. The hauling business was a disguise.

A concentration of events had brought it about that, at one and the same time, Abalene, after a dazzling run of the dice, found the hauling business an actual danger to the preservation of his liberty. He won seventeen dollars and sixty cents, and within the hour found himself in trouble with an officer of the Humane Society on account of an altercation with Whitey. Abalene had been offered four dollars for Whitey some ten days earlier; wherefore he at

once drove to the shop of the junk-dealer who had made
the offer and announced his acquiescence in the sacrifice.

"*No*, suh!" the junk-dealer said, with emphasis, "I aw-
ready done got me a good mule fer my deliv'ry hoss, 'n'at
ole Whitey hoss ain' wuff no fo' dollah nohow! I 'uz a fool
when I talk 'bout th'owin' money roun' that a-way. *I* know
what *you* up to, Abalene. Man come by here li'l bit ago tole
me all 'bout white man try to 'rest you, ovah on the
avvynoo. Yessuh; he say white man goin' to git you yit an'
th'ow you in jail 'count o' Whitey. White man tryin' to
fine out who you *is*. He say, nemmine, he'll know Whitey
ag'in, even if he don' know you! He say he ketch you by the
hoss; so you come roun' tryin' fix me up with Whitey so
white man grab me, th'ow *me* in 'at jail. G'on 'way f'um
hyuh, you Abalene! You cain' sell an' you cain' give Whitey
to no cullud man 'n 'is town. You go an' drowned 'at ole
hoss, 'cause you sutny goin' to jail if you git ketched driv-
in' him."

The substance of this advice seemed good to Abalene,
especially as the seventeen dollars and sixty cents in his
pocket lent sweet colours to life out of jail at this time.
At dusk he led Whitey to a broad common at the edge of
town, and spoke to him finally.

"G'on 'bout you biz'nis," said Abalene; "you ain' *my*
hoss. Don' look roun' at me, 'cause *I* ain't got no 'quaintance
wif you. I'm a man o' money, an' I got my own frien's; I'm
a-lookin' fer bigger cities, hoss. You got you biz'nis an' I
got mine. Mista' Hoss, good-night!"

Whitey found a little frosted grass upon the common
and remained there all night. In the morning he sought the
shed where Abalene had kept him; but that was across the
large and busy town, and Whitey was hopelessly lost. He
had but one eye, a feeble one, and his legs were not to be
depended upon; but he managed to cover a great deal of
ground, to have many painful little adventures, and to get
monstrously hungry and thirsty before he happened to
look in upon Penrod and Sam.

When the two boys chased him up the alley they had no intention to cause pain; they had no intention at all. They were no more cruel than Duke, Penrod's little old dog, who followed his own instincts, and, making his appearance hastily through a hole in the back fence, joined the pursuit with sound and fury. A boy will nearly always run after anything that is running, and his first impulse is to throw a stone at it. This is a survival of primeval man, who must take every chance to get his dinner. So, when Penrod and Sam drove the hapless Whitey up the alley, they were really responding to an impulse thousands and thousands of years old—an impulse founded upon the primordial observation that whatever runs is likely to prove edible. Penrod and Sam were not "bad"; they were never that. They were something that was not their fault; they were historic.

At the next corner Whitey turned to the right into the cross-street; thence, turning to the right again and still warmly pursued, he zigzagged down a main thoroughfare until he reached another cross-street, which ran alongside the Schofields' yard and brought him to the foot of the alley he had left behind in his flight. He entered the alley, and there his dim eye fell upon the open door he had previously investigated. No memory of it remained; but the place had a look associated in his mind with hay, and, as Sam and Penrod turned the corner of the alley in panting yet still vociferous pursuit, Whitey stumbled up the inclined platform before the open doors, staggered thunderously across the carriage-house and through another open door into a stall, an apartment vacant since the occupancy of Mr. Schofield's last horse, now several years deceased.

CHAPTER XXXI

SALVAGE

THE two boys shrieked with excitement as they beheld the coincidence of this strange return. They burst into the stable, making almost as much noise as Duke, who had become frantic at the invasion. Sam laid hands upon a rake.

"You get out o' there, you ole horse, you!" he bellowed. "I ain't afraid to drive him out. I——"

"*Wait* a minute!" Penrod shouted. "Wait till I——"

Sam was manfully preparing to enter the stall.

"You hold the doors open," he commanded, "so's they won't blow shut and keep him in here. I'm goin' to hit him with——"

"Quee-*yut!*" Penrod shouted, grasping the handle of the rake so that Sam could not use it. "Wait a *minute,* can't you?" He turned with ferocious voice and gestures upon Duke. "*Duke!*" And Duke, in spite of his excitement, was so impressed that he prostrated himself in silence, and then unobtrusively withdrew from the stable. Penrod ran to the alley doors and closed them.

"My gracious!" Sam protested. "What you goin' to do?"

"I'm goin' to keep this horse," said Penrod, whose face showed the strain of a great idea.

"What *for?*"

"For the reward," said Penrod simply.

Sam sat down in the wheelbarrow and stared at his friend almost with awe.

"My gracious," he said, "I never thought o' that! How —how much do you think we'll get, Penrod?"

Sam's thus admitting himself to a full partnership in the enterprise met no objection from Penrod, who was absorbed in the contemplation of Whitey.

"Well," he said judicially, "we might get more and we might get less."

Sam rose and joined his friend in the doorway opening upon the two stalls. Whitey had preëmpted the nearer, and was hungrily nuzzling the old frayed hollows in the manger.

"Maybe a hunderd dollars—or sumpthing?" Sam asked in a low voice.

Penrod maintained his composure and repeated the new-found expression that had sounded well to him a moment before. He recognized it as a symbol of the non-committal attitude that makes people looked up to. "Well"—he made it slow, and frowned—"we might get more and we might get less."

"More'n a hunderd *dollars?*" Sam gasped.

"Well," said Penrod, "we might get more and we might get less." This time, however, he felt the need of adding something. He put a question in an indulgent tone, as

though he were inquiring, not to add to his own information but to discover the extent of Sam's. "How much do you
think horses are worth, anyway?"

"I don't know," Sam said frankly, and, unconsciously,
he added, "They might be more and they might be less."

"Well, when our ole horse died," Penrod said, "Papa
said he wouldn't taken five hunderd dollars for him. That's
how much *horses* are worth!"

"My gracious!" Sam exclaimed. Then he had a practical afterthought. "But maybe he was a better horse than
this'n. What colour was he?"

"He was bay. Looky here, Sam"—and now Penrod's manner changed from the superior to the eager—"you look
what kind of horses they have in a circus, and you bet a
circus has the *best* horses, don't it? Well, what kind of
horses do they have in a circus? They have some black
and white ones; but the best they have are white all over.
Well, what kind of a horse is this we got here? He's perty
near white right now, and I bet if we washed him off and
got him fixed up nice he *would* be white. Well, a bay horse
is worth five hunderd dollars, because that's what Papa said,
and this horse——"

Sam interrupted rather timidly.

"He—he's awful bony, Penrod. You don't guess they'd
make any——"

Penrod laughed contemptuously.

"Bony! All he needs is a little food and he'll fill right up
and look good as ever. You don't know much about horses,
Sam, I expect. Why, *our* ole horse——"

"Do you expect he's hungry now?" asked Sam, staring
at Whitey.

"Let's try him," said Penrod. "Horses like hay and oats
the best; but they'll eat most anything."

"I guess they will. He's tryin' to eat that manger up
right now, and I bet it ain't good for him."

"Come on," said Penrod, closing the door that gave

entrance to the stalls. "We got to get this horse some drinkin'-water and some good food."

They tried Whitey's appetite first with an autumnal branch that they wrenched from a hardy maple in the yard. They had seen horses nibble leaves, and they expected Whitey to nibble the leaves of this branch; but his ravenous condition did not allow him time for cool discriminations. Sam poked the branch at him from the passageway, and Whitey, after one backward movement of alarm, seized it venomously.

"Here! You stop that!" Sam shouted. "You stop that, you ole horse, you!"

"What's the matter?" called Penrod from the hydrant, where he was filling a bucket. "What's he doin' now?"

"Doin'! He's eatin' the wood part, too! He's chewin' up sticks as big as baseball bats! He's crazy!"

Penrod rushed to see this sight, and stood aghast.

"Take it away from him, Sam!" he commanded sharply.

"Go on, take it away from him yourself!" was the prompt retort of his comrade.

"You had no biz'nuss to give it to him," said Penrod. "Anybody with any sense ought to know it'd make him sick. What'd you want to go and give it to him for?"

"Well, you didn't say not to."

"Well, what if I didn't? I never said I did, did I? You go on in that stall and take it away from him."

"*Yes*, I will!" Sam returned bitterly. Then, as Whitey had dragged the remains of the branch from the manger to the floor of the stall, Sam scrambled to the top of the manger and looked over. "There ain't much left to *take* away! He's swallered it all except some splinters. Better give him the water to try and wash it down with." And, as Penrod complied, "My gracious, look at that horse *drink!*"

They gave Whitey four buckets of water, and then debated the question of nourishment. Obviously, this horse could not be trusted with branches, and, after getting their knees black and their backs sodden, they gave up trying to pull enough grass to sustain him. Then Penrod remembered that horses like apples, both "cooking-apples" and "eating-apples", and Sam mentioned the fact that every autumn his father received a barrel of "cooking-apples" from a cousin who owned a farm. That barrel was in the Williams' cellar now, and the cellar was providentially supplied with "outside doors", so that it could be visited without going through the house. Sam and Penrod set forth for the cellar.

They returned to the stable bulging, and, after a discussion of Whitey's digestion (Sam claiming that eating the core and seeds, as Whitey did, would grow trees in his inside) they went back to the cellar for supplies again—and again. They made six trips, carrying each time a capacity cargo of apples, and still Whitey ate in a famished manner. They were afraid to take more apples from the barrel, which began to show conspicuously the result of their raids, wherefore Penrod made an unostentatious visit to the cellar of his own house. From the inside he opened a window and passed vegetables out to Sam, who placed them in a bucket and carried them hurriedly to the stable, while Penrod returned in a casual manner through the house. Of his *sang-froid* under a great strain it is sufficient to relate that, in the kitchen, he said suddenly to Della, the cook, "Oh, look behind you!" and by the time Della discovered that there was nothing unusual behind her, Penrod was gone, and a loaf of bread from the kitchen table was gone with him.

Whitey now ate nine turnips, two heads of lettuce, one cabbage, eleven raw potatoes and the loaf of bread. He ate the loaf of bread last and he was a long time about it; so the boys came to a not unreasonable conclusion.

"Well, sir, I guess we got him filled up at last!" said Penrod. "I bet he wouldn't eat a saucer of ice-cream now, if we'd give it to him!"

"He looks better to me," said Sam, staring critically at Whitey. "I think he's kind of begun to fill out some. I expect he must like us, Penrod; we been doin' a good deal for this horse."

"Well, sir, I guess we got him filled up at last!"
said Penrod.

"Well, we got to keep it up," Penrod insisted rather pompously. "Long as *I* got charge o' this horse, he's goin' to get good treatment."

"What we better do now, Penrod?"

Penrod took on the outward signs of deep thought.

"Well, there's plenty to *do*, all right. I got to think."

Sam made several suggestions, which Penrod—maintaining his air of preoccupation—dismissed with mere gestures.

"Oh, *I* know!" Sam cried finally. "We ought to wash him so's he'll look whiter'n what he does now. We can turn the hose on him acrost the manger."

"No; not yet," Penrod said. "It's too soon after his meal. You ought to know that yourself. What we got to do is to make up a bed for him—if he wants to lay down or anything."

"Make up a what for him?" Sam echoed, dumfounded. "What you talkin' about? How can——"

"Sawdust," Penrod said. "That's the way the horse we used to have used to have it. We'll make this horse's bed in the other stall, and then he can go in there and lay down whenever he wants to."

"How we goin' to do it?"

"Look, Sam; there's the hole into the sawdust-box! All you got to do is walk in there with the shovel, stick the shovel in the hole till it gets full of sawdust, and then sprinkle it around on the empty stall."

"All *I* got to do!" Sam cried. "What are you goin' to do?"

"I'm goin' to be right here," Penrod answered reassuringly. "He won't kick or anything, and it isn't goin' to take you half a second to slip around behind him to the other stall."

"What makes you think he won't kick?"

"Well, I *know* he won't, and, besides, you could hit him with the shovel if he tried to. Anyhow, I'll be right here, won't I?"

"I don't care where you are," Sam said earnestly. "What difference would that make if he ki——"

"Why, you were goin' right in the stall," Penrod reminded him. "When he first came in, you were goin' to take the rake and——"

"I don't care if I was," Sam declared. "I was excited then."

"Well, you can get excited now, can't you?" his friend urged. "You can just as easy get——"

He was interrupted by a shout from Sam, who was keeping his eye upon Whitey throughout the discussion.

"Look! Looky there!" And undoubtedly renewing his excitement, Sam pointed at the long, gaunt head beyond the manger. It was disappearing from view. "Look!" Sam shouted. "He's layin' down!"

"Well, then," said Penrod, "I guess he's goin' to take a nap. If he wants to lay down without waitin' for us to get the sawdust fixed for him, that's his lookout, not ours."

On the contrary, Sam perceived a favourable opportunity for action.

"I just as soon go and make his bed up while he's layin' down," he volunteered. "You climb up on the manger and watch him, Penrod, and I'll sneak in the other stall and fix it all up nice for him, so's he can go in there any time when he wakes up, and lay down again, or anything; and if he starts to get up, you holler and I'll jump out over the other manger."

Accordingly, Penrod established himself in a position to observe the recumbent figure. Whitey's breathing was rather laboured but regular, and, as Sam remarked, he looked "better", even in his slumber. It is not to be doubted that although Whitey was suffering from a light attack of colic his feelings were in the main those of contentment. After trouble, he was solaced; after exposure, he was sheltered; after hunger and thirst, he was fed and watered. He slept.

The noon whistles blew before Sam's task was finished; but by the time he departed for lunch there was made a bed of such quality that Whitey must needs have been a born faultfinder if he complained of it. The friends parted, each urging the other to be prompt in returning; but Penrod got into threatening difficulties as soon as he entered the house.

CHAPTER XXXII

REWARD OF MERIT

"PENROD," said his mother, "what did you do with that loaf of bread Della says you took from the table?"

"Ma'am? *What* loaf o' bread?"

"I believe I can't let you go outdoors this afternoon," Mrs. Schofield said severely. "If you were hungry, you know perfectly well all you had to do was to——"

"But I wasn't hungry; I——"

"You can explain later," Mrs. Schofield said. "You'll have all afternoon."

Penrod's heart grew cold.

"I *can't* stay in," he protested. "I've asked Sam Williams to come over."

"I'll telephone Mrs. Williams."

"Mamma!" Penrod's voice became agonized. "I *had* to give that bread to a—to a poor ole man. He was starving and so were his children and his wife. They were all just *starving*—and they couldn't wait while I took time to come and ask you, Mamma. I *got* to go outdoors this afternoon. I *got* to! Sam's——"

She relented.

In the carriage-house, half an hour later, Penrod gave an account of the episode.

"Where'd we been, I'd just like to know," he concluded, "if I hadn't got out here this afternoon?"

"Well, I guess I could managed him all right," Sam said. "I was in the passageway, a minute ago, takin' a look at him. He's standin' up again. I expect he wants more to eat."

"Well, we got to fix about that," said Penrod. "But what I mean—if I'd had to stay in the house, where would we been about the most important thing in the whole biz'nuss?"

"What you talkin' about?"

"Well, why can't you wait till I tell you?" Penrod's tone had become peevish. For that matter, so had Sam's; they were developing one of the little differences, or quarrels, that composed the very texture of their friendship.

"Well, why don't you tell me, then?"

"Well, how can I?" Penrod demanded. "You keep talkin' every minute."

"I'm not talkin' *now*, am I?" Sam protested. "You can tell me *now*, can't you? I'm not talk——"

"You are, too!" Penrod shouted. "You talk all the time! You——"

He was interrupted by Whitey's peculiar cough. Both boys jumped and forgot their argument.

"He means he wants some more to eat, I bet," said Sam.

"Well, if he does, he's got to wait," Penrod declared. "We got to get the most important thing of all fixed up first."

"What's that, Penrod?"

"The reward," said Penrod mildly. "That's what I was tryin' to tell you about, Sam, if you'd ever give me half a chance."

"Well, I *did* give you a chance. I kept *tellin'* you to tell me, but——"

"You never! You kept sayin'——"

They renewed this discussion, protracting it indefinitely; but as each persisted in clinging to his own interpretation of the facts, the question still remains unsettled. It was abandoned, or rather, it merged into another during the later stages of the debate, this other being concerned with which of the debaters had the least "sense". Each made the plain statement that if he were more deficient than his opponent in that regard, self-destruction would be his only refuge. Each declared that he would "rather die than be talked to death"; and then, as the two approached a point bluntly recriminative, Whitey coughed again, whereupon they were miraculously silent, and went into the passage-way in a perfectly amiable manner.

"I got to have a good look at him, for once," Penrod said, as he stared frowningly at Whitey. "We got to fix up about that reward."

"I want to take a good ole look at him myself," Sam said.

After supplying Whitey with another bucket of water, they returned to the carriage-house and seated themselves thoughtfully. In truth, they were something a shade more than thoughtful; the adventure to which they had committed themselves was beginning to be a little overpowering. If Whitey had been a dog, a goat, a fowl, or even a stray calf, they would have felt equal to him; but now that the earlier glow of their wild daring had disappeared, vague apprehensions stirred. Their "good look" at Whitey had not reassured them—he seemed large, Gothic and unusual.

Whisperings within them began to urge that for boys to undertake an enterprise connected with so huge an animal as an actual horse was perilous. Beneath the surface of their musings, dim but ominous prophecies moved; both boys began to have the feeling that, somehow, this affair was going to get beyond them and that they would be in heavy trouble before it was over—they knew not why. They knew why no more than they knew why they felt it imperative to keep the fact of Whitey's presence in the stable a secret from their respective families; but they did begin to realize that keeping a secret of that size was going to be attended with some difficulty. In brief, their sensations were becoming comparable to those of the man who stole a house.

Nevertheless, after a short period given to unspoken misgivings, they returned to the subject of the reward. The money-value of bay horses, as compared to white, was again discussed, and each announced his certainty that nothing less than "a good ole hunderd dollars" would be offered for the return of Whitey.

But immediately after so speaking they fell into another silence, due to sinking feelings. They had spoken loudly and confidently, and yet they knew, somehow, that such things were not to be. According to their knowledge, it was perfectly reasonable to suppose that they would receive this fortune; but they frightened themselves in speaking of it. They knew that they *could* not have a hundred dollars for their own. An oppression, as from something awful and criminal, descended upon them at intervals.

Presently, however, they were warmed to a little cheerfulness again by Penrod's suggestion that they should put a notice in the paper. Neither of them had the slightest idea how to get it there; but such details as that were beyond the horizon; they occupied themselves with the question of what their advertisement ought to "say". Finding that they differed irreconcilably, Penrod went to his cache in the sawdust-box and brought two pencils and a supply of paper. He gave one of the pencils and several sheets to Sam; then both boys bent themselves in silence to the labour of practical composition. Penrod produced the briefer paragraph. (See Fig. I.) Sam's was more ample. (See Fig. II.)

Neither Sam nor Penrod showed any interest in what the other had written; but both felt that something praiseworthy had been accomplished. Penrod exhaled a sigh, as of relief, and, in a manner he had observed his father use sometimes, he said:

"Thank goodness, *that's* off my mind, anyway!"

"What we goin' do next, Penrod?" Sam asked deferentially, the borrowed manner having some effect upon him.

"I don't know what *you're* goin' to do," Penrod returned, picking up the old cigarbox that had contained the paper and pencils. "*I'm* goin' to put mine in here, so's it'll come in handy when I haf to get at it."

"Well, I guess I'll keep mine there, too," Sam said. Thereupon he deposited his scribbled slip beside Penrod's in the cigarbox, and the box was solemnly returned to the secret place whence it had been taken. "There, *that's* 'tended to!" Sam said, and, unconsciously imitating his friend's imitation, he gave forth audibly a breath of satisfaction and relief.

Both boys felt that the financial side of their great affair had been conscientiously looked to, that the question of the reward was settled, and that everything was proceeding in a businesslike manner. Therefore, they were able to turn their attention to another matter.

This was the question of Whitey's next meal. After their exploits of the morning, and the consequent imperilment of Penrod, they decided that nothing more was to be done in apples, vegetables or bread; it was evident that Whitey must be fed from the bosom of nature.

"We couldn't pull enough o' that frostbit ole grass in the yard to feed him," Penrod said gloomily. "We could work a week and not get enough to make him swaller more'n about twice. All we got this morning, he blew most of it away. He'd try to scoop it in toward his teeth with his lip, and then he'd haf to kind of blow out his breath, and after

FIG I

Reward.

White horse yn Schofields
ally finders got him in
Schofields stable and will
let him taken away by by ~~paying~~
paying for good food he
has aten while ~~wat~~
while ~~wat~~ waiting and
Reward of ~~$100~~ ~~$20~~
~~$15~~ ~~$5~~ $10

FIG II

FOND

Horse on Satarday moring
onwer can get him by ~~aply~~ replyng at
stable bhind Mr Schofield. You will have
to proov he is your horse he is whit with
kind of brown ~~spec~~ speks and worout
~~tail~~ tale he is geting good care and food
reword ~~$100~~ ~~$20~~ seventy five cents to
each one or we will keep him loked up.

that all the grass that'd be left was just some wet pieces stickin' to the outsides of his face. Well, and you know how he acted about that maple branch. We can't trust him with branches."

Sam jumped up.

"*I* know!" he cried. "There's lots of leaves left on the branches. We can give them to him."

"I just said——"

"I don't mean the branches," Sam explained. "We'll leave the branches on the trees, but just pull the leaves off the branches and put 'em in the bucket and feed 'em to him out the bucket."

Penrod thought this plan worth trying, and for three-quarters of an hour the two boys were busy with the lower branches of various trees in the yard. Thus they managed to supply Whitey with a fair quantity of wet leaves, which he ate in a perfunctory way, displaying little of his earlier enthusiasm. And the work of his purveyors might have been more tedious if it had been less damp, for a boy is seldom bored by anything that involves his staying-out in the rain without protection. The drizzle had thickened; the leaves were heavy with water, and at every jerk the branches sent fat drops over the two collectors. They attained a note-worthy state of sogginess.

Finally, they were brought to the attention of the authorities indoors, and Della appeared upon the back porch.

"Musther Penrod," she called, "y'r mamma says ye'll c'm in the house this minute an' change y'r shoes an' stock-in's an' everythun' else ye got on! D'ye hear me?"

Penrod, taken by surprise and unpleasantly alarmed, darted away from the tree he was depleting and ran for the stable.

"You tell her I'm dry as toast!" he shouted over his shoulder.

Della withdrew, wearing the air of a person gratuitously insulted; and a moment later she issued from the kitchen, carrying an umbrella. She opened it and walked resolutely to the stable.

"She says I'm to bring ye in the house," said Della, "an' I'm goin' to bring ye!"

Sam had joined Penrod in the carriage-house, and, with the beginnings of an unnamed terror, the two beheld this grim advance. But they did not stay for its culmination. Without a word to each other they hurriedly tiptoed up the stairs to the gloomy loft, and there they paused, listening.

They heard Della's steps upon the carriage-house floor.

"Ah, there's plenty places t'hide in," they heard her say; "but I'll show ye! She tole me to bring ye, and I'm——"

She was interrupted by a peculiar sound—loud, chilling, dismal, and unmistakably not of human origin. The boys knew it for Whitey's cough; but Della had not their experience. A smothered shriek reached their ears; there was a scurrying noise, and then, with horror, they heard Della's footsteps in the passageway that ran by Whitey's manger. Immediately there came a louder shriek, and even in the anguish of knowing their secret discovered, they were shocked to hear distinctly the words, "O Lard in hivvin!" in the well-known voice of Della. She shrieked again, and they heard the rush of her footfalls across the carriage-house floor. Wild words came from the outer air, and the kitchen door slammed violently. It was all over. She had gone to "tell".

Penrod and Sam plunged down the stairs and out of the stable. They climbed the back fence and fled up the alley. They turned into Sam's yard, and, without consultation, headed for the cellar doors, nor paused till they found themselves in the farthest, darkest and gloomiest recess of the cellar. There, perspiring, stricken with fear, they sank down upon the earthen floor, with their moist backs against the stone wall.

Thus with boys. The vague apprehensions that had been

creeping upon Penrod and Sam all afternoon had become monstrous; the unknown was before them. How great their crime would turn out to be (now that it was in the hands of grown people) they did not know; but, since it concerned a horse, it would undoubtedly be considered of terrible dimensions.

Their plans for a reward, and all the things that had seemed both innocent and practical in the morning, now staggered their minds as manifestations of criminal folly. A new and terrible light seemed to play upon the day's exploits; they had chased a horse belonging to strangers, and it would be said that they deliberately drove him into the stable and there concealed him. They had, in truth, virtually stolen him, and they had stolen food for him. The waning light through the small window above them warned Penrod that his inroads upon the vegetables in his own cellar must soon be discovered. Della, that Nemesis, would seek them in order to prepare them for dinner, and she would find them not. But she would recall his excursion to the cellar, for she had seen him when he came up; and also the truth would be known concerning the loaf of bread. Altogether, Penrod felt that his case was worse than Sam's —until Sam offered a suggestion that roused such horrible possibilities concerning the principal item of their offense that all thought of the smaller indictments disappeared.

"Listen, Penrod," Sam quavered: "What—what if that —what if that ole horse maybe b'longed to a—policeman!" Sam's imagination was not of the comforting kind. "What'd they—do to us, Penrod, if it turned out he was some policeman's horse?"

Penrod was able only to shake his head. He did not reply in words; but both boys thenceforth considered it almost inevitable that Whitey *had* belonged to a policeman, and, in their sense of so ultimate a disaster, they ceased for a time to brood upon what their parents would probably do to them. The penalty for stealing a policeman's horse would be only a step short of capital, they were sure. They would not be hanged; but vague, looming sketches of something called the penitentiary began to flicker before them.

It grew darker in the cellar, so that finally they could not see each other.

"I guess they're huntin' for us by now," Sam said huskily. "I don't—I don't like it much down here, Penrod."

Penrod's hoarse whisper came from the profound gloom: "Well, who ever said you did?"

"Well——" Sam paused; then he said plaintively, "I wish we'd never *seen* that dern ole horse."

"It was every bit his fault," said Penrod. "*We* didn't do anything. If he hadn't come stickin' his ole head in our stable, it'd never happened at all. Ole fool!" He rose. "I'm goin' to get out of here; I guess I've stood about enough for one day."

"Where—where you goin', Penrod? You aren't goin' *home*, are you?"

"No; I'm not! What you take me for? You think I'm crazy?"

"Well, where *can* we go?"

How far Penrod's desperation actually would have led him is doubtful; but he made this statement: "I don't know where *you're* goin', but *I'm* goin' to walk straight out in the country till I come to a farmhouse and say my name's George and live there!"

"I'll do it, too," Sam whispered eagerly. "I'll say my name's Henry."

"Well, we better get started," said the executive Penrod. "We got to get away from here, anyway."

But when they came to ascend the steps leading to the "outside doors", they found that those doors had been closed and locked for the night.

"It's no use," Sam lamented, "and we can't bust 'em, cause I tried to, once before. Fanny always locks 'em about five o'clock—I forgot. We got to go up the stairway and try to sneak out through the house."

They tiptoed back, and up the inner stairs. They paused

at the top, then breathlessly stepped out into a hall that was entirely dark. Sam touched Penrod's sleeve in warning, and bent to listen at a door.

Immediately that door opened, revealing the bright library, where sat Penrod's mother and Sam's father.

It was Sam's mother who had opened the door. "Come into the library, boys," she said. "Mrs. Schofield is just telling us about it."

And as the two comrades moved dumbly into the lighted room, Penrod's mother rose, and, taking him by the shoulder, urged him close to the fire.

"You stand there and try to dry off a little, while I finish telling Mr. and Mrs. Williams about you and Sam," she said. "You'd better make Sam keep near the fire, too, Mrs. Williams, because they both got wringing wet. Think of their running off just when most people would have wanted to stay! Well, I'll go on with the story, then. Della told me all about it, and what the cook next door said *she'd* seen, how they'd been trying to pull grass and leaves for the poor old thing all day—and all about the apples they carried from *your* cellar, and getting wet and working in the rain as hard as they could—and they'd given him a loaf of bread! Shame on you, Penrod!" She paused to laugh; but there was a little moisture about her eyes, even before she laughed. "And they'd fed him on potatoes and lettuce and cabbage and turnips out of *our* cellar! And I wish you'd seen the sawdust bed they made for him! Well, when I'd telephoned, and the Humane Society man got there, he said it was the most touching thing he ever knew. It seems he *knew* this horse, and had been looking for him. He said ninety-nine boys out of a hundred would have chased the poor old thing away; he said he thought Sam and Penrod were the finest boys in town."

Mr. Williams coughed. "Well, I declare," he said. "Why, boys, that's splendid!"

Sam and Penrod were too busy looking modestly noble to look at each other.

CHAPTER XXXIII

CONSCIENCE

MRS. SCHOFIELD had been away for three days, visiting her sister in Dayton, Illinois, and on the train, coming back, she fell into a reverie. Little dramas of memory were reënacted in her pensive mind, and through all of them moved the figure of Penrod as a principal figure, or star. These little dramas did not present Penrod as he really was, much less did they glow with the uncertain but glamorous light in which Penrod saw himself. No; Mrs. Schofield had indulged herself in absence from her family merely for her own pleasure, and, now that she was homeward bound, her conscience was asserting itself; the fact that she had enjoyed her visit began to take on the aspect of a crime.

She had heard from her family only once during the three days—the message "All well don't worry enjoy yourself" telegraphed by Mr. Schofield, and she had followed his suggestions to a reasonable extent. Of course she had worried—but only at times; wherefore she now suffered more and more poignant pangs of shame because she had not worried constantly. Naturally, the figure of Penrod, in her railway reverie, was that of an invalid.

She recalled all the illnesses of his babyhood and all those of his boyhood. She reconstructed scene after scene, with the hero always prostrate and the family physician opening the black case of phials. She emphatically renewed her recollection of accidental misfortunes to the body of Penrod Schofield, omitting neither the considerable nor the inconsiderable, forgetting no strain, sprain, cut, bruise or dislocation of which she had knowledge. And running this film in a sequence unrelieved by brighter interludes, she produced a biographical picture of such consistent and unremittent gloom that Penrod's past appeared to justify disturbing thoughts about his present and future.

She became less and less at ease, reproaching herself for having gone away, wondering how she had brought herself to do such a crazy thing, for it seemed to her that the members of her family were almost helpless without her guidance; they were apt to do anything—anything at all—or to catch anything. The more she thought about her having left these irresponsible harebrains unprotected and undirected for three days, the less she was able to account for her action. It seemed to her that she must have been a little flighty; but, shaking her head grimly, she decided that flightiness was not a good excuse. And she made up her mind that if, upon her arrival, she found poor little neglected Penrod (and Margaret and Mr. Schofield) spared to her, safe and sound, she would make up to them—especially to Penrod—for all her lack of care in the past, and for this present wild folly of spending three whole days and nights with her sister, far away in Dayton, Illinois.

Consequently, when Mrs. Schofield descended from that train, she wore the hurried but determined expression that was always the effect upon her of a guilty conscience.

"You're *sure* Penrod is well now?" she repeated, after Mr. Schofield had seated himself at her side in a vehicle known to its driver as a "deepoe hack".

"'Well *now?*'" he said. "He's been well all the time. I've told you twice that he's all right."

"Men can't always see." She shook her head impatiently. "I haven't been a bit sure he was well lately. I don't think he's been really well for two or three months. How has he seemed to-day?"

"In fair health," Mr. Schofield replied thoughtfully. "Della called me up at the office to tell me that one of the telephone-men had come into the house to say that if that durn boy didn't quit climbing their poles they'd have him arrested. They said he——"

"That's it!" Mrs. Schofield interrupted quickly. "He's nervous. It's some nervous trouble makes him act like that. He's not like himself at all."

"Sometimes," Mr. Schofield said, "I wish he weren't."

"When he's himself," Mrs. Schofield went on anxiously, "he's very quiet and good; he doesn't go climbing telegraph-poles and reckless things like that. And I noticed before I went away that he was growing twitchy, and seemed to be getting the habit of making unpleasant little noises in his throat."

"Don't fret about that," her husband said. "He was trying to learn Sam Williams's imitation of a bullfrog's croak. I used to do that myself when I was a boy. Gl-glump, gallump! No; I can't do it now. But nearly all boys feel obliged to learn it."

"You're entirely mistaken, Henry," she returned a little sharply. "That isn't the way he goes in his throat. Penrod is getting to be a *very* nervous boy, and he makes noises because he can't help it. He works part of his face, too,

sometimes, so much that I've been afraid it would interfere
with his looks."

"Interfere with his what?" For the moment, Mr. Schofield seemed to be dazed.

"When he's himself," she returned crisply, "he's quite a
handsome boy."

"He is?"

"Handsomer than the average, anyhow," Mrs. Schofield
said firmly. "No wonder you don't see it—when we've let
his system get all run down like this!"

"Good heavens!" the mystified Mr. Schofield murmured.
"Penrod's system hasn't been running down; it's just the
same as it always was. He's absolutely all right."

"Indeed he is not!" she said severely. "We've got to take
better care of him than we have been."

"Why, how could——"

"I know what I'm talking about," she interrupted. "Penrod is anything but a strong boy, and it's all our fault. We
haven't been watchful enough of his health; that's what's
the matter with him and makes him so nervous."

Thus she continued, and, as she talked on, Mr. Schofield
began, by imperceptible processes, to adopt her views. As
for Mrs. Schofield herself, these views became substantial
by becoming vocal. This is to say, with all deference, that
as soon as she heard herself stating them she was convinced that they accurately represented facts. And the determined look in her eyes deepened when the "deepoe hack"
turned the familiar corner and she saw Penrod running to
the gate, followed by Duke.

Never had Penrod been so glad to greet his mother. Never
was he more boisterous in the expression of happiness of that
kind. And the tokens of his appetite at dinner, a little later,
were extraordinary. Mr. Schofield began to feel reassured
in spite of himself; but Mrs. Schofield shook her head.

"Don't you see? It's abnormal!" she said, in a low, decisive voice.

★   ★   ★

That night Penrod awoke from a sweet, conscienceless slumber—or, rather, he was awakened. A wrappered form lurked over him in the gloom.

"Uff—ow——" he muttered, and turned his face from the dim light that shone through the doorway. He sighed and sought the depths of sleep again.

"Penrod," his mother said softly, and, while he resisted feebly, she turned him over to face her.

"Gawn lea' me 'lone," he muttered.

Then, as a little sphere touched his lips, he jerked his head away, startled.

"Whassat?"

Mrs. Schofield replied in tones honeysweet and coaxing: "It's just a nice little pill, Penrod."

"Doe waw 'ny!" he protested, keeping his eyes shut, clinging to the sleep from which he was being riven.

"Be a good boy, Penrod," she whispered. "Here's a glass of nice cool water to swallow it down with. Come, dear; it's going to do you lots of good."

And again the little pill was placed suggestively against his lips; but his head jerked backward, and his hand struck out in blind, instinctive self-defense.

"I'll *bust* that ole pill," he muttered, still with closed eyes. "Lemme get my han's on it an' I will!"

"Penrod!"

"*Please* go on away, Mamma!"

"I will, just as soon as you take this little pill."

"I *did!*"

"No, dear."

"I did," Penrod insisted plaintively. "You made me take it just before I went to bed."

"Oh, yes; *that* one. But, dearie," Mrs. Schofield explained, "I got to thinking about it after I went to bed, and I decided you'd better have another."

"I don't *want* another."

"Yes, dearie."

"Please go 'way and let me sleep."

"Not till you've taken the little pill, dear."

"Oh, *golly!*" Groaning, he propped himself upon an elbow and allowed the pill to pass between his lips. (He would have allowed anything whatever to pass between them, if that passing permitted his return to slumber.) Then, detaining the pill in his mouth, he swallowed half a glass of water, and again was recumbent.

"G'-night, Mamma."

"Good-night, dearie. Sleep well."

"Yes'm."

After her departure Penrod drowsily enjoyed the sugar coating of the pill; but this was indeed a brief pleasure. A bitterness that was like a pang suddenly made itself known to his sense of taste, and he realized that he had dallied too confidingly with the product of a manufacturing chemist who should have been indicted for criminal economy. The medicinal portion of the little pill struck the wall with a faint tap, then dropped noiselessly to the floor, and, after a time, Penrod slept.

Some hours later he began to dream; he dreamed that his feet and legs were becoming uncomfortable as a result of Sam Williams's activities with a red-hot poker.

"You *quit* that!" he said aloud, and awoke indignantly. Again a dark, wrappered figure hovered over the bed.

"It's only a hot-water bag, dear," Mrs. Schofield said, still labouring under the covers with an extended arm. "You mustn't hunch yourself up that way, Penrod. Put your feet down on it."

And, as he continued to hunch himself, she moved the bag in the direction of his withdrawal.

"Ow, murder!" he exclaimed convulsively. "What you tryin' to do? Scald me to death?"

"Penrod——"

"My goodness, Mamma," he wailed; "can't you let me sleep a *minute?*"

"It's very bad for you to let your feet get cold, dear."

"They *weren't* cold. I don't want any ole hot-wat——"

"Penrod," she said firmly, "you must put your feet against the bag. It isn't too hot."

"Oh, isn't it?" he retorted. "I don't s'pose you'd care if I burned my feet right off! Mamma, won't you please, pul-*leeze* let me get some sleep?"

"Not till you——"

She was interrupted by a groan that seemed to come from an abyss.

"All right, I'll do it! Let 'em burn, then!" Thus spake the desperate Penrod; and Mrs. Schofield was able to ascertain that one heel had been placed in light contact with the bag.

"No; both feet, Penrod."

With a tragic shiver he obeyed.

"*That's* right, dear! Now, keep them that way. It's good for you. Good-night."

"G'-night!"

The door closed softly behind her, and the body of Penrod, from the hips upward, rose invisibly in the complete darkness of the bedchamber. A moment later the hot-water bag reached the floor in as noiseless a manner as that previously adopted by the remains of the little pill, and Penrod once more bespread his soul with poppies. This time he slept until the breakfast-bell rang.

He was late to school, and at once found himself in difficulties. Government demanded an explanation of the tardiness; but Penrod made no reply of any kind. Taciturnity is seldom more strikingly out of place than under such circumstances, and the penalties imposed took account not only of Penrod's tardiness but of his supposititious defiance of authority in declining to speak. The truth was that Penrod did not know why he was tardy, and, with mind still lethargic, found it impossible to think of an excuse—his continuing silence being due merely to the persistence of his efforts to invent one. Thus were his meek searchings misinterpreted, and the unloved hours of improvement in science and the arts made odious.

"They'll *see!*" he whispered sorely to himself, as he bent low over his desk, a little later. Some day he would "show 'em". The picture in his mind was of a vast, vague assembly of people headed by Miss Spence and the superior pupils who were never tardy, and these multitudes, representing persecution and government in general, were all cringing before a Penrod Schofield who rode a grim black horse up and down their miserable ranks, and gave curt orders.

"Make 'em step back there!" he commanded his myrmidons savagely. "Fix it so's your horses'll step on their feet if they don't do what I say!" Then, from his shining saddle, he watched the throngs slinking away. "I guess they know who I am *now!*"

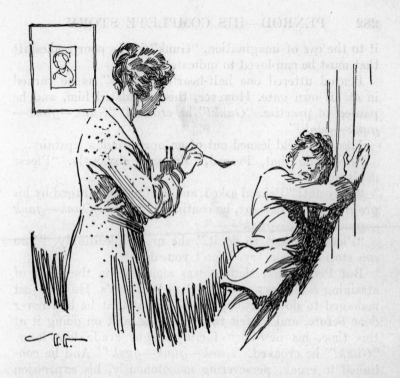

CHAPTER XXXIV

THE TONIC

THESE broodings helped a little; but it was a severe
morning, and on his way home at noon he did not
recover heart enough to practise the bullfrog's croak,
the craft that Sam Williams had lately mastered to inspiring perfection. This sonorous accomplishment Penrod had
determined to make his own. At once guttural and reso-
nant, impudent yet plaintive, with a barbaric twang like
the plucked string of a Congo war-fiddle, the sound had
fascinated him. It is made in the throat by processes utterly
impossible to describe in human words, and no alphabet as
yet produced by civilized man affords the symbols to vocalize

it to the ear of imagination. "Gunk" is the poor makeshift that must be employed to indicate it.

Penrod uttered one half-hearted *"Gunk"* as he turned in at his own gate. However, this stimulated him, and he paused to practise. *"Gunk!"* he croaked. *"Gunk—gunk—gunk—gunk!"*

Mrs. Schofield leaned out of an open window upstairs.

"Don't do that, Penrod," she said anxiously. "Please don't do that."

"Why not?" Penrod asked, and, feeling encouraged by his progress in the new art, he continued: *"Gunk! Gunk—gunk—gunk! Gunk—gunk——"*

"Please try not to do it," she urged pleadingly. "You *can* stop it if you try. Won't you, dear?"

But Penrod felt that he was almost upon the point of attaining a mastery equal to Sam Williams's. He had just managed to do something in his throat that he had never done before, and he felt that unless he kept on doing it at this time, his new-born facility might evade him later. *"Gunk!"* he croaked. *"Gunk—gunk—gunk!"* And he continued to croak, persevering monotonously, his expression indicating the depth of his preoccupation.

His mother looked down solicitously, murmured in a melancholy undertone, shook her head; then disappeared from the window, and, after a moment or two, opened the front door.

"Come in, dear," she said; "I've got something for you."

Penrod's look of preoccupation vanished; he brightened and ceased to croak. His mother had already given him a small leather pocketbook with a nickel in it, as a souvenir of her journey. Evidently she had brought another gift as well, delaying its presentation until now. "I've got something for you!" These were auspicious words.

"What is it, Mamma?" he asked, and, as she smiled tenderly upon him, his gayety increased. "Yay!" he shouted. "Mamma, is it that reg'lar carpenter's tool chest I told you about?"

"No," she said. "But I'll show you, Penrod. Come on, dear."

He followed her with alacrity to the dining-room, and the bright anticipation in his eyes grew more brilliant— until she opened the door of the china-closet, simultaneously with that action announcing cheerily:

"It's something that's going to do you lots of good, Penrod."

He was instantly chilled, for experience had taught him that when predictions of this character were made, nothing pleasant need be expected. Two seconds later his last hope departed as she turned from the closet and he beheld in her hands a quart bottle containing what appeared to be a section of grassy swamp immersed in a cloudy brown liquor. He stepped back, grave suspicion in his glance.

"What *is* that?" he asked, in a hard voice.

Mrs. Schofield smiled upon him. "It's nothing," she said. "That is, it's nothing you'll mind at all. It's just so you won't be so nervous."

"I'm not nervous."

"You don't think so, of course, dear," she returned, and, as she spoke, she poured some of the brown liquor into a tablespoon. "People often can't tell when they're nervous themselves; but your Papa and I have been getting a little anxious about you, dear, and so I got this medicine for you."

"*Where'd* you get it?" he demanded.

Mrs. Schofield set the bottle down and moved toward him, insinuatingly extending the full tablespoon.

"Here, dear," she said; "just take this little spoonful, like a goo——"

"I want to know where it came from," he insisted darkly, again stepping backward.

"Where?" she echoed absently, watching to see that nothing was spilled from the spoon as she continued to move toward him. "Why, I was talking to old Mrs. Wottaw at market this morning, and she said her son Clark used to have nervous trouble, and she told me about this medicine and how to have it made at the drug store. She told me it cured Clark, and——"

"I don't want to be cured," Penrod said, adding inconsistently, "I haven't got anything to be cured of."

"Now, dear," Mrs. Schofield began, "you don't want your Papa and me to keep on worrying about——"

"I don't care whether you worry or not," the heartless boy interrupted. "I don't want to take any horrable ole medicine. What's that grass and weeds in the bottle for?"

Mrs. Schofield looked grieved. "There isn't any grass and there aren't any weeds; those are healthful herbs."

"I bet they'll make me sick."

She sighed. "Penrod, we're trying to make you well."

"But I *am* well, I tell you!"

"No, dear; your Papa's been very much troubled about you. Come, Penrod; swallow this down and don't make such a fuss about it. It's just for your own good."

And she advanced upon him again, the spoon extended toward his lips. It almost touched them, for he had retreated until his back was against the wall-paper. He could go no farther; but he evinced his unshaken repugnance by averting his face.

"What's it taste like?" he demanded.

"It's not unpleasant at all," she answered, poking the spoon at his mouth. "Mrs. Wottaw said Clark used to be very fond of it. 'It doesn't taste like ordinary medicine at all,' she said."

"How often I got to take it?" Penrod mumbled, as the persistent spoon sought to enter his mouth. "Just this once?"

"No, dear; three times a day."

"I won't do it!"

"Penrod!" She spoke sharply. "You swallow this down and stop making such a fuss. I can't be all day. Hurry!"

She inserted the spoon between his lips, so that its rim touched his clenched teeth; he was still reluctant. Moreover, his reluctance was natural and characteristic, for a boy's sense of taste is as simple and as peculiar as a dog's, though, of course, altogether different from a dog's. A boy, passing through the experimental age, may eat and drink astonishing things; but they must be of his own choosing. His palate is tender, and, in one sense, might be called fastidious; nothing is more sensitive or more easily shocked. A boy tastes things much *more* than grown people taste them: what is merely unpleasant to a man is sheer broth of hell to a boy. Therefore, not knowing what might be encountered, Penrod continued to be reluctant.

"Penrod," his mother exclaimed, losing patience, "I'll call your Papa to make you take it, if you don't swallow it right down! Open your mouth, Penrod! It isn't going to taste bad at all. Open your mouth—*there!*"

The reluctant jaw relaxed at last, and Mrs. Schofield dexterously elevated the handle of the spoon so that the brown liquor was deposited within her son.

"There!" she repeated triumphantly. "It wasn't so bad after all, was it?"

Penrod did not reply. His expression had become odd, and the oddity of his manner was equal to that of his expression. Uttering no sound, he seemed to distend, as if he had suddenly become a pneumatic boy under dangerous pressure. Meanwhile, his reddening eyes, fixed awfully upon his mother, grew unbearable.

"Now, it wasn't such a bad taste," Mrs. Schofield said rather nervously. "Don't go acting *that* way, Penrod!"

But Penrod could not help himself. In truth, even a grown person hardened to all manner of flavours, and able to eat caviar or liquid Camembert, would have found the cloudy brown liquor virulently repulsive. It contained in solution, with other things, the vital element of surprise, for it was comparatively odourless, and, unlike the chivalrous rattlesnake, gave no warning of what it was about to do. In the case of Penrod, the surprise was complete and its effect visibly shocking.

The distention by which he began to express his emotion appeared to be increasing; his slender throat swelled as his cheeks puffed. His shoulders rose toward his ears; he lifted his right leg in an unnatural way and held it rigidly in the air.

"Stop that, Penrod!" Mrs. Schofield commanded. "You stop it!"

He found his voice.

"Uff! *Oooff!*" he said thickly, and collapsed—a mere, ordinary, every-day convulsion taking the place of his pneumatic symptoms. He began to writhe, at the same time opening and closing his mouth rapidly and repeatedly, waving his arms, stamping on the floor.

"Ow! Ow-ow-*ow!*" he vociferated.

Reassured by these normal demonstrations, of a type with which she was familiar, Mrs. Schofield resumed her fond smile.

"*You're* all right, little boysie!" she said heartily. Then, picking up the bottle, she replenished the tablespoon, and told Penrod something she had considered it undiplomatic to mention before.

"Here's the other one," she said sweetly.

"Uuf!" he sputtered. "Other—uh—what?"

"Two tablespoons before each meal," she informed him.

Instantly Penrod made the first of a series of passionate efforts to leave the room. His determination was so intense, and the manifestations of it were so ruthless, that Mrs. Schofield, exhausted, found herself obliged to call for the official head of the house—in fact, she found herself obliged to shriek for him; and Mr. Schofield, hastily entering the room, beheld his wife apparently in the act of sawing his son back and forth across the sill of an open window.

Penrod made a frantic effort to reach the good green earth, even after his mother's clutch upon his ankle had been reënforced by his father's. Nor was the lad's revolt subdued when he was deposited upon the floor and the window closed. Indeed, it may be said that he actually never gave up, though it is a fact that the second potion was successfully placed inside him. But by the time this feat was finally accomplished, Mr. Schofield had proved that, in spite of middle age, he was entitled to substantial claims and honours both as athlete and orator—his oratory being founded less upon the school of Webster and more upon that of Jeremiah.

So the thing was done, and the double dose put within the person of Penrod Schofield. It proved not ineffective there, and presently, as its new owner sat morosely at table, he began to feel slightly dizzy and his eyes refused him perfect service. This was natural, because two tablespoons of the cloudy brown liquor contained about the amount of alcohol to be found in an ordinary cocktail. Now a boy does not enjoy the effects of intoxication; enjoyment of that kind is obtained only by studious application. Therefore, Penrod spoke of his symptoms complainingly, and even showed himself so vindictive as to attribute them to the new medicine.

His mother made no reply. Instead, she nodded her head as if some inner conviction had proven well founded.

"*Bilious, too,*" she whispered to her husband.

That evening, during the half-hour preceding dinner, the dining-room was the scene of another struggle, only a little less desperate than that which had been the prelude to lunch, and again an appeal to the head of the house was found necessary. Muscular activity and a liberal imitation of the jeremiads once more subjugated the rebel—and the same rebellion and its suppression in a like manner took place the following morning before breakfast. But this was Saturday, and, without warning or apparent reason, a remarkable change came about at noon. However, Mr. and Mrs. Schofield were used to inexplicable changes in Penrod, and they missed its significance.

When Mrs. Schofield, with dread in her heart, called Penrod into the house "to take his medicine" before lunch, he came briskly, and took it like a lamb!

"Why, Penrod, that's splendid!" she cried. "You see it isn't bad, at all."

"No'm," he said meekly. "Not when you get used to it."

"And aren't you ashamed, making all that fuss?" she went on happily.

"Yes'm, I guess so."

"And don't you feel better? Don't you see how much good it's doing you already?"

"Yes'm, I guess so."

Upon a holiday morning, several weeks later, Penrod and Sam Williams revived a pastime that they called "drug store", setting up display counters, selling chemical, cosmetic and other compounds to imaginary customers, filling prescriptions and variously conducting themselves in a pharmaceutical manner. They were in the midst of affairs when Penrod interrupted his partner and himself with a cry of recollection.

"*I* know!" he shouted. "I got some mighty good ole stuff we want. You wait!" And, dashing to the house, he disappeared.

Returning immediately, Penrod placed upon the principal counter of the "drug store" a large bottle. It was a quart bottle, in fact; and it contained what appeared to be a section of grassy swamp immersed in a cloudy brown liquor.

"There!" Penrod exclaimed. "How's that for some good ole medicine?"

"It's good ole stuff," Sam said approvingly. "Where'd you get it? Whose is it, Penrod?"

"It *was* mine," said Penrod. "Up to about serreval days ago, it was. They quit givin' it to me. I had to take two bottles and a half of it."

"What did you haf to take it for?"

"I got nervous, or sumpthing," said Penrod.

"You all well again now?"

"I guess so. I expect she got too busy to think about it,

or sumpthing. Anyway, she quit makin' me take it, and said I was lots better. She's forgot all about it by this time."

Sam was looking at the bottle with great interest.

"What's all that stuff in there, Penrod?" he asked. "What's all that stuff in there looks like grass?"

"It *is* grass," said Penrod.

"How'd it get there?"

"I stuck it in there," the candid boy replied. "First they had some horrable ole stuff in there like to killed me. But after they got three doses down me, I took the bottle out in the yard and cleaned her all out and pulled a lot o' good ole grass and stuffed her pretty full and poured in a lot o' good ole hydrant water on top of it. Then, when they got the next bottle, I did the same way, and——"

"It don't look like water," Sam objected.

Penrod laughed a superior laugh.

"Oh, that's nothin'," he said, with the slight swagger of young and conscious genius. "Of course, I had to slip in and shake her up sometimes, so's they wouldn't notice."

"But what did you put in it to make it look like that?"

Penrod, upon the point of replying, happened to glance toward the house. His gaze, lifting, rested for a moment upon a window. The head of Mrs. Schofield was framed in that window. She nodded gayly to her son. She could see him plainly, and she thought that he seemed perfectly healthy, and as happy as a boy could be. She was right.

"What *did* you put in it?" Sam insisted.

And probably it was just as well that, though Mrs. Schofield could see her son, the distance was too great for her to hear him.

"Oh, nothin'," Penrod replied. "Nothin' but a little good ole mud."

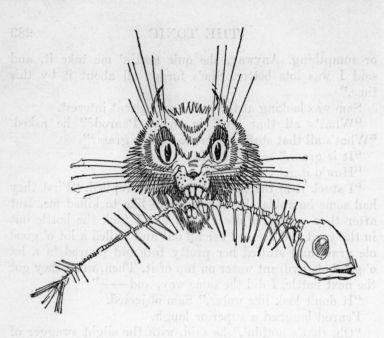

CHAPTER XXXV

GIPSY

ON A fair Saturday afternoon in November Penrod's little old dog Duke returned to the ways of his youth and had trouble with a strange cat on the back porch. This indiscretion, so uncharacteristic, was due to the agitation of a surprised moment, for Duke's experience had inclined him to a peaceful pessimism, and he had no ambition for hazardous undertakings of any sort. He was given to musing but not to avoidable action, and he seemed habitually to hope for something that he was pretty sure would not happen. Even in his sleep, this gave him an air of wistfulness.

Thus, being asleep in a nook behind the metal refuse-can, when the strange cat ventured to ascend the steps of the porch, his appearance was so unwarlike that the cat felt

encouraged to extend its field of reconnaissance—for the
cook had been careless, and the backbone of a three-pound
whitefish lay at the foot of the refuse-can.

This cat was, for a cat, needlessly tall, powerful, independent and masculine. Once, long ago, he had been a
roly-poly pepper-and-salt kitten; he had a home in those
days, and a name, "Gipsy", which he abundantly justified.
He was precocious in dissipation. Long before his adolescence, his lack of domesticity was ominous, and he had
formed bad companionships. Meanwhile, he grew so rangy,
and developed such length and power of leg and such traits
of character, that the father of the little girl who owned him
was almost convincing when he declared that the young cat
was half broncho and half Malay pirate—though, in the
light of Gipsy's later career, this seems bitterly unfair to
even the lowest orders of bronchos and Malay pirates.

No; Gipsy was not the pet for a little girl. The rosy
hearthstone and sheltered rug were too circumspect for
him. Surrounded by the comforts of middle-class respect-
ability, and profoundly oppressed, even in his youth, by the
Puritan ideals of the household, he sometimes experienced
a sense of suffocation. He wanted free air and he wanted
free life; he wanted the lights, the lights and the music. He
abandoned the *bourgeoisie* irrevocably. He went forth in a
May twilight, carrying the evening beefsteak with him, and
joined the underworld.

His extraordinary size, his daring and his utter lack of
sympathy soon made him the leader—and, at the same time,
the terror—of all the loose-lived cats in a wide neighbourhood. He contracted no friendships and had no confidants.
He seldom slept in the same place twice in succession, and
though he was wanted by the police, he was not found. In
appearance he did not lack distinction of an ominous sort;
the slow, rhythmic, perfectly controlled mechanism of his
tail, as he impressively walked abroad, was incomparably
sinister. This stately and dangerous walk of his, his long,
vibrant whiskers, his scars, his yellow eye, so ice-cold, so

fire-hot, haughty as the eye of Satan, gave him the deadly air of a mousquetaire duellist. His soul was in that walk and in that eye; it could be read—the soul of a bravo of fortune, living on his wits and his valour, asking no favours and granting no quarter. Intolerant, proud, sullen, yet watchful and constantly planning—purely a militarist, believing in slaughter as in a religion, and confident that art, science, poetry and the good of the world were happily advanced thereby—Gipsy had become, though technically not a wild-cat, undoubtedly the most untamed cat at large in the civilized world. Such, in brief, was the terrifying creature that now elongated its neck, and, over the top step of the porch, bent a calculating scrutiny upon the wistful and slumberous Duke.

The scrutiny was searching but not prolonged. Gipsy muttered contemptuously to himself, "Oh, sheol; I'm not afraid o' *that!*" And he approached the fishbone, his padded feet making no noise upon the boards. It was a desirable fishbone, large, with a considerable portion of the fish's tail still attached to it.

It was about a foot from Duke's nose, and the little dog's dreams began to be troubled by his olfactory nerve. This faithful sentinel, on guard even while Duke slept, signalled that alarums and excursions by parties unknown were tak-ing place, and suggested that attention might well be paid. Duke opened one drowsy eye. What that eye beheld was monstrous.

Here was a strange experience—the horrific vision in the midst of things so accustomed. Sunshine fell sweetly upon porch and backyard; yonder was the familiar stable, and from its interior came the busy hum of a carpenter shop, established that morning by Duke's young master, in association with Samuel Williams and Herman. Here, close by, were the quiet refuse-can and the wonted brooms and mops leaning against the latticed wall at the end of the porch, and there, by the foot of the steps, was the stone slab of the cistern, with the iron cover displaced and lying beside the round opening, where the carpenters had left it, not half an hour ago, after lowering a stick of wood into the water, "to season it". All about Duke were these usual and reassuring environs of his daily life, and yet it was his fate to behold, right in the midst of them, and in ghastly juxtaposition to his face, a thing of nightmare and lunacy.

Gipsy had seized the fishbone by the middle. Out from one side of his head, and mingling with his whiskers, projected the long, spiked spine of the big fish; down from the other side of that ferocious head dangled the fish's tail, and from above the remarkable effect thus produced shot the intolerable glare of two yellow eyes. To the gaze of Duke, still blurred by slumber, this monstrosity was all of one piece—the bone seemed a living part of it. What he saw was like those interesting insect-faces that the magnifying glass reveals to great M. Fabre. It was impossible for Duke to maintain the philosophic calm of M. Fabre, however; there was no magnifying glass between him and this spined and spiky face. Indeed, Duke was not in a position to think the matter over quietly. If he had been able to do that, he would have said to himself: "We have here an animal of most peculiar and unattractive appearance, though, upon examination, it seems to be only a cat stealing a fishbone. Nevertheless, as the thief is large beyond all my recollection of cats and has an unpleasant stare, I will leave this spot at once."

On the contrary, Duke was so electrified by his horrid awakening that he completely lost his presence of mind. In the very instant of his first eye's opening, the other eye and his mouth behaved similarly, the latter loosing upon the quiet air one shriek of mental agony before the little dog scrambled to his feet and gave further employment to his voice in a frenzy of profanity. At the same time the subterranean diapason of a demoniac bass viol was heard; it rose to a wail, and rose and rose again till it screamed like a small siren. It was Gipsy's war-cry, and, at the sound of it, Duke became a frothing maniac. He made a convulsive frontal attack upon the hobgoblin—and the massacre began.

Never releasing the fishbone for an instant, Gipsy laid back his ears in a chilling way, beginning to shrink into himself like a concertina, but rising amidships so high that he appeared to be giving an imitation of that peaceful beast, the dromedary. Such was not his purpose, however, for, having attained his greatest possible altitude, he partially sat down and elevated his right arm after the manner of a semaphore. This semaphore arm remained rigid for a second, threatening; then it vibrated with inconceivable rapidity, feinting. But it was the treacherous left that did the work. Seemingly this left gave Duke three lightning little pats upon the right ear; but the change in his voice indicated that these were no love-taps. He yelled "help!" and "bloody murder!"

Never had such a shattering uproar, all vocal, broken out upon a peaceful afternoon. Gipsy possessed a vocabulary for cat-swearing certainly second to none out of Italy, and probably equal to the best there, while Duke remembered and uttered things he had not thought of for years.

The hum of the carpenter shop ceased, and Sam Williams appeared in the stable doorway. He stared insanely.

"My gorry!" he shouted. "Duke's havin' a fight with the biggest cat you ever saw in your life! C'mon!"

His feet were already in motion toward the battlefield, with Penrod and Herman hurrying in his wake. Onward they sped, and Duke was encouraged by the sight and sound of these reënforcements to increase his own outrageous clamours and to press home his attack. But he was ill-advised. This time it was the right arm of the semaphore that dipped—and Duke's honest nose was but too conscious of what happened in consequence.

A lump of dirt struck the refuse-can with violence, and Gipsy beheld the advance of overwhelming forces. They rushed upon him from two directions, cutting off the steps of the porch. Undaunted, the formidable cat raked Duke's nose again, somewhat more lingeringly, and prepared to depart with his fishbone. He had little fear for himself, because he was inclined to think that, unhampered, he could whip anything on earth; still, things seemed to be growing rather warm and he saw nothing to prevent his leaving.

And though he could laugh in the face of so unequal an antagonist as Duke, Gipsy felt that he was never at his best or able to do himself full justice unless he could perform that feline operation inaccurately known as "spitting". To his notion, this was an absolute essential to combat; but, as all cats of the slightest pretensions to technique perfectly understand, it can neither be well done nor produce the best effects unless the mouth be opened to its utmost capacity so as to expose the beginnings of the alimentary canal, down which—at least that is the intention of the threat—the opposing party will soon be passing. And Gipsy could not open his mouth without relinquishing his fishbone.

Therefore, on small accounts he decided to leave the field to his enemies and to carry the fishbone elsewhere. He took two giant leaps. The first landed him upon the edge of the porch. There, without an instant's pause, he gathered his fur-sheathed muscles, concentrated himself into one big steel spring, and launched himself superbly into space. He made a stirring picture, however brief, as he left the solid porch behind him and sailed upward on an ascending curve into the sunlit air. His head was proudly up; he was the incarnation of menacing power and of self-confidence. It is possible that the whitefish's spinal column and flopping tail had interfered with his vision, and in launching himself he may have mistaken the dark, round opening of the cistern for its dark, round cover. In that case, it was a leap calculated and executed with precision, for as the boys clamoured their pleased astonishment, Gipsy descended accurately into the orifice and passed majestically from public view, with the fishbone still in his mouth and his haughty head still high.

There was a grand splash!

CHAPTER XXXVI

CONCERNING TROUSERS

DUKE, hastening to place himself upon the stone slab, raged at his enemy in safety; and presently the indomitable Gipsy could be heard from the darkness below, turning on the bass of his siren, threatening the water that enveloped him, returning Duke's profanity with interest, and cursing the general universe.

"You hush!" Penrod stormed, rushing at Duke. "You go 'way from here! You *Duke!*"

And Duke, after prostrating himself, decided that it would be a relief to obey and to consider his responsibilities in this matter at an end. He withdrew beyond a corner of the house, thinking deeply.

"Why'n't you let him bark at the ole cat?" Sam Williams inquired, sympathizing with the oppressed. "I guess you'd want to bark if a cat had been treatin' you the way this one did Duke."

"Well, we got to get this cat out o' here, haven't we?" Penrod demanded crossly.

"What fer?" Herman asked. "Mighty mean cat! If it was me, I let 'at ole cat drownd."

"My goodness," Penrod cried. "What you want to let it drown for? Anyways, we got to use this water in our house, haven't we? You don't s'pose people like to use water that's got a cat drowned in it, do you? It gets pumped up into the tank in the attic and goes all over the house, and I bet you wouldn't want to see your father and mother usin' water a cat was drowned in. I guess I don't want my father and moth——"

"Well, how *can* we get it out?" Sam asked, cutting short this virtuous oration. "It's swimmin' around down there," he continued, peering into the cistern, "and kind of roaring, and it must of dropped its fishbone, 'cause it's spittin' just awful. I guess maybe it's mad 'cause it fell in there."

"I don't know how it's goin' to be got out," said Penrod; "but I know it's *got* to be got out, and that's all there is to it! I'm not goin' to have my father and mother——"

"Well, once," said Sam, "once when a kitten fell down *our* cistern, Papa took a pair of his trousers, and he held 'em by the end of one leg, and let 'em hang down through the hole till the end of the other leg was in the water, and the kitten went and clawed hold of it, and he pulled it right up, easy as anything. Well, that's the way to do now, 'cause if a kitten could keep hold of a pair of trousers, I guess this ole cat could. It's the biggest cat *I* ever saw! All you got to do is to go and ast your mother for a pair of your father's trousers, and we'll have this ole cat out o' there in no time."

Penrod glanced toward the house perplexedly.

"She ain't home, and I'd be afraid to——"

"Well, take your own, then," Sam suggested briskly.

"You take 'em off in the stable, and wait in there, and I and Herman'll get the cat out."

Penrod had no enthusiasm for this plan; but he affected to consider it.

"Well, I don't know 'bout that," he said, and then, after gazing attentively into the cistern and making some eye measurements of his knickerbockers, he shook his head. "They'd be too short. They wouldn't be *near* long enough!"

"Then neither would mine," said Sam promptly.

"Herman's would," said Penrod.

"No, suh!" Herman had recently been promoted to long trousers, and he expressed a strong disinclination to fall in with Penrod's idea. "My Mammy sit up late nights sewin' on 'ese britches fer me, makin' 'em outen of a pair o' Pappy's, an' they mighty good britches. Ain' goin' have no wet cat climbin' up 'em! No, suh!"

Both boys began to walk toward him argumentatively, while he moved slowly backward, shaking his head and denying them.

"I don't keer how much you talk!" he said. "Mammy give my *ole* britches to Verman, an' 'ese here ones on'y britches I got now, an' I'm go' to keep 'em on me—not take 'em off an' let ole wet cat splosh all over 'em. My Mammy, she sewed 'em fer *me*, I reckon—din' sew 'em fer no cat!"

"Oh, *please*, come on, Herman!" Penrod begged pathetically. "You don't want to see the poor cat drown, do you?"

"Mighty mean cat!" Herman said. "Bet' let 'at ole pussy-cat 'lone whur it is."

"Why, it'll only take a minute," Sam urged. "You just wait inside the stable and you'll have 'em back on again before you could say 'Jack Robinson'."

"I ain' got no use to say no Jack Robason," said Herman. "An' I ain' go' to han' over my britches fer *no* cat!"

"Listen here, Herman," Penrod began pleadingly. "You can watch us every minute through the crack in the stable door, can't you? We ain' goin' to *hurt* 'em any, are we? You can see everything we do, can't you? Look at here, Herman: you know that little saw you said you wished it was yours, in the carpenter shop? Well, honest, if you'll just let us take your trousers till we get this poor ole cat out the cistern, I'll give you that little saw."

Herman was shaken; he yearned for the little saw.

"You gimme her to keep?" he asked cautiously. "You gimme her befo' I han' over my britches?"

"You'll see!" Penrod ran into the stable, came back with the little saw, and placed it in Herman's hand. Herman could resist no longer, and two minutes later he stood in the necessary negligée within the shelter of the stable door, and watched, through the crack, the lowering of the surrendered garment into the cistern. His gaze was anxious, and surely nothing could have been more natural, since the removal had exposed Herman's brown legs, and, although the weather was far from inclement, November is never quite the month for people to be out of doors entirely without leg-covering. Therefore, he marked with impatience that Sam and Penrod, after lowering the trousers partway to the water, had withdrawn them and fallen into an argument.

"Name o' goo'ness!" Herman shouted. "I ain' got no time fer you all do so much talkin'. If you go' git 'at cat out, why'n't you *git* him?"

"Wait just a minute," Penrod called, and he came running to the stable, seized upon a large wooden box, which the carpenters had fitted with a lid and leather hinges, and returned with it cumbersomely to the cistern. "There!" he said. "That'll do to put it in. It won't get out o' that, I bet you!"

"Well, I'd like to know what you want to keep it for," Sam said peevishly, and, with the suggestion of a sneer, he added, "I s'pose you think somebody'll pay about a hunderd dollars reward or something, on account of a cat!"

"I don't, either!" Penrod protested hotly. "I know what I'm doin', I tell you."

"Well, what on earth——"

"I'll tell you some day, won't I?" Penrod cried. "I got my reasons for wantin' to keep this cat, and I'm goin' to keep it. *You* don't haf to ke——"

"Well, all right," Sam said shortly. "Anyways, it'll be dead if you don't hurry."

"It won't, either," Penrod returned, kneeling and peering down upon the dark water. "Listen to him! He's growlin' and spittin' away like anything! It takes a mighty fine-blooded cat to be as fierce as that. I bet you most cats would 'a' given up and drowned long ago. The water's awful cold, and I expect he was perty supprised when he lit in it."

"Herman's makin' a fuss again," Sam said. "We better get the ole cat out o' there if we're goin' to."

"Well, this is the way we'll do," Penrod said authoritatively: "I'll let you hold the trousers, Sam. You lay down and keep hold of one leg, and let the other one hang down till its end is in the water. Then you kind of swish it around till it's somewheres where the cat can get hold of it, and soon as he does, you pull it up, and be mighty careful so's it don't fall off. Then I'll grab it and stick it in the box and slam the lid down."

Rather pleased to be assigned to the trousers, Sam accordingly extended himself at full length upon the slab and proceeded to carry out Penrod's instructions. Meanwhile, Penrod, peering from above, inquired anxiously for information concerning this work of rescue.

"Can you see it, Sam? Why don't it grab hold? What's it doin' now, Sam?"

"It's spittin' at Herman's trousers," said Sam. "My gracious, but it's a fierce cat! If it's mad all the time like this, you better not ever try to pet it much. Now it's kind o' sniffin' at the trousers. It acks to me as if it was goin' to ketch hold. Yes, it's stuck one claw in 'em—— *Ow!*"

Sam uttered a blood-curdling shriek and jerked convulsively. The next instant, streaming and inconceivably gaunt, the ravening Gipsy appeared with a final bound upon Sam's shoulder. It was not in Gipsy's character to be drawn up peaceably; he had ascended the trousers and Sam's arm without assistance and in his own way. Simultaneously—for this was a notable case of everything happening at once— there was a muffled, soggy splash, and the unfortunate Herman, smit with prophecy in his seclusion, uttered a dismal yell. Penrod laid hands upon Gipsy, and, after a struggle suggestive of sailors landing a man-eating shark, succeeded in getting him into the box, and sat upon the lid thereof.

Sam had leaped to his feet, empty handed and vociferous.

"Ow, ow, *ouch!*" he shouted, as he rubbed his suffering arm and shoulder. Then, exasperated by Herman's lamentations, he called angrily: "Oh, what *I* care for your ole britches? I guess if you'd 'a' had a cat climb up *you,* you'd 'a' dropped 'em a hunderd times over!"

However, upon excruciating entreaty, he consented to explore the surface of the water with a clothes-prop, but reported that the luckless trousers had disappeared in the depths, Herman having forgotten to remove some "fishin' sinkers" from his pockets before making the fated loan.

Penrod was soothing a lacerated wrist in his mouth.

"That's a mighty fine-blooded cat," he remarked. "I expect it'd got away from pretty near anybody, 'specially if they didn't know much about cats. Listen at him, in the box, Sam. I bet you never heard a cat growl as loud as that in your life. I shouldn't wonder it was part panther or sumpthing."

Sam began to feel more interest and less resentment.

"I tell you what we can do, Penrod," he said: "Let's take it in the stable and make the box into a cage. We can take off the hinges and slide back the lid a little at a time, and nail some o' those laths over the front for bars."

"That's just exackly what I was goin' to say!" Penrod exclaimed. "I already thought o' that, Sam. Yessir, we'll make it just like a reg'lar circus-cage, and our good ole cat can look out from between the bars and growl. It'll come in pretty handy if we ever decide to have another show. Anyways, we'll have her in there, good and tight, where we can watch she don't get away. I got a mighty good reason to keep this cat, Sam. You'll see."

"Well, why don't you——" Sam was interrupted by a vehement appeal from the stable. "Oh, we're comin'!" he shouted. "We got to bring our cat in its cage, haven't we?"

"Listen, Herman," Penrod called absent-mindedly. "Bring us some bricks, or something awful heavy to put on the lid of our cage, so we can carry it without our good ole cat pushin' the lid open."

Herman explained with vehemence that it would not be right for him to leave the stable upon any errand until just restorations had been made. He spoke inimically of the cat that had been the occasion of his loss, and he earnestly requested that operations with the clothes-prop be resumed in the cistern. Sam and Penrod declined, on the ground that this was absolutely proven to be of no avail, and Sam went to look for bricks.

These two boys were not unfeeling. They sympathized with Herman; but they regarded the trousers as a loss about which there was no use in making so much outcry. To them, it was part of an episode that ought to be closed. They had done their best, and Sam had not intended to drop the trousers; that was something no one could have helped, and therefore no one was to be blamed. What they were now interested in was the construction of a circus-cage for their good ole cat.

"It's goin' to be a cage just exactly like circus-cages, Herman," Penrod said, as he and Sam set the box down on the stable floor. "You can help us nail the bars and——"

"I ain' studyin' 'bout no bars!" Herman interrupted fiercely. "What good you reckon nailin' bars go' do me if Mammy holler fer me? You white boys sutn'y show me bad day! I try treat people nice, 'n'en they go th'ow my britches down cistern!"

"I did not!" Sam protested. "That ole cat just kicked 'em out o' my hand with its hind feet while its front ones were stickin' in my arm. I bet *you'd* of——"

"Blame it on cat!" Herman sneered. "'At's nice! Jes' looky here minute: Who'd I len' 'em britches to? D' I len' 'em britches to thishere cat? No, suh; you know I didn'! You know well's any man I len' 'em britches to you—an' you tuck an' th'owed 'em down cistern!"

"Oh, *please* hush up about your old britches!" Penrod said plaintively. "I got to think how we're goin' to fix our cage up right, and you make so much noise I can't get my mind on it. Anyways, didn't I give you that little saw?"

"Li'l saw!" Herman cried, unmollified. "Yes; an' thishere li'l saw go' do me lot o' good when I got to go home!"

"Why, it's only across the alley to your house, Herman!" said Sam. "That ain't anything at all to step over there, and you've got your little saw."

"Aw right! You jes' take off you' clo'es an' step 'cross the alley," said Herman bitterly. "I give you li'l saw to carry!"

Penrod had begun to work upon the cage.

"Now listen here, Herman," he said: "if you'll quit talkin' so much, and kind of get settled down or sumpthing, and help us fix a good cage for our panther, well, when Mamma comes home about five o'clock, I'll go and tell her there's a poor boy got his britches burned up in a fire, and how he's waitin' out in the stable for some, and I'll tell her I promised him. Well, she'll give me a pair I wore for summer; honest she will, and you can put 'em on as quick as anything."

"There, Herman," said Sam; "now you're all right again!"

"*Who* all right?" Herman complained. "I like feel sump'm' roun' my laigs befo' no five o'clock!"

"Well, you're sure to get 'em by then," Penrod promised. "It ain't winter yet, Herman. Come on and help saw these laths for the bars, Herman, and Sam and I'll nail 'em on. It ain't long till five o'clock, Herman, and then you'll just feel fine!"

Herman was not convinced; but he found himself at a disadvantage in the argument. The question at issue seemed a vital one to him—and yet his two opponents evidently considered it of minor importance. Obviously, they felt that the promise for five o'clock had settled the whole matter conclusively; but to Herman this did not appear to be the fact. However, he helplessly suffered himself to be cajoled back into carpentry, though he was extremely ill at ease and talked a great deal of his misfortune. He shivered and grumbled, and, by his passionate urgings, compelled Penrod to go into the house so many times to see what time it was by the kitchen clock that both his companions almost lost patience with him.

"There!" said Penrod, returning from performing this errand for the fourth time. "It's twenty minutes after three, and I'm not goin' in to look at that ole clock again if I haf to die for it! I never heard anybody make such a fuss in my life, and I'm gettin' tired of it. Must think we want to be all night fixin' this cage for cur panther! If you ask me to go and see what time it is again, Herman, I'm a-goin' to take back about askin' Mamma at five o'clock, and *then* where'll you be?"

"Well, it seem like mighty long aft'noon to me," Herman sighed. "I jes' like to know what time it *is* gettin' to be now!"

"Look out!" Penrod warned him. "You heard what I was just tellin' you about how I'd take back——"

"Nemmine," Herman said hurriedly. "I wasn' astin' you. I jes' sayin' sump'm' kind o' to myse'f like."

CHAPTER XXXVII

CAMERA WORK IN THE JUNGLE

T HE completed cage, with Gipsy behind the bars, framed a spectacle sufficiently thrilling and panther-like. Gipsy raved, "spat", struck virulently at taunting fingers, turned on his wailing siren for minutes at a time, and he gave his imitation of a dromedary almost continuously. These phenomena could be intensified in picturesqueness, the boys discovered, by rocking the cage a little, tapping it with a hammer, or raking the bars with a stick. Altogether, Gipsy was having a lively afternoon.

There came a vigorous rapping on the alley door of the stable, and Verman was admitted.

"Yay, Verman!" cried Sam Williams. "Come and look at our good ole panther!"

Another curiosity, however, claimed Verman's attention. His eyes opened wide, and he pointed at Herman's legs.

"Wha' ma' oo? Mammy hay oo hip ap hoe-woob."

"Mammy tell *me* git 'at stove-wood?" Herman interpreted resentfully. "How'm I go' git 'at stove-wood when my britches down bottom 'at cistern, I like you answer *me* please? You shet 'at do' behime you!"

Verman complied, and again pointing to his brother's legs, requested to be enlightened.

"Ain' I tole you once they down bottom 'at cistern?" Herman shouted, much exasperated. "You wan' know how come so, you ast Sam Williams. He say thishere cat tuck an' th'owed 'em down there!"

Sam, who was busy rocking the cage, remained cheerfully absorbed in that occupation.

"Come look at our good ole panther, Verman," he called. "I'll get this circus-cage rockin' right good, an' then——"

"Wait a minute," said Penrod; "I got sumpthing I got to think about. Quit rockin' it! I guess I got a right to think about sumpthing without havin' to go deaf, haven't I?"

Having obtained the quiet so plaintively requested, he knit his brow and gazed intently upon Verman, then upon Herman, then upon Gipsy. Evidently his idea was fermenting. He broke the silence with a shout.

"*I* know, Sam! I know what we'll do *now!* I just thought of it, and it's goin' to be sumpthing I bet there aren't any other boys in this town could do, because where would they get any good ole panther like we got, and Herman and Verman? And they'd haf to have a dog, too—and we got our good ole Dukie, I guess. I bet we have the greatest ole time this afternoon we ever had in our lives!"

His enthusiasm roused the warm interest of Sam and Verman, though Herman, remaining cold and suspicious, asked for details.

"An' I like to hear if it's sump'm'," he concluded, "what's go' git me my britches back outen 'at cistern!"

"Well, it ain't exackly that," said Penrod. "It's different from that. What I'm thinkin' about, well, for us to have it the way it ought to be, so's you and Verman would look like natives—well, Verman ought to take off his britches, too."

"Mo!" said Verman, shaking his head violently. "Mo!"

"Well, wait a minute, can't you?" Sam Williams said. "Give Penrod a chance to say what he wants to, first, can't you? Go on, Penrod."

"Well, you know, Sam," said Penrod, turning to this sympathetic auditor; "you remember that movin'-pitcher show we went to, 'Fortygraphing Wild Animals in the Jungle'. Well, Herman wouldn't have to do a thing more to look like those natives we saw that the man called the 'beaters'. They were dressed just about like the way he is now, and if Verman——"

"Mo!" said Verman.

"Oh, wait a minute, Verman!" Sam entreated. "Go on, Penrod."

"Well, we can make a mighty good jungle up in the loft," Penrod continued eagerly. "We can take that ole dead tree that's out in the alley and some branches, and I bet we could have the best jungle you ever saw. And then we'd fix up a kind of place in there for our panther, only, of course, we'd haf to keep him in the cage so's he wouldn't run away; but we'd pretend he was loose. And then you remember how they did with that calf? Well, we'd have Duke for the tied-up calf for the panther to come out and jump on, so they could fortygraph him. Herman can be the chief beater, and we'll let Verman be the other beaters, and I'll——"

"Yay!" shouted Sam Williams. "I'll be the fortygraph man!"

"No," said Penrod; "you be the one with the gun that guards the fortygraph man, because I'm the fortygraph man already. You can fix up a mighty good gun with this carpenter shop, Sam. We'll make spears for our good ole beaters, too, and I'm goin' to make me a camera out o' that little starch-box and a bakin'-powder can that's goin' to be a mighty good ole camera. We can do lots more things——"

"Yay!" Sam cried. "Let's get started!" He paused. "Wait a minute, Penrod. Verman says he won't——"

"Well, he's got to!" said Penrod.

"I momp!" Verman insisted, almost distinctly.

They began to argue with him; but, for a time, Verman remained firm. They upheld the value of dramatic consistency, declaring that a beater dressed as completely as he was "wouldn't look like anything at all". He would "spoil the whole biznuss", they said, and they praised Herman for the faithful accuracy of his costume. They also insisted that the garment in question was much too large for Verman, anyway, having been so recently worn by Herman and turned over to Verman with insufficient alteration, and they expressed surprise that "anybody with any sense" should make such a point of clinging to a misfit.

Herman sided against his brother in this controversy, perhaps because a certain loneliness, of which he was conscious, might be assuaged by the company of another trouserless person—or it may be that his motive was more sombre. Possibly he remembered that Verman's trousers were his own former property and might fit him in case the promise for five o'clock turned out badly. At all events, Verman finally yielded under great pressure, and consented to appear in the proper costume of the multitude of beaters it now became his duty to personify.

Shouting, the boys dispersed to begin the preparation of their jungle scene. Sam and Penrod went for branches and the dead tree, while Herman and Verman carried the panther in his cage to the loft, where the first thing that Verman did was to hang his trousers on a nail in a conspicuous and accessible spot near the doorway. And with the arrival of Penrod and Sam, panting and dragging no inconsiderable thicket after them, the coloured brethren began to take a livelier interest in things. Indeed, when Penrod, a little later, placed in their hands two spears, pointed with tin, their good spirits were entirely restored, and they even began to take a pride in being properly uncostumed beaters.

Sam's gun and Penrod's camera were entirely satisfactory, especially the latter. The camera was so attractive, in fact, that the hunter and the chief beater and all the other beaters immediately resigned and insisted upon being photographers. Each had to be given a "turn" before the jungle project could be resumed.

"Now, for goodnesses' sakes," said Penrod, taking the camera from Verman, "I hope you're done, so's we can get started doin' something like we ought to! We got to have Duke for a tied-up calf. We'll have to bring him and tie him out here in front the jungle, and then the panther'll come out and jump on him. Wait, and I'll go bring him."

Departing upon this errand, Penrod found Duke enjoying the declining rays of the sun in the front yard.

"Hyuh, Duke!" called his master, in an indulgent tone. "Come on, good ole Dukie! Come along!"

Duke rose conscientiously and followed him.

"I got him, men!" Penrod called from the stairway. "I got our good ole calf all ready to be tied up. Here he is!" And he appeared in the doorway with the unsuspecting little dog beside him.

Gipsy, who had been silent for some moments, instantly raised his banshee battlecry, and Duke yelped in horror. Penrod made a wild effort to hold him; but Duke was not to be detained. Unnatural strength and activity came to him in his delirium, and, for the second or two that the struggle lasted, his movements were too rapid for the eyes of the spectators to follow—merely a whirl and blur in the air could be seen. Then followed a sound of violent scrambling —and Penrod sprawled alone at the top of the stairs.

"Well, why'n't you come and help me?" he demanded indignantly. "I couldn't get him back now if I was to try a million years!"

"What we goin' to do about it?" Sam asked.

Penrod rose and dusted his knees. "We got to get along without any tied-up calf—that's certain! But I got to take those fortygraphs *some* way or other!"

"Me an' Verman aw ready begin 'at beatin'," Herman suggested. "You tole us we the beaters."

"Well, wait a minute," said Penrod, whose feeling for realism in drama was always alert. "I want to get a mighty good pitcher o' that ole panther this time." As he spoke, he threw open the wide door intended for the delivery of hay into the loft from the alley below. "Now, bring the cage over here by this door so's I can get a better light; it's gettin' kind of dark over where the jungle is. We'll pretend there isn't any cage there, and soon as I get him fortygraphed, I'll holler, 'Shoot, men!' Then you must shoot, Sam—and Herman, you and Verman must hammer on the cage with your spears, and holler: 'Hoo! Hoo!' and pretend you're spearin' him."

"Well, we aw ready!" said Herman. "Hoo! Hoo!"

"Wait a minute," Penrod interposed, frowningly surveying the cage. "I got to squat too much to get my camera fixed right." He assumed various solemn poses, to be interpreted as those of a photographer studying his subject. "No," he said finally; "it won't take good that way."

"My goo'ness!" Herman exclaimed. "When we goin' begin 'at beatin'?"

"Here!" Apparently Penrod had solved a weighty problem. "Bring that busted ole kitchen chair, and set the panther up on it. There! *That's* the ticket! This way, it'll make a mighty good pitcher!" He turned to Sam importantly. "Well, Jim, is the chief and all his beaters here?"

"Yes, Bill; all here," Sam responded, with an air of loyalty.

"Well, then, I guess we're ready," said Penrod, in his deepest voice. "Beat, men."

Herman and Verman were anxious to beat. They set up
the loudest uproar of which they were capable. "Hoo! Hoo!
Hoo!" they bellowed, flailing the branches with their spears
and stamping heavily upon the floor. Sam, carried away by
the *élan* of the performance, was unable to resist joining
them. "Hoo! Hoo! Hoo!" he shouted. "Hoo! Hoo! Hoo!"
And as the dust rose from the floor to their stamping, the
three of them produced such a din and hoo-hooing as could
be made by nothing on earth except boys.

"Back, men!" Penrod called, raising his voice to the
utmost. "Back for your lives. The *pa-a-anther!* Now I'm
takin' his pitcher. Click, click! Shoot, men; shoot!"

"Bing! Bing!" shouted Sam, levelling his gun at the
cage, while Herman and Verman hammered upon it, and
Gipsy cursed boys, the world and the day he was born.
"Bing! Bing! Bing!"

"You missed him!" screamed Penrod. "Give *me* that
gun!" And snatching it from Sam's unwilling hand, he
levelled it at the cage.

"Bing!" he roared.

Simultaneously there was the sound of another report;
but this was an actual one and may best be symbolized by
the statement that it was a whack. The recipient was Herman, and, outrageously surprised and pained, he turned
to find himself face to face with a heavily built coloured
woman who had recently ascended the stairs and approached
the preoccupied hunters from the rear. In her hand was
a lath, and, even as Herman turned, it was again wielded,
this time upon Verman.

"*Mammy!*"

"Yes; you bettuh holler, 'Mammy!'" she panted. "My
goo'ness, if yo' Pappy don' lam you to-night! Ain' you got
no mo' sense 'an to let white boys 'suade you play you
Affikin heathums? Whah you britches?"

"Yonnuh Verman's," quavered Herman.

"Whah y'own?"

Choking, Herman answered bravely:

" 'At ole cat tuck an' th'owed 'em down cistern!'"

Exasperated almost beyond endurance, she lifted the lath again. But unfortunately, in order to obtain a better field of action, she moved backward a little, coming in contact with the bars of the cage, a circumstance that she overlooked. More unfortunately still, the longing of the captive to express his feelings was such that he would have welcomed the opportunity to attack an elephant. He had been striking and scratching at inanimate things and at boys out of reach for the past hour; but here at last was his opportunity. He made the most of it.

"I learn you tell me cat th'owed—*ooooh!*"

The coloured woman leaped into the air like an athlete, and, turning with a swiftness astounding in one of her weight, beheld the semaphoric arm of Gipsy again extended between the bars and hopefully reaching for her. Beside herself, she lifted her right foot briskly from the ground, and allowed the sole of her shoe to come in contact with Gipsy's cage.

The cage moved from the tottering chair beneath it. It passed through the yawning hay-door and fell resoundingly to the alley below, where—as Penrod and Sam, with cries of dismay, rushed to the door and looked down—it burst asunder and disgorged a large, bruised and chastened cat. Gipsy paused and bent one strange look upon the broken box. Then he shook his head and departed up the alley, the two boys watching him till he was out of sight.

Before they turned, a harrowing procession issued from the carriage-house doors beneath them. Herman came first, hurriedly completing a temporary security in Verman's trousers. Verman followed, after a little reluctance that departed coincidentally with some inspiriting words from the rear. He crossed the alley hastily, and his Mammy stalked behind, using constant eloquence and a frequent lath. They went into the small house across the way and closed the door.

Then Sam turned to Penrod.

"Penrod," he said thoughtfully, "was it on account of fortygraphing in the jungle you wanted to keep that cat?"

"No; that was a mighty fine-blooded cat. We'd of made some money."

Sam jeered.

"You mean when we'd sell tickets to look at it in its cage?"

Penrod shook his head, and if Gipsy could have overheard and understood his reply, that atrabilious spirit, almost broken by the events of the day, might have considered this last blow the most overwhelming of all.

"No," said Penrod; "when she had kittens."

CHAPTER XXXVIII

A MODEL LETTER TO A FRIEND

ON MONDAY morning Penrod's faith in the coming of another Saturday was flaccid and lustreless. Those Japanese lovers who were promised a reunion after ten thousand years in separate hells were brighter with hope than he was. On Monday Penrod was virtually an agnostic.

Nowhere upon his shining morning face could have been read any eager anticipation of useful knowledge. Of course he had been told that school was for his own good; in fact, he had been told and told and told, but the words conveying this information, meaningless at first, assumed, with each repetition, more and more the character of dull and unsolicited insult.

He was wholly unable to imagine circumstances, present or future, under which any of the instruction and training he was now receiving could be of the slightest possible use or benefit to himself; and when he was informed that such circumstances would frequently arise in his later life, he but felt the slur upon his coming manhood and its power to prevent any such unpleasantness.

If it were possible to place a romantic young Broadway actor and athlete under hushing supervision for six hours a day, compelling him to bend his unremittent attention upon the city directory of Sheboygan, Wisconsin, he could scarce be expected to respond genially to frequent statements that the compulsion was all for his own good. On the contrary, it might be reasonable to conceive his response as taking the form of action, which is precisely the form that Penrod's smouldering impulse yearned to take.

To Penrod school was merely a state of confinement, envenomed by mathematics. For interminable periods he was forced to listen to information concerning matters about which he had no curiosity whatever; and he had to read over and over the dullest passages in books that bored him into stupors, while always there overhung the preposterous task of improvising plausible evasions to conceal the fact that he did not know what he had no wish to know. Likewise, he must always be prepared to avoid incriminating replies to questions that he felt nobody had a real and natural right to ask him. And when his gorge rose and his inwards revolted, the hours became a series of ignoble misadventures and petty disgraces strikingly lacking in privacy.

It was usually upon Wednesday that his sufferings culminated; the nervous strength accumulated during the holiday hours at the end of the week would carry him through Monday and Tuesday; but by Wednesday it seemed ultimately proven that the next Saturday actually *never* was coming, "this time", and the strained spirit gave way. Wednesday was the day averaging highest in Penrod's list of absences; but the time came when he felt that the advantages attendant upon his Wednesday "sick headache" did not compensate for its inconveniences.

For one thing, this illness had become so symmetrically recurrent that even the cook felt that he was pushing it too far, and the liveliness of her expression, when he was able to leave his couch and take the air in the backyard at about ten o'clock, became more disagreeable to him with each convalescence. There visibly increased, too, about the whole household, an atmosphere of uncongeniality and suspicion so pronounced that every successive illness was necessarily more severe, and at last the patient felt obliged to remain bedded until almost eleven, from time to time giving forth pathetic little sounds eloquent of anguish triumphing over Stoic endurance, yet lacking a certain conviction of utterance.

Finally, his father enacted, and his mother applied, a new and distinctly special bit of legislation, explaining it with simple candour to the prospective beneficiary.

"Whenever you really *are* sick," they said, "you can go out and play as soon as you're well—that is, if it happens on Saturday. But when you're sick on a school-day, you'll stay in bed till the next morning. This is going to do you good, Penrod."

Physically, their opinion appeared to be affirmed, for Wednesday after Wednesday passed without any recurrence of the attack; but the spiritual strain may have been damaging. And it should be added that if Penrod's higher nature did suffer from the strain, he was not unique. For, confirming the effect of Wednesday upon boys in general, it is probable that, if full statistics concerning cats were available, they would show that cats dread Wednesdays, and that their fear is shared by other animals, and would be shared, to an extent by windows, if windows possessed nervous systems. Nor must this probable apprehension on the part of cats and the like be thought mere superstition. Cats have superstitions, it is true; but certain actions inspired by the sight of a boy with a missile in his hand are better evidence of the workings of logic upon a practical nature than of faith in the supernatural.

Moreover, the attention of family physicians and specialists should be drawn to these significant though obscure phenomena; for the suffering of cats is a barometer of the nerve-pressure of boys, and it may be accepted as sufficiently established that Wednesday—after school-hours —is the worst time for cats.

After the promulgation of that parental edict, "You'll stay in bed till the next morning", four weeks went by unflawed by a single absence from the field of duty; but, when the fifth Wednesday came, Penrod held sore debate within himself before he finally rose. In fact, after rising, and while actually engaged with his toilet, he tentatively emitted the series of little moans that was his wonted preliminary to a quiet holiday at home; and the sound was heard (as intended) by Mr. Schofield, who was passing Penrod's door on his way to breakfast.

"*All* right!" the father said, making use of peculiar and unnecessary emphasis. "Stay in bed till to-morrow morning. Castor-oil, this time, too."

Penrod had not hoped much for his experiment; nevertheless his rebellious blood was sensibly inflamed by the failure, and he accompanied his dressing with a low murmuring—apparently a bitter dialogue between himself and some unknown but powerful patron.

Thus he muttered:

"Well, they better *not!*" "Well, what can I *do* about it?" "Well, *I'd* show 'em!" "Well, I *will* show 'em!" "Well, you *ought* to show 'em; that's the way *I* do! I just shake 'em around, and say, 'Here! I guess you don't know who you're talkin' to like that! You better look out!'" "Well, that's the way *I'm* goin' to do!" "Well, go on and *do* it, then!" "Well, I *am* goin'——"

The door of the next room was slightly ajar; now it swung wide, and Margaret appeared.

"Penrod, what on earth are you talking about?"

"Nothin'. None o' your——"

"Well, hurry to breakfast, then; it's getting late."

Lightly she went, humming a tune, leaving the door of her room open, and the eyes of Penrod, as he donned his jacket, chanced to fall upon her desk, where she had thoughtlessly left a letter—a private missive just begun, and intended solely for the eyes of Mr. Robert Williams, a senior at a far university.

In such a fashion is coincidence the architect of misfortune. Penrod's class in English composition had been instructed, the previous day, to concoct at home and bring to class on Wednesday morning, "a model letter to a friend on some subject of general interest." Penalty for omission to perform this simple task was definite; whosoever brought no letter would inevitably be "kept in" after school, that afternoon, until the letter was written, and it was precisely a premonition of this misfortune that had prompted Penrod to attempt his experimental moaning upon his father, for, alas! he had equipped himself with no model letter, nor any letter whatever.

In stress of this kind, a boy's creed is that anything is worth a try; but his eye for details is poor. He sees the future too sweepingly and too much as he would have it, seldom providing against inconsistencies of evidence that may damage him. For instance, there is a well-known case of two brothers who exhibited to their parents, with pathetic confidence, several imported dried herring on a string, as a proof that the afternoon had been spent, not at a forbidden circus, but with hook and line upon the banks of a neighbouring brook.

So with Penrod. He had vital need of a letter, and there, before his eyes, upon Margaret's desk, was apparently the precise thing he needed!

From below rose the voice of his mother urging him to the breakfast-table, warning him that he stood in danger of tardiness at school; he was pressed for time, and acted upon an inspiration that failed to prompt him even to read the letter.

Hurriedly he wrote "Dear freind" at the top of the page Margaret had partially filled. Then he signed himself "Yours respectfuly, Penrod Schofield" at the bottom, and enclosed the missive within a battered volume entitled, "Principles of English Composition." With that and other books compacted by a strap, he descended to a breakfast somewhat oppressive but undarkened by any misgivings concerning a "letter to a friend on some subject of general interest." He felt that a difficulty had been encountered and satisfactorily disposed of; the matter could now be dismissed from his mind. He had plenty of other difficulties to take its place.

No; he had no misgivings, nor was he assailed by anything unpleasant in that line, even when the hour struck for the class in English composition. If he had been two or three years older, experience might have warned him to take at least the precaution of copying his offering, so that it would appear in his own handwriting when he "handed it in"; but Penrod had not even glanced at it.

"I think," Miss Spence said, "I will ask several of you to read your letters aloud before you hand them in. Clara Raypole, you may read yours."

Penrod was bored but otherwise comfortable; he had no apprehension that he might be included in the "several", especially as Miss Spence's beginning with Clara Raypole, a star performer, indicated that her selection of readers would be made from the conscientious and proficient division at the head of the class. He listened stoically to the beginning of the first letter, though he was conscious of a dull resentment, inspired mainly by the perfect complacency of Miss Raypole's voice.

" 'Dear Cousin Sadie,' " she began smoothly, " 'I thought I would write you to-day on some subject of general interest, and so I thought I would tell you about the subject of our court-house. It is a very fine building situated in the centre of the city, and a visit to the building after school hours well repays for the visit. Upon entrance we find upon our left the office of the county clerk and upon our right a number of windows affording a view of the street. And so we proceed, finding on both sides much of general interest. The building was begun in 1886 A. D. and it was through in 1887 A. D. It is four stories high and made of stone, pressed brick, wood, and tiles, with a tower, or cupola, one hundred and twenty-seven feet seven inches from the ground. Among other subjects of general interest told by the janitor, we learn that the architect of the building was a man named Flanner, and the foundations extend fifteen feet five inches under the ground——' "

Penrod was unable to fix his attention upon these statistics; he began moodily to twist a button of his jacket and to concentrate a new-born and obscure but lasting hatred upon the court-house. Miss Raypole's glib voice continued to press upon his ears; but, by keeping his eyes fixed upon the twisting button he had accomplished a kind of self-hypnosis, or mental anæsthesia, and was but dimly aware of what went on about him.

The court-house was finally exhausted by its visitor, who resumed her seat and submitted with beamish grace to praise. Then Miss Spence said, in a favourable manner:

"Georgie Bassett, you may read your letter next."

The neat Georgie rose, nothing loath, and began: " 'Dear Teacher——' "

There was a slight titter, which Miss Spence suppressed. Georgie was not at all discomfited.

" 'My mother says,' " he continued, reading his manuscript, " 'we should treat our teacher as a friend, and so *I* will write *you* a letter.' "

This penetrated Penrod's trance, and he lifted his eyes to fix them upon the back of Georgie Bassett's head in a long and inscrutable stare. It was inscrutable, and yet if Georgie had been sensitive to thought waves, it is probable that he would have uttered a loud shriek; but he remained placidly unaware, continuing:

"'I thought I would write you about a subject of general interest, and so I will write you about the flowers. There are many kinds of flowers, spring flowers, and summer flowers, and autumn flowers, but no winter flowers. Wild flowers grow in the woods, and it is nice to hunt them in springtime, and we must remember to give some to the poor and hospitals, also. Flowers can be made to grow in flower-beds and placed in vases in houses. There are many names for flowers, but *I* call them "nature's ornaments"——' "

Penrod's gaze had relaxed, drooped to his button again, and his lethargy was renewed. The outer world grew vaguer; voices seemed to drone at a distance; sluggish time passed heavily—but some of it did pass.

"Penrod!"

Miss Spence's searching eye had taken note of the bent head and the twisting button. She found it necessary to speak again.

"Penrod Schofield!"

He came languidly to life.

"Ma'am?"

"You may read your letter."

"Yes'm."

And he began to paw clumsily among his books, whereupon Miss Spence's glance fired with suspicion.

"Have you prepared one?" she demanded.

"Yes'm," said Penrod dreamily.

"But you're going to find you forgot to bring it, aren't you?"

"I got it," said Penrod, discovering the paper in his "Principles of English Composition."

"Well, we'll listen to what you've found time to prepare," she said, adding coldly, "for once!"

The frankest pessimism concerning Penrod permeated the whole room; even the eyes of those whose letters had not met with favour turned upon him with obvious assurance that here was every prospect of a performance that would, by comparison, lend a measure of credit to the worst preceding it. But Penrod was unaffected by the general gaze; he rose, still blinking from his lethargy, and in no true sense wholly alive.

He had one idea: to read as rapidly as possible, so as to be done with the task, and he began in a high-pitched monotone, reading with a blind mind and no sense of the significance of the words.

" 'Dear friend,' " he declaimed. " 'You call me beautiful, but I am not really beautiful, and there are times when I doubt if I am even pretty, though perhaps my hair is beautiful, and if it is true that my eyes are like blue stars in heaven——' "

Simultaneously he lost his breath and there burst upon him a perception of the results to which he was being committed by this calamitous reading. And also simultaneous was the outbreak of the class into cachinnations of delight, severely repressed by the perplexed but indignant Miss Spence.

"Go on!" she commanded grimly, when she had restored order.

"Ma'am?" he gulped, looking wretchedly upon the rosy faces all about him.

"Go on with the description of yourself," she said. "We'd like to hear some more about your eyes being like blue stars in heaven."

Here many of Penrod's little comrades were forced to clasp their faces tightly in both hands; and his dismayed gaze, in refuge, sought the treacherous paper in his hand.

What it beheld there was horrible.

"Proceed!" Miss Spence said.

" 'I—often think,' " he faltered, " 'and a-a tree-more thu-thrills my bein' when I *re*call your last words to me that last—that last—that——' "

"*Go on!*"

" 'That last evening in the moonlight when you—you—
you——' "

"Penrod," Miss Spence said dangerously, "you go on, and
stop that stammering."

" 'You—you said you would wait for—for years to—to—
to—to——' "

"Penrod!"

" 'To win me!' " the miserable Penrod managed to gasp.
" 'I should not have pre—premitted—permitted you to
speak so until we have our—our parents' con-consent; but
oh, how sweet it——' " He exhaled a sigh of agony, and
then concluded briskly, " 'Yours respectfully, Penrod Schofield.' "

But Miss Spence had at last divined something, for she
knew the Schofield family.

"Bring me that letter!" she said.

And the scarlet boy passed forward between rows of
mystified but immoderately uplifted children.

Miss Spence herself grew rather pink as she examined the
missive, and the intensity with which she afterward extended her examination to cover the complete field of Penrod Schofield caused him to find a remote centre of interest
whereon to rest his embarrassed gaze. She let him stand
before her throughout a silence, equalled, perhaps, by the
tenser pauses during trials for murder, and then, containing herself, she sweepingly gestured him to the pillory
—a chair upon the platform, facing the school.

Here he suffered for the unusual term of an hour, with
many jocular and cunning eyes constantly upon him; and,
when he was released at noon, horrid shouts and shrieks
pursued him every step of his homeward way. For his
laughter-loving little schoolmates spared him not—neither
boy nor girl.

"Yay, Penrod!" they shouted. "How's your beautiful
hair?" And, "Hi, Penrod! When you goin' to get your
parents' consent?" And, "Say, blue stars in heaven, how's
your beautiful eyes?" And, "Say, Penrod, how's your tree-

mores?" "Does your tree-mores thrill your bein', Penrod?"
And many other facetious inquiries, hard to bear in public.

And when he reached the temporary shelter of his home,
he experienced no relief upon finding that Margaret was out
for lunch. He was as deeply embittered toward her as
toward any other, and, considering her largely responsible
for his misfortune, he would have welcomed an opportunity
to show her what he thought of her.

CHAPTER XXXIX

WEDNESDAY MADNESS

HOW long he was "kept in" after school that afternoon is not a matter of record; but it was long. Before he finally appeared upon the street, he had composed an ample letter on a subject of general interest, namely "School Life", under the supervision of Miss Spence; he had also received some scorching admonitions in respect to honourable behaviour regarding other people's letters; and Margaret's had been returned to him with severe instructions to bear it straight to the original owner accompanied by full confession and apology. As a measure of insurance that these things be done, Miss Spence stated definitely her intention to hold a conversation by telephone with Margaret that evening. Altogether, the day had been unusually awful, even for Wednesday, and Penrod left the school-house with the heart of an anarchist throbbing in his hot bosom. It were more accurate, indeed, to liken him to the anarchist's characteristic weapon; for as Penrod came out to the street he was, in all inward respects, a bomb, loaded and ticking.

He walked moodily, with a visible aspect of soreness. A murmurous sound was thick about his head, wherefore it is to be surmised that he communed with his familiar, and one vehement, oft-repeated phrase beat like a tocsin of revolt upon the air: "Daw-gone 'em!"

He meant everybody—the universe.

Particularly included, evidently, was a sparrow, offensively cheerful upon a lamp-post. This self-centred little bird allowed a pebble to pass overhead and remained unconcerned, but, a moment later, feeling a jar beneath his feet, and hearing the tinkle of falling glass, he decided to leave. Similarly, and at the same instant, Penrod made the same decision, and the sparrow in flight took note of a boy likewise in flight.

The boy disappeared into the nearest alley and emerged therefrom, breathless, in the peaceful vicinity of his own home. He entered the house, clumped upstairs and down, discovered Margaret reading a book in the library, and flung the accursed letter toward her with loathing.

"You can take the old thing," he said bitterly. "*I* don't want it!"

And before she was able to reply, he was out of the room. The next moment he was out of the house.

"Daw-*gone* 'em!" he said.

And then, across the street, his soured eye fell upon his true comrade and best friend leaning against a picket fence and holding desultory converse with Mabel Rorebeck, an attractive member of the Friday Afternoon Dancing Class, that hated organization of which Sam and Penrod were both members. Mabel was a shy little girl; but Penrod had a vague understanding that Sam considered her two brown pigtails beautiful.

Howbeit, Sam had never told his love; he was, in fact, sensitive about it. This meeting with the lady was by chance, and, although it afforded exquisite moments, his heart was beating in an unaccustomed manner, and he was suffering from embarrassment, being at a loss, also, for subjects of conversation. It is, indeed, no easy matter to chat easily with a person, however lovely and beloved, who keeps her face turned the other way, maintains one foot in rapid and continuous motion through an arc seemingly perilous to her equilibrium, and confines her responses, both affirmative and negative, to "Uh-huh."

Altogether, Sam was sufficiently nervous without any help from Penrod, and it was with pure horror that he heard his own name and Mabel's shrieked upon the ambient air with viperish insinuation.

"Sam-my and May-bul! *Oh*, oh!"

Sam started violently. Mabel ceased to swing her foot, and both, encarnadined, looked up and down and everywhere for the invisible but well-known owner of that voice. It came again, in taunting mockery:

> "Sammy's mad, and I am glad,
>   And I know what will please him:
> A bottle o' wine to make him shine,
>   And Mabel Rorebeck to squeeze him!"

"Fresh ole thing!" said Miss Rorebeck, becoming articulate. And unreasonably including Sam in her indignation, she tossed her head at him with an unmistakable effect of scorn. She began to walk away.

"Well, Mabel," Sam said plaintively, following, "it ain't *my* fault. *I* didn't do anything. It's Penrod."

"I don't care," she began pettishly, when the viperish voice was again lifted:

> "Oh, oh, oh!
> Who's your beau?
> Guess *I* know:
> Mabel and Sammy, oh, oh, oh!
> *I* caught you!"

Then Mabel did one of those things that eternally perplex the slower sex. She deliberately made a face, not at the tree behind which Penrod was lurking, but at the innocent and heart-wrung Sam. "You needn't come limpin' after *me*, Sam Williams!" she said, though Sam was approaching upon two perfectly sound legs. And then she ran away at the top of her speed.

"Run, nigger, run!" Penrod began inexcusably. But Sam cut the persecutions short at this point. Stung to fury, he charged upon the sheltering tree in the Schofields' yard.

Ordinarily, at such a juncture, Penrod would have fled, keeping his own temper and increasing the heat of his pursuer's by back-flung jeers. But this was Wednesday, and he was in no mood to run from Sam. He stepped away from the tree, awaiting the onset.

"Well, what you goin' to do so much?" he said.

Sam did not pause to proffer the desired information. "Tcha got'ny *sense!*" was the total extent of his vocal preliminaries before flinging himself headlong upon the taunter; and the two boys went to the ground together. Embracing, they rolled, they pommelled, they hammered, they kicked. Alas, this was a fight.

They rose, flailing a while, then renewed their embrace, and, grunting, bestowed themselves anew upon our ever too receptive Mother Earth. Once more upon their feet, they beset each other sorely, dealing many great blows, ofttimes upon the air, but with sufficient frequency upon resentful flesh. Tears were jolted to the rims of eyes, but technically they did not weep. "Got'ny sense," was repeated chokingly many, many times; also, "Dern ole fool!" and, "I'll *show* you!"

The peacemaker who appeared upon the animated scene was Penrod's great-uncle Slocum. This elderly relative had come to call upon Mrs. Schofield, and he was well upon his way to the front door when the mutterings of war among some shrubberies near the fence caused him to deflect his course in benevolent agitation.

"Boys! Boys! Shame, boys!" he said; but, as the originality of these expressions did not prove striking enough to attract any great attention from the combatants, he felt obliged to assume a share in the proceedings. It was a share entailing greater activity than he had anticipated, and, before he managed to separate the former friends, he intercepted bodily an amount of violence to which he was wholly unaccustomed. Additionally, his attire was disarranged; his hat was no longer upon his head, and his temper was in a bad way. In fact, as his hat flew off, he made use of words that under less extreme circumstances would have caused both boys to feel a much profounder interest than they did in great-uncle Slocum.

"I'll *get* you!" Sam babbled. "Don't you ever dare to speak to me again, Penrod Schofield, long as you live, or I'll whip you worse'n I have this time!"

Penrod squawked. For the moment he was incapable of coherent speech, and then, failing in a convulsive attempt to reach his enemy, his fury culminated upon an innocent object that had never done him the slightest harm. Great-uncle Slocum's hat lay upon the ground close by, and Penrod was in the state of irritation that seeks an outlet too blindly—as people say, he "*had* to do *something!*" He kicked great-uncle Slocum's hat with such sweep and precision that it rose swiftly, and, breasting the autumn breeze, passed over the fence and out into the street.

Great-uncle Slocum uttered a scream of anguish, and, immediately ceasing to peacemake, ran forth to a more

important rescue; but the conflict was not renewed. Sanity
had returned to Sam Williams; he was awed by this colossal
deed of Penrod's and filled with horror at the thought that
he might be held as accessory to it. Fleetly he fled, pursued
as far as the gate by the whole body of Penrod, and thereafter by Penrod's voice alone.

"You *better* run! You wait till I catch you! You'll see
what you get next time! Don't you ever speak to me again
as long as you——"

Here he paused abruptly, for great-uncle Slocum had
recovered his hat and was returning toward the gate. After
one glance at great-uncle Slocum, Penrod did not linger to
attempt any explanation—there are times when even a boy
can see that apologies would seem out of place. Penrod ran
round the house to the backyard.

Here he was enthusiastically greeted by Duke. "You get
away from me!" Penrod said hoarsely, and with terrible
gestures he repulsed the faithful animal, who retired philo-
sophically to the stable, while his master let himself out of
the back gate. Penrod had decided to absent himself from
home for the time being.

The sky was gray, and there were hints of coming
dusk in the air; it was an hour suited to his turbulent soul,
and he walked with a sombre swagger. "Ran like a c'ardy-
calf!" he sniffed, half aloud, alluding to the haste of Sam
Williams in departure. "All he is, ole c'ardy-calf!"

Then, as he proceeded up the alley, a hated cry smote
his ears: "Hi, Penrod! How's your tree-mores?" And two
jovial schoolboy faces appeared above a high board fence.
"How's your beautiful hair, Penrod?" they vociferated.
"When you goin' to git your parents' consent? What makes
you think you're only pretty, ole blue stars?"

Penrod looked about feverishly for a missile, and could
find none to his hand, but the surface of the alley sufficed;
he made mud balls and fiercely bombarded the vociferous
fence. Naturally, hostile mud balls presently issued from
behind this barricade; and thus a campaign developed that

offered a picture not unlike a cartoonist's sketch of a political campaign, wherein this same material is used for the decoration of opponents. But Penrod had been unwise; he was outnumbered, and the hostile forces held the advantageous side of the fence.

Mud balls can be hard as well as soggy; some of those that reached Penrod were of no inconsiderable weight and substance, and they made him grunt despite himself. Finally, one, at close range, struck him in the pit of the stomach, whereupon he clasped himself about the middle silently, and executed some steps in seeming imitation of a quaint Indian dance.

His plight being observed through a knothole, his enemies climbed upon the fence and regarded him seriously.

"Aw, *you're* all right, ain't you, old tree-mores?" inquired one.

"I'll *show* you!" bellowed Penrod, recovering his breath; and he hurled a fat ball—thoughtfully retained in hand throughout his agony —to such effect that his interrogator disappeared backward from the fence without having taken any initiative of his own in the matter. His comrade impulsively joined him upon the ground, and the battle continued.

Through the gathering dusk it went on. It waged but the hotter as darkness made aim more difficult—and still Penrod would not be driven from the field. Panting, grunting, hoarse from returning insults, fighting on and on, an indistinguishable figure in the gloom, he held the back alley against all comers.

For such a combat darkness has one great advantage; but it has an equally important disadvantage—the combatant cannot see to aim; on the other hand, he cannot see to dodge. And all the while Penrod was receiving two for one. He became heavy with mud. Plastered, impressionistic and sculpturesque, there was about him a quality of the tragic, of the magnificent. He resembled a sombre masterpiece by Rodin. No one could have been quite sure what he was meant for.

Dinner bells tinkled in houses. Then they were rung from kitchen doors. Calling voices came urging from the distance, calling boys' names into the darkness. They called, and a note of irritation seemed to mar their beauty.

Then bells were rung again—and the voices renewed appeals more urgent, much more irritated. They called and called and called.

Thud! went the mud balls.

Thud! Thud! Blunk!

"*Oof!*" said Penrod.

. . . . Sam Williams, having dined with his family at their usual hour, seven, slipped unostentatiously out of the kitchen door, as soon as he could, after the conclusion of the meal, and quietly betook himself to the Schofields' corner.

Here he stationed himself where he could see all avenues of approach to the house, and waited. Twenty minutes went by, and then Sam became suddenly alert and attentive, for the arc-light revealed a small, grotesque figure slowly approaching along the sidewalk. It was brown in colour, shaggy and indefinite in form; it limped excessively, and paused to rub itself, and to meditate.

Peculiar as the thing was, Sam had no doubt as to its identity. He advanced.

" 'Lo, Penrod," he said cautiously, and with a shade of formality.

Penrod leaned against the fence, and, lifting one leg, tested the knee-joint by swinging his foot back and forth, a process evidently provocative of a little pain. Then he rubbed the left side of his encrusted face, and, opening his mouth to its whole capacity as an aperture, moved his lower jaw slightly from side to side, thus triumphantly settling a question in his own mind as to whether or no a suspected dislocation had taken place.

Having satisfied himself on these points, he examined both shins delicately by the sense of touch, and carefully tested the capacities of his neck-muscles to move his head in a wonted manner.

Then he responded somewhat gruffly:

" 'Lo!"

"Where you been?" Sam said eagerly, his formality vanishing.

"Havin' a mud-fight."

"I guess you did!" Sam exclaimed, in a low voice. "What you goin' to tell your——"

"Oh, nothin'."

"Your sister telephoned to our house to see if I knew where you were," said Sam. "She told me if I saw you before you got home to tell you sumpthing; but not to say anything about it. She said Miss Spence had telephoned to her, but *she* said for me to tell you it was all right about that letter, and she wasn't goin' to tell your mother and father on you, so you needn't say anything about it to 'em."

"All right," said Penrod indifferently.

"She says you're goin' to be in enough trouble without that," Sam went on. "You're goin' to catch fits about your Uncle Slocum's hat, Penrod."

"Well, I guess I know it."

"And about not comin' home to dinner, too. Your mother telephoned twice to Mamma while we were eatin' to see if you'd come in our house. And when they *see* you—*my*, but you're goin' to get the *dickens*, Penrod!"

Penrod seemed unimpressed, though he was well aware that Sam's prophecy was no unreasonable one.

"Well, I guess I know it," he repeated casually. And he moved slowly toward his own gate.

His friend looked after him curiously—then, as the limping figure fumbled clumsily with bruised fingers at the latch of the gate, there sounded a little solicitude in Sam's voice.

"Say, Penrod, how—how do you feel?"

"What?"

"Do you feel pretty bad?"

"No," said Penrod, and, in spite of what awaited him beyond the lighted portals just ahead, he spoke the truth. His nerves were rested, and his soul was at peace. His Wednesday madness was over.

"No," said Penrod; "I feel bully!"

CHAPTER XL

PENROD'S BUSY DAY

ALTHOUGH the pressure had thus been relieved and Penrod found peace with himself, nevertheless there were times during the rest of that week when he felt a strong distaste for Margaret. His schoolmates frequently reminded him of such phrases in her letter as they seemed least able to forget, and for hours after each of these experiences he was unable to comport himself with human courtesy when constrained (as at dinner) to remain for any length of time in the same room with her. But by Sunday these moods had seemed to pass; he attended church in her close company, and had no thought of the troubles brought upon him by her correspondence with a person who throughout remained unknown to him.

Penrod slumped far down in the pew with his knees against the back of that in front, and he also languished to one side, so that the people sitting behind were afforded a view of him consisting of a little hair and one bored ear. The sermon—a noble one, searching and eloquent—was but a persistent sound in that ear, though, now and then, Penrod's attention would be caught by some detached portion of a sentence, when his mind would dwell dully upon the phrases for a little while—and lapse into a torpor. At intervals his mother, without turning her head, would whisper, "Sit up, Penrod", causing him to sigh profoundly and move his shoulders about an inch, this mere gesture of compliance exhausting all the energy that remained to him.

The black backs and gray heads of the elderly men in the congregation oppressed him; they made him lethargic with a sense of long lives of repellent dullness. But he should have been grateful to the lady with the artificial cherries upon her hat. His gaze lingered there, wandered away, and hopelessly returned again and again, to be a little refreshed by the glossy scarlet of the cluster of tiny globes. He was not so fortunate as to be drowsy; that would have brought him some relief—and yet, after a while, his eyes became slightly glazed; he saw dimly, and what he saw was distorted.

The church had been built in the early 'Seventies, and it contained some naïve stained glass of that period. The arch at the top of a window facing Penrod was filled with a gigantic Eye. Of oyster-white and raw blues and reds, inflamed by the pouring sun, it had held an awful place in the infantile life of Penrod Schofield, for in his tenderer years he accepted it without question as the literal Eye of Deity. He had been informed that the church was the divine dwelling—and there was the Eye!

Nowadays, being no longer a little child, he had somehow come to know better without being told, and, though the great flaming Eye was no longer the terrifying thing it had been to him during his childhood, it nevertheless re-

tained something of its ominous character. It made him feel
spied upon, and its awful glare still pursued him, sometimes, as he was falling asleep at night. When he faced the
window his feeling was one of dull resentment.

His own glazed eyes, becoming slightly crossed with an
ennui that was peculiarly intense this morning, rendered
the Eye more monstrous than it was. It expanded to horrible
size, growing mountainous; it turned into a volcano in the
tropics, and yet it stared at him, indubitably an Eye implacably hostile to all rights of privacy forever. Penrod
blinked and clinched his eyelids to be rid of this dual image,
and he managed to shake off the volcano. Then, lowering
the angle of his glance, he saw something most remarkable
—and curiously out of place.

An inverted white soup-plate was lying miraculously
balanced upon the back of a pew a little distance in front
of him, and upon the upturned bottom of the soup-plate
was a brown cocoanut. Mildly surprised, Penrod yawned,
and, in the effort to straighten his eyes, came to life
temporarily. The cocoanut was revealed as Georgie Bassett's
head, and the soup-plate as Georgie's white collar. Georgie
was sitting up straight, as he always did in church, and
Penrod found this vertical rectitude unpleasant. He knew
that he had more to fear from the Eye than Georgie had,
and he was under the impression (a correct one) that
Georgie felt on intimate terms with it and was actually fond
of it.

Penrod himself would have maintained that he was fond
of it, if he had been asked. He would have said so because
he feared to say otherwise; and the truth is that he never
consciously looked at the Eye disrespectfully. He would
have been alarmed if he thought the Eye had any way of
finding out how he really felt about it. When not off his
guard, he always looked at it placatively.

By and by, he sagged so far to the left that he had
symptoms of a "stitch in the side", and, rousing himself,
sat partially straight for several moments. Then he rubbed

his shoulders slowly from side to side against the back of the seat, until his mother whispered, "Don't do that, Penrod."

Upon this, he allowed himself to slump inwardly till the curve in the back of his neck rested against the curved top of the back of the seat. It was a congenial fit, and Penrod again began to move slowly from side to side, finding the friction soothing. Even so slight a pleasure was denied him by a husky, "Stop that!" from his father.

Penrod sighed, and slid farther down. He scratched his head, his left knee, his right biceps and his left ankle, after which he scratched his right knee, his right ankle and his left biceps. Then he said, "Oh, hum!" unconsciously, but so loudly that there was a reproving stir in the neighbourhood of the Schofield pew, and his father looked at him angrily.

Finally, his nose began to trouble him. It itched, and after scratching it, he rubbed it harshly. Another "Stop that!" from his father proved of no avail, being greeted by a desperate-sounding whisper, "I *got* to!"

And, continuing to rub his nose with his right hand, Penrod began to search his pockets with his left. The quest proving fruitless, he rubbed his nose with his left hand and searched with his right. Then he abandoned his nose and searched feverishly with both hands, going through all of his pockets several times.

"What *do* you want?" whispered his mother.

But Margaret had divined his need, and she passed him her own handkerchief. This was both thoughtful and thoughtless—the latter because Margaret was in the habit of thinking that she became faint in crowds, especially at the theatre or in church, and she had just soaked her handkerchief with spirits of ammonia from a small phial she carried in her muff.

Penrod hastily applied the handkerchief to his nose and even more hastily exploded. He sneezed stupendously; he choked, sneezed again, wept, passed into a light convulsion of coughing and sneezing together—a mergence of sound that attracted much attention—and, after a few recurrent spasms, convalesced into a condition marked by silent tears and only sporadic instances of sneezing.

By this time his family were unanimously scarlet—his father and mother with mortification, and Margaret with the effort to control the almost irresistible mirth that the struggles and vociferations of Penrod had inspired within her. And yet her heart misgave her, for his bloodshot and tearful eyes were fixed upon her from the first and remained upon her, even when half-blinded with his agony; and their expression—as terrible as that of the windowed Eye confronting her—was not for an instant to be misunderstood. Absolutely, he believed that she had handed him the ammonia-soaked handkerchief deliberately and with malice, and well she knew that no power on earth could now or at any time henceforth persuade him otherwise.

"Of course I didn't mean it, Penrod," she said, at the first opportunity upon their homeward way. "I didn't notice —that is, I didn't think——" Unfortunately for the effect of sincerity she hoped to produce, her voice became tremulous and her shoulders moved suspiciously.

"Just you wait! You'll see!" he prophesied, in a voice now choking, not with ammonia, but with emotion. "Poison a person, and then laugh in his face!"

He spake no more until they had reached their own house, though she made some further futile efforts at explanation and apology.

And after brooding abysmally throughout the meal that followed, he disappeared from the sight of his family, having answered with one frightful look his mother's timid suggestion that it was almost time for Sunday-school. He retired to his eyry—the sawdust box in the empty stable— and there gave rein to his embittered imaginings, incidentally forming many plans for Margaret.

Most of these were much too elaborate; but one was so alluring that he dwelt upon it, working out the details with gloomy pleasure, even after he had perceived its defects. It involved some postponement—in fact, until Margaret should have become the mother of a boy about Penrod's present age. This boy would be precisely like Georgie Bassett—Penrod conceived that as inevitable—and, like Georgie, he would be his mother's idol. Penrod meant to take him to church and force him to blow his nose with an ammonia-soaked handkerchief in the presence of the Eye and all the congregation.

Then Penrod intended to say to this boy, after church, "Well, that's exackly what your mother did to me, and if you don't like it, you better look out!"

And the real Penrod in the sawdust box clenched his fists. "Come ahead, then!" he muttered. "You talk too much!" Whereupon, the Penrod of his dream gave Margaret's puny son a contemptuous thrashing under the eyes of his mother, who besought in vain for mercy.

"That'll show you how you better treat me after this," Penrod said to the imagined Margaret. "Now take that ole cry-baby home and keep him there!"

The day became bright; Penrod climbed out of the box, and, with a heart at peace, went to look for Sam Williams.

CHAPTER XLI

ON ACCOUNT OF THE WEATHER

THERE is no boredom (not even an invalid's) comparable to that of a boy who has nothing to do. When a man says he has nothing to do, he speaks idly; there is always more than he can do. Grown women never say they have nothing to do, and when girls or little girls say they have nothing to do, they are merely airing an affectation. But when a boy has nothing to do, he has actually nothing at all to do; his state is pathetic, and when he complains of it his voice is haunting.

Mrs. Schofield was troubled by this uncomfortable quality in the voice of her son, who came to her thrice, in his search for entertainment or even employment, one Saturday afternoon during the February thaw. Few facts are better estab-

lished than that the February thaw is the poorest time of
year for everybody. But for a boy it is worse than poorest;
it is bankrupt. The remnant streaks of old soot-speckled
snow left against the north walls of houses have no power
to inspire; rather, they are dreary reminders of sports long
since carried to satiety. One cares little even to eat such
snow, and the eating of icicles, also, has come to be a flaccid
and stale diversion. There is no ice to bear a skate; there
is only a vast sufficiency of cold mud, practically useless.
Sunshine flickers shiftily, coming and going without any
honest purpose; snow-squalls blow for five minutes, the
flakes disappearing as they touch the earth; half an hour
later rain sputters, turns to snow and then turns back to
rain—and the sun disingenuously beams out again, only
to be shut off like a rogue's lantern. And all the wretched
while, if a boy sets foot out of doors, he must be harassed
about his overcoat and rubbers; he is warned against tracking up the plastic lawn and sharply advised to stay inside
the house. Saturday might as well be Sunday.

Thus the season. Penrod had sought all possible means
to pass the time. A full half-hour of vehement yodelling
in the Williams' yard had failed to bring forth comrade
Sam; and at last a coloured woman had opened a window
to inform Penrod that her intellect was being unseated by
his vocalizations, which surpassed in unpleasantness, she
claimed, every sound in her previous experience—and, for
the sake of definiteness, she stated her age to be fifty-three
years and four months. She added that all members of
the Williams family had gone out of town to attend the
funeral of a relative, but she wished that they might have
remained to attend Penrod's, which she confidently predicted
as imminent if the neighbourhood followed its natural impulse.

Penrod listened for a time, but departed before the conclusion of the oration. He sought other comrades, with no
success; he even went to the length of yodelling in the yard
of that best of boys, Georgie Bassett. Here was failure

again, for Georgie signalled to him, through a closed window, that a closeting with dramatic literature was preferable to the society of a playmate; and the book that Georgie exhibited was openly labelled, "300 Choice Declamations." Georgie also managed to convey another reason for his refusal of Penrod's companionship, the visitor being conversant with lip-reading through his studies at the "movies".

"Too muddy!"

Penrod went home.

"Well," Mrs. Schofield said, having almost exhausted a mother's powers of suggestion, "well, why don't you give Duke a bath?" She was that far depleted when Penrod came to her the third time.

Mothers' suggestions are wonderful for little children but sometimes lack lustre when a boy approaches twelve—an age to which the ideas of a Swede farm-hand would usually prove more congenial. However, the dim and melancholy eye of Penrod showed a pale gleam, and he departed. He gave Duke a bath.

The entertainment proved damp and discouraging for both parties. Duke began to tremble even before he was lifted into the water, and after his first immersion he was revealed to be a dog weighing about one-fourth of what an observer of Duke, when Duke was dry, must have guessed his weight to be. His wetness and the disclosure of his extreme fleshly insignificance appeared to mortify him profoundly. He wept. But, presently, under Penrod's thorough ministrations—for the young master was inclined to make this bath last as long as possible—Duke plucked up a heart and began a series of passionate attempts to close the interview. As this was his first bath since September, the effects were lavish and impressionistic, both upon Penrod and upon the bathroom. However, the imperious boy's loud remonstrances contributed to bring about the result desired by Duke.

Mrs. Schofield came running, and eloquently put an end

to Duke's winter bath. When she had suggested this cleansing as a pleasant means of passing the time, she assumed that it would take place in a washtub in the cellar; and Penrod's location of the performance in her own bathroom was far from her intention.

Penrod found her language oppressive, and, having been denied the right to rub Duke dry with a bath-towel—or even with the cover of a table in the next room—the dismal boy, accompanied by his dismal dog, set forth, by way of the kitchen door, into the dismal weather. With no purpose in mind, they mechanically went out to the alley, where Penrod leaned morosely against the fence, and Duke stood shivering close by, his figure still emaciated and his tail absolutely withdrawn from view.

There was a cold, wet wind, however; and before long Duke found his condition unendurable. He was past middle age and cared little for exercise; but he saw that something must be done. Therefore, he made a vigorous attempt to dry himself in a dog's way. Throwing himself, shoulders first, upon the alley mud, he slid upon it, back downward; he rolled and rolled and rolled. He began to feel lively and rolled the more; in every way he convinced Penrod that dogs have no regard for appearances. Also, having discovered an ex-fish near the Herman and Verman cottage, Duke confirmed an impression of Penrod's that dogs have a peculiar fancy in the matter of odours that they like to wear.

Growing livelier and livelier, Duke now wished to play with his master. Penrod was anything but fastidious; nevertheless, under the circumstances, he withdrew to the kitchen, leaving Duke to play by himself, outside.

Della, the cook, was comfortably making rolls and entertaining a caller with a cup of tea. Penrod lingered a few moments, but found even his attention to the conversation ill received, while his attempts to take part in it met outright rebuff. His feelings were hurt; he passed broodingly to the front part of the house, and flung himself wearily into an armchair in the library. With glazed eyes he stared at shelves of books that meant to him just what the wall-paper meant, and he sighed from the abyss. His legs tossed and his arms flopped; he got up, scratched himself exhaustively, and shuffled to a window. Ten desolate minutes he stood there, gazing out sluggishly upon a soggy world. During this time two wet delivery-wagons and four elderly women under umbrellas were all that crossed his field of vision. Somewhere in the world, he thought, there was probably a boy who lived across the street from a jail or a fire-engine house, and had windows worth looking out of. Penrod rubbed his nose up and down the pane slowly, continuously, and without the slightest pleasure; and he again scratched himself wherever it was possible to do so, though he did not even itch. There was nothing in his life.

Such boredom as he was suffering can become agony, and an imaginative creature may do wild things to escape it; many a grown person has taken to drink on account of less pressure than was upon Penrod during that intolerable Saturday.

A faint sound in his ear informed him that Della, in the kitchen, had uttered a loud exclamation, and he decided to go back there. However, since his former visit had resulted in a rebuff that still rankled, he paused outside the kitchen door, which was slightly ajar, and listened. He did this idly, and with no hope of hearing anything interesting or helpful.

"Snakes!" Della exclaimed. "Didja say the poor man was seein' snakes, Mrs. Cullen?"

"No, Della," Mrs. Cullen returned dolorously; "jist one. Flora says he niver see more th'n one—jist one big, long, ugly-faced horr'ble black one; the same one comin' back an' makin' a fizzin' n'ise at um iv'ry time he had the fit on um. 'Twas alw'ys the same snake; an' he'd holler at Flora. 'Here it comes ag'in, *oh*, me soul!' he'd holler. 'The big, black, ugly-faced thing; it's as long as the front fence!' he'd holler, 'an' it's makin' a fizzin' n'ise at me, an' breathin' in me face!' he'd holler. 'Fer th' love o' hivin', Flora,' he'd

holler, 'it's got a little black man wit' a gassly white forehead a-pokin' of it along wit' a broom-handle, an' a-sickin'
it on me, the same as a boy sicks a dog on a poor cat. Fer
the love o' hivin', Flora,' he'd holler, 'cantcha fright it
away from me before I go out o' me head?' "

"Poor Tom!" said Della with deep compassion. "An' the
poor man out of his head all the time, an' not knowin' it!
'Twas awful fer Flora to sit there an' hear such things in
the night like that!"

"You may believe yerself whin ye say it!" Mrs. Cullen
agreed. "Right the very night the poor soul died, he was
hollerin' how the big black snake and the little black man
wit' the gassly white forehead a-pokin' it wit' a broomstick
had come fer um. 'Fright 'em away, Flora!' he was
croakin', in a v'ice that hoarse an' husky 'twas hard to
make out what he says. 'Fright 'em away, Flora!' he says.
' 'Tis the big, black, ugly-faced snake, as black as a black
stockin' an' thicker round than me leg at the thigh before
I was wasted away!' he says, poor man. 'It's makin' the
fizzin' n'ise awful to-night,' he says. 'An' the little black
man wit' the gassly white forehead is a-laughin',' he says.
'He's a-laughin' an' a-pokin' the big, black, fizzin', ugly-
faced snake wit' his broomstick——' "

Della was unable to endure the description.

"Don't tell me no more, Mrs. Cullen!" she protested.
"Poor Tom! I thought Flora was wrong last week whin she
hid the whisky. 'Twas takin' it away from him that killed
him—an' him already so sick!"

"Well," said Mrs. Cullen, "he hardly had the strengt' to
drink much, she tells me, after he see the big snake an' the
little black divil the first time. Poor woman, she says he
talked so plain she sees 'em both herself, iv'ry time she
looks at the poor body where it's laid out. She says——"

"Don't tell me!" cried the impressionable Della. "Don't
tell me, Mrs. Cullen! I can most see 'em meself, right here
in me own kitchen! Poor Tom! To think whin I bought me

new hat, only last week, the first time I'd be wearin' it'd be to his funeral. To-morrow afternoon, it is?"

"At two o'clock," said Mrs. Cullen. "Ye'll be comin' to th' house to-night, o' course, Della?"

"I will," said Della. "After what I've been hearin' from ye, I'm 'most afraid to come, but I'll do it. Poor Tom! I remember the day him an' Flora was married——"

But the eavesdropper heard no more; he was on his way up the back stairs. Life and light—and purpose—had come to his face once more.

Margaret was out for the afternoon. Unostentatiously, he went to her room, and for the next few minutes occupied himself busily therein. He was so quiet that his mother, sewing in her own room, would not have heard him except for the obstinacy of one of the drawers in Margaret's bureau. Mrs. Schofield went to the door of her daughter's room.

"What are you doing, Penrod?"

"Nothin'."

"You're not disturbing any of Margaret's things, are you?"

"No, ma'am," said the meek lad.

"What did you jerk that drawer open for?"

"Ma'am?"

"You heard me, Penrod."

"Yes, ma'am. I was just lookin' for sumpthing."

"For what?" Mrs. Schofield asked. "You know that nothing of yours would be in Margaret's room, Penrod, don't you?"

"Ma'am?"

"What was it you wanted?" she asked, rather impatiently.

"I was just lookin' for some pins."

"Very well," she said, and handed him two from the shoulder of her blouse.

"I ought to have more," he said. "I want about forty."

"What for?"

"I just want to *make* sumpthing, Mamma," he said

plaintively. "My goodness! Can't I even want to have a few pins without everybody makin' such a fuss about it you'd think I was doin' a srime!"

"Doing a what, Penrod?"

"A *srime!*" he repeated, with emphasis; and a moment's reflection enlightened his mother.

"Oh, a crime!" she exclaimed. "You *must* quit reading the murder trials in the newspapers, Penrod. And when you read words you don't know how to pronounce you ought to ask either your papa or me."

"Well, I am askin' you about sumpthing now," Penrod said. "Can't I even have a few *pins* without stoppin' to talk about everything in the newspapers, Mamma?"

"Yes," she said, laughing at his seriousness; and she took him to her room, and bestowed upon him five or six rows torn from a paper of pins. "That ought to be plenty," she said, "for whatever you want to make."

And she smiled after his retreating figure, not noting that he looked softly bulky around the body, and held his elbows unnaturally tight to his sides. She was assured of the innocence of anything to be made with pins, and forbore to press investigation. For Penrod to be playing with pins seemed almost girlish. Unhappy woman, it pleased her to have her son seem girlish!

Penrod went out to the stable, tossed his pins into the wheelbarrow, then took from his pocket and unfolded six pairs of long black stockings, indubitably the property of his sister. (Evidently Mrs. Schofield had been a little late in making her appearance at the door of Margaret's room.)

Penrod worked systematically; he hung the twelve stockings over the sides of the wheelbarrow, and placed the wheelbarrow beside a large packing-box that was half full of excelsior. One after another, he stuffed the stockings with excelsior, till they looked like twelve long black sausages. Then he pinned the top of one stocking securely over the stuffed foot of another, pinning the top of a third to the foot of the second, the top of a fourth to the foot of the third—and continued operations in this fashion until the twelve stockings were the semblance of one long and sinuous black body, sufficiently suggestive to any normal eye.

He tied a string to one end of this unpleasant-looking thing, led it around the stable, and, by vigorous manipulations, succeeded in making it wriggle realistically; but he was not satisfied, and, dropping the string listlessly, sat down in the wheelbarrow to ponder. Penrod sometimes proved that there were within him the makings of an artist; he had become fascinated by an idea, and could not be content until that idea was beautifully realized. He had meant to create a big, long, ugly-faced horrible black snake with which to interest Della and her friend, Mrs. Cullen; but he felt that results, so far, were too crude for exploitation. Merely to lead the pinned stockings by a string was little to fulfill his ambitious vision.

Finally, he rose from the wheelbarrow.

"If I only had a cat!" he said dreamily.

CHAPTER XLII

CREATIVE ART

H E WENT forth, seeking.

The Schofield household was catless this winter; but there was a nice white cat at the Williams'. Penrod strolled thoughtfully over to the Williams's yard.

He was entirely successful, not even having been seen by the sensitive coloured woman, aged fifty-three years and four months.

But still Penrod was thoughtful. The artist within him was unsatisfied with his materials: and upon his return to the stable he placed the cat beneath an overturned box, and once more sat down in the inspiring wheelbarrow, pondering. His expression, concentrated and yet a little anxious, was like that of a painter at work upon a portrait that may or may not turn out to be a masterpiece. The cat did not disturb him by her purring, though she was, indeed, already purring. She was one of those cozy, youngish cats—plump, even a little full-bodied, perhaps, and rather conscious of the figure—that are entirely conventional and domestic by nature, and will set up a ladylike housekeeping anywhere without making a fuss about it. If there be a fault in these cats, overcomplacency might be the name for it; they are a shade too sure of themselves, and their assumption that the world means to treat them respectfully has just a little taint of the *grande dame*. Consequently, they are liable to great outbreaks of nervous energy from within, engendered by the extreme surprises that life sometimes holds in store for them. They lack the pessimistic imagination.

Mrs. Williams's cat was content upon a strange floor and in the confining enclosure of a strange box. She purred for a time, then trustfully fell asleep. 'Twas well she slumbered; she would need all her powers presently.

She slumbered, and dreamed not that she would wake to mingle with events that were to alter her serene disposition radically and cause her to become hasty-tempered and abnormally suspicious for the rest of her life.

Meanwhile, Penrod appeared to reach a doubtful solution of his problem. His expression was still somewhat clouded as he brought from the storeroom of the stable a small fragment of a broken mirror, two paint brushes and two old cans, one containing black paint and the other white. He regarded himself earnestly in the mirror; then, with some reluctance, he dipped a brush into one of the cans, and slowly painted his nose a midnight black. He was on the point of spreading this decoration to cover the lower part of his face, when he paused, brush halfway between can and chin.

What arrested him was a sound from the alley—a sound of drumming upon tin. The eyes of Penrod became significant of rushing thoughts; his expression cleared and

brightened. He ran to the alley doors and flung them open.
"Oh, Verman!" he shouted.

Marching up and down before the cottage across the
alley, Verman plainly considered himself to be an army.
Hanging from his shoulders by a string was an old tin
wash-basin, whereon he beat cheerily with two dry bones,
once the chief supports of a chicken. Thus he assuaged his
ennui.

"Verman, come on in here," Penrod called. "I got sumpthing for you to do you'll like awful well."

Verman halted, ceased to drum, and stared. His gaze was
not fixed particularly upon Penrod's nose, however, and
neither now nor later did he make any remark or gesture
referring to this casual eccentricity. He expected things like
that upon Penrod or Sam Williams. And as for Penrod
himself, he had already forgotten that his nose was painted.

"Come on, Verman!"

Verman continued to stare, not moving. He had received
such invitations before, and they had not always resulted
to his advantage. Within that stable things had happened
to him the like of which he was anxious to avoid in the
future.

"Oh, come ahead, Verman!" Penrod urged, and, divining
logic in the reluctance confronting him, he added, "This
ain't goin' to be anything like last time, Verman. I got
sumpthing just *splendud* for you to do!"

Verman's expression hardened; he shook his head decisively.

"Mo," he said.

"Oh, *come* on, Verman?" Penrod pleaded. "It isn't anything goin' to *hurt* you, is it? I tell you it's sumpthing you'd
give a good deal to *get* to do, if you knew what it is."

"Mo!" said Verman firmly. "I mome maw woo!"

Penrod offered arguments.

"Look, Verman!" he said. "Listen here a minute, can't
you? How d'you know you don't want to until you know
what it is? A person *can't* know they don't want to do a

thing even before the other person tells 'em what they're goin' to get 'em to do, can they? For all you know, this thing I'm goin' to get you to do might be sumpthing you wouldn't miss doin' for anything there is! For all you know, Verman, it might be sumpthing like this: well, f'rinstance, s'pose I was standin' here, and you were over there, sort of like the way you are now, and I says, 'Hello, Verman!' and then I'd go on and tell you there was sumpthing I was goin' to get you to do; and you'd say you wouldn't do it, even before you heard what it was, why where'd be any sense to *that?* For all you know, I might of been goin' to get you to eat a five-cent bag o' peanuts."

Verman had listened obdurately until he heard the last few words; but as they fell upon his ear, he relaxed, and advanced to the stable doors, smiling and extending his open right hand.

"Aw wi," he said. "Gi'm here."

"Well," Penrod returned, a trifle embarrassed, "I didn't say it *was* peanuts, did I? Honest, Verman, it's sumpthing you'll like better'n a few old peanuts that most of 'em'd prob'ly have worms in 'em, anyway. All I want you to do is——"

But Verman was not favourably impressed; his face hardened again.

"Mo!" he said, and prepared to depart.

"Look here, Verman," Penrod urged. "It isn't goin' to hurt you just to come in here and see what I got for you, is it? You can do *that* much, can't you?"

Surely such an appeal must have appeared reasonable, even to Verman, especially since its effect was aided by the promising words, "See what I got for you." Certainly Verman yielded to it, though perhaps a little suspiciously. He advanced a few cautious steps into the stable.

"Look!" Penrod cried, and he ran to the stuffed and linked stockings, seized the leading-string, and vigorously illustrated his further remarks. "How's that for a big, long, ugly-faced horr'ble black ole snake, Verman? Look at her follow me all round anywhere I feel like goin'! Look at her wiggle, will you, though? Look how I make her do anything I tell her to. Lay down, you ole snake, you! See her lay down when I tell her to, Verman? Wiggle, you ole snake, you! See her wiggle, Verman?"

"Hi!" Undoubtedly Verman felt some pleasure.

"Now, listen, Verman!" Penrod continued, hastening to make the most of the opportunity. "Listen! I fixed up this good ole snake just for you. I'm goin' to give her to you."

"*Hi!*"

On account of a previous experience not unconnected with cats, and likely to prejudice Verman, Penrod decided to postpone mentioning Mrs. Williams's pet until he should have secured Verman's coöperation in the enterprise irretrievably.

"All you got to do," he went on, "is to chase this good ole snake around, and sort o' laugh and keep pokin' it with the handle o' that rake yonder. I'm goin' to saw it off just so's you can poke your good ole snake with it, Verman."

"Aw wi," said Verman, and, extending his open hand again, he uttered a hopeful request. "Peamup?"

His host perceived that Verman had misunderstood him. "Peanuts!" he exclaimed. "My goodness! I didn't say I *had* any peanuts, did I? I only said s'pose f'rinstance I *did* have some. My goodness! You don't expeck me to go round here all day workin' like a dog to make a good ole snake for you and then give you a bag o' peanuts to hire you to *play* with it, do you, Verman? My goodness!"

Verman's hand fell, with a little disappointment.

"Aw wi," he said, consenting to accept the snake without the bonus.

"That's the boy! *Now* we're all right, Verman; and pretty soon I'm goin' to saw that rake-handle off for you, too; so's you can kind o' guide your good ole snake around with it; but first—well, first there's just one more thing's got to be done. I'll show you—it won't take but a minute." Then, while Verman watched him wonderingly, he went to the can of white paint and dipped a brush therein. "It won't get on your clo'es much, or anything, Verman," he explained. "I only just got to——"

But as he approached, dripping brush in hand, the wondering look was all gone from Verman; determination took its place.

"Mo!" he said, turned his back, and started for outdoors.

"Look here, Verman," Penrod cried. "I haven't done anything to you yet, have I? It isn't goin' to hurt you, is it? You act like a little teeny bit o' paint was goin' to kill you! What's the matter of you? I only just got to paint the top part of your face; I'm not goin' to *touch* the other part of it—nor your hands or anything. All *I* want——"

"*Mo!*" said Verman from the doorway.

"Oh, my goodness!" moaned Penrod; and in desperation he drew forth from his pocket his entire fortune. "All right, Verman," he said resignedly. "If you won't do it any other way, here's a nickel, and you can go and buy you some peanuts when we get through. But if I give you this money, you got to promise to wait till we *are* through, and you got to promise to do anything I tell you to. You goin' to promise?"

The eyes of Verman glistened; he returned, gave bond, and, grasping the coin, burst into the rich laughter of a gourmand.

Penrod immediately painted him dead white above the eyes, all round his head and including his hair. It took all the paint in the can.

Then the artist mentioned the presence of Mrs. Williams's cat, explained in full his ideas concerning the docile animal, and the long black snake, and Della and her friend, Mrs. Cullen, while Verman listened with anxiety, but remained true to his oath.

They removed the stocking at the end of the long black snake, and cut four holes in the foot and ankle of it. They removed the excelsior, placed Mrs. Williams's cat in the stocking, shook her down into the lower section of it; drew her feet through the four holes there, leaving her head in the toe of the stocking; then packed the excelsior down on top of her, and once more attached the stocking to the rest of the long, black snake.

How shameful is the ease of the historian! He sits in his dressing-gown to write: "The enemy attacked in force——" The tranquil pen, moving in a cloud of tobacco smoke, leaves upon the page its little hieroglyphics, serenely summing up the monstrous deeds and sufferings of men of action. How cold, how niggardly, to state merely that Penrod and the painted Verman succeeded in giving the long, black snake a motive power, or tractor, apparently its own but consisting of Mrs. Williams's cat!

She was drowsy when they lifted her from the box; she was still drowsy when they introduced part of her into the orifice of the stocking; but she woke to full, vigorous young life when she perceived that their purpose was for her to descend into the black depths of that stocking head first.

Verman held the mouth of the stocking stretched, and Penrod manipulated the cat; but she left her hearty mark on both of them before, in a moment of unfortunate inspiration, she humped her back while she was upside down, and Penrod took advantage of the concavity to increase it even more than she desired. The next instant she was assisted downward into the gloomy interior, with excelsior already beginning to block the means of egress.

Gymnastic moments followed; there were times when both boys hurled themselves full-length upon the floor, seizing the animated stocking with far-extended hands; and even when the snake was a complete thing, with legs growing from its unquestionably ugly face, either Penrod or Verman must keep a grasp upon it, for it would not be soothed, and refused, over and over, to calm itself, even when addressed as, "Poor pussy!" and "Nice 'ittle kitty!"

Finally, they thought they had their good ole snake "about quieted down", as Penrod said, because the animated head had remained in one place for an unusual length of time, though the legs produced a rather sinister effect of crouching, and a noise like a distant planing-mill came from the interior—and then Duke appeared in the doorway.

He was still feeling lively.

CHAPTER XLIII

THE DEPARTING GUEST

B Y THE time Penrod returned from chasing Duke to the next corner, Verman had the long, black snake down from the rafter where its active head had taken refuge, with the rest of it dangling; and both boys agreed that Mrs. Williams's cat must certainly be able to "see *some*, anyway", through the meshes of the stocking.

"Well," said Penrod, "it's gettin' pretty near dark, what with all this bother and mess we been havin' around here, and I expeck as soon as I get this good ole broom-handle fixed out of the rake for you, Verman, it'll be about time to begin what we had to go and take all this trouble *for*."

. . . . Mr. Schofield had brought an old friend home to dinner with him: "Dear old Joe Gilling," he called this friend when introducing him to Mrs. Schofield. Mr. Gilling, as Mrs. Schofield was already informed by telephone, had just happened to turn up in town that day, and had called on his classmate at the latter's office. The two had not seen each other in eighteen years.

Mr. Gilling was a tall man, clad highly in the mode, and brought to a polished and powdered finish by barber and manicurist; but his colour was peculiar, being almost unhumanly florid, and, as Mrs. Schofield afterward claimed to have noticed, his eyes "wore a nervous, apprehensive look", his hands were tremulous, and his manner was "queer and jerky"—at least, that is how she defined it.

She was not surprised to hear him state that he was travelling for his health and not upon business. He had not been really well for several years, he said.

At that, Mr. Schofield laughed and slapped him heartily on the back.

"Oh, mercy!" Mr. Gilling cried, leaping in his chair. "What *is* the matter?"

"Nothing!" Mr. Schofield laughed. "I just slapped you the way we used to slap each other on the campus. What I was going to say was that you have no business being a bachelor. With all your money, and nothing to do but travel and sit around hotels and clubs, no wonder you've grown bilious."

"Oh, no; I'm not bilious," Mr. Gilling said uncomfortably. "I'm not bilious at all."

"You ought to get married," Mr. Schofield returned. "You ought——" He paused, for Mr. Gilling had jumped again. "What's the trouble, Joe?"

"Nothing. I thought perhaps—perhaps you were going to slap me on the back again."

"Not this time," Mr. Schofield said, renewing his laughter. "Well, is dinner about ready?" he asked, turning to his wife. "Where are Margaret and Penrod?"

"Margaret's just come in," Mrs. Schofield answered.

"She'll be down in a minute, and Penrod's around some-where."

"Penrod?" Mr. Gilling repeated curiously, in his nervous, serious way. "What is Penrod?"

And at this, Mrs. Schofield joined in her husband's laughter. Mr. Schofield explained.

"Penrod's our young son," he said. "He's not much for looks, maybe; but he's been pretty good lately, and some-times we're almost inclined to be proud of him. You'll see him in a minute, old Joe!"

Old Joe saw him even sooner. Instantly, as Mr. Schofield finished his little prediction, the most shocking uproar ever heard in that house burst forth in the kitchen. Distinctly Irish shrieks unlimited came from that quarter—together with the clashing of hurled metal and tin, the appealing sound of breaking china, and the hysterical barking of a dog.

The library door flew open, and Mrs. Cullen appeared as a mingled streak crossing the room from one door to the other. She was followed by a boy with a coal-black nose; and between his feet, as he entered, there appeared a big, long, black, horr'ble snake, with frantic legs springing from what appeared to be its head; and it further fulfilled Mrs. Cullen's description by making a fizzin' noise. Accompany-ing the snake, and still faithfully endeavouring to guide it with the detached handle of a rake, was a small black demon with a gassly white forehead and gasslier white hair. Duke, evidently still feeling his bath, was doing all in his power to aid the demon in making the snake step lively. A few kitchen implements followed this fugitive procession through the library doorway.

The long, black snake became involved with a leg of the heavy table in the centre of the room. The head developed spasms of agility; there were clawings and rippings; then the foremost section of the long, black snake detached itself, bounded into the air, and, after turning a number of somer-saults, became, severally, a torn stocking, excelsior, and a lunatic cat. The ears of this cat were laid back flat upon its head and its speed was excessive upon a fairly circular track it laid out for itself in the library. Flying round this orbit, it perceived the open doorway; passed through it, thence to the kitchen, and outward and onward—Della having left the kitchen door open in her haste as she retired to the backyard.

The black demon with the gassly white forehead and hair, finding himself in the presence of grown people who were white all over, turned in his tracks and followed Mrs. Williams's cat to the great outdoors. Duke preceded Ver-man. Mrs. Cullen vanished. Of the apparition, only wreckage and a rightfully apprehensive Penrod were left.

"But where—" Mrs. Schofield began, a few minutes later, looking suddenly mystified—"where—where——"

"Where what?" Mr. Schofield asked testily. "What are you talking about?" His nerves were jarred, and he was rather hoarse after what he had been saying to Penrod. (That regretful necromancer was now upstairs doing unhelpful things to his nose over a washstand.) "What do you mean by, 'Where, where, where?' " Mr. Schofield demanded. "I don't see any sense to it."

"But where is your old classmate?" she cried. "Where's Mr. Gilling?"

She was the first to notice this striking absence.

"By George!" Mr. Schofield exclaimed. "Where *is* old Joe?"

Margaret intervened. "You mean that tall, pale man who was calling?" she asked.

"Pale, no!" said her father. "He's as flushed as——"

"He was pale when *I* saw him," Margaret said. "He had his hat and coat, and he was trying to get out of the front door when I came running downstairs. He couldn't work the catch for a minute; but before I got to the foot of the steps he managed to turn it and open the door. He went out before I could think what to say to him, he was in such a hurry. I guess everything was so confused you didn't notice—but he's certainly gone."

Mrs. Schofield turned to her husband.

"But I thought he was going to stay to dinner!" she cried.

Mr. Schofield shook his head, admitting himself floored. Later, having mentally gone over everything that might shed light on the curious behaviour of old Joe, he said, without preface: "He wasn't at all dissipated when we were in college."

Mrs. Schofield nodded severely. "Maybe this was just the best thing could have happened to him, after all," she said.

"It may be," her husband returned. "I don't say it isn't. *But* that isn't going to make any difference in what I'm going to do to Penrod!"

CHAPTER XLIV

THE PARTY

> *Miss Amy Rennsdale*
>
> *At Home*
> *Saturday, the twenty-third*
> *from three to six*
> R. s. v. p.   *Dancing*

THIS little card, delicately engraved, betokened the
hospitality incidental to the ninth birthday anniversary of Baby Rennsdale, youngest member of the
Friday Afternoon Dancing Class, and, by the same token,
it represented the total social activity (during that season)

of a certain limited bachelor set consisting of Messrs. Penrod Schofield and Samuel Williams. The truth must be faced: Penrod and Sam were seldom invited to small parties; they were considered too imaginative. But in the case of so large an affair as Miss Rennsdale's, the feeling that their parents would be sensitive outweighed fears of what Penrod and Sam might do at the party. Reputation is indeed a bubble, but sometimes it is blown of sticky stuff.

The comrades set out for the fête in company, final maternal outpourings upon deportment and the duty of dancing with the hostess evaporating in their freshly cleaned ears. Both boys, however, were in a state of mind, body, and decoration appropriate to the gala scene they were approaching. Their collars were wide and white; inside the pockets of their overcoats were glistening dancing-pumps, wrapped in tissue-paper; inside their jacket pockets were pleasant-smelling new white gloves, and inside their heads solemn timidity commingled with glittering anticipations. Before them, like a Christmas tree glimpsed through lace curtains, they beheld joy shimmering—music, ice-cream, macaroons, tinsel caps, and the starched ladies of their hearts. Penrod and Sam walked demurely yet almost boundingly; their faces were shining but grave—they were on their way to the Party!

"Look at there!" said Penrod. "There's Carlie Chitten!"

"Where?" Sam asked.

" 'Cross the street. Haven't you got any eyes?"

"Well, whyn't you say he was 'cross the street in the first place?" Sam returned plaintively. "Besides, he's so little you can't hardly see him." This was, of course, a violent exaggeration, though Master Chitten, not yet eleven years old, was an inch or two short for his age. "He's all dressed up," Sam added. "I guess he must be invited."

"I bet he does sumpthing," said Penrod.

"I bet he does, too," Sam agreed.

This was the extent of their comment upon the small person across the street; but, in spite of its non-committal character, the manner of both commentators seemed to indicate that they had just exchanged views upon an interesting and even curious subject. They walked along in silence for several minutes, staring speculatively at Master Chitten.

His appearance was pleasant and not remarkable. He was a handsome, dark little boy, with quick eyes and a precociously reserved expression; his air was "well-bred"; he was exquisitely neat, and he had a look of manly competence that grown people found attractive and reassuring. In short, he was a boy of whom a timid adult stranger would have inquired the way with confidence. And yet Sam and Penrod had mysterious thoughts about him—obviously there was something subterranean here.

They continued to look at him for the greater part of a block, when, their progress bringing them in sight of Miss Amy Rennsdale's place of residence their attention was directed to a group of men bearing festal burdens—encased violins, a shrouded harp and other beckoning shapes. There were signs, too, that most of "those invited" intended to miss no moment of this party; guests already indoors watched from the windows the approach of the musicians. Washed boys in black and white, and girls in tender colours converged from various directions, making gayly for the thrilling gateway—and the most beautiful little girl in all the world, Marjorie Jones, of the amber curls, jumped from a carriage step to the curbstone as Penrod and Sam came up. She waved to them.

Sam responded heartily; but Penrod, feeling real emotion and seeking to conceal it, muttered, " 'Lo, Marjorie!" gruffly, offering no further demonstration. Marjorie paused a moment, expectant, and then, as he did not seize the opportunity to ask her for the first dance, she tried not to look disappointed and ran into the house ahead of the two boys. Penrod was scarlet; he wished to dance the first dance with Marjorie, and the second and the third and all the other dances, and he strongly desired to sit with her "at refreshments"; but he had been unable to ask for a single one of these privileges. It would have been impossible for him to state why he was thus dumb, although the reason was simple and wholly complimentary to Marjorie: she had looked so overpoweringly pretty that she had produced in the bosom of her admirer a severe case of stage fright. That was "all the matter with him"; but it was the beginning of his troubles, and he did not recover until he and Sam reached the "gentlemen's dressing-room", whither they were directed by a polite coloured man.

Here they found a cloud of acquaintances getting into pumps and gloves, and, in a few extreme cases, readjusting hair before a mirror. Some even went so far—after removing their shoes and putting on their pumps—as to wash traces of blacking from their hands in the adjacent bathroom before assuming their gloves. Penrod, being in a strange mood, was one of these, sharing the basin with little Maurice Levy.

"Carlie Chitten's here," said Maurice, as they soaped their hands.

"I guess I know it," Penrod returned. "I bet he does sumpthing, too."

Maurice shook his head ominously. "Well, I'm gettin' tired of it. I know he was the one stuck that cold fried egg in P'fesser Bartet's overcoat pocket at dancin'-school, and ole p'fesser went and blamed it on me. Then, Carlie, he c'm up to me, th' other day, and he says, 'Smell my buttonhole bokay.' He had some vi'lets stickin' in his buttonhole, and I went to smell 'em and water squirted on me out of 'em. I guess I've stood about enough, and if he does another thing I don't like, he better look out!"

Penrod showed some interest, inquiring for detrils, whereupon Maurice explained that if Master Chitten displeased him further, Master Chitten would receive a blow upon one of his features. Maurice was simple and homely about it, seeking rhetorical vigour rather than elegance; in fact, what he definitely promised Master Chitten was "a bang on the snoot."

"Well," said Penrod, "he never bothered *me* any. I expect he knows too much for that!"

A cry of pain was heard from the dressing-room at this juncture, and, glancing through the doorway, Maurice and Penrod beheld Sam Williams in the act of sucking his right thumb with vehemence, the while his brow was contorted and his eyes watered. He came into the bathroom and held his thumb under a faucet.

"That darn little Carlie Chitten!" he complained. "He ast me to hold a little tin box he showed me. He told me to hold it between my thumb and fingers and he'd show me sumpthing. Then he pushed the lid, and a big needle came out of a hole and stuck me half through my thumb. That's a *nice* way to act, isn't it?"

Carlie Chitten's dark head showed itself cautiously beyond the casing of the door.

"How's your thumb, Sam?" he asked.

"You wait!" Sam shouted, turning furiously; but the small prestidigitator was gone. With a smothered laugh, Carlie dashed through the groups of boys in the dressing-room and made his way downstairs, his manner reverting to its usual polite gravity before he entered the drawing-room, where his hostess waited. Music sounding at about this time, he was followed by the other boys, who came trooping down, leaving the dressing-room empty.

Penrod, among the tail-enders of the procession, made his dancing-school bow to Miss Rennsdale and her grown-up supporters (two maiden aunts and a governess) then he looked about for Marjorie, discovering her but too easily. Her amber curls were swaying gently in time to the music; she looked never more beautiful, and her partner was Master Chitten!

A pang of great penetrative power and equal unexpectedness found the most vulnerable spot beneath the simple black of Penrod Schofield's jacket. Straightway he turned his back upon the crash-covered floors where the dancers were, and moved gloomily toward the hall. But one of the maiden aunts Rennsdale waylaid him.

"It's Penrod Schofield, isn't it?" she asked. "Or Sammy Williams? I'm not sure which. Is it Penrod?"

"Ma'am?" he said. "Yes'm."

"Well, Penrod, I can find a partner for you. There are several dear little girls over here, if you'll come with me."

"Well——" He paused, shifted from one foot to the other, and looked enigmatic. "I better not," he said. He meant no offence; his trouble was only that he had not yet learned how to do as he pleased at a party and, at the same time, to seem polite about it. "I guess I don't want to," he added.

"Very well!" And Miss Rennsdale instantly left him to his own devices.

He went to lurk in the wide doorway between the hall and the drawing-room—under such conditions the universal refuge of his sex at all ages. There he found several boys of notorious shyness, and stood with them in a mutually protective group. Now and then one of them would lean upon another until repelled by action and a husky "What's matter 'th you? Get off o' me!" They all twisted their slender necks uneasily against the inner bands of their collars, at intervals, and sometimes exchanged facetious blows under cover. In the distance Penrod caught glimpses of amber curls flashing to and fro, and he knew himself to be among the derelicts.

He remained in this questionable sanctuary during the next dance; but, edging along the wall to lean more comfortably in a corner, as the music of the third sounded, he overheard part of a conversation that somewhat concerned him. The participants were the governess of his hostess, Miss Lowe, and that one of the aunts Rennsdale who had offered to provide him with a partner. These two ladies were standing just in front of him, unconscious of his nearness.

"I never," Miss Rennsdale said, "*never* saw a more

fascinating little boy than that Carlie Chitten. There'll be some heartaches when he grows up; I can't keep my eyes off him."

"Yes; he's a charming boy," Miss Lowe said. "His manners are remarkable."

"He's a little man of the world," the enthusiastic Miss Rennsdale went on, "very different from such boys as Penrod Schofield!"

"Oh, *Penrod!*" Miss Lowe exclaimed. "Good gracious!"

"I don't see why he came. He declines to dance—rudely, too!"

"I don't think the little girls will mind *that* so much!" Miss Lowe said. "If you'd come to the dancing class some Friday with Amy and me, you'd understand why."

They moved away. Penrod heard his name again mentioned between them as they went, and, though he did not catch the accompanying remark, he was inclined to think it unfavourable. He remained where he was, brooding morbidly.

He understood that the government was against him, nor was his judgment at fault in this conclusion. He was affected, also, by the conduct of Marjorie, who was now dancing gayly with Maurice Levy, a former rival of Penrod's. The fact that Penrod had not gone near her did not make her culpability seem the less; in his gloomy heart he resolved not to ask her for one single dance. He would not go near her. He would not go near *any of 'em!*

His eyes began to burn, and he swallowed heavily; but he was never one to succumb piteously to such emotion, and it did not even enter his head that he was at liberty to return to his own home. Neither he nor any of his friends had ever left a party until it was officially concluded. What his sufferings demanded of him now for their alleviation was not departure but action!

Underneath the surface, nearly all children's parties contain a group of outlaws who wait only for a leader to hoist the black flag. The group consists mainly of boys too shy to be at ease with the girls, but who wish to distinguish themselves in some way; and there are others, ordinarily well behaved, whom the mere actuality of a party makes drunken. The effect of music, too, upon children is incalculable, especially when they do not hear it often—and both a snare-drum and a bass drum were in the expensive orchestra at the Rennsdale party.

Nevertheless, the outlawry at any party may remain incipient unless a chieftain appears; but in Penrod's corner were now gathering into one anarchical mood all the necessary qualifications for leadership. Out of that bitter corner there stepped, not a Penrod Schofield subdued and hoping to win the lost favour of the Authorities, but a hot-hearted rebel determined on an uprising.

Smiling a reckless and challenging smile, he returned to the cluster of boys in the wide doorway and began to push one and another of them about. They responded hopefully with counter-pushes, and presently there was a tumultuous surging and eddying in that quarter, accompanied by noises that began to compete with the music. Then Penrod allowed himself to be shoved out among the circling dancers, so that he collided with Marjorie and Maurice Levy, almost oversetting them.

He made a mock bow and a mock apology, being inspired to invent a jargon phrase.

"Excuse me," he said, at the same time making vocal his own conception of a taunting laugh. "Excuse me, but I must 'a' got your bumpus!"

Marjorie looked grieved and turned away with Maurice; but the boys in the doorway squealed with maniac laughter.

"Gotcher bumpus! Gotcher bumpus!" they shrilled. And they began to push others of their number against the dancing couples, shouting, " 'Scuse me! Gotcher bumpus!"

It became a contagion and then a game. As the dances went on, strings of boys, led by Penrod, pursued one another across the rooms, howling, "Gotcher bumpus!" at the top of their lungs. They dodged and ducked, and seized upon dancers as shields; they caromed from one couple into another, and even into the musicians of the orchestra. Boys who were dancing abandoned their partners and joined the marauders, shrieking, "Gotcher bumpus!" Potted plants went down; a slender gilt chair refused to support the hurled body of Master Roderick Magsworth Bitts, and the sound of splintering wood mingled with other sounds. Dancing became impossible; Miss Amy Rennsdale wept in the midst of the riot, and everybody knew that Penrod Schofield had "started it".

Under instructions, the leader of the orchestra, clapping his hands for attention, stepped to the centre of the drawing-room, and shouted,

"A moment silence, if you bleace!"

Slowly the hubbub ceased; the virtuous and the wicked paused alike in their courses to listen. Miss Amy Rennsdale was borne away to have her tearful face washed, and Marjorie Jones and Carlie Chitten and Georgie Bassett came forward consciously, escorted by Miss Lowe. The musician waited until the return of the small hostess; then he announced in a loud voice:

"A fency dence called 'Les Papillons', denced by Miss Amy Rennstul, Miss Chones, Mister Chorch Passett, ant Mister Jitten. Some young chentlemen haf mate so much noise ant confoosion Miss Lowe wish me to ask bleace no more such a nonsense. Fency dence, 'Les Papillons'."

Thereupon, after formal salutations, Mr. Chitten took Marjorie's hand, Georgie Bassett took Miss Rennsdale's, and they proceeded to dance "Les Papillons" in a manner that made up in conscientiousness whatever it may have lacked in abandon. The outlaw leader looked on, smiling a smile intended to represent careless contempt, but in reality he was unpleasantly surprised. A fancy dance by Georgie Bassett and Baby Rennsdale was customary at every party attended by members of the Friday Afternoon Dancing Class; but Marjorie and Carlie Chitten were new performers, and Penrod had not heard that they had learned *to* dance "Les Papillons" together. He was the further embittered.

Carlie made a false step, recovering himself with some difficulty, whereupon a loud, jeering squawk of laughter was heard from the insurgent cluster, which had been awed to temporary quiet but still maintained its base in the drawing-room doorway. There was a general "*Sh!*" followed by a shocked whispering, as well as a general turning of eyes toward Penrod. But it was not Penrod who had laughed, though no one would have credited him with an alibi. The laughter came from two throats that breathed as one with such perfect simultaneousness that only one was credited with the disturbance. These two throats belonged respectively to Samuel Williams and Maurice Levy, who were standing in a strikingly Rosencrantz-and-Guildenstern attitude.

"He got me with his ole tin-box needle, too," Maurice muttered to Sam. "He was goin' to do it to Marjorie, and I told her to look out, and he says, 'Here, *you* take it!' all of a sudden, and he stuck it in my hand so quick I never thought. And then, *bim!* his ole needle shot out and perty near went through my thumb-bone or sumpthing. He'll be sorry before this day's over!"

"Well," said Sam darkly, "he's goin' to be sorry he stuck *me*, anyway!" Neither Sam nor Maurice had even the vaguest plan for causing the desired regret in the breast of Master Chitten; but both derived a little consolation from these prophecies. And they, too, had aligned themselves with the insurgents. Their motives were personal—Carlie Chitten had wronged both of them, and Carlie was conspicuously in high favour with the Authorities. Naturally Sam and Maurice were against the Authorities.

"Les Papillons" came to a conclusion. Carlie and Georgie bowed; Marjorie Jones and Baby Rennsdale curtesied, and there was loud applause. In fact, the demonstration became so uproarious that some measure of it was open to suspicion, especially as hisses of reptilian venomousness were commingled with it, and also a hoarse but vociferous repetition of the dastard words, "Carlie dances *rotten!*" Again it was the work of Rosencrantz and Guildenstern; but the plot was attributed to another.

"*Shame*, Penrod Schofield!" said both the aunts Rennsdale publicly, and Penrod, wholly innocent, became scarlet with indignant mortification. Carlie Chitten himself, however, marked the true offenders. A slight flush tinted his cheeks, and then, in his quiet, self-contained way, he slipped through the crowd of girls and boys, unnoticed, into the hall, and ran noiselessly up the stairs and into the "gentlemen's dressing-room", now inhabited only by hats, caps, overcoats, and the temporarily discarded shoes of the dancers. Most of the shoes stood in rows against the wall, and Carlie examined these rows attentively, after a time discovering a pair of shoes with patent leather tips. He knew them; they belonged to Maurice Levy, and, picking them up, he went to a corner of the room where four shoes had been left together under a chair. Upon the chair were overcoats and caps that he was able to identify as the property of Penrod Schofield and Samuel Williams; but, as he was not sure which pair of shoes belonged to Penrod and which to Sam, he added both pairs to Maurice's and carried them into the bathroom. Here he set the plug in the tub, turned the faucets, and, after looking about him and discovering large supplies of all sorts in a wall cabinet, he tossed six cakes of green soap into the tub. He let the soap remain in the water to soften a little, and, returning to the dressing room, whiled away the time in mixing and mismating pairs of shoes along the walls, and also in tying the strings of the mismated shoes together in hard knots.

Throughout all this, his expression was grave and intent; his bright eyes grew brighter, but he did not smile. Carlie Chitten was a singular boy, though not unique: he was an "only child", lived at a hotel, and found life there favourable to the development of certain peculiarities in his nature. He played a lone hand, and with what precocious diplomacy he played that curious hand was attested by the fact that Carlie was brilliantly esteemed by parents and guardians in general.

It must be said for Carlie that, in one way, his nature was liberal. For instance, having come upstairs to prepare a vengeance upon Sam and Maurice in return for their slurs upon his dancing, he did not confine his efforts to the belongings of those two alone. He provided every boy in the house with something to think about later, when shoes should be resumed; and he was far from stopping at that. Casting about him for some material that he desired, he opened a door of the dressing-room and found himself confronting the apartment of Miss Lowe. Upon a desk he beheld the bottle of mucilage he wanted, and, having taken possession of it, he allowed his eye the privilege of a rapid glance into a dressing table drawer, accidentally left open.

He returned to the dressing-room, five seconds later, carrying not only the mucilage but a "switch" worn by Miss Lowe when her hair was dressed in a fashion different from that which she had favoured for the party. This "switch" he placed in the pocket of a juvenile overcoat unknown to him, and then he took the mucilage into the bathroom. There he rescued from the water the six cakes of soap, placed one in each of the six shoes, pounding it down securely into the toe of the shoe with the handle of a back brush. After that, Carlie poured mucilage into all six shoes impartially until the bottle was empty, then took them back to their former positions in the dressing-room. Finally, with careful forethought, he placed his own shoes in the pockets of his overcoat, and left the overcoat and his cap upon a chair near the outer door of the room. Then he went quietly downstairs, having been absent from the festivities a little less than twelve minutes. He had been energetic—only a boy could have accomplished so much in so short a time. In fact, Carlie had been so busy that his forgetting to turn off the faucets in the bathroom is not at all surprising.

No one had noticed his absence. That infectious pastime, "Gotcher bumpus", had broken out again, and the general dancing, which had been resumed upon the conclusion of "Les Papillons", was once more becoming demoralized. Despairingly the aunts Rennsdale and Miss Lowe brought forth from the rear of the house a couple of waiters and commanded them to arrest the ringleaders, whereupon hilarious terror spread among the outlaw band. Shouting tauntingly at their pursuers, they fled—and bellowing, trampling flight swept through every quarter of the house.

Refreshments quelled this outbreak for a time. The orchestra played a march; Carlie Chitten and Georgie Bassett, with Amy Rennsdale and Marjorie, formed the head of a procession, while all the boys who had retained their sense of decorum immediately sought partners and fell in behind. The outlaws, succumbing to ice cream hunger, followed suit, one after the other, until all of the girls were provided with escorts. Then, to the moral strains of "The Stars and Stripes Forever", the children paraded out to the dining-room. Two and two they marched, except at the extreme tail end of the line, where, since there were three more boys than girls at the party, the three left-over boys were placed. These three were also the last three outlaws to succumb and return to civilization from outlying portions of the house after the pursuit by waiters. They were Messieurs Maurice Levy, Samuel Williams, and Penrod Schofield.

They took their chairs in the capacious dining-room quietly enough, though their expressions were eloquent of bravado, and they jostled one another and their neighbours intentionally, even in the act of sitting. However, it was not long before delectable foods engaged their whole attention and Miss Amy Rennsdale's party relapsed into etiquette for the following twenty minutes. The refection concluded with the mild explosion of paper "crackers" that erupted bright-coloured, fantastic headgear, and, during the snapping of the "crackers", Penrod heard the voice of Marjorie calling from somewhere behind him, "Carlie and Amy, will you change chairs with Georgie Bassett and me—just for fun?" The chairs had been placed in rows, back to back, and Penrod would not even turn his head to see if Master Chitten and Miss Rennsdale accepted Marjorie's proposal, though they were directly behind him and Sam; but he grew red and breathed hard. A moment later, the liberty-cap that he had set upon his head was softly removed, and a little crown of silver paper put in its place.

"*Penrod?*"

The whisper was close to his ear, and a gentle breath cooled the back of his neck.

CHAPTER XLV

THE HEART OF MARJORIE JONES

"WELL, what you want?" Penrod asked, brusquely.
Marjorie's wonderful eyes were dark and mysterious, like still water at twilight.

"What makes you behave so *awful?*" she whispered.

"I don't either! I guess I got a right to do the way I want to, haven't I?"

"Well, anyway," said Marjorie, "you ought to quit bumping into people so it hurts."

"Poh! It wouldn't hurt a fly!"

"Yes, it did. It hurt when you bumped Maurice and me that time."

"It didn't either. *Where'd* it hurt you? Let's see if it——"

"Well, I can't show you, but it did. Penrod, are you going to keep on?"

Penrod's heart had melted within him; but his reply was pompous and cold. "I will if I feel like it, and I won't if I feel like it. You wait and see."

But Marjorie jumped up and ran around to him abandoning her escort. All the children were leaving their chairs and moving toward the dancing-rooms; the orchestra was playing dance-music again.

"Come on, Penrod!" Marjorie cried. "Let's go dance this together. Come on!"

With seeming reluctance, he suffered her to lead him away. "Well, I'll go with you; but I won't dance," he said. "I wouldn't dance with the President of the United States!"

"Why, Penrod?"

"Well—because—well, I won't *do* it!"

"All right. I don't care. I guess I've danced plenty, anyhow. Let's go in here." She led him into a room too small for dancing, used ordinarily by Miss Amy Rennsdale's father as his study, and now vacant. For a while there was silence; but finally Marjorie pointed to the window and said shyly:

"Look, Penrod, it's getting dark. The party'll be over pretty soon, and you've never danced one single time!"

"Well, I guess I know that, don't I?"

He was unable to cast aside his outward truculence, though it was but a relic. However, his voice was gentler, and Marjorie seemed satisfied. From the other rooms came the swinging music, shouts of "Gotcher bumpus!" sounds of stumbling, of scrambling, of running, of muffled concussions and squeals of dismay. Penrod's followers were renewing the wild work, even in the absence of their chief.

"Penrod Schofield, you bad boy," said Marjorie, "you started every bit of that! You ought to be ashamed of yourself."

"*I* didn't do anything," he said—and he believed it. "Pick on me for everything!"

"Well, they wouldn't if you didn't do so much," said Marjorie.

"They would, too."

"They wouldn't, either. Who would?"

"That Miss Lowe," he specified bitterly. "Yes, and Baby Rennsdale's aunts. If the house'd burn down, I bet they'd say Penrod Schofield did it! Anybody does anything at *all*, they say, 'Penrod Schofield, shame on you!' When you and Carlie were dan——"

"Penrod, I just hate that little Carlie Chitten. P'fesser Bartet made me learn that dance with him; but I just hate him."

Penrod was now almost completely mollified; nevertheless, he continued to set forth his grievance. "Well, they all turned around to me and they said, 'Why, Penrod Schofield, shame on you!' And I hadn't done a single thing! I was just standin' there. They got to blame *me*, though!"

Marjorie laughed airily. "Well, if you aren't the foolishest——"

"They would, too," he asserted, with renewed bitterness. "If the house was to fall down, you'd see! They'd all say——"

Marjorie interrupted him. She put her hand on the top of her head, looking a little startled.

"What's that?" she said.

"What's what?"

"Like rain!" Marjorie cried. "Like it was raining in here! A drop fell on my——"

"Why, it couldn't——" he began. But at this instant a drop fell upon his head, too, and, looking up, they beheld a great oozing splotch upon the ceiling. Drops were gathering upon it and falling; the tinted plaster was cracking, and a little stream began to patter down and splash upon the floor. Then there came a resounding thump upstairs, just above them, and fragments of wet plaster fell.

"The roof must be leaking," said Marjorie, beginning to be alarmed.

"Couldn't be the roof," said Penrod. "Besides there ain't any rain outdoors."

As he spoke, a second slender stream of water began to patter upon the floor of the hall outside the door.

"Good gracious!" Marjorie cried, while the ceiling above them shook as with earthquake—or as with boys in numbers jumping, and a great uproar burst forth overhead.

"I believe the house *is* falling down, Penrod!" she quavered.

"Well, they'll blame *me* for it!" he said. "Anyways, we better get out o' here. I guess sumpthing must be the matter."

His guess was accurate, so far as it went. The dance-music had swung into "Home Sweet Home" some time before, the children were preparing to leave, and Master Chitten had been the first boy to ascend to the gentlemen's dressing-room for his cap, overcoat and shoes, his motive being to avoid by departure any difficulty in case his earlier activities should cause him to be suspected by the other boys. But in the doorway he halted, aghast.

The lights had not been turned on; but even the dim windows showed that the polished floor gave back reflections no floor-polish had ever equalled. It was a gently steaming lake, from an eighth to a quarter of an inch deep. And Carlie realized that he had forgotten to turn off the faucets in the bathroom.

For a moment, his *savoir faire* deserted him, and he was filled with ordinary, human-boy panic. Then, at a sound of voices behind him, he lost his head and rushed into the bathroom. It was dark, but certain sensations and the splashing of his pumps warned him that the water was deeper in there. The next instant the lights were switched on in both bathroom and dressing-room, and Carlie beheld Sam Williams in the doorway of the former.

"Oh, look, Maurice!" Sam shouted, in frantic excitement. "Somebody's let the tub run over, and it's about ten feet deep! Carlie Chitten's sloshin' around in here. Let's hold the door on him and keep him in!"

Carlie rushed to prevent the execution of this project; but he slipped and went swishing full length along the floor, creating a little surf before him as he slid, to the demoniac happiness of Sam and Maurice. They closed the door, however, and, as other boys rushed, shouting and splashing, into the flooded dressing-room, Carlie began to hammer upon the panels. Then the owners of shoes, striving to rescue them from the increasing waters, made discoveries.

The most dangerous time to give a large children's party is when there has not been one for a long period. The Rennsdale party had that misfortune, and its climax was the complete and convulsive madness of the gentlemen's dressing-room during those final moments supposed to be given to quiet preparations, on the part of guests, for departure.

In the upper hall and upon the stairway, panic-stricken little girls listened, wild-eyed, to the uproar that went on, while waiters and maid servants rushed with pails and towels into what was essentially the worst ward in Bedlam. Boys who had behaved properly all afternoon now gave way and joined the confraternity of lunatics. The floors of the house shook to tramplings, rushes, wrestlings, falls and collisions. The walls resounded to chorused bellowings and roars. There were pipings of pain and pipings of joy; there was whistling to pierce the drums of ears; there were hootings and howlings and bleatings and screechings, while over all bleated the heathen battle-cry incessantly: *"Gotcher bumpus! Gotcher bumpus!"* For the boys had been inspired by the unusual water to transform Penrod's game of "Gotcher bumpus" into an aquatic sport, and to induce one another, by means of superior force, dexterity, or stratagems, either to sit or to lie at full length in the flood, after the example of Carlie Chitten.

One of the aunts Rennsdale had taken what charge she could of the deafened and distracted maids and waiters who were working to stem the tide, while the other of the aunts Rennsdale stood with her niece and Miss Lowe at the foot of the stairs, trying to say good-night reassuringly to those of the terrified little girls who were able to tear themselves away. This latter aunt Rennsdale marked a dripping figure that came unobtrusively, and yet in a self-contained and gentlemanly manner, down the stairs.

"Carlie Chitten!" she cried. "You poor dear child, you're soaking! To think those outrageous little fiends wouldn't even spare *you!*" As she spoke, another departing male guest came from behind Carlie and placed in her hand a snakelike article—a thing that Miss Lowe seized and concealed with one sweeping gesture.

"It's some false hair somebody must of put in my overcoat pocket," said Roderick Magsworth Bitts. "Well, g'-night. Thank you for a very nice time."

"Good-night, Miss Rennsdale," said Master Chitten demurely. "Thank you for a——"

But Miss Rennsdale detained him. "Carlie," she said earnestly, "you're a dear boy, and I know you'll tell me something. It was all Penrod Schofield, wasn't it?"

"You mean he left the——"

"I mean," she said, in a low tone, not altogether devoid of ferocity. "I mean it was Penrod who left the faucets running, and Penrod who tied the boys' shoes together, and filled some of them with soap and mucilage, and put Miss Lowe's hair in Roddy Bitts's overcoat. No; look me in the eye, Carlie! They were all shouting that silly thing he started. Didn't he do it?"

Carlie cast down thoughtful eyes. "I wouldn't like to tell, Miss Rennsdale," he said. "I guess I better be going or I'll catch cold. Thank you for a very nice time."

"There!" said Miss Rennsdale vehemently, as Carlie went

on his way. "What did I tell you? Carlie Chitten's too manly to say it, but I just *know* it was that terrible Penrod Schofield."

Behind her, a low voice, unheard by all except the person to whom it spoke, repeated a part of this speech: "What did I tell you?"

This voice belonged to one Penrod Schofield.

Penrod and Marjorie had descended by another stairway, and he now considered it wiser to pass to the rear of the little party at the foot of the stairs. As he was still in his pumps, his choked shoes occupying his overcoat pockets, he experienced no difficulty in reaching the front door, and getting out of it unobserved, although the noise upstairs was greatly abated. Marjorie, however, made her curtseys and farewells in a creditable manner.

"There!" Penrod said again, when she rejoined him in the darkness outside. "What did I tell you? Didn't I say I'd get the blame of it, no matter if the house went and fell down? I s'pose they think I put mucilage and soap in my own shoes."

Marjorie delayed at the gate until some eagerly talking little girls had passed out. The name "Penrod Schofield" was thick and scandalous among them.

"Well," said Marjorie, "*I* wouldn't care, Penrod. 'Course, about soap and mucilage in *your* shoes, anybody'd know some other boy must of put 'em there to get even for what you put in his."

Penrod gasped.

"But I *didn't!*" he cried. "I didn't do *anything!* That ole Miss Rennsdale can say what she wants to, I didn't do a——"

"Well, anyway, Penrod," said Marjorie, softly, "they can't ever *prove* it was you."

He felt himself suffocating in a coil against which no struggle availed.

"But I never *did* it!" he wailed, helplessly. "I never did anything at all!"

She leaned toward him a little, and the lights from her waiting carriage illumined her dimly, but enough for him to see that her look was fond and proud, yet almost awed.

"Anyway, Penrod," she whispered, "*I* don't believe there's any other boy in the whole world could of done *half* as much!"

Part Three

PENROD JASHBER

CHAPTER XLVI

THE NEW PUP

ON A Friday in April, Penrod Schofield, having returned from school at noon promptly, on account of
an earnest appetite, found lunch considerably delayed and himself (after a bit of simple technique) alone in
the pantry with a large, open, metal receptacle containing
about two-thirds of a peck of perfect doughnuts just come
into the world.

The history of catastrophe is merely the history of irresistible juxtapositions. When Penrod left the pantry he
walked slowly. In the large metal receptacle were left a small
number of untouched doughnuts; while upon the shelf beside it were two further doughnuts, each with a small bite
experimentally removed—and one of these bites, itself, lay,
little mangled, beside the parent doughnut.

Nothing having been discovered, he seated himself gently at the lunch-table, and, making no attempt to take part in the family conversation, avoided rather than sought attention. This decorum on his part was so unusual as to be the means of defeating its object, for his mother and father and Margaret naturally began to stare at him. Nevertheless, his presence continued to be unobtrusive and his manner preoccupied. Rallied by Margaret, he offered for reply only a smile, faint, courteous and strange, followed, upon further badinage, by an almost imperceptible shake of the head, which he seemed to fear might come off if more decisively agitated.

"But, Penrod dear," his mother insisted, "you *must* eat a little something or other."

For the sake of appearances, Penrod made a terrible effort to eat a little something or other.

When they had got him to his bed, he said, with what resentful strength remained to him, that it was all the fault of his mother, and she was indeed convinced that her insistence had been a mistake. For several hours the consequences continued to be more or less demonstrative; then they verged from physical to mental, as the thoughts of Penrod and the thoughts of his insides merged into one. Their decision was unanimous—a conclusive horror of doughnuts. Throughout ghastly durations of time there was no thought possible to him but the intolerable thought of doughnuts. There was no past but doughnuts; there was no future but doughnuts. He descended into the bottomest pit of an abyss of doughnuts; he lay suffocating in a universe of doughnuts. He looked back over his dreadful life to that time, before lunch, when he had been alone with the doughnuts in the pantry, and it seemed to him that he must have been out of his mind. How could he have endured even the noxious smell of the things? It was incredible to him that any human being could ever become hardy enough to bear the mere sight of a doughnut.

Not until the next morning did Penrod Schofield quit his bed and come out into the fair ways of mankind again, and then his step was cautious; there was upon his brow the trace of an experience. For a little while after his emergence to the air he had the look of one who has discovered something alarming in the pleasant places of life, the look of one who has found a scorpion hiding under a violet. He went out into the yard through the front door, and, even with his eyes, avoided the kitchen.

"Yay, Penrod!" a shout greeted him. "Look! Looky here! Look what *I* got!"

Upon the sidewalk was Sam Williams in a state of unmistakable elation. His right hand grasped one end of a taut piece of clothes-line; the other end had been tied round the neck of a pup; but, owing to the pup's reluctance, the makeshift collar was now just behind his ears, so that his brow was furrowed, his throat elongated and his head horizontal. As a matter of fact, he was sitting down; nevertheless, Sam evidently held that the pup was being led.

"This good ole dog o' mine not so easy to *lead*, I can tell you!"

These were Sam's words, in spite of the pup's seated attitude. On the other hand, to support the use of "lead", the pup was certainly moving along at a fair rate of speed. In regard to his state of mind, any beholder must have hesitated between two guesses: his expression denoted either resignation or profound obstinacy, and, by maintaining silence throughout what could not possibly have been other than a spiritual and bodily trial, he produced an impression of reserve altogether deceptive. There do exist reserved pups, of course; but this was not one of them.

Sam brought him into the yard. "How's *that* for high, Penrod?" he cried.

Penrod forgot doughnuts temporarily. "Where'd you get him?" he asked. "Where'd you get that fellow, Sam?"

"Yay!" shouted Master Williams. "He belongs to me."

"Where'd you *get* him? Didn't you hear me?"

"You just look him over," Sam said importantly. "Take a good ole look at him and see what you got to say. He's a full-blooded dog, all right! You just look this good ole dog over."

With warm interest, Penrod complied. He looked the good ole dog over. The pup, released from the stress of the rope, lay placidly upon the grass. He was tan-coloured over most of him, though interspersed with black; and the fact that he had nearly attained his adolescence was demonstrated by the cumbersomeness of his feet and the half-knowing look of his eye. He was large; already he was much taller and heavier than Duke.

"How do you know he's full-blooded?" asked Penrod cautiously, before expressing any opinion.

"My goodness!" Sam exclaimed. "Can't you look at him? Don't you know a full-blooded dog when you see one?"

Penrod frowned. "Well, who told you he was?"

"John Carmichael."

"Who's John Carmichael?"

"He's the man works on my uncle's farm. John Carmichael owns the mother o' this dog here; and he said he took a fancy to me and he was goin' to give me this dog's mother and all the other pups besides this one, too, only my fam'ly wouldn't let me. John says they were all pretty full-blooded, except the runt; but this one was the best. This one is the most full-blooded of the whole kitamaboodle."

For the moment Penrod's attention was distracted from the pup. "Of the whole what?" he inquired.

"Of the whole kitamaboodle," Sam repeated carelessly.

"Oh," said Penrod, and he again considered the pup. "I bet he isn't as full-blooded as Duke. I bet he isn't anyway *near* as full-blooded as Duke."

Sam hooted. "Duke!" he cried. "Why, I bet Duke isn't a *quarter* full-blooded! I bet Duke hasn't got any full blood in him at all! All you'd haf to do'd be look at Duke and this dog together; then you'd see in a minute. I bet you, when this dog grows up, he could whip Duke four times out o' five. I bet he could whip Duke now, only pups won't fight. All I ast is, you go get Duke and just *look* which is the most full-blooded."

"All right," said Penrod. "I'll get him, and I guess maybe you'll have sense enough to see yourself which is. Duke's got more full blood in his hind feet than that dog's got all over him."

He departed hotly, calling and whistling for his own, and Duke, roused from a nap on the back porch, loyally obeyed the summons. A moment or two later, he made his appearance, following his master to the front yard, where Sam and the new pup were waiting. However, upon his first sight of this conjuncture, Duke paused at the corner of the house, then quietly turned to withdraw. Penrod was obliged to take him by the collar.

"Well, *now* you're satisfied, I guess!" said Sam Williams, when Penrod had dragged Duke to a spot about five feet from the pup. "I expeck you can tell which is the full-bloodedest now, can't you?"

"Yes; I guess I can!" Penrod retorted. "Look at that ole cur beside good ole Dukie, and anybody can see he isn't full-blooded a-*tall!*"

"He isn't?" Sam cried indignantly, and, as a conclusive test, he gathered in both hands a large, apparently unoccupied area of the pup's back, lifting it and displaying it proudly, much as a clerk shows goods upon a counter. "Look at that!" he shouted. "Look how loose his hide is! You never saw a looser-hided dog in your life, and you can't any more do that with Duke'n you could with a potato-bug! Just try it once; that's all I ast."

"That's nothing. Any pup can do that. When Duke was a pup——"

"Just try it once, I said. That's all I ast."

"I got a right to talk, haven't I?" Penrod demanded bitterly. "I guess this is my own father's yard, and I got a ri——"

"Just try it, once," Sam repeated, perhaps a little irritatingly. "That's all I ast."

"My goodness HEAVENS!" Penrod bellowed. "I never heard such a crazy racket as you're makin'! Haven't you got enough sense to——"

"Just try it once. That's all I——"

"Dry UP!" Penrod was furious.

Sam relapsed into indignant silence. Penrod similarly relapsed. Each felt that the other knew nothing whatever about full-blooded dogs.

"Well," Sam said finally, "what you want to keep aholt o' Duke for? *My* dog ain't goin' to hurt him."

"I guess not! You said yourself he couldn't fight."

"I did not! I said *no* pup will——"

"All right then," said Penrod. "I was only holdin' him to keep him from chewin' up that poor cur. Better let him loose so's he can get away if good ole Dukie takes after him."

"Let's let 'em both loose," Sam said, forgetting animosity. "Let's see what they'll do."

"All right," Penrod, likewise suddenly amiable, agreed. "I expeck they kind of like each other, anyways."

Released, both animals shook themselves. Then Duke approached the pup and sniffed carelessly and without much interest at the back of his neck. Duke was so bored by the information thus obtained that he yawned and once more made evident his intention to retire to the backyard. The new pup, however, after having presented up to this moment an appearance uninterruptedly lethargic, suddenly took it into his head to play the jolly rogue. At a pup's gallop, he proceeded to a point directly in Duke's line of march, and halted. Then he placed his muzzle flat upon the ground between his wide-spread paws and showed the whites of his eyes in a waggish manner. Duke also halted, confronting the joker and emitting low sounds of warning and detestation.

Then, for the sake of peace, he decided to go round the house the other way; in fact, he was in the act of turning to do so when the pup rushed upon him and frolicsomely upset him. Thereupon, Duke swore, cursing all the pups in the world and claiming blasphemously to be a dangerous person whom it were safer not again to jostle. For a moment, the pup was startled by the elderly dog's intensive oratory; then he decided that Duke was joking, too, and returned to his clowning. Again and again he charged ponderously upon, into and over Duke, whose words and actions now grew wild indeed. But he was helpless. The pup's humour expressed itself in a fever of physical badinage, and Duke no sooner rose than he was upset again. When he lay upon his back, raving and snapping, the disregardful pup's large feet would flop weightily upon the pit of his stomach or upon his very face with equal unconcern. Duke had about as much chance with him as an elderly gentleman would have with a jocular horse. Never before was a creature of settled life so badgered.

Both boys were captivated by the pup's display of gaiety, and Penrod, naturally prejudiced against the blithe animal, unwillingly felt his heart warming. It was impossible to preserve any coldness of feeling toward so engaging a creature, and, besides, no boy can long resist a pup. Penrod began to yearn toward this one. He wished that John Carmichael had worked on a farm belonging to *his* uncle.

"That *is* a pretty good dog, Sam," he said, his eyes following the pup's merry violence. "I guess you're right— he's proba'ly *part* full-blooded, maybe not as much as Duke, but a good deal, anyhow. What you goin' to name him?"

"John Carmichael."

"I wouldn't," said Penrod. "I'd name him sumpthing nice. I'd name him Frank, or Walter or sumpthing."

"No, sir," Sam said firmly. "I'm goin' to name him John Carmichael. I told John Carmichael I would."

"Well, all right," Penrod returned, a little peevishly. "Always got to have your own way!"

"Well, haven't I got a right to?" Sam inquired, with justifiable heat. "I'd like to know why I oughtn't to have my own way about my own dog!"

"I don't care," said Penrod. "You can call him John Carmichael when you speak to him; but, when *I* speak to him, I'm goin' to call him Walter."

"You can if you want to," Sam returned. "It won't be his name."

"Well, Walter'll be his name long as I'm talkin' to him."

"It won't, either!"

"Why won't it? Just answer me, why."

"Because," said Sam, "his name'll be John Carmichael all the time, no matter who's talkin' to him."

"That's what you think," said Penrod, and he added, in a tone of determination, "His name'll be Walter whenever I say a word to him."

Sam began to wear a baffled expression, for the controversy was unusual and confusing. "It won't," he said. "Do you s'pose Duke's name'd be Walter, if you called him Walter while you were talkin' to him, and then change back to Duke the rest o' the time when you aren't talkin' to him?"

"What?"

"I said—well, suppose Duke's name was Walter"—Sam paused, finding himself unable to recall the details of the argumentative illustration he had offered.

"What's all that stuff you were talkin' about?" Penrod insisted.

"His name's John Carmichael," Sam said curtly. "Hyuh, John!"

"Hyuh, Walter!" cried Penrod.

"Hyuh, John! Hyuh, John Carmichael!"

"Hyuh, Walter, Walter! *Come* here, good ole Walter, Walter, Walter!"

"Hyuh, John! *Good* ole Johnny!"

The pup paid no attention to either of the rival godfathers, but continued to clown it over Duke, whose mood was beginning to change. His bad temper had exhausted

itself, and, little by little, the pup's antics began to stir the
elderly dog's memory of his own puphood. He remembered
the glad unconventionality, the long days of irresponsible
romping, and he wished that he might live those days again.
By imperceptible degrees, his indignation diminished; he
grew milder and milder until, finally, he found himself actually collaborating in the pup's hoydenish assaults. Duke's
tone of voice became whimsical; he lay upon his back and
pretended to swear and snap; but the swearing and snapping were now burlesque and meant to be understood as
such. Duke ended by taking a decided fancy to Walter-
John Carmichael.

The moral influence of dogs upon one another is profound
- -a matter seldom estimated at its value. People are often
mystified by a change of character in a known and tried
dog; they should seek to discover with whom he has been
associating himself. Sometimes the change in a dog's character is permanent; sometimes it is merely temporary. In
the latter case, when the animal returns to his former habit
of mind, it is usually a sign that the source of influence has
vanished—the other dog has moved away. Or it may be
merely that the influenced dog has concluded that his new
manner does not pay. One thing, however, is certain: when a
dog goes wrong late in life, it is almost invariably due to
the influence and example of some other dog—usually a
younger one, odd as that may seem.

Walter-John Carmichael proved his light-headedness by
forgetting Duke abruptly and galloping off after a sparrow that had flown near the ground. The sparrow betook
himself to the limb of a tree, while the pup continued to
careen and zigzag over the grass in the lunatic belief that
he was still chasing the sparrow. Duke thereupon scampered
upon an imaginary track, shaped like a large figure eight,
and then made a jovial rush at Walter-John, bowling him
over and over. Finding that the thing could be done, Duke
knocked Walter-John over as often as the latter rose to his

feet. Duke had caught the infection of youth; he had been lifted out of himself by Walter-John's simple happiness, and the little old dog was in great spirits. Of course, he did not weigh the question of his conduct carefully; later events proved that he acted on the spur of emotion and paused neither to reason nor to estimate consequences. His promptings were, indeed, physical rather than mental—simply, he felt like a pup once more and in all things behaved like one.

Meanwhile, the two boys sat upon the grass and watched the friendly battle. "I'm goin' to train John to be a trick dog," Sam said.

"What you goin' to train him?"

"Oh, like dogs in the dog show," Sam replied, with careless ease. "I'm goin' to make him do all those tricks."

"Yes, you are!"

"I am, too!"

"Well, *how* are you?" asked the skeptical Penrod. "How you goin' to train him?"

"Lots o' ways."

"Well, what are they?"

"Why, it's the easiest thing in the world to train a pup," said Sam. "Take an ole dog like Duke, and 'course you can't train him. First thing I'm goin' to train John is to catch a ball when I throw it to him."

"You mean catch it in his mouth the same as a baseball player does with his hands?"

"Yes, sir!"

Penrod laughed scornfully.

"You wait and see!" Sam cried.

"Well, how are you goin' to? Just answer me that!"

"You'll *see* how."

"Well, why can't you answer how you're goin' to do so much? Just answer me that; that's all I——"

"Well, I'll tell you how," Sam began, speaking thoughtfully.

"Well, why'n't you *tell* me, then, instead o' talkin' so mu——"

"How can I, when you won't let me? You talk yourself all the ti——"

"You don't *know* how! That's the reason you talk so much," Penrod asserted. "You couldn't any more teach a dog to catch a ball than——"

"I could, too! I'd put sumpthing on it."

Penrod's loud laugh was again scornful. " 'Put sumpthing on it!' " he mocked. "*That'd* teach a dog to catch a ball, wouldn't it? What you goin' to put on it? Tar? So it'd stick in his mouth?" And overcome by the humour of this satire, Penrod rolled in the grass, shouting derisively.

Not at all disconcerted, his friend explained: "No; I wouldn't put any ole tar on it. I'd take a ball and rub sumpthing that tastes good to him on the ball."

"What for?"

"Then I'd throw it to him, and he'd catch it just like he would a piece o' beefsteak. Haven't you ever seen a dog catch meat?"

Penrod's laughter ceased; the idea fascinated him at once. "Look here, Sam," he said. "Let's teach both our dogs to do that. Let's go round to the barn and start gettin' 'em all trained up so's we can have a dog show."

"*That's* the ticket!" cried Sam.

Within five minutes, the unfortunate Duke and Walter-John, interrupted in their gambols, were beginning to undergo a course of instruction. The two trainers agreed to avoid all harshness; the new method of teaching by attractive deceptions was to be followed throughout the course, and, for a while, they were consistently persuasive and diplomatic. Penrod brought a bit of raw meat and a solid-rubber ball from the house. The meat was rubbed on the ball, which was then presented to the two dogs for inspection and sniffing. Both took some interest in it, and Duke licked it casually.

The ball was tossed first to Duke, who moved aside and would have taken his unobtrusive departure had he not been detained. Next, Sam tossed the ball to Walter-John, who, without budging, placidly watched its approach through the air, and yet seemed surprised and troubled when it concluded its flight upon his right eye. Meat was freshly rubbed upon the ball and the experiment repeated again and again, so that after a little experience Walter-John learned to watch the ball and to move as soon as he saw it coming toward him. After half an hour, he was almost as able a dodger as Duke.

It may not be denied that by this time the trainers were irritated. Their theory was so plausible—it had sounded so simple, so inevitable—that the illogical conduct of the two dogs could not fail to get more and more upon the theorists' nerves. Naturally, then, in spite of all agreements never to resort to harshness, there were times when, instead of tossing, Penrod threw the ball to Duke, and Sam to Walter-John. In fact, to an observer who had no knowledge of dog-training, the instruction finally might have seemed to be a contest in accuracy between the two trainers, especially as they had found it necessary to tie both Walter-John and Duke rather closely to the stable wall. Indeed, that was the view of the matter ignorantly taken by Della.

"I niver see th' beat!" she exclaimed, coming out upon the back porch from the kitchen. "Chainin' thim two poor dogs ag'inst the wall and throwin' big rocks at 'em to see which can hit 'em the most times and——"

"Rocks!" Penrod interrupted angrily. "Who's throwin' rocks? You tell me who's throwin' any rocks!"

"I'll tell you to come to lunch," Della retorted. "And Mrs. Williams has been telephonin' a quawter'v an hour. They're waitin' lunch at the Williamses; so you let thim two poor dogs go—if they still got the strenk to walk. Are you comin' to yer lunch, Musther Penrod, or not? Come in and try to eat like a human person and not like a rhinoceros the way you did yesterday, and you know what you got fer it, too—I'm glad, praise hiven!" She returned into the house, slamming the door.

"What's she mean, Penrod?" Sam inquired, as he released Walter-John from the wall. "What did you get for what, that she says she was so glad about?"

"Nothin'," said Penrod, though his expression had become momentarily unpleasant. "Those Irish always got to be sayin' sumpthing or other."

"Yep," Sam agreed. "Let's go ahead and train our dogs some more this afternoon. You bring Duke over to our yard, Penrod, and let's get started early."

CHAPTER XLVII

BAD INFLUENCE OF WALTER-JOHN

PENROD assented, and, at a little after one o'clock, the training began again in the Williams's yard. Duke and Walter-John passed two hours comparable to hours human beings pass at the dentist's, and both the trainers gradually became hoarse, though they still maintained that their method continued to be humane and persuasive. Experiments with the ball were finally postponed to another day, as both dogs persisted in their dodging and each refused to grasp the idea of a ball's purpose—even when it was forcibly placed in his mouth and held there for minutes at a time.

Duke had long ago mastered the art of "sitting-up", and

to-day, upon command, he "sat up" till he was ready to drop, while Walter-John was held up in a similar position and bidden to learn from the example of Duke, but would not even look at him. No progress being perceptible in this, a barrel-hoop was procured, and one trainer held the hoop, while the other accustomed the dogs to passing through it. Patiently, until his back ached, Penrod again and again threw Duke and the cumbersome Walter-John in turn through the hoop; then held it while Sam manipulated the dogs.

"*Now* I expeck they unnerstand what we want 'em to do," said Sam, at last, straightening up with a gasp. "Anyways, they cert'nly ought to!"

"Jump, Dukie!" Penrod urged. "Jump through the hoop just like you been doin'! *Come* on, old Dukie—*jump!*"

Again the patience of the instructors was strained. Both Duke and Walter-John could be coaxed to pass under the hoop or upon either side of it; but each refused to pass through it of his free will. Manifestly, they had, for inexplicable reasons, conceived a prejudice against hoop-jumping, and nothing served to remove their aversion.

"I'll tell you what we can train 'em," Penrod suggested, after a long pause of discouragement. "We can train 'em to walk the tight-rope. We could do that, anyway!"

After the setbacks received in processes apparently so much simpler (especially for dogs) than tight-rope walking, Penrod's proposal naturally produced a feeling of surprise in Sam. "What on earth you talkin' about now?"

"Why, look!" said Penrod. "Listen, Sam—you listen here a minute! We can teach 'em to walk the tight-rope *easy!* It won't be anything at all, the way *I* got fixed up to do it. *Then* just look where we'll be, when our good ole dogs get so's all we got to do'll just be to say, 'Hyuh, Dukie, jump up on that clo'es-line and walk it!' And then you can say, Hyuh, Walter, jump up——' "

"I wouldn't, neither!" Sam interrupted. "His name's John!"

"Well, anyway," Penrod continued evasively, "you could tell him to jump up on a clo'es-line and walk it just like Duke, and he'd do it. *Oh*, oh!" Penrod's eyes sparkled; he gesticulated joyously—to his mind, the gorgeous performance was already taking place. "*Oh*, oh! That wouldn't be any good ole show—I guess not! Why, we could charge a *dollar* for anybody to come in! *Oh*, oh! Laydeez and gentlemun, the big show is about to commence! *Get* up on that tight-rope now, you good ole Duke! Laydeez and gentlemun, you now see before your very eyes the only two tight-rope-walking dogs ever trained to——"

"Well, can't you wait a minute?" Sam cried. "I'd like to know how we're goin' to train 'em to walk any tight-rope when they don't show any more sense'n they did about that hoop and catchin' a ball and——"

"*Listen*, I told you, didn't I?" said Penrod. "Look, Sam! First, we'll train 'em to walk the fence-rail here in your yard. We'll take one of 'em at a time and put him on the rail. Then one of us'll hold him from jumpin' off while the other pushes him along from behind so's he's got to keep goin'. Well, if he *can't* get off, and if he's *got* to keep goin' —so, well, if we do that enough, say so often a day for so many weeks—well, he can't *help* himself from learning how to walk a fence-rail, can he?"

"No. But how——"

"*Listen*—didn't I tell you? Well, when he's got that much good and learned, all we do is get a board half the size of the fence-rail and do the same thing with him on *it*—and then get another one half the size of that one, and so on till we get him trained to walk on a board that's just the same size as a rope. I'd like to know *then* if he couldn't walk just as well on a rope as on a board he couldn't tell the *difference* from a rope from."

"Well, I don't care," Sam said. "I bet it'll take pretty near forever, though."

"It would if we just sit around here and never do anything."

"Oh, I'm willing to give it a *try*," Sam said.

Sam's mother, coming out into the yard, half an hour
later, preserved her composure, though given cause for
abandoning it. Walter-John was seated upon the fence-rail
but moving steadily. Sam distrained him from leaving the
rail, while Penrod's two extended hands, applying serious
and constant pressure at the base of Walter-John's spine,
compelled Walter-John to progress along the fence-rail.
Walter-John's expression was concerned and inquiring, and
Duke, tied to a tree, near by, stood in an attitude of depression.

"Let the dogs go now, boys," Mrs. Williams called. "I've
got something for you, and then Sam has to come in and get
dressed to go and spend an hour or so at his grandmother's.
It's after three o'clock."

"What you got for us?" Sam asked.

She displayed a plate covered with a napkin.

"*Oh*, oh!" Both boys trotted to Mrs. Williams.

"What's under that napkin?" cried the eager Sam.

"Look!" and she withdrew the napkin, while Sam
shouted.

"Doughnuts!"

He dashed at them; but his mother fended him off. "Wait,
Sam!" she said. "Shame on you! See how polite Penrod is!
He doesn't grab and——"

"That's only because he's company," Sam interrupted.
"Gimme those doughnuts!"

"No," she said. "There are five apiece, and you'll divide
evenly. Here, Penrod; you take your five first."

"Ma'am?" said Penrod, his face flushing painfully.

"Don't be bashful." Mrs. Williams laughed, and she extended the plate toward him. "You're Sam's guest and you
must choose your five first."

Penrod was anxious to prevent his recent misfortune from becoming known, and he felt that to decline these doughnuts would arouse suspicion. Yet he was uncertain whether or not he could, with physical security, hold five doughnuts even in his hands.

"Hurry, Penrod! I know you want them."

At arm's length he took five doughnuts, two in one hand and three in the other. Then his arms fell at his sides, and he stood very straight, holding his head high and his nose to the clouds.

"There!" said Mrs. Williams, departing. "All right, Sammy! As soon as you've finished them, you must come to dress. Not more than ten minutes."

Sam carolled and capered with his doughnuts, stuffing his mouth full, so that he carolled no more, but capered still, in greater ecstasy. No pleasures of contemplation for Sam, or dwelling long and delicately upon morsels! What was sweet to his flesh he took, and consumed as he took. The five doughnuts sped to the interior almost *en masse*. Within four minutes there remained of them but impalpable tokens upon Sam's cheeks.

"Hah!" he shouted. "Those were *good!*" Then, his eye falling upon Penrod's drooping hands, "Well, for gray-*shus* sakes!" he exclaimed. "Aren't you goin' to *eat* 'em?"

Penrod's voice was lifeless. He responded: "Well, some days I kind o' like to save mine up and eat 'em when I feel like it." He swallowed twice, coughed twice.

"I wish I'd saved mine," Sam said. "Come on, John, ole doggie!" he added, beginning to drag the pup toward the house.

"What you goin' to do with him?" Penrod asked.

"I'm goin' to lock him up in the cellar while I'm gone. That's where they said I could keep him."

"What for? Let me have him till you get back. I'll bring him over here before dinner-time."

Sam thought this request outrageous. "*No*, sir!" he cried. "Haven't you got a dog o' your own? You want to go and get mine so's he knows you better'n he would me? I guess not! John Carmichael's goin' to stay right in our cellar every minute I'm not here to be trainin' him!"

"Oh, come on, Sam!" Penrod urged, for he had become more and more fascinated by Walter-John throughout the day. "It isn't goin' to *hurt* him any, is it?"

"I won't do it."

"Oh, come on, Sam! What's the use actin' that way to a poor dog—lockin' him up in a dark ole cellar when he ought to be out in the fresh air so's he could keep strong? He likes Duke, and he ought to be allowed to stay with him. I call it mighty mean, lockin' him up in that ole ugly cellar just because *you* want to go and have a good time at your grandmother's."

"I don't care what you call it; he's goin' to be locked up," Sam said. "And I don't either want to go and have a good time at my grandmother's. I *got* to go."

Whereupon, having thus uttered his final decision in the matter, and defended his character against the charge of selfishness, Sam towed Walter-John as far as the cellar door.

"Wait a minute, Sam," Penrod urged. "If you'll let me have him till you get back, I'll give you some o' these dough-nuts."

"How many?"

"I'll give you," said Penrod, "the whole kitamaboodle!"

"*Yay!*"

Blithely the doughnuts passed from Penrod's hands to Sam's, and the end of the bit of clothes-line from Sam's to Penrod's.

"Come on, Walter!" Penrod cried.

Though his utterance was already thick, Sam protested instantly. "Stop that!" he commanded. "His name's John Carmichael, and you got to call him John. You can't have him if you're goin' to call him Walter."

Penrod began to argue rather bitterly. "My goodness, gracious heavens! He's just the same as *my* dog till you get back, isn't he?"

"He is not!"

"Didn't I just pay you for him? It's just the same as buyin' him till you get back from your grandmother's, and whatever time he's my dog, he's got to be named Walter. If you don't like it, you can give me back my doughnuts!"

"Oh, goodness!" Sam groaned. "Well, you got to quit callin' him Walter after to-day, anyways. The poor dog's got to learn his name *some*time."

Penrod, wearing an unassuming air of triumph, released Duke from the tree to which he had been tied, and, leading both dogs, proceeded toward the back gate; but before he went out into the alley Sam was amazed to see him pause at the hydrant and wash his hands exhaustively. Then Penrod opened the alley gate and passed from sight with his two charges, leaving Sam staring, open-mouthed.

Duke trotted obediently after his master; but Walter-John still misconceived the purposes of a leash and progressed for the most part in his seated or semi-seated attitude. However, Penrod reached his own yard—the front yard, away from the kitchen—without much difficulty, and paused there, regarding Walter-John with pleasure and affection.

He sat down on the grass, a dog under each arm. His imagination stepped quietly out of the present into the gold-clouded future. He saw himself in the filtered light of a great tent, addressing in a magnificent bass voice the fanning multitude.

"Laydeez and gentlemun, allow me to interodoos to your attainshon, the great tight-rope-walking dog, Walter!" And straightway, from the "dressing-room tent", Walter-John came hopping on hind legs, white ruff about his neck. Then Penrod proclaimed: "And now, laydeez and gentlemun, let me interodoos to your attainshon, Walter's little boy, Duke, the greatest tight-rope dog on EARTH!" Whereupon, Duke, similarly hopping and similarly beruffed, came forward to the side of the ringmaster in the ring, and the three bowed low, to twenty-thousand plaudits. Anxious attendants in uniform ran to their posts to support the tight-rope, and Penrod, smiling negligently——

His bubble broke. The clatter of a brazen gong and a staccato of iron-shod hoofs—sounds increasing, coming nearer—startled him from the proud day-dream. A hose-cart, then a fire-engine, then a hook-and-ladder wagon careened in turn round the corner, passed furiously and roared up the street, followed by panting boys with faces alight.

Penrod leaped to his feet. The stable was too far. He dragged Duke and Walter-John up the front steps and across the verandah; he tried the front door, found it un-locked, opened it, thrust Walter-John and Duke into the hall, slammed the door and made off to the fire.

In the cool hall, Duke and Walter-John looked at each other vaguely; then discovered that they were free. A frolic-some look bloomed upon the fertile face of Walter-John. With no motive, he dashed into a large room that opened from the hall, and knocked over a tall silver vase of lilies that somebody had set upon the floor directly in his way. Then he charged upon Duke, upset him, left him kicking at the air, and scampered to and fro for the love of mo-tion. Duke was instantly infected; his puphood of the morn-ing returned in full flood, and he, in his turn, charged upon Walter-John.

Both dogs had been through a great deal that day; in fact, their trainers had shown them a poor time, and noth-ing could have been more natural than that Duke and Walter-John should wish to liven things up after their pro-tracted experience as apprentices in baseball, sitting-up, hoop-jumping and tight-rope-walking. They made it an orgy. The house was empty of human life, upstairs and down, as far as the kitchen door, which was closed. Walter-John and Duke engaged in mimic battle all over this empty house, and wherever there was anything that could be upset, they upset it, for Walter-John was undoubtedly cumber-some.

Exhausting for a time this pleasure, Walter-John found matter of interest on a low table in the library. This consisted of a new encyclopedia, limp-leather covers, gilt tops, thin paper, seven volumes, purchased by Mr. Schofield the week before. Walter-John dragged down two volumes, one labelled "Ala-Con", the other, "Mon-Pyx". Walter-John began to eat "Ala-Con", and Duke—all culture fallen from him now in his rejuvenation—Duke began to eat "Mon-Pyx". That is, they did not eat except accidentally, for neither of them actually swallowed much of the paper; but the effect upon "Ala-Con" and "Mon-Pyx" was none the less radical.

Growing tired of this learned work, they found some semi-edible slippers in Margaret's room upstairs, also a table-cover—which frightened Walter-John on account of the noise the things made when he dragged the cover from the table. Next, he discovered, hanging in an open closet in the same room, a beady substance that proved enjoyable. In this, as in everything, the senile Duke joined him with gusto. The orgy continued.

Penrod found the fire an unusually satisfactory one. In fact, a large warehouse, almost full of hides and leather, burned all up, and dusk was falling when Penrod, smelling intensely, again reached his place of residence. As he opened the gate, he saw Duke coming round a corner of the house with a peculiar air. There was something regretful and haunted about the little old dog; he advanced hesitatingly, seeming to be without confidence, and when Penrod spoke to him, he disappeared instantly. In the darkness, his young master could not see where or even in which direction he went. Suddenly a chill struck upon Penrod's spine. He remembered. Where, oh, where, was Walter-John?

Penrod entered the front hall impetuously; but paused there at once—and more cold chills touched his young spine. A sound of lamentation—his mother's voice—came from the library, and evidently she was addressing Mr. Schofield.

"You never *saw* such a house! *Oh*, if I'd only followed my instinct and not let Margaret persuade me to go to that reception with her! We had Della give Duke a whipping, because he had a shred of Margaret's best party dress sticking to his nose, and he *must* have helped that horrible pup! Della threw lumps of coal at *him* when she chased him out, and I do hope she hit him. It seems utterly impossible that there were only *two* dogs in the house. Look at that encyclopedia—why anybody would think it must have taken two of them all afternoon to do just *that* much damage, let alone all the other awful things! Della says she's sure Penrod let them into the house, and this time I certainly don't intend to say one word against it if you think you ought to——"

"Yes, of course I ought to," Mr. Schofield said; and, to the dismayed ears listening in the hallway, his voice was the executioner's.

With infinite precaution, Penrod returned to the front door, let himself out, and no one could have heard a footfall as he crossed the verandah.

He found Sam closing the door of the Williams's cellar upon Walter-John. "Where'd you come across him?" Penrod asked, in a preoccupied tone. He was not much interested.

"*Nice* way to bring him home like you promised, wasn't it?" Sam returned indignantly. "I found him out in the alley, 'way up by the corner, and he acted like he was scared to death. He didn't even ack like he knew me."

"See here a minute, Sam," Penrod said, in a friendly though still preoccupied tone. "On account of all those doughnuts I gave you, and everything, I don't s'pose your mother would mind if I stayed over here for dinner much, would she?"

CHAPTER XLVIII

BEGINNINGS OF JASHBER

NO DOUBT many of us, like Penrod, live not so much in one commingled world as in two interchangeable worlds, the one able instantly to replace the other with such smooth rapidity as to produce not the slightest jar. In youth especially, the interchanging of these two worlds is so continuous, so facile, and accomplished with so quick and sleek a movement that it is like the play of light and shadow when young grasses flutter and twinkle, reflected in a clear stream, itself unruffled by the April breeze. Penrod's most striking interchangeability was with George B. Jashber, the supreme figure of all the *dramatis personæ* he created for himself and out of himself. The great Jashber period did not come upon him spontaneously, full born out of a single emotion; George B. Jashber came on by fits and starts, as it were, developing slowly and irregularly, dropped altogether for days at a time, and then returning to life, becoming at last so well conceived and complete as to be powerful in the affairs of people whole decades older and more experienced than Penrod.

In that sequestered hermitage, the sawdust-box in the woodshed adjoining the horseless stable, the secret, romantic manuscript, "Harold Ramorez," was from time to time exhumed. Perhaps the exhumation would take place upon a day when Penrod was gloomy through some oppression, and several chapters—or, it might be, only part of a chapter, or no more than the beginning of a sentence—would be added.

The earlier portions of the narrative were concerned with the escapes of the handsome bandit, Harold Ramorez, from detectives and other vicious and inept enemies, including ghosts, and the reader (if a reader may be imagined for the manuscript) was led to place his sympathies entirely with Ramorez; for Penrod worked after the manner of all child-of-nature authors, picturing his idealed self as the hero, which unconscious system, when followed with sufficient artlessness and a little craftsmanship, leads the child-of-nature reader to picture *his* idealed self as the hero, so that reader and author meet and fuse in the fiction, separating with reluctance at the end, yet consoled by the shared belief that the story was "good". Thus, although Penrod did not know that he had a method, he did have one; but, unfortunately, something happened to it—no infrequent disaster in cases like his.

He had what is sometimes defined in *argot* as a "change of heart", and it radically affected his hero at a high point in the narrative. Penrod began to admire detectives more than he admired bandits, and, although the author never realized what he had done, the too plastic Ramorez became the villain, while the hitherto malevolent but futile detective, Jashber, or Jasber, burst unexpectedly into noble bloom as the hero—this in the course of one chapter, short enough in the reading. However, in the writing of it Penrod consumed the greatest part of two mornings that were a full month apart, and, in the meantime, he had been to two matinées, had read several paper novels, and, moreover, had strained his young eyes at more than several unusually violent "movies". To be definite, this chapter was:

CHAPTER XIIII

HAROLD RAMOREZ decied he would go away from where was all such blodshed and plots of the scondrel Jashber so biding goodby to some of his freinds he got on the cars, he looked all around and cooly lit a cigrette. Well said the conduter this is not the place where anybody is alowed to smoke and you have no tiket I guess I know that as well as anybody said our hero but you need not talk so much I got money and will pay $5 bill for a tiket

The conduter took hold of the $5 and put it in his pocket. Then the conduter went on out Soon harold Ramorez had reached the city and he was just walkin arond looking at the stores and houses and not hurting anything when a shot rang out stratling our hero What could that be said Harold I wonder why anybody would shoot at me here where I do not know anybody bing Bing went the old pistol bing bing bing it went bing bing

one hole went through our heros coat and one went in his hat shightly crazing his scalp and porduc a flech wond Harld smiled at this O said he a flech wond is nothing and will soon heal up but I wold like to know what anybody is shootin at me here for where I never came before in my life and my emenies did not know I was going to any such a place.

O no they didn't O no not at all I guess said a tanting voice O no it said

Harold whished to know who it was tanting him so he looked around Soon he saw the foul Jashber still holding the smoking revoler in his hands He was behind a tree exept part of his face and the old pistol Well I would like to know what did you have to come all the way here for our hero said to him I was not doing anything to you and you have no busines to go shooting at me said he I guess I got some rights arond here

There folowed a deep curse Well go ahead and swear all you want to because that will not hurt me but remeber when you go to meet your maker each vile oth you say now he will know about and probaly do somthing you will not like

Well I will not stand this kind of talk said Jashber There flowed a curse and some more vile oths I hate you Harold Ramorez and I bet I get you yet said he

Our hero cooly tanted him for what he said then You are the worst yet said Harold and you are double whatever you call me yes and I bet you wold not come half way

I will shoot you throgh and throgh said the scondrel you are a ———— ———— ———— ———— ———— (*The dashes are Penrod's.*)

Our hero smiled cooly at this No I am not any such thing said he but you are a double ———— ———— ———— ———— ———— because I just said so

Well I will not stand this said the scondrel He took a whistle out of his pocket and blew on it, there was another detective hiding behind some bushs and 4 more were also hid around there somwheres and all of a suden they jumped out

Soon our hero was fighting for his very life He had left all his wapons in the house when he came away on the cars He hardly knew what he better do so he took the foul Jasbers old pistol away from him and shot it off three of the scondrels went to meet their maker but now he did not have any more cartridges There was one scondrel left besides Jashber and these two scondrels bit him till thier teeth met in the flech makin flech wonds which he would soon get well from

He stabed the other one and now his emeny Jashber the detective was the only one left I guess your sorry you began it now said Ramorez Soon hunting around he found a long peice of rope and he fixed it arond the scondrels neck I am going to fix you sos you quit folling me when I go on the cars said he

The scondrel began to cry and our hero gave him a kick and tanted him O yes you wold folow me but I guess I'll show you this time said he

Jashber went on crying some more he got down on his knees and begged and begged but after all his persetcums Harold was not going to do anything such a scondrel so he fixed the rope the right way to hang poeple Soon he tied it up in the tree The scondrel holowed loud as he could but soon he was dead Soon Harold walked on off and fond a good place to sleep and made a fire to cook some bacon because he was tired now.

At this point, work upon the manuscript was interrupted, and not resumed until a Saturday morning four weeks later.

Soon after this some man came along and tacked up a sign that said $500000 reward paid to anybody for geting this crook Harold Ramorez put in the pentenartyry So Jashber the detective thougt he wold go upon the trail once more On the door of his ofice it read George B Jasber detective ofice on a sign because his first name was George B Well said George I would like to have $5000 Reward he is at his old tricks again and I better go after him Jashber the detective went on out of his ofice and the first thing he knew a young lady in an automobile wanted him to go with her so he got in and they went a long ways What do you want of me now that I have come out ridding with you said Jashber The young lady got to crying and all and took on Soon she said well I will tell you.

It is about the crooks is not your name George B Jashber the notted detective So George said yes he was and ask her what did she want of him besides Soon the young lady kept on crying and all and she said probaly he had heard the name of Harold Ramorez Yes I have heard the name of Harold Ramorez said George and he is a —— —— —— —— and I am after him because I will get a reward of $50000 for killin him How do you hapen to know the name of Harold Ramorez That scondrel has riuned the lifes of pretty near everybody

Well said this young lady now I will now tell you because my father is an old bank and Harold Ramorez has got this poor old man in his pouer sos he can get all the money that people have put in the bank and uless you will save my poor old father Harold Ramorez will proaly kill him and get the money and I will have to mary him If you will save this poor old man you can have the money and I will mary you

Soon they went in the house and the old bank said if George would save him he could mary the young lady and have the money himself Soon Harold Ramorez came in there because he had been looking through a hole in the cieling Yes sneered he you are a nice one coming arond here this way Ill just show you O no you dont

sneered our Hero yes I will to sneered Harold and he began to
shoot at George with his ottomatick Soon six more crooks ran on
in because they had been lookin through the hole and wish to kill
George B Jasber the notted detective but the young lady got a
dager off the wall and pretty soon the old bank got killed by Harold Ramorez and Jashber killed the crooks by stabbing them in
their abodmen

Look what you have been doing here sneered Ramorez and there
folowed a deep curse You just wait said George and you will see
what you get your vile oths are not doing me any harm and he
went on and tanted some more with a smile

The scondrel called him names a while but George cooly lit a
ciggrett and was going to put his arms over the young lady but
soon Ramorez grabed her and pushed her out of a window where
she fell in a mortarboat the rest of the crooks put there Soon
Ramorez jumped after her and George had to go on back to his
ofice Soon a secert message came on the wall like this it said this
young lady was in the pouer of the scondrel Harold Ramorez and
the gang of crooks under the east peir of the river Wenever our
hero wish to know about anything a secert mesage would come on
the wall of his ofice printed in large letters and then it would fad
out Sometimes it said different things and all such.

Jashber decied he would have to shadow some man he saw
when he looked out the window. He shadowed this crook day and
night till the scondrel went to the secret den of the conterfiters
under the east peir First he was shadowing the crook night and
day before he went to the den

George took some sailor cloths and put them on and fixed himself all up sos nobody would know him in disguise and when he
got to the den the scondrel Harold Ramorez was twising the
young lady's arm and starting to whip her. She was mad but she
did not want to fight

Our hero told him he better not do any more like that but the
scondrel went on ahead pushing her all around because he did not
know it was Jashber the detective but soon the scondrel had to go
out a minute and George told the young lady who he was Now I
will tell you what we better do said the detective Well what said
the young lady Well you put my sailor suit on and I will put yours
on and you can go on out and go to my ofce and when he comes
back he will think I am the young lady and try to whip me but I

am lots stronger than and he will see what he gets So they changed thier clothes and the young lady went on out because the crooks thought she was a sailor and she went up to George B Jasbers ofice and sat there while our hero was wating in the conterfiters den Soon the scondrel Ramorez came back so he thought George was the young lady and began again but soon Jashber got him down on the floor and choked him till his hands met in the flech Yes you try to whip me said he I could whip you any day in the week because you are mistaken and I am not any young lady

Well who are you you talk so much sneered Harold I will show you who I am said he I am Jashber the detective I guess you know who I am now Soon they were fightin for thier very life Soon some more crooks came in and he had to let him up and went on back to his ofice So ther the young lady asked him if he arested Harold Ramorez

No I did not yet said our hero but I am going to the next time because I want to have $500000 Reward.

So he put on some better clothes and they decided they would go to a party that Harold Ramorez was going to be at

CHAPTER XIIIII

THIS party was a party at some poeples house a band was playing and all and soon our hero and the young lady——

Here the manuscript was again buried beneath the surface of the sawdust, upon a peremptory summons from the back porch, and Penrod repaired to the house for lunch. He was thoughtful during the meal, ate absently and did not return to the sawdust-box afterwards. Instead, he wandered about the yard for a time, then sat upon the steps of the back porch, his elbows on his knees, his cheeks in the palms of his hands, and gazed unseeingly at the empty stable.

His thoughts were those that such a manuscript as "Harold Ramorez" might be expected to stimulate in its producer; but they so far outran the speed of a writing hand that he had no desire to return to the composition. All his old ambitions had faded. He no longer cared to play the biggest horn in the band; no more did he picture himself in flashing uniform—not even as a General on a white horse. No; through tortuous adventures in his vivid mind's eye he wandered, cool, expressionless, resourceful, always turning up at the theatrical moment, shadowing male and female crooks night and day, a soft hat pulled low over steely eyes that nothing escaped, his coat collar pulled up to disguise the back of his head. A cigarette was ever ready to his hand (to be smoked for the purpose of concealing watchfulness of expression) and an automatic pistol always lay in his pocket (to be glanced at before he left his office or entered any door whatsoever). Yes; Penrod's childish ideals of circuses and bands and tinsel Generals were now discarded pinchbeck indeed, ignominious and almost incredible. He had decided to be a detective.

So far as facts go—and they do not go very far at Penrod's age—he had never seen an actual detective; but he did not realize that. If you had asked him, he would have said that he had seen hundreds, and he would have been conscious of no untruth in the reply. In the theatre, it was the day of "crooks" and detectives. Our plot-playwrights, being driven out of the "costume" centuries, yet being as ever dependent for thrill upon weapons, and the imminence of death and prison, had discovered with joy and gratitude that stage criminals can be made so virtuous in certain respects that audiences will love them, and wherever there is a criminal in a play, there must, of course, be a detective, sometimes many detectives. At this same time, there was a revival of detective plays—old-fashioned ones and new-fashioned ones, for many new kinds of detectives were invented. Not only upon the stage were detectives ubiquitous; many magazines ran overflowing with detectives; the Sunday newspapers were always an ounce or so heavier with detectives; they had daily serials about detectives; the billboards everywhere shouted with posters of detectives, and, above all, the "movies" filled the land, up and down, and sideways and across, with detectives and detectives and detectives—they could live no hour of the day or night without detectives. So what wonder that Penrod would have said he had seen great numbers of detectives?

And considering the nature of the most powerful influences under which he came (at his age, those that affect the imagination being always the most powerful) it is not inconsiderably to his credit that he decided to be a detective and not a "crook". Perhaps—especially at the matinées—perhaps he wavered; for, on the stage, in many of these plays, the criminals were incomparably more attractive than the law-abiding people, who naturally must appear as persecutors and take the place formerly filled by villains in tan coats. But the "movies" (which nearly always punish or kill the "crooks") and the stories and plays wherein detectives were the heroes—these won the day, and Penrod's decision was upon the side of the law.

Now, as Penrod sat on the steps of the back porch, his imagined self—the Penrod in his mind—began to shift and alter. By the very act of writing (which is an act comparable to the changing of plaster-of-Paris from a plastic to a fixed state) Penrod had solidified his nebulous studies of the notted detective, George B. Jashber, into a fixed contour, and, by the same process, the more he thought of Jashber, the more he miraculously forgot himself. He became less and less conscious of the actual Penrod, and, when his far-away eye glanced downward, what it physically saw —his knickerbockers and stockings and stubby shoes—bore no meaning. Penrod thought that he was wearing long trousers, rubber-soled shoes, a soft hat with the brim turned down, a long overcoat with the collar turned up, and that he had an automatic pistol in one of the outer pockets of that coat always ready to be taken forth and levelled at (or pressed against) a crook's abdomen. During this long, mystic sitting upon the back steps, the individuality of Penrod and the individuality of the notted detective were merging. Penrod was becoming George B. Jashber, or Jasber.

After a while he rose, glanced sharply over his shoulder,

then, his right hand in the right pocket of his jacket, walked with affected carelessness as far as the door of the stable. Here he paused, looked right and left quickly, drew forth his hand from his pocket, glanced at it vigilantly, then, not in conscious imitation at all but by inspiration, gave the abrupt sag and heave to his shoulders of a "movie" actor about to make an exit. Penrod had not the slightest idea why he did this, and indeed, in the truest sense, it was not Penrod but George B. Jashber who did it. George B. having done it, Penrod passed determinedly into the stable.

He sat upon a box, facing the wheelbarrow; but the box was a swivel-chair and the wheelbarrow a large and polished desk, while the battered old door of the disused harness-closet gleamed mahogany and opaque glass with a sign upon it. This sign, in fact, became actual, for there was paint in a can in the woodshed, and the harness-closet door bore this rubric:

GEORGE B. JASHBER
DETECTIVE OFICE
WALK IN

CHAPTER XLIX

JASHBER DEVELOPS

IN HIS day-dreams and his night-dreams, more and
more, Penrod merged into the character of George B.
Even when he played or romped in ordinary pastimes
with comrade Sam Williams or Herman and Verman, or
with Roddy Bitts and Georgie Bassett, he did not entirely
forget his new significance; there was about him the superiority of one possessing a fateful secret, and there were
times, when (perhaps offended by some action of his play-
mates) he would mutter inaudibly, "I bet they better not
do that if they knew who I was!" And once Margaret overheard him communing with himself as he slowly dressed for
school.

"Well, George, you got *your* eyes open all right? Yes,

sir; I guess I have! Well, George, we got to watch out! Oh, we'll watch *out*, all right!"

Margaret laughed and called to him. "Who's George, Penrod?" she asked.

There was a silence, and then his voice came indistinctly, "Nothin'."

Now befell one of those coincidences in which life abounds, though we are beginning to be cynical about them when we see them on the stage or read of them in fiction. Thus it happened: Della, the cook, had an appanage of some vagueness, though definitely known as "Jarge". Jarge was a golden-haired, pale-eyed, strangely freckled young man, whose chin and Adam's apple knew but one difference, and that was merely geographical. On Sundays, Jarge wore a blue-satin tie, manufactured in the permanent estate of a tiny flat bow-knot, and, as the newspapers are so fond of pointing out, he wore more than this tie—but nothing else so noticeable. The tie and Jarge's chin and Adam's apple had a strong fascination for Penrod; he thought Jarge a remarkable person, and felt favoured by Jarge's conversations with him. Jarge came for Della every Sunday afternoon and was not infrequently to be discovered at other times, sitting solemn and non-committal in the kitchen, when some member of the Schofield family had occasion to go there. To this family he was known, through Della's reserved account of him, as "Jarge", simply; and, as he was evidently much younger than Della, he was accepted by the Schofields as her nephew—or something; for so they alluded to him upon occasion.

Jarge was waiting on the back porch for his presumable aunt, on a fair Sunday afternoon in May, when Penrod approached him and in a rather guarded manner opened a conversation upon the subject of detectives. Jarge proved congenial, and presently informed Penrod that he, Jarge, himself, was a detective no less. However, he stated that the experience had proved disappointing and of no financial benefit whatever. He added that for three dollars anybody

could be a detective. It was only necessary to send three
dollars to an address in Wisconsin, and a badge, a certificate and a book of instructions would be the certain result,
unless the United States mail-car ran off the track. Jarge
had proved this to be the fact, more than a year ago, by
responding with three dollars to an advertisement; but now
he wished he had his three dollars back. His gloom in the
matter had anything but a discouraging effect on Penrod;
on the contrary, an electric opportunity sparkled before
him.

"Look here!" he said solemnly, his eyes grown abnormally
large. "What'll you take for those things?"

Jarge had lost the book, and the certificate had been
accidentally used by his landlady to start a fire in the stove;
but he believed that the badge was somewhere in his trunk.
It passed into Penrod's possession the following Thursday
evening, the exchange being thirty-five cents in the form
of two dimes, two nickels and five pennies. Jarge had polished the badge for good measure, and it was as bright as
quicksilver. It was shaped like an ornamental shield and
bore in black intaglio the awing device:

MEM

GRAY BROS

PVT

DETEC AGCY

NO

103

From that moment, Penrod believed that he was Detective No. 103. That was as far as he went, and it was sufficient—the rest of the organization remained in his mind
as something powerful behind a curtain of Wisconsin mist;
it was enough for him that he was Detective No. 103. And
yet, in spite of the fact that he did not at all question his
official rank as Detective No. 103, he did not think of himself as Penrod Schofield, No. 103; he thought of himself
as George B. Jashber—George B. Jashber, No. 103. None

of his family saw the badge, and, for a time, neither did any
of his comrades—not even Sam Williams. He wore it under
his jacket, near his left armpit, and kept it beneath his pillow at night—to be handy, perhaps, in case of burglars.

There was one person, however, who was granted, not
precisely a look at the portent but at least a glimpse of it.
This was Marjorie Jones, and the glimpse came at the end
of a short interview across Marjorie's picket fence, Penrod
lingering upon the sidewalk there, in the course of a detour
he made on his way home from school. He was so preoccupied—or, at least, he appeared to be so preoccupied—that
Marjorie inquired about it.

"Penrod, what *is* the matter of you?" she cried.

"Well—" he said, neither removing the pucker in his
forehead nor turning his watchful gaze to her. "Nothin'.
Anyway, nothin' you could understand about."

"There is, too!" Marjorie insisted. "I believe you been
havin' a fight with some boy and keep watchin' out maybe
he'll come round the corner."

"Not," Penrod returned, relaxing no more than that.

"Well, what *is* the matter? You acted this way last time,
too."

"Well, what of it?"

"I know you got sumpthing the matter of you, Penrod,"
she persisted. "I bet your mother's found out sumpthing
you *did!*"

"She has not!"

"Well, then, you think she's goin' to."

"I do not!"

"I bet you do, too! I bet that's just it." And she began
to sing an improvisation in a sweet, taunting voice:

> "Penrod knows they'll ketch him yet.
> Penrod's 'fraid what he will *get.*"

Thus mocked, he was sufficiently stung to abandon
George B. Jashber for the moment and turn upon her in the

true likeness of Penrod Schofield aggrieved. "You stop that, Marjorie!"

Marjorie felt encouraged to proceed with her successful treatment, seeing that it had dispersed his rather lofty preoccupation, so she chanted again:

> "Penrod knows they'll ketch him yet,
> So he's 'fraid what he will get.
> *Oh,* Penrod Schofield!"

"You *better* stop that, Marjorie!"

She leaned across the fence, laughing, and pointed at him with a clean little forefinger. "Why had I? Who'll make me, Mister Penrod Schofield? I'll sing it all I want to! I'm goin' to sing it all day! I'm goin' to sing it all night! I'm goin' to sing it from now till the Fourth o' July! Listen!

> "Penrod knows they'll get him yet,
> So he's 'fraid what——"

"All right!" said Penrod, and, turning a pathetic back upon her, began to walk away. But Marjorie checked her mockeries at that and called to him.

"Wait, Penrod! *Please* wait a minute!"

"Well, you goin' to quit?" he demanded, halting tentatively.

"Well, I *have* quit," she said. "Penrod, what *is* the matter of you?"

And as she leaned once more across the fence, her head close to his, he cast one quick, severe glance to the south down the street, and a second to the north up the street. Then, frowning, he said, "Will you cross your heart never to tell anybody long as you live?"

Marjorie was suddenly impressed; her lovely eyes widened. "Yes, I will!" she whispered, crossed herself, and stood waiting, breathless.

"Well—look here!"

Penrod flicked back the left lapel of his jacket, and Marjorie caught a glitter from near his armpit. He allowed time for no more than this glitter to reach her eye, but instantly flicked his jacket back into position, buttoned it, turned and immediately walked away. He walked rapidly and paid no attention to several appeals from Marjorie, who had but the vaguest idea of what she had seen and no conception whatever of its significance. A moment later, he had passed round the corner, never looking back and leaving her completely mystified.

She was not the only person whom his behaviour amazed. Miss Spence was pretty well hardened to Penrod; but his present developments gave her quite a turn. She would have been unobservant indeed had she seen nothing new in his eye; frequently she caught that eye bent upon her, or upon one and another of his fellow pupils, in the long, enigmatic looks full of undecipherable calculations. She noticed, too, that whenever he left the schoolroom he first became obviously furtive, heaved his shoulders as if about to do something desperate, and then departed with an odd intensity. He entered the room with the same intensity and, she got the impression, whenever he came in, that he had previously heaved his shoulders in the cloak-room. There was nothing technically contrary to her rules of discipline in these symptoms of his, and she found herself at a loss. He made her uncomfortable; but she did not know what to do about it, or even in just what terms she could speak to him about it.

Toward the closing days of the school-term (vacation now being at hand) Miss Spence found something to puzzle over that apparently had little connection with the part of her life concerned in her profession of teacher. She finally thought the matter serious enough to be mentioned, and one evening she spoke of it to a fellow boarder, a teacher in the same school.

"I'm sure I haven't imagined it, Miss Carter," she said, shaking her head. "I'm not that sort of a person. I didn't decide that there could be no other explanation until it had happened several times; but every evening I went out last week I had that curious and uncomfortable sensation of being followed."

"How awful!" said Miss Carter.

"At first, I didn't see anything or even hear anything," Miss Spence went on. "It was on my way to the eight-o'clock lecture, Monday evening of last week, and all at once I just got that feeling of someone following me. 'I'm being followed,' I said to myself—just like that. Then I decided it must be nonsense, and laughed at myself and went on. Well, you know I went to those lectures every night except Saturday of last week, and Tuesday, Thursday and Friday the same thing happened—and twice I distinctly heard steps behind me, and once I turned quickly and saw somebody jump behind a tree."

"What did you do?"

"I turned right round and walked back—and there was nobody there. He'd got away somehow."

"What did he look like?" Miss Carter asked eagerly.

"It was too dark to see much; I couldn't tell. Well, I went on to the lecture, and pretty soon I was sure he was behind me again, following me all the way."

"And when you came home from the lecture, did——"

"No," Miss Spence said. "That's the odd part of it. I never got the feeling at all, or heard or saw anything, on the way home from the lecture any of those nights, though, of course, coming home it was later, and you'd think if he was a criminal of any kind, then's when he would be around."

"But do you know of any enemy that would want to follow you?"

"I can't think of any enemy exactly."

"And what would they want to follow you for to a lecture?" Miss Carter cried. "It's the strangest thing I ever heard of!"

"I've thought back over all my family history and everything I've ever done," Miss Spence said, "and I can think of only one person who could have any possible object in doing such a thing."

"Who is that?"

"It's a cousin of mine; his name is William Bote. He drank so much that nobody would speak to him, and finally he got to be sort of a tramp and disappeared. Well, my aunt Milly lives in this town, and she has a little property, and she is William's aunt, too. He might have heard somewhere that she's talked about leaving it to me, and he might have come here to try to do something about it; maybe——"

Miss Carter was an intuitive woman, instant in her decisions. "That's it!" she exclaimed. "If you can't think of anybody else it *could* be, why, of course it's this William What's-his-name——"

"William Bote."

"I'm *sure* it's this William Bote," Miss Carter declared. "A woman outside of an experience like this has more perspective than the woman who is actually having the experience; and I felt all the time you were talking that it was this Bote." She glanced at the clock. "It's a quarter to eight, and you say this was about the time he followed you all last week. Do you suppose he's somewhere out there now?"

"He might be."

"Let's find out," Miss Carter suggested.

"What!"

"Come on! Put on your hat, and go out alone. I'll wait two minutes and come after you, and, if he's following you, he'll be in between us. How large is he?"

"William? Oh, he was a little thin man, and very shaky."

"I'll grab him," said Miss Carter impulsively. "I'm not afraid. Let's hurry. Walk straight down the street and go slowly, and we'll show this William Bote that the age of terrorizing women has passed."

The two determined teachers proceeded at once to set the trap for Mr. Bote. Miss Spence left the house at a leisurely gait, and exactly two minutes later her friend set forth somewhat more rapidly. Before the latter had gone half of a block, she drew a sudden breath, partly nervous, partly triumphant, for in the near distance she perceived and identified Miss Spence, who was passing beneath a street-lamp, while between Miss Spence and herself a figure indistinctly yet undeniably flitted from one to another of the shade trees that lined the sidewalk. There was no question about it: Miss Spence *was* being followed!

Instantly Miss Carter determined upon her action. "Miss Spence! Cornelia Spence!" she shouted loudly. "We've *got* him!"

And she rushed forward while Miss Spence turned and ran back at full speed, and the mysterious stranger, thus waylaid and cut off between them, might have found himself a sudden prisoner if the mouth of an alley had not been opposite the tree where he lurked, and only about ten feet away. Both ladies screamed loudly as they saw a shadow streaking into this refuge; but both resolutely followed it at top speed and went shouting down the alley.

"Look!" cried Miss Carter. "I think he's climbing the fence!" And then, at a clatter of shoes scampering over wood, "He's got on top of this woodshed! I know he's up there!"

"He is!" Miss Spence rejoined. "I heard him! I can hear him now!"

The woodshed was a humble part of a property well known to both of them as the home of Samuel Williams, who was a pupil of Miss Carter's, and the two indomitable teachers, halting beside the shed, hammered upon its reso-nant outer wall—Miss Spence with an umbrella, which she had carried in lieu of weapons, and Miss Carter with a piece of brick she had discovered underfoot. Both also freely used their strong young voices.

"William!" Miss Spence shouted into the upper dark-ness. "William, you better come down from up there! You know we've got you!"

And Miss Carter went so far as to hurl her brick bat upon the roof of the shed. "You William Bote!" she cried fiercely. "We know you're up there! You might as well come down! We're going to have you *arrested!*"

Then both of them shrieked, for a flashlight first silhouetted the sky-line of the woodshed with light, and, rising, as its holder mounted the adjacent fence, illuminated the ominous roof, but disclosed only a vacant expanse of shingles.

"There's no one up there now," said a voice. Then an alley gate opened, and Mr. Williams and Mrs. Williams and Sam and two suddenly vociferous coloured women appeared. Several people from neighbouring houses, some pedestrians from the street, a small touring car and a patrolman likewise arrived, and shouts indicated that more were coming.

Penrod decided that he had made a mistake. As he crawled through an aperture in the farther line of Mr. Williams's fence, and made his way toward home as rapidly as possible, but painfully withal (on account of a gratuitous nail on the roof of Mr. Williams's woodshed) sounds of agitation and excitement came increasingly to his ears, indicating the beginnings of a neighbourhood perturbation he had little anticipated; and, in spite of an almost unbearable anxiety to know who William Bote was, he felt that he would not do well to linger.

It became plain to him that he would have to give up shadowing Miss Spence. She was too excitable to serve as a Harold Ramorez; and George B. Jashber would have to find some other scondrel to shadow.

CHAPTER L

JASHBER IS INTERRUPTED

THE days were longer now, and there was more time for detective work after school. Until Friday of the week after the fiasco, Penrod employed the daylight hours following the afternoon dismissal of school in shadowing schoolmates and acquaintances, and also practised this art during the earlier part of the evenings; but with results on the whole unsatisfactory and far from exciting. On Thursday evening, in the twilight after dinner, he did a little better; unperceived, he followed Sam Williams and Walter-John to a corner drug store, and, peering through the window, made note of the fact that Sam purchased a bag of salted peanuts. When Sam came out, Penrod concealed himself from view, and again took up the trail, pursuing in silence, until Sam and Walter-John came almost to their own purlieus. Then Penrod made his presence known, stepping suddenly to his friend's side.

"You give me some o' those salted peanuts, Sam Williams!" he said commandingly. At the moment Sam was not eating; the bag was in his pocket; therefore he was astonished.

"Where'd you come from? How'd you know I got peanuts?"

"Never mind," Penrod returned darkly. "I got ways o' knowin'. I know everything you do."

"You do not!"

"I'll prove it. You and Walter-John went over to Smith and Muhlbach's and bought a dime's worth o' salted peanuts. When they handed 'em to you you could hardly reach 'em because Walter-John was pullin' you the other way on account he wanted to smell at Smith and Muhlbach's cat, and she had her back all humped up and was fixin' to take a crack at him. You hand out that bag o' peanuts!"

Sam proffered the bag; Penrod helped himself, and there followed some moments of silence broken only by sounds of eating. "Well," Sam said, at length, "you might know that, but you don't know everything I do, because you couldn't."

"I do, too. I told you I got ways o' knowin' all about what anybody does I want to."

"All right then," Sam said challengingly. "You know so much, tell me what I ate for dinner and what my mother said to my father when he asked her when was my brother Robert goin' to get home from college this year. You just answer me that, you know so much!"

"I could if I wanted to; but that's sumpthing I wouldn't want to. I said I know everything about anybody I want to, because I got ways to find out—ways nobody else knows about."

"I bet you haven't! What are they?"

"You wait and see. Maybe I'll show you some day, Sam."

"When?"

"Well, maybe pretty soon." Penrod had become thoughtful. "Maybe to-morrow after school, and Saturday. I got to think it over, though; but I guess I will, Sam."

Sam seemed to be satisfied with this tentative promise, though not greatly excited by the prospect offered, and Penrod departed, ruminating. He had about made up his mind that George B. Jashber needed something of an organization behind him—subordinates, in fact, minor officials to be commanded, sent here and there, and set to trail criminals when George B. Jashber, himself, might be engaged with other matters, or perhaps preoccupied with duties at home. For such services, Sam Williams was easily available, and so were Herman and Verman. The idea appeared to be excellent, and, before falling to sleep that night, Penrod decided to begin the organization of his subordinate force on the following day after school. Unfortunately, however, the carrying out of this plan had to be postponed; an interruption occurred that even banished George B. Jashber, himself, for the time being, and, when Sam Williams made his appearance in the Schofields' backyard, the next afternoon, he had to be informed of unavoidable events indefinitely postponing the fulfillment of Penrod's promises.

Penrod sat gloomily upon the back steps with his elbows upon his knees and his cheeks supported by his hands, while not far away a bright-eyed little boy, nine years old, seemed to find pleasure in pulling Duke about by the collar, and otherwise annoying the patient little old dog.

"Watch me, Penrod!" the strange little boy shouted continually. "Look at me, Penrod! Look how I do with this crazy ole dog! Look how I do, Penrod!"

"It's my little cousin," Penrod explained sadly. "His name's Ronald Passloe, and he's here on a visit with his father, and he's an orphan or sumpthing, because he hasn't got any mother, and I haf to put in all my time with him. They didn't tell me anything about it until I got home from school. I don't know how long he's goin' to stay—maybe a week or sumpthing—and I got to be polite to him and everything all the time he's here. I already did take a walk with him, but that's all, and I s'pose I got to keep on hangin' around him. You want to go and get Walter-John and let him play with him a while, Sam?"

Sam glanced again at Master Ronald Passloe, and evidently received an unfavourable impression. "Well, I guess not, Penrod. I guess what you were tellin' me about last night—how to find out everything you want to about anybody—I guess you couldn't——"

"No," Penrod said morosely. "I got to keep hangin' around him because he's my little cousin and visitin' us."

Sam looked once more at little Ronald; then he said, "Well, g'bye, Penrod," and went away.

"Hey, Penrod!" little Ronald cried, and, abandoning Duke, came running to his cousin. "Le'ss go in the lib'ary where Papa is and make him give us the money to buy that little gun we saw in the drug store window. C'mon!"

He dashed into the house, and Penrod followed more slowly, so that by the time he reached the door of the library little Ronald had already begun his pleadings.

"Papa, please," said little Ronald. "Please, please, please! Won'tcha, Papa, please? Please! Oh, please, Papa!"

"No; I will not," said Mr. Passloe, who was writing a letter at a desk by a window.

Penrod remained in the doorway and watched the beginning of a process never in his own case followed by pleasant results. But little Ronald kept at it.

"Papa," he resumed quietly, "it's only twenty-five cents. That's all we need."

"I don't care if it is," his father coldly returned. "Go out and play some more with Penrod. I'm busy writing. Don't bother me."

"But, Papa——"

"Go out and play, I tell you."

"But, Papa, how can we play when you won't give us anything we want to play with?"

"I don't care what you play with," Mr. Passloe said crossly. "I want to finish this letter. Go and play."

Ronald's tone became weary, but retained its affectation of patient reasonableness. "Papa, I've explained to you time and again—how can we play when we haven't got anything we like? And if you'd only just give me a quarter this once, I promise I'll never ask you for——"

"I won't do it. Didn't you hear me say I wouldn't?"

"Yes. But, Papa——"

"That's all there is to it! When I say a thing I mean it, and you might just as well not waste any more of my time. I've said I wouldn't, and I won't."

Ronald became more plaintive. "Papa, you don't under-*stand!* It's just a little squirt-gun that Penrod and I——"

"I don't allow you to play with any kind of a gun, and you know it."

"It isn't a gun, Papa. It makes just a little water come out of the end of it. It wouldn't hurt a flea. It's kind of useful, more than just to play with, Papa. Honest it is! If you were out walking or anything and had to have a drink of water, why, if you had this little gun with you, why, you could get a *good* drink out of it and be all right again. 'N' then, s'pose you were goin' along somewheres, and kind of looked around somewheres, and s'pose there was a house on fire somewheres, where some poor people lived, and they were all burning up or sumpthing, why, if I had my good little water-gun with me, I'd turn it on that ole fire——"

"Stop it!" Mr. Passloe commanded bitterly. "If you say one more word about that gun, I'll——"

"*Please*, Papa!"

"Not one single word!"

Ronald's manner and voice suddenly became passionate. "Papa, I *got* to get that little gun!" he cried.

"Well, you won't!"

"Papa! *Pop*-puh!"

"Be quiet!" Mr. Passloe shouted. "Be quiet!"

"Pop-*puh!*"

"You don't get it! No!"

"*Please!*"

Mr. Passloe uttered dismal sounds, and, having dropped his pen, massaged his hair with both hands. "If you're not out of this room before I count ten, I'll take you upstairs, myself, and put you to bed for the rest of the day! One—two——"

"Pop-*puh!*"

"Three—four—five——"

"Please! Oh, *please* let me get that little—oh!—gun." Ronald's voice was now syncopated with sobs. He seemed to suffer horribly. "Oh, Papa, you *know* how I want that little—oh!—gun! You *know* you do, Poppuh! You—oh!—*know* you do! Please, please, please, please——"

"Eight—nine—*ten!*" Mr. Passloe finished his counting with a great air of grimness, and Penrod gave Ronald up for lost. (He had long ago abandoned all hope of the squirt-gun.)

"There!" said Passloe. "I've counted the ten, and you know the consequences, Ronald. I told you what I'd do, and you deliberately——"

"I *haf* to have that little—oh!—gun!" sobbed Ronald. "It wouldn't *hurt* you to give it to me, either! I'd like to know what—oh!—harm it'd ever do *you* just to let me get that little gun—oh! If I was *your* father and I had a boy that wanted a little—oh!—gun—I bet you'd think I was perty mean if I said—oh!—I wouldn't! The only reason you say you won't do it's because you don't *want* me to have a good time! You *don't* want me to! Pleose, please, please, *please!* PLEASE——"

"O Lord!" Then the dumfounded Penrod observed the hand of Mr. Passloe seeking a pocket. "Here! Hush! Be quiet! For heaven's sake go and *get* your little gun!"

Ronald, with no more words upon the matter, instantly grasped the resplendent coin emerging from that pocket, and the two boys departed, leaving the sacked parent mur-

murous behind closed doors. Briskly they went into the
bright air, and lightly sped gateward.

"That was easy," said Ronald, in a businesslike tone.

Penrod looked with interest upon this type, hitherto unfamiliar to him. He said nothing, but stared at Ronald almost continuously as they walked along; and there was
approbation in this gaze.

Ronald made several other allusions to his victory, down-
right contempt for his late adversary mingling with a little
justifiable swagger. "Why, that was nothin' at all!" he said
scornfully. "When *I* want anything, I *get* it!"

Meanwhile, the approbation in the eyes of Penrod increased in lustre. However, it was somewhat dimmed by
various occurrences after their return in possession of the
squirt-gun. This implement proved even more fascinating
in actual operation than in anticipation, especially as each
of the boys wished to operate it while the other remained
a spectator, and neither was willing to remain a spectator
for an instant. But, for once, Penrod found himself hopelessly out-talked. Ronald claimed possession on the reasonable ground of ownership; he reminded Penrod severely of
certain dogmas of etiquette concerning the treatment of
visitors, citing many instances to establish his rights as a
guest, and finally became so vociferous, as well as verbose,
in a reminiscence covering the whole history of their relations to the squirt-gun that Penrod despairingly proposed
a compromise somewhat to his own disadvantage.

"Well, what if it *was* your own father's money?" he said.
"What if you *did* see our good ole gun first in the window?
I was the one said I wished it was ours first, wasn't I? And
you got to use water in a bucket out of *my* own father's
hydrant, don't you? Whose *bucket* is it, I'd like to know?
I guess that bucket belongs to my own father, doesn't it? I
guess this is my own father's yard, isn't it? Well, I got jus'
much right to use that gun any way I want to as you have
—and better, too! I guess you got sense enough to see that,
haven't you? Well, I tell you the way we'll fix it. Each of

us'll take turns ten minutes long, and you can have the first turn. The one that's not got the gun can stand in the kitchen doorway where they can see the clock, and then, when the ten minutes is up, I can come and get the gun, and *my* turn'll begin."

Having thus spoken, he abandoned the hand-grip that until then he had maintained upon the squirt-gun as a sort of legal protest, and, turning his back upon Ronald, sought the doorway, where he came to a stand with his eyes conscientiously upon the face of the clock.

Ronald capered over the yard, squirting fluently. "Look, Penrod!" he shouted. "Watch me, Penrod! I got her workin' great now. Watch, Penrod! I'm ole hose-reel Number Nine. Clang! Clang! Clang! Fire! Fire! Fire! *Git* that horness on them horses there, you men, you! Hurry up, now! Think I want to be all day gettin' to that fire? Click, click —horness, horness, horness!" He fastened imaginary buckles, and mounted to an imaginary seat. "All ready, boys! *Gallump, gallump, gallumpety—glump!*" Here, he not only gave this vocal imitation of a gallop but galloped simultaneously with his legs, contriving with his arms and shoulders the impersonation of a most passionate fireman in the act of driving, the squirt-gun now enacting the rôle of a whip. "Gong! Gong! Gong! *Hi*, there, you white horse, can't you keep up with that black horse o' mine! Go, you devils, go! Gallump! Gallump! Gallumpety-glump! *Whoa* there, you ole black horse, you! Here's the fire! Gimme that hose; I'll show you how *I* put fires out! *Fz-z-z-z-z!* That's the ole fire blazin' away. Look, Penrod! Watch me! *Listen*, Penrod! *Fz-z-z-z!* That's the fire, Penrod! Why don't you look? Look at the way I put houses out when they're on fire? *Fz-z-z-z!* Squirt! Squirt! Squirt! Pen-rod! What's the matter o' you? Whyn't you look see the way I'm puttin' this fire out? Looky here! *Fz-z-z-z-z——*"

At last Penrod looked. He had kept his eyes steadfastly, even sternly, upon the clock throughout the interminable period. "My turn!" And with an altered face, joy upon it, he ran and captured the squirt-gun from Ronald's clinging hands. "My turn now, Ronald! You go stand where you can see the clock!"

"I won't!" Ronald declared vehemently. "You gimme that little gun!"

"But it's my turn. We said we'd each keep it ten minutes for you and then ten minutes for me."

"I did not! You said so. I never said anything about it at all. You gimme my little gun! I——"

"I won't do it," said Penrod stoutly. "Not till you go look at the clock ten minutes. I looked at it ten minutes, didn't I?"

"You gimme my little gun!" Ronald insisted, growing visibly and audibly more intense. "It's my little gun, I guess! And whose quarter paid for it? You just answer me that, I'd like to ask!"

"I don't care who!" Penrod returned lightly. "Look, Ronald: I'm chief o' the Fire Department. This is the way I do!" And he began to romp over the grass with the replenished squirt-gun. "Watch, Ronald! Here's me!"

But Ronald showed even less interest in Penrod's performance than Penrod had shown in Ronald's, and, while Penrod—ever inspired to excel—now brought forth from his creative soul and painted upon the empty air not one mere hose-reel alone but the complex machineries of a completely equipped metropolitan Fire Department, including motor-driven ladder-trucks, chemical engines and something he called a "fire-tower", Ronald brooded near by with obvious malevolence.

He was not wholly unwatchful, however, as he proceeded to prove, about four minutes after the beginning of Penrod's "turn". The new fireman happened to be holding the squirt-gun somewhat loosely in his left hand, gesticulating for the moment with his right, and his back was toward Ronald. Ronald darted upon him, captured the squirt-gun with one swift and stealthy jerk, then sped away, laughing tauntingly.

"You give that back here!" Penrod cried, pursuing. "It ain't half a minute since my turn began! You never went near the clock! If I catch you, I'll——"

But Ronald was fleet. He disappeared round a corner of the house, and Penrod beheld the squirt-gun no more that day. Ronald scrambled through an open window before his pursuer turned the corner, and, half an hour later, leaving the squirt-gun securely hidden within the house, the visitor again sought the backyard, discovering his host gloomily beginning the mastication of an apple.

"Biters!" Ronald immediately vociferated. "Biters! I got you, Penrod! Biters!"

"Yes, you will!" Penrod returned sardonically. "You got no more chance to get biters on this apple than——" But here he was forced to interrupt himself by a cry of sincere emotion. Ronald swooped upon him, this time in a frontal attack, and, with a motion as rapid as a prestidigitator's, snatched the apple from Penrod's hand. Again Ronald disappeared, cackling, round the corner of the house, safely in advance.

"All right for you!" Penrod called bitterly after him, abandoning the chase. "Go on; keep it! What I care! I know where's sumpthing better'n any ole apple, and just because you haf to go and act a pig, you don't get any what *I'm* goin' to get!"

Never was he less a true prophet. As he emerged from the kitchen, a few minutes later, triumphant in the contemplation of half a dozen cookies, cajoled from Della and intended to be eaten tantalizingly in the presence of Ronald, this latter lay in wait behind the outward-swinging screen door, and again a surprise attack was successful. Ronald was one of those bright-eyed little boys who are as quick and as sly as cats.

Penrod was so deftly robbed of the six cookies that he remained staring incredulously at the crumby and still feebly gesticulating fingers of his left hand until a hastily massed portion of the ravished delicacies had already passed

Ronald's esophagus and epiglottis and established itself as a through tourist for the whole route of his alimentary canal. The dazed eyes of Penrod lifted from his vacant hand and perceived the undulations of Ronald's slender throat as this journey was thus begun. Then Penrod made outcry and tried to retrieve what might be retrievable.

But Ronald had discovered that he was easily the fleeter. Disdaining to seek cover, this time, he dodged, ducked and zigzagged, eating spasmodically the while, and not failing to describe in rich words the ecstasies produced in his insides by the food, which he maddeningly affected to believe Penrod had presented to him. He ate the cakes to the last infuriating crumb, dancing just beyond arm's length, while Penrod formed a plan of retaliation, deciding that he would obtain a fresh supply from Della, and, behind a closed window, eat cookies at Ronald. He went to the length of rehearsing mentally the scornful gestures to accompany this performance, which might have proven an effective one if Della had been a woman with a real heart in her bosom. Unfortunately, she was of those whom no pathos moves except their own, and for to-day she had founded herself stonily upon the senseless and arbitrary dogma, "Six is enough", her only variation being quite as discouraging— "Well, annyway, you'll git no more!"

Following this chilling siege, Penrod spent half an hour satisfying himself that when Della really intended to hide a pan of cookies she was able to do it. After this, he returned to the yard gloomily, but with his hurt somewhat healed by time.

New injuries awaited him at the hands of Ronald. The latter found it amusing to snatch things from his cousin, and Penrod could not pick up a stick or twig or even a pebble to throw, but Ronald made his attempt upon it, and always (unless Penrod was alertly upon his guard) successfully. By sunset, Penrod had begun to wear a badgered look.

He was silent, not to say heavy, at the evening meal;

there was upon his youthful front something not unsugges-
tive of the careworn expression of Mr. Passloe, Ronald's
father. And when Mrs. Schofield, with a mother's absent
smile, asked her son if he and Ronald had enjoyed a "happy
afternoon, playing together", Penrod's answer was naught.
One would have said he did not hear.

Ronald, on the other hand, was talkative. He dominated
the table—though Mr. Passloe frequently offered nervous
protest—while the Schofield family (except Penrod) listened to the boyish chatter with the indulgent responsiveness that all polite people show to other people's children.

As Ronald talked on, disjointedly interrupting, squeak-
ing, yipping, sometimes almost shouting, Penrod's parents
and sister Margaret exhibited every token of friendly and
approving interest. They wore the air of people greatly
pleased by the conversation of a witty and distinguished
person, and yet, all the while, little seemed plainer to Penrod than the fact that Ronald was, definitely, nothing but
the freshest little smart Aleck on earth. Penrod became,
first, embittered; next, envious and jealous; then he began
to ponder, though dimly. Ronald's ways appeared to be
successful. It might pay to be like that!

This impression was confirmed during the service of des-
sert. Ronald announced that he wished to attend a "pitcher-
show" that evening, and his father promptly and sharply
denied the consequent application for funds. He denied per-
mission as well, concluding decidedly, "You'll be in bed before half-past eight, or I'll know the reason why!"

"But, Papa——"

"Not another word, Ronald. You can't go, and we don't
wish to hear anything more about it."

"But, Papa," Ronald persevered, "it's only ten cents, and
Penrod's papa will give *him* ten cents, and——"

"No, he won't," said Mr. Passloe.

"Well, then," Ronald responded briskly, "*I* don't care if
I haf to go alone."

"No; you can't go——"

"Well, then, you can give us twenty cents and I'll buy a ticket for Penrod, too."

"Didn't you hear me say you couldn't go?"

"Pop-puh!"

"Not another word now!"

"*Please*, Papa!"

"I said——"

"Pop-*puh!*"

"I told you——"

At this point Ronald became emotional; his young voice quavered piteously. "Papa, it's *only* twenty cents! I should think you could spare *that* much when——you know what a nice time I and Penrod would have! Papa, I *got* to go to that pitcher-show! I *got* to!"

"Shame on you," said his father sternly, "making such a fuss at the table when you're on a visit! Look at Penrod, how nicely he sits and how quiet he keeps."

"Well, that's not so usual," Mr. Schofield felt called upon to say, coming to the rescue of Ronald. "Ronald seems to me a very nice little boy."

"I'm ashamed of him," said Mr. Passloe. "The idea of his making such a distur——"

"*Pop*-puh!" Ronald interrupted vehemently. "Pop-*puh!* You *got* to gimme that twenty cents! You got to *do* it!"

Here Mrs. Schofield attempted to mediate. She smilingly offered a compromise. "But dear," she said sweetly to Ronald, "if your papa doesn't want you to go this evening because it's dark and late——and I'd just a little rather Penrod didn't go, either——think what a nice time you can have to-morrow! When to-morrow comes, and all nice, bright sunshine——"

She continued to expand this theme, offering rewards and enticements——for the morrow. Even in the silent Penrod these evoked no responsive anticipations. A boy can look forward ecstatically to his birthday, to the Fourth of July, to Thanksgiving dinner and to Christmas. Those are the only morrows that weigh greatly with him, and grown

people are seldom less intelligent than when they follow
that eternal custom of theirs—offering boys beauteous morrows, invented on the spur of the moment, and easily recognizable as mere dismal words to offset immediate pleasures
already within grasp. Ronald was moved by Mrs. Schofield's
soft eloquence—moved to break out in a yell.

"*Rats!*" he vociferated, and set an exclamation point
upon the shocking word—a heartrending sob. "Oh! I don't
—*oh!*—want to go to any crazy ole matinée to—oh!—to-
morrow!" he wailed. "I want to go to that pitcher-show
to-night!"

"Ronald," his father warned him sharply, "you're dis-
gustingly rude!"

"Oh, no," said Mrs. Schofield lightly, "Ronald didn't
mean to be impolite at all. He's a very good boy—aren't
you, Ronald?"

Ronald paid no attention to her, renewing the attack
upon his father with vehemence. But the murky glance of
Penrod swept Mrs. Schofield; he gave her a long look wherein strong injury mingled with perplexity.

And why should he not have been injured and perplexed?
To a boy, a visitor is a visitor for only the first hour or so;
after that, you know him about as well as you know anybody. Penrod was unable to perceive that his family was
being indulgent toward Ronald because the latter was a
guest in the house, and, if he had perceived this, the point
of etiquette involved would have seemed founded upon
vicious unreason; he could not understand why a guest
should be treated better than anybody else. But he saw,
all too plainly, that Ronald was behaving in a way that
would have insured punishment for Penrod Schofield—and
here were Penrod's parents making excuses for Ronald and
calling him "good" and "nice"! Evidently they liked this
sort of thing.

"*Pop*-puh!" screamed Ronald.

"One—two—three—four—" Mr. Passloe began ominously.

"Pop-*puh!* Oh, please, please, please, *please!* Papa, you *know* how I want to go to that pitcher-show! It wouldn't hurt *you* to let me go! What *harm* would it do you—unless you don't *want* me to have a nice time! Papa, you *don't* want me to! You *don't!* You *don't!* Oh, Pop-puh, *please, please!* Please!"

His passion had become acute. Mr. Passloe groaned, "Oh, good heavens!" and plunged his hand into his pocket, drawing forth two dimes.

"C'm on, Penrod!" said Ronald briskly.

"Can I, Mamma?"

"Well—since Ronald wants to go so much," Mrs. Schofield said affably.

And, as the two boys passed out of the front door, Penrod happened to sneeze, and therefore drew forth his handkerchief; but before he had time to make it of any service to him, Ronald, with a malicious yell, snatched it out of his hand, and ran carolling down the walk and through the gateway—a sprightly soul with never a care in the world.

CHAPTER LI

LITTLE RONALD

THIS snatching habit of Ronald's, jocular as it was, palled so heavily upon Penrod the next morning that he withdrew from his visitor's company, and, leaving Ronald the whole of the Schofields' yard as a playground, put several fences between himself and the snatcher, then emerged to the comforting, secluded alley, where he walked, inwardly communing. Ere long he encountered one Herman, who, in recognition of summer's approach, walked with brown feet bare and would go thus unshod until October. To-day his feet moved slowly in the alley dust, for Herman was preoccupied with a turtle, an intelligent animal about the size of the palm of the brown hand upon which it rested.

445

"Yay!" shouted Penrod, his troubles forgotten. "Where'd you get that turtle, Herman?"

"I trade him off'n Cubena Howliss," Herman replied.

"Who's Cubena Howliss?"

"Cubena live ovuh on canal bank," said Herman. "She say, 'Look, what settin' right in pie-pan on kitchum flo' las' night!' She say she mos' yell her neck off. So she say she don' want him so *much*, but she ain' go' *give* no turkle away to nobody. I trade' him off'n her."

"What'd you trade?"

"I tuck an' give her a good. piece o' kin'lin'-wood an' a nice bode I foun' ovuh where's buil'n' a house, an' a nice knife-blade."

Penrod touched the turtle's head, which had protruded from the shell adventurously. "Yay!" he shouted. "A turtle's mighty smart, Herman. All you got to do is just to touch 'em on the head or their tail or one o' their feet or anything, and they'll stick 'em right back in again, unless you grab it and hold on so's they can't."

"My goo'ness, you think I don' know that!" Herman exclaimed. "Whut I goin' *own* a turkle fer ef I don' know that much about 'em? Whut I want go an' han' ovuh 'at stick o' kin'lin'-wood an' 'at bode an' nice knife-blade to Cubena Howliss fer, ef I don' know no mo' 'bout a turkle 'n what you say I do?"

"I didn't say anything, Herman," Penrod protested. "What you goin' to do with him, Herman?"

"I'm go' cut my 'nitials on his back, an' 'en I'm go' to put him in a bucket in ow woodshed an' wait fer him to grow. When he git big, my 'nitials go' to grow same as he do. Be two feet long some day!"

Penrod's eyes glowed and enlarged. The idea he had just absorbed was more than fascinating; it was compelling. "Look here, Herman," he said breathlessly. "Has this Cubena Howliss got any more turtles? Where's she live?"

"She ain' got no mo'," said Herman. " 'Iss here turkle on'y one she own, an' she ain' got air' one lef'."

"My!" Penrod exclaimed. "I *would* like to own that turtle, Herman! What'll you trade for him?"

"Ain' go' trade fer him. I done trade to git him. Ain' go' trade to lose him."

"Why not?"

Herman was both obdurate and unenlightening; he seemed to love the sound of the words he had just uttered, and to consider them sufficient. "I done trade to git him," he repeated. "Ain' go' trade to lose him!"

"Aw, Herman!" Penrod remonstrated.

"I done trade to git him. Ain' go' trade to lose him!"

"How much'll you take?"

Herman plunged into calculations. "Well, suh, 'at nice bode uz wuff dime; 'at knife-blade wuff nickel—'at's fifteem—an' 'at nice kin'lin'-wood uz wuff two cents easy. 'At's sevumteem. I take sevumteem cents fer 'iss here turkle."

"I'll buy him," said Penrod eagerly. "I'll give you the seventeen cents for him."

"You got 'at money?" Herman was surprised; perhaps a little skeptical.

"No; but I will have when Papa comes home at noon. I can get him to give it to me." He smiled reassuringly—almost swaggeringly, in fact, and added, "Easy!"

"You kin?"

"Yes. And, look here, Herman: don't you go and cut your 'nitials on this turtle, Herman, because he'll be my turtle soon as I pay you for him, and I don't want anybody else's 'nitials on any turtle of mine except my own 'nitials. You won't cut yours on him, will you?"

"Tell you whut I do," said Herman: "I wait till six o'clock 's even'. 'F you pay me down 'at sevumteem cents 'fo six 'clock's even', he ain' go' to have nuff'm 'tall cut on him. You don' pay me down 'at sevumteem cents 'fo' no six 'clock's even', I'm go' to begin cuttin'. 'At's all a way I'm willin' to fix it."

"Oh, that's all right!" Penrod assured him. "I'll have that seventeen cents long before any ole six o'clock. Don't you worry!" And the contract thus comprehended by both the party of the first part and the party of the second part, Herman proceeded homeward with the property under consideration, while Penrod continued his walk in the alley. His spirits had risen decidedly. Already he felt the turtle to be virtually his own, and he had been convinced by the mere sight of it—in another boy's possession—that a turtle is the most delightful animal in the world. He wondered why he had never owned one before, and he determined never to be without one again.

His vision roamed the future; he saw the little turtle growing year by year, the initials, P.S., growing with him. He saw the turtle following him about the yard, large, docile, obedient. He would train the turtle to do tricks; the turtle and Duke and Walter-John (borrowed) would do tricks together. He would invite a large crowd—and Marjorie Jones—to a show in the stable. He saw himself as ringmaster coming forward with Duke and Walter-John upon one side of him and the turtle upon the other. "Laydeez and gentlemun, permit me to interodoos to your attainshon ——" There was a warmth in his bosom as he walked. Already affection for this turtle was springing in the heart of Penrod Schofield.

A little before the hour for lunch, he slid over the back fence, and made his way into the house without being noticed by Ronald, who, squirt-gun in hand, was treacherously approaching Duke in the front yard. Penrod ascended to his father's room and found both his parents there, engaged in conversation.

"Papa," he began at once, "I'd like you to please give me seventeen cents."

"Would you?" Mr. Schofield returned unenthusiastically.

"Yes, Papa, please."

"That's a strange coincidence," said the father. "I've just been wishing some one would give me seventeen thousand dollars; but I don't believe anybody will."

"Papa, please give me seventeen cents."

"No, sir."

"Papa——"

Mrs. Schofield interrupted. "What do you want seventeen cents for?"

"To buy a turtle."

"A what?" Mr. Schofield inquired.

"That coloured boy Herman's got the finest turtle I ever did see," Penrod explained. "He traded some good kindling-wood and a nice board and a nice knife-blade to Cubena Howliss for it, and the board was worth ten cents, and the knife-blade was worth five cents, and the wood was worth two cents, and that makes seventeen cents. He won't take a cent under seventeen cents for the turtle."

Mr. Schofield had begun to wear a look of irritation. "He won't?" he inquired dangerously.

"No, sir; and I do want that turtle."

"Well, you can't have it. It's time you learned you can't spend money idiotically, no matter how much or how little. You can find all the turtles you want, anyhow."

"I never did find a turtle in my life," Penrod asserted stoutly, "except one time at a picnic, and you made me put it back in the creek." His tone became more insistent. "Papa, *please* give me seventeen cents."

"No."

"Papa, it's the finest turtle I ever——"

"That's enough! You don't *need* a turtle! What on earth do you want a turtle for, anyhow? *We* don't want a nasty turtle around the house. You can't——"

"It could sleep in the stable," Penrod urged. "I'd fix a place for it. It wouldn't be any trouble or anything to *you*, Papa."

Mr. Schofield raised his voice. "Didn't I tell you you couldn't have it?"

But now Penrod's tone became almost excruciatingly plaintive. "Papa, *please* give me seventeen cents! That's all I want you to do. Can't you just give me seven*teen* cents?"

"No!"

"*Pop*-puh!"

"No!"

"*Pop-puh!*"

"Didn't you hear what I said?"

"Papa, please, please, *please*——"

Mr. Schofield sent a sharp glance at his wife, who had begun to look serious beyond her wont. "What's the matter with him?"

Before Mrs. Schofield could express an opinion, Penrod intervened. He uttered a sudden howl; a passion took possession of him. "*Pop*-puh!" he bleated. "I *got* to get that turtle! I *haf* to have seventeen cents! What harm would it do *you* for me to have that turtle? You don't *want* me to have a nice time with that turtle! You *don't!* Oh, Papa—oh!—Pop-*puh*—oh!—*please!* Please, please, please, *please*, PLEASE!"

Mr. Schofield rushed upon his son. By the shoulders he caught Penrod, and the latter found it impossible to continue his imitation, one all the more remarkable because it was only partially a conscious imitation. Most of it was instinctive.

His father shook him. "By George, he's caught it!" and he impelled the unfortunate Penrod toward a door that Mrs. Schofield sorrowfully opened, in response to a grim command from her husband. It was the door of a drear and dark closet, utterly without resources to aid an inmate in passing the time.

"You stay in there till you get over it!" Mr. Schofield said, as he closed this painful door. Then he turned to his wife. "By George, we want to cure him of *that*, right at the start! We don't want to be driven as crazy as poor cousin Henry."

Penrod was released by Mrs. Schofield subsequent to his father's departure after lunch. He was allowed to partake of some chilled remains of the meal but informed of a decree that he should curtail his activities until four o'clock; he was to stay indoors until that hour. Thereafter, he could go out; but not until the next day outside the yard. And upon this additional sentence, he spake not, yet his eyes were fierce and almost unbearable.

He underwent his penalties to the full, enigmatically looking out of windows most of the long, horrid time, his expression merely concentrating a little when across his field of vision Ronald went sweeping over the lawn, in further squirt-gun persecutions of Duke. But at eight seconds after four o'clock, Penrod threw open the rear doors of the stable and gazed earnestly at the abode of Herman across the alley.

"Yay, Herman!" Penrod shouted.

Herman appeared.

"Herman, I can't come out. I got to stay in our yard till to-morrow; but the stable's just the same as the yard. Where's that turtle?"

Herman's air was morbid; injuries lay heavy upon him. "You kin' keep 'at sevumteem cents," he said. "*Hain't* no turkle! I laid him down nice in dish-pan. Pappy sen' me to drug sto' to git him some 'at brain-medicine; Mammy tuck 'at turkle an' frew him in ash-pile. Man come 'long; clean up ash-pile. Tuck an' tuck 'at turkle an' done ca'y him off! I tell Mammy 'at's nice way treat sevumteem-cent turkle, a'n' she done slosh me ovuh my haid wif' a dish-towel. Go on keep you' sevumteem cents; I ain' got no turkle!"

Penrod sighed. "I only wanted to look at him, anyway, Herman. I couldn't get the seventeen cents. I tried but—I couldn't fix it."

"Well, Mammy done fix my turkle," the coloured boy said, withdrawing gloomily.

Penrod sighed again, closed the stable doors, and stood in the melancholy half-darkness of the carriage-house to ponder. Then a pleasant aroma came slenderly upon the air, warm and spicy, arousing some interest in the dejected boy; and he followed it to its source in the kitchen.

"G'wan away!" said Della. "Thim little cakes is f'r dinner, an' if yer pa eats 'em the way he use'ly does, th'r 'ain't more'n enough to go round."

"Oh, just one, Della!" Penrod pleaded. The little cakes were fat brown little cakes, not flat cookies. They were beautiful to look upon, exquisite to smell. "Can't I have just *one?*"

"If I give you wan, will you eat it an' g'wan away?"

"Honest!"

Della gave him one. "Well, keep yer word f'r wanst!" she said.

Penrod lifted the cake toward his mouth, and, as he did so, a yelp from Duke was heard outside the kitchen window, followed by the shrill triumphant cry of Ronald. Then, at this sound, reminder of the cause of all his woes, Penrod's hand, holding the cake, paused. A strange look came upon the face of Penrod.

"Well, if yer goin' to eat it, why don't you eat it an' g'wan away?" Della inquired.

"Guess I—I'll wait," Penrod muttered hastily, and, with the cake intact, walked quickly out of the kitchen and into the dining-room.

Here, engaged in a delicate semi-chemical operation, with the sideboard as laboratory, he remained not more than seven busy minutes, and when he issued forth the cake was still apparently intact; certainly he had not taken a bite of it. He went out into the yard and displayed himself before Ronald.

"Hey, Penrod!" cried the small visitor. "Watch me! I've learned how I can get Duke so mad with my little gun he almost bites himself!"

"I don't care anything about your ole gun," Penrod said languidly. "I got sumpthing better to think about."

"What you got?"

Penrod carelessly displayed the cake; in fact, his carelessness was incredible after the lessons Ronald had taught him. Penrod gazed absently skyward, opened his mouth, and, with thumb and forefinger, delicately lifted the cake toward the orifice.

Ronald's bright eyes emitted a purposeful gleam; he swooped like an arrow; his small hand shot out at Penrod's, and, in a flash, he had the cake and was away, his taunting cackle streaming behind him.

"I'll catch you this time!" Penrod shouted. "I been practising running, and I got you now. I'm goin' to take that cake away from you or break my neck!"

To settle this point and insure the latter alternative, Ronald, even in the act of ducking under Penrod's clumsily reaching arm, opened his mouth to its capacity, plunged the whole cake therein and with one great masticatory action attempted to swallow the thing in the forceful manner of an anaconda.

He did not succeed. Instead, he uttered a dreadful cry; his eyes protruded, and, after a period of terrible activity, he turned the squirt-gun straight into his mouth and there discharged it. This seeming but to increase his distress, he rushed, bellowing, to the hydrant and ardently applied his mouth thereto.

Showers of water sparkled up into the air, descending with rainbow effects lovely to the gaze of Penrod, and, in the midst of this aquatic display, Ronald contorted himself into grotesque shapes of protest, squealing like some wild thing of the woods.

Greater suffering finally convinced him that water was not the remedy for his ailment, and he tried great drafts of air taken between heroic gasps. Then, relieved no more by air than by water, he gesticulated insanely for a time and finally became coherent in one vociferous word.

"*Pop*-PUH!"

He ran to the house, and the kitchen door slammed behind him; but still from the interior could be heard his searching appeals to his parent. Penrod stood listening for a few moments, while a better and a nobler expression shed a radiance upon his simple features; it was the look that comes to one who, after great turbulence, finds peace in his own soul. Nevertheless, there slowly penetrated an apprehension that the Authorities might consider that he had gone too far, and he sought seclusion in the disused hayloft of the stable.

He returned to the house unostentatiously at dusk, softly ascending by the rear stairs to his own room. But his mother had heard him, and she came in. The faded light of a western window revealed a small, meek form, sitting with folded hands.

"Ma'am?" he said gently.

"What on earth did you do to Ronald?"

"Nothing."

"He says you poisoned him. He came in screaming, and he wanted us to send for the doctor, but his papa wouldn't. Then he insisted on being put to bed. What did you *do* to him?"

"*I* didn't do anything."

"Penrod!" She spoke warningly.

"No'm; I didn't. I had a cake and I just put a spoonful of red pepper and a little tabasco in the middle of it, and——"

"And you gave such a horrible thing as that to——"

"No'm. He came and grabbed it away from me, and ate it up before I could stop him!"

Mrs. Schofield shook her head sorrowfully. "We knew it must have been pepper," she said. "Penrod, I don't know what your father means to do to you."

However, just at this moment, Mr. Passloe and Mr. Schofield passed through the hall. "I was looking out of the window," Penrod and his mother heard Mr. Passloe say, "and I saw Ronald snatch it out of Penrod's hand. Served him right; he has a disgusting trick of snatching. And anyhow, we'll have one meal in peace; he won't be down to dinner."

"Is he still suffering a little?" Mr. Schofield asked, and

no one could have mistaken the hopefulness in his voice for anything else.

"Oh, I think he's convalescent."

There came a smothered laugh from each of these gentlemen; they seemed to be in the best of spirits, indeed. And then, as they were heard descending the stairs, Mrs. Schofield turned to Penrod with a last attempt to preserve her severity. "Penrod, you did a very dangerous thing to let poor little Ronald eat——"

"I *didn't* 'let' him."

"He's a very nice little boy," she said. "It was a shame!"

But a strange thing happened as she was speaking. Her words and her expression were at complete variance. The befogged Penrod saw this extraordinary contrast plainly, as she opened the door and the light from the hall fell upon her face. He perceived that she could not speak of poor little Ronald's sufferings without smiling.

CHAPTER LII

HERMAN MISSES A TREAT

THE next day at noon Penrod came home from church, accompanying his mother and sister, and walking sedately, pleased to be wearing an entirely new straw hat that was circled with a blue and white ribbon. Little Ronald sat between Mr. Passloe and Mr. Schofield upon the verandah and without apparent emotion watched the arrival of the small party from church; but after a moment he got up and quietly followed Penrod into the hall.

"Let me try on that new hat to see if it'd fit me?" he said, in a tone almost respectful. "Will you, Penrod?"

"No, I will not," Penrod returned promptly, and, as he put the new hat upon the hall table, he added with severity, "You let that hat alone!"

"Of course, if you say so," the little cousin said, curiously meek. "Penrod, what's it mean out on that ole horness-closet in the stable where it's painted up 'George B. Jash-ber' and all that stuff?"

"Never mind! You 'tend to your own affairs."

"All right," Ronald said thoughtfully. "I guess you got the paint for it from those cans in the woodshed, didn't you, Penrod?"

"You 'tend to your own affairs!"

"I will. Did you know I and Papa are goin' away on the railroad train right after lunch, Penrod? I guess maybe after I'm gone away you'll be sorry you played that trick on me and made me sick yesterday, won't you, Penrod? Maybe sumpthing'll happen that'll make you feel sorry about that." Then, as Penrod only stared at him, he turned toward the open front door, intending to rejoin his father and Mr. Schofield on the verandah; but paused. "Sump-thing *might* make you sorry, don't you think so, Cousin Penrod?"

He spoke so gently that Penrod almost felt a pang of re-morse; Ronald's meekness perplexed him, and so did the little boy's well-behaved silence at luncheon. Afterward, when a taxicab came to take the visitors away, Ronald could not be found immediately and failed to respond even when impatient calls for him resounded through the house; how-ever, he made his appearance rather suddenly, running from the back yard where he had gone, he said, "To say good-bye to Duke." Then, having expressed his farewells courte-ously to all the members of the Schofield family, he followed his father into the taxicab and drove away, with a final ges-ture that strikingly nullified the good impression he had just begun to make. Leaning from the open window of the taxicab, with his thumb to his nose and spread fingers wig-gling, he tauntingly and insultingly squealed "Yah! Yah! Yah!" over and over until the vehicle passed out of hearing.

Something triumphant in this departing cry brought misgiving to the heart of his boy cousin, and Penrod remembered little Ronald's interest in the new straw hat. The hat was not upon the hall table where it had been left, nor did a search of the house reveal its whereabouts; but Penrod had a fatal premonition when he discovered Duke in the back yard trying to remove a variegated coat of paint by rolling himself passionately in the grass. The new hat was in the woodshed, and only a glance at it was needed to show that the paint upon Duke had been little Ronald's mere afterthought. Penrod lifted the wreck upon the point of a stick, carried it round the house to the verandah where he found his father and mother, lodged a formal but indignant protest against the vandalism of the recent guest, and received some sympathy. Then he returned gloomily to the back yard, left the ruined hat in the woodshed, and went to seek Sam Williams.

Sam was not at home, and Penrod returned by way of the alley. Upon the doorstep of a humble cottage that faced the Schofields' stable Herman sat sleepily, his eyes half closed, enjoying the strong sunshine of the afternoon. "Hey, whi' boy," he said in a drowsy voice.

Penrod stopped for converse. "Where's Verman?"

"Verman way down in Tennasee. Mammy done tuck an' gone way down to Tennasee 'cause Gran'mammy up an' tuck sick, an' Mammy gone to take keer of her an' tucken Verman along wif her."

"When's he comin' back?"

"Come back soon as Gran'mammy git well. Whaτ you want o' Verman?"

"Well——" Penrod said, and paused to frown importantly. "I kind of wanted both of you, maybe. I was thinkin' about tellin' you about it last week; but I had a little cousin visitin' me that made a lot o' trouble around here and's goin' to grow up to be proba'ly the worst crook in the United States, I expeck. Anyhow, I guess there's mighty few crooks that could behave any worse than he did. It was sumpthing like that I was goin' to tell you and Verman about, Herman."

"Like what? Like you havin' a mean l'il whi' boy come to visit you?"

"No. I mean about crooks. You know what they are, don't you, Herman? I mean if we got after one, f'r instance——"

"Where any?" Herman inquired, but without much interest, for he continued to be drowsy. "Where any we go' to git after?"

Penrod scraped the dust with the side of his shoe. "Well, there wouldn't be any trouble about that if I made up my mind to tell you and Verman about it when Verman comes back. This is the way it is, you see, Herman, about shadowin' crooks: I got to decide first what gang o' crooks we better go after; then maybe sometime I'll let you and Verman and Sam Williams maybe get on their trail or sumpthing when I'm busy."

Herman appeared to be too languid to make any response; one of his eyes had closed entirely and the drowsy lid hung low upon the other. He muttered indistinguishably; but, after a time, roused himself enough to make an inquiry. "Whut 'at l'il whi' boy done do to you?"

Penrod gave an account of the spitefulness of the recent visitor's final exploit. "I bet you never had anybody visit you that was as mean as that little Ronald," he said in conclusion. "I bet you never had any little cousin that painted a brand new hat and your dog, and then went away makin' that sign at you and your whole family, the way he did!"

Herman roused himself a little more. " 'At ain' nuff'm. Pappy tuck an' stay all night one time where my Uncle Ben live'. When night come Pappy tuck his coat an' pants an' stuck 'em under his haid to sleep on 'cause his pants had fo'teen dolluhs in 'em. When he wake up nex' day he ain' got nuff'm under him but a bundle o' rags—coat an' pants an' fo'teen dolluhs done gone. 'Where my coat an' pants an' fo'teen dolluhs done gone?' he ast Uncle Ben. Uncle Ben say they done gone. 'I knows they gone,' Pappy say. 'Whut I wan' to know is where is they gone!' Uncle Ben say Oofus got 'em."

"Who?" Penrod asked, struck by this name. "Who was Oofus? Did he mean somebody named Rufus?"

"How I know?" Herman said. "All I know is Uncle Ben say Oofus done tuck an' come an' git 'em. He say Oofus done come an' tuck 'at coat an' pants an' fo'teen dolluhs while Pappy's sleepin', an' tuck an' gone outdoors an' buil' him a bonfire an' burn 'at coat an' pants an' fo'teen dolluhs all up. Pappy say, 'Where's 'em ashes? Where's 'em ashes?' Pappy say. Ef Oofus done tuck an' buil' him a bonfire an' burn my pants an' coat an' fo'teen dolluhs all up, where's 'em ashes?' Uncle Ben say Oofus done tuck an' scatter all 'em ashes. Uncle Ben say he len' Pappy pair of overalls to go home in. 'Tain' his fault, Uncle Ben say, 'cause he cain' he'p whut Oofus do."

Penrod felt that little Ronald's vandalism was out-matched by the misbehaviour of Oofus; Herman seemed to have scored a point of superiority in possessing a relative more damaging than young Master Passloe. However, the point was not entirely settled in Herman's favour. "Listen, Herman, was Oofus your Uncle Ben's little boy?"

"How I know? Uncle Ben ain' say who Oofus is. All he say, 'Oofus done tuck an' buil' him a bonfire an' burn' 'em all up'."

"Well, then," Penrod returned, "he proba'ly wasn't your father's little cousin or else your Uncle Ben would of told him he was, so I guess that proves it, Herman."

"Prove whut?" Herman inquired sleepily, and now both his eyelids were closed. "Who prove whut?" he murmured.

"Your Uncle Ben would of told your father that Oofus was his little boy if he had been, wouldn't he? So that proves you haven't got any little cousin as bad as the one that's just been visitin' at our house. Oofus must of been a pretty mean person but he wasn't any relation to your father, or to you either, Herman." Penrod undoubtedly found a little solace in this thought; his voice took on the tone of one who triumphs in an argument. "It doesn't matter how bad this Oofus was, Herman. I got the worst little cousin in the

world, and I bet I can prove it, because Oofus wasn't your
father's cousin, and anyhow proba'ly your father's clothes
were kind of old. Oofus didn't ruin anything that was brand
new, the way Ronald ruined my hat, and Oofus didn't cover
a poor ole dog that couldn't help himself with a lot of sticky
paint and all different colours and everything. Besides, Oofus
didn't make any sign at your father with his thumb on his
nose, and ride away in a taxicab yelling 'Yah! Yah! Yah!'
at him and all his family, the way my little cousin Ronald
did. Oofus might of been a crook maybe, Herman; but I
bet he wouldn't of been very hard to manage if your father
had known how. That's what you haf to know about man-
agin' crooks, Herman; you haf to know how to do it." Here
Penrod became mysterious; he glanced up and down the
alley, frowned and passed his right hand over the left part
of his chest under his jacket. "Herman," he said confidentially, in a low voice, "I got a notion to show you sumpthing, if you'll never tell. It's a secret; but it's got sumpthing to do with what I was tellin' you about a while ago.
It's got sumpthing to do with what I said maybe I'd tell you
and Verman and Sam Williams some day, if I decide to. I
guess you'll be surprised, Herman; but I'll show it to you."

Again he glanced under a frowning brow to right and
left, up and down the alley; then dramatically tossed back
the left side of his jacket, exposing, for one moment only,
the shield upon his breast, "Look, Herman!"

The effect was disappointing; Herman was not surprised,
nor impressed, nor moved in any manner whatever. He was
now sound asleep, a fact that slowly and somewhat chillingly
became apparent. Penrod was disconcerted; the feeling he
experienced was not wholly unlike that of an actor who
finds himself minus an audience at a moment of crisis. He
buttoned his jacket, scuffed dust again with the side of his
shoe, and, oddly embarrassed, seemed to need to do or say
something that would reduce a mortifying effect of anticlimax. He looked down darkly upon the unconscious figure
on the doorstep.

"Huh!" he said grimly. "I guess it's a good thing for you I didn't let you see this badge, you old Herman you!"

Then, not quite sure what he meant by that threatening exit-speech, but nevertheless restored by it to a Jashberish frame of mind, he strode away, to fill in an hour of this long Sunday afternoon with a bath for Duke. "I guess you better not try to go to sleep while I'm talkin' to you," he said fiercely to the gayly coloured little dog, as he drew him toward the necessary bucket of soapy water. "You hold still, you ole crook you!"

CHAPTER LIII

WAYS OF KNOWING THINGS

THE June-time moon hung over the town, and, in a wicker chair upon the ample front verandah of Mr. Schofield's house, a young man sat and sometimes struck little harmonies and chimes from the strings of a light guitar; sometimes, too, he sang to this accompaniment in an unobtrusive tenor voice, and at other times—and oftener—made as much love as she would permit to Mr. Schofield's pretty daughter. But in this he encountered difficulties that presently became part of a crisis.

"I can't and I won't," she said, after listening patiently to an appeal that would easily have reached those heights defined as "impassioned oratory", if it had not been delivered in a whisper. "It's just ridiculous, Robert. You've only had your Bachelor's degree three or four days, and next fall you've got to begin law school for three years, and after that you've got to go into somebody's office and wait to get a practice. I won't hear of such nonsense—not now."

"But why not?" Mr. Robert Williams urged huskily.

"Good gracious!" Margaret cried. "Haven't I just told you? It would be *absurd* for us to consider ourselves absolutely engaged. You ought to have your utter freedom."

"*I?*" he said, astonished. "*I* ought to? But I don't want to have my utter freedom!"

"Yes; you might," she returned gently. "You might see somebody else you wanted to marry, and you ought to be entirely free of all entanglements until you're established as a lawyer."

"But if I *should* see somebody else and wanted to marry her——"

"You see!" Margaret cried triumphantly. "You admit right away that you might!"

"I don't anything of the kind; I was just arguing. I was pointing out that if I got engaged to somebody else, as you say I ought to have the right to, I wouldn't be 'free' from entanglements, as you say I should be, until I'm an established lawyer."

"I never heard anything so mixed up," she declared.

"Neither did I," Robert returned, with some bitterness. "That's just what I'm trying to make clear. You say I ought to be free——"

"Of course you ought! At your age, a man just starting in the world, and with his way to make, ought not to have the burden of any obliga——"

"Well, what would I be asking you for, if it were a burden?"

"It's no use, Robert," she said firmly. "If I let you hamper yourself with this engagement now, I couldn't look your mother and father in the face, and I nearly always see both of them three or four times a day. I couldn't face them, knowing that I had allowed their only son——"

"Margaret!" he protested. "What *is* the matter with you? When I was home at Christmas you didn't talk through your hat like this."

"Well, perhaps not an only son," she admitted placidly. "I just said that, and, besides, Sam's so much younger he doesn't count. Anyhow, it can't affect the truth of what I was saying. I simply couldn't look your mother and father in the face if I let you saddle yourself with——"

"Margaret!" he interrupted, in a voice of such feeling that she paused to listen. "Margaret, you're only making excuses for something you don't want to confess—something in your own soul."

Margaret sat up straight in her chair. "I think," she said, with sudden frigidity, "I think when you bring such charges against me, you had better explain what you mean."

"Why, I wasn't bringing any charges," Robert protested unhappily. "I only meant that last summer I thought you were pretty fond of me, and when I came home for the holidays, you were so—so——"

"So what?" she inquired sharply. "What was I?"

"So—so friendly—that I thought we'd pretty well settled things. And your letters, up to three weeks ago, were—were the same way. Then you didn't write any more——"

"I knew your time was occupied with Commencement."

"It wasn't," said Robert. "Not for three whole weeks. Didn't I write to you—seven or eight *long* letters?"

"You should have been working on your thesis or something," she returned primly. "You shouldn't have been hampered——"

This word at such a juncture was too much for Robert. "Hampered!" he cried indignantly. "Margaret, how can you sit there and go on with such barefaced hypocrisy?"

"What!" she said. " 'Hypocrisy'? Is that what you're charging me with?"

"You know it! You've changed toward me—that's the truth of it—and you're ashamed to admit it. You don't want to be engaged to me, and you put it on the score of *my* future, so you can take a high, altruistic ground, instead of confessing that there's somebody *else!*"

"What!"

"It's true! It's *you* who want to be free, for your own sake, not mine. I feared it; but I wouldn't believe it, not even when I was told so!"

" 'Told so'!" she echoed sharply. "Who told you?"

"I decline to state. But it's true. I was told yesterday that you'd gone everywhere for the last four or five weeks with a new man that's come here to live, named Dade."

"Mr. Dade!" Margaret cried angrily. "He has nothing whatever to do with it, and I wish you'd please leave Mr. Herbert Hamilton Dade out of this conversation. Besides that, I wish you would kindly use a little self-control— unless you *want* father and mother to overhear you inside the house. With all this fuss and excitement you're making, I should think you'd prefer that they didn't."

Robert dropped the guitar unheeded to the floor of the verandah as he rose in agitation. "It's true! I see it must be the truth!" he said; and he paced up and down, running his hands through his hair. "You never spoke in that tone to me before in your whole life! It *is* this Dade! And you sat there pretending you were thinking of *my* future, and that I oughtn't to be 'hampered'—oh, Margaret, I should think you'd be ashamed!"

"You—you are so unjust. I couldn't have believed—I couldn't—I——"

Robert, in his pacing, had reached the other end of the verandah; but, at this faltering in her voice, he turned, came rapidly back to her, and saw that her form was bowed to the arms of her chair and that her handkerchief was pressed upon her eyes by both trembling hands. She was weeping—weeping almost vehemently.

Stricken, the miserable young man threw himself upon his knees beside her, imploring. "*Margaret!* For God's sake, don't cry! I take it back! I didn't mean it! Don't! Don't! Oh, dearest, dearest, *please* don't!"

"You're so—so cruel!" she sobbed. "You—you have no right—it's not so. You mustn't call me 'dearest'—you said such awful things! There are times in every girl's life when she doesn't understand herself; but—but Mr. Dade hasn't been here since early in the week—he *was* here one evening— I admit it——"

Robert sprang to his feet. "You do!" he said harshly. "I thought so!" And he broke into bitter laughter. "Fool that I was!" he cried. "Yes; a fool in a fool's paradise, there at college—believing you *loved* me——"

"I never told you so," she protested. "You have no right to charge me with that, Robert!"

"No; you never told me in so many words. It was only the flirt's way to let a poor fool guess it for himself, while she never signs a document." And he struck the palm of his left hand a passionate blow with his clenched right fist. "Yes; it's only the old story of the flirt and one of her fools, one of her *playthings!*"

Moaning, Margaret lifted imploring hands, caught his arm and clung to it. "You *mustn't*, Robert!" she besought him, in a choked voice. "I can't bear it! You mustn't charge me with making playthings of men—you can't dream how miserable I am!" And the moonlight glinted on tears upon the anguished face she lifted to him. "I've told you"—she choked—"I've told you, Robert, that Mr. Dade *was* here Tuesday——"

At this moment there came an interruption that produced in both of these young people a condition of shock. A human voice spoke from just on the other side of a large Bath chair that stood against the verandah railing, about four feet away. "It wasn't either Tuesday," this voice said, in tones of warmest interest. "It was Wednesday he was here."

Margaret leaped to her feet. "Penrod!" she shrieked.

"What you want?" Penrod inquired, coming out from the shadow of the Bath chair.

"*How long have you been there?*"

"Well, just while you and Bob been talkin'," he replied

casually, and continued, "I remember well as anything it was Wednesday and not Tuesday he was here, because Tuesday I and Papa went to the movies and——"

But Margaret remained for no further introduction of corroborative evidence. "*Oh!*" she cried. With a tumultuous rush, she disappeared into the open front door.

"I guess she feels mad," Penrod said placidly, turning to Mr. Williams. "Well, anyway, I know I'm right," he continued, dropping comfortably into Margaret's chair. "I know I am, because I and Papa——"

He paused as Mr. Williams, gathering up his guitar and a straw hat, seemed to be hardly more in a mood for conversation than Margaret had been.

"Well, you goin' home?" Penrod inquired, mildly surprised.

But the visitor only muttered something incoherent and descended the steps of the verandah.

Penrod hopped up and, quite unsolicited, accompanied him to the gate. "I know I'm right," he said, "because, after the movies, I and Papa went to bring Mamma from prayer-meeting Wednesday night, and, when we got back, that Dade was here, and Papa heard him call her a Princess or sumpthing and told her so at breakfast next morning until she got up and left the table. Well, after that—well, good-night."

Penrod added this farewell a little breathlessly, owing to the abruptness with which Robert swung out of the gate and closed it after him. Then the little brother watched the tall figure growing quickly dimmer under the shadow of the maple trees that lined the sidewalk; but, moved by a charitable impulse before it passed out of hearing, he leaned over the gate and called loudly, "He's around here all the time, anyway!"

After that, Penrod waited in silence, expecting the courtesy of a comment, or, at least, a brief expression of gratitude for his information—but nothing came.

CHAPTER LIV

THE SCONDREL'S DEN

THIS lack of responsiveness on the part of one whom he felt to be fully his equal caused him some surprise, especially as complete cordiality had always existed between them; but, upon reflection, he decided that Margaret's conduct was responsible. Of course, Bob Williams's feelings were hurt by the way she switched into the house without saying good-night or anything.

Penrod had liked and admired Bob Williams faithfully, above all other suitors, for more than a year—in fact, ever since the preceding summer when Mr. Williams had given him a dollar, and the seeming curtness of this present departure caused no abatement in the liking and admiration. Besides, in the matter of Margaret, Penrod was firmly on

Robert's side and even more firmly not on Mr. Dade's side. How a girl "with any sense" could hesitate between these two was a question he answered with too brotherly promptness—"Hasn't got a grain!" being his permanent decision.

However, she had influence inside the house, and he delayed before entering it, because he gloomily supposed she would be stirring up the authorities there against him, as she usually did when he happened to interrupt one of her conversations with a caller; and her manner had led him to conclude that she was more than ordinarily upset this time.

He was cheerfully surprised, therefore, upon repairing to the library, where his mother and father were engaged at cribbage, to be greeted casually, no reference whatever to Margaret being made. She had gone directly to her own room, and, as Penrod, in the character of George B. Jashber, presently discovered, she had locked her door and preserved a complete silence on the other side of it. Moreover, there gradually came to the great detective a sense of reassurance. He began vaguely to perceive that Margaret had no desire to make the episode of the evening known to her parents, and he was amply content with the mere fact of this reticence, which he did not feel it necessary to comprehend.

George B. Jashber was emphatically present at the Schofield family dinner-table the following evening, though the family and Mr. Herbert Hamilton Dade, a guest upon this occasion, were unconscious of the honour. Mrs. Schofield did indeed notice a peculiarity in her son's manner; but she misinterpreted it.

"Do your eyes hurt you, Penrod?" she whispered to him.

"No," he said. "Why?"

"You keep making that pucker in your forehead, I've noticed lately; and you keep looking out of your eyes sideways, as though it hurt you to look at anything straight in front of you. Does it?"

"No, it don't."

"Then don't do it, Penrod. You *will* injure your eyes, doing it so much."

"I won't either, Mamma."

"I don't know, but I think it might; I'm going to ask the doctor. What makes you do it, if they don't pain you?"

Penrod was annoyed. "Nothin'," he muttered.

After dinner, he disappeared (as was his summer privilege) until nine o'clock, his bedtime, and presently he was moving slowly on all fours along the latticework below the front verandah. Unfortunately for his mystic purposes, Margaret glanced down over the railing in the course of a little tour she appeared to be making to points of interest about the verandah.

"Don't play around here, Penrod," she said, and there was a businesslike tone in her voice. "You'll catch cold from the dew on the grass, and if you don't find something healthier to do, I'll have to call Mother."

Penrod made no audible reply, but rose and sauntered away. However, she seated herself on the railing, and glanced frequently over her shoulder, chatting gaily with Mr. Dade all the while, and George B. Jashber, after watching for some time this exhibition of a vigilance equal to his own, extricated himself noiselessly from a clump of lilac, entered the house by way of the kitchen, went up the back stairs, came down the front stairs, then, after a moment's debate, tiptoed through the hall and seated himself quietly upon the floor just outside the open door of the library. He had caught words from the two cribbage players that acutely interested him.

"Well, I'd just like to know who he *is*," Mr. Schofield was saying. "I don't like to have every Tom, Dick and Harry to dinner without knowing anything at all about them."

"But Mr. Dade seems to be a very pleasant young man," Mrs. Schofield said mildly. "He has nice manners——"

" 'Manners'!" Mr. Schofield interrupted. "Anybody can

have good manners. Why, I knew a horse-thief once that had beautiful manners."

A low vocal flutter, soprano, betokened Mrs. Schofield's amusement. "Mr. Dade isn't a horse-thief, I fancy," she murmured.

"There's something a little slick about him," her husband grumbled. "I'd like to know more about him if he's going on coming to the house this much."

"Why, Margaret met him at the church fair last month," Mrs. Schofield explained.

"Anybody can go to a church fair; that's what they're for."

"But he knows *all* the girls of Margaret's set."

"Met 'em all at the church fair?"

Mrs. Schofield laughed again. "They're all excited about him, because he's so good-looking and different. You're worse than Penrod. As soon as a young man shows the slightest interest in Margaret, you decide there's something queer about him. Mr. Dade has good manners; he dresses well; he's very good-looking—in fact, he's handsome—and he's travelled, because he speaks familiarly of every city in the country; but——"

"But we don't know," he took her up emphatically, "what business he's in, where he comes from, or even where he stays in this town. He hasn't mentioned——"

"But he did! The last time he was here, he told me he came from Gosport, Illinois."

"Well, where does he live here in town?"

"I don't know."

"No," Mr. Schofield said grimly. "And what business is he in?"

Mrs. Schofield, a little piqued, replied, with satire: "He didn't happen to mention that either, so I suppose that leaves us no option. Probably you're right; he must be a professional horse-thief."

Naturally, she had little expectation that this remark would be accepted at its face value; but it was not the habit of George B. Jashber to take sarcasm into account, except when uttered in either a savage or a mocking tone of voice; and he forthwith came to the simple conclusion that both his parents suspected Mr. Herbert Hamilton Dade's business, or profession, to be that of stealing horses. This conclusion, coinciding with the trend of his own impressions, gave him a great moment. He rose in silence; his fingers stole to his jacket pocket and took therefrom a well-whittled object of wood—the sketchy likeness of an ottomatick. He returned it to his pocket, and, after the proper heave of his shoulders, moved silently toward the open front door.

He halted, hearing his name spoken from the verandah.

"You mean Penrod?" Margaret said.

"If that's what you call your little brother—yes."

"Why, no; I don't think he goes downtown often. I think he plays around the neighbourhood here, most of the time. Why?"

"I didn't know," Mr. Dade replied carelessly. "It just struck me that I've run across him downtown almost every time I go out lately. I wondered if your mother knew about it; that's all. I thought possibly she wouldn't want him to be——"

"She wouldn't," Margaret agreed decidedly. "I'll tell her about it. Of course, a child of his age shouldn't be wandering around down there among street-urchins and newsboys."

At this, Penrod's expression became so scornful, and continued in that contortion so long, that he was forced to relax it because his nose hurt him. Meantime, after a silence and some murmured words, the verandah was the scene of a departure.

Margaret spoke regretfully. "It's awfully mean of you to go so soon!"

And Mr. Dade replied airily from the foot of the steps: "Too bad! But I've got to be on long-distance at eight-thirty sharp, Princess."

"Telephoning to—to someone in another town?"

Mr. Dade had a rich voice and a rich laugh, musically barytone and perhaps a shade conscious; he protracted his laugh now, as if he heard it with some pleasure, himself. "It's only business—but important in spite of that, Princess."

She made a small exclamation, half smothered but impatient; he laughed again, and then his voice came from near the gate. "Good-night! Good-night, Princess!"

Margaret came in, looking pink and perplexed and cross; but Penrod did not see her—nor did she see Penrod. He had slipped into an unlit room adjacent to the hall, had slid down from a window and was now crossing the front lawn, hot on the trail. Mr. Herbert Hamilton Dade had indeed become the bandit selected by George B. Jashber for a ruthless running to earth; but this was the first opportunity Penrod had found to shadow him except in the daytime, and daytime shadowing had so far failed to reveal (on account of Penrod's various engagements to lunch and dine at home) the whereabouts and nature of Mr. Dade's dwelling-place. George B. meant to discover the secret lodging of the scondrel this very night; and, not only that, but where he kept his stolen horses.

Mr. Herbert Hamilton Dade walked down the street, humming thoughtfully to himself and lightly swinging from a hand gloved in chamois a polished yellow cane that flashed streaks of high light as he passed the street-lamps. Surely no detective could have wished for a more easily shadowed scondrel, and, since Mr. Dade not once glanced over his shoulder to ascertain if he were followed, many of George B. Jashber's precautions to avoid being seen might have struck an observer as unnecessary.

George B. took advantage, so to speak, of every bit of cover; he flitted from the trunk of one shade-tree to the next; anon, stooping low, he darted into the mouths of alleys and out again; several times he threw himself full-length upon the grass-plots beside the pavement and crawled a few feet before rising; and in these various alarums and excursions he covered almost as much ground as if he had been an inquisitive poodle out walking with his master.

Not less ingenious was he when the marts of the town were reached. In this illuminated region he sheltered himself among groups of citizens, or walked behind strolling couples, or flattened himself in entryways, not forgetting to put frequently into practise that detectivest of street devices, the affectation of interest in a shop window; but never letting his eye wander, for more than three or four seconds at a time, from the flashing yellow walking-stick and the yellow chamois glove that held it.

Proceeding in this manner, he traced the sinister peregrinations of Herbert Hamilton Dade for more than an hour. Mr. Dade went into a hotel lobby, purchased a package of cigarettes at the news-stand (as Penrod was able to observe from the entrance to the lobby) and then spoke to the telephone operator. After this, he took a seat near by, and lit a cigarette and smoked it. Presently, the telephone operator spoke to him in a low voice, and Mr. Dade went into one of the booths. He remained therein for almost a quarter of an hour and came out looking annoyed and perspiring suspiciously. He gave the telephone operator a sum of money, left the hotel and crossed the street to a drug store, where he purchased a glass (with spoon) of soda-water, ice-cream and a flavouring sirup not to be identified from outside the show-window. Then he left the drug store, walked to the next corner and stood there for several minutes, apparently thinking. Suddenly, he decided to go on again, and walked twice round the block with no object discernible to Penrod, whose feet were beginning to be painful. Yet he would not give up. He was determined to see this thing through to the end.

At last, he uttered a low exclamation—that is to say, he uttered a moral exclamation in a low voice—and quickened his pace; for Mr. Dade, having yawned audibly, had quickened his own pace and had turned into a dark and silent side street that led away from the main thoroughfare of the town. Before he had gone a dozen paces in this direction, he encountered a man whose lower features were wholly curtained behind a black beard, as easily supposed false as real, and both Mr. Dade and this bearded man came to a halt. Every word of their conversation was audible to George B. Jashber, who was sitting below the level of the pavement upon some steps leading down to a basement barber-shop.

"Well, good-evening," said the bearded man.

"Hello!" Mr. Dade returned.

"Any news?"

"Nothing in particular."

"Well, it's warm weather."

"Yes, it is," said Mr. Dade. "I'm going home to bed. Good-night."

And the other, passing onward, called back, in a voice not perceptibly muffled by his whiskers, "Well, good-night."

Breathlessly, Penrod waited until the black-bearded man was safely beyond the entrance to the barber's stairway; then he crept forth upon the pavement and once more took up the trail. Dade had distinctly said, "I'm going home to bed." Very well! George B. Jashber might have to defer to another occasion the discovery of where the stolen horses were kept; but at least he was certain of one thing: a short time—perhaps only a few minutes—would reveal the location of the scondrel's den. He was going there now!

Mr. Dade proceeded as far as the middle of the block; then he crossed the street and halted before a broad, arched doorway, rather dimly revealed by a faintly luminous globe above the arch. Then he opened the door, passed noiselessly into an entryway, and the door closed behind him.

Penrod darted across the street and marked the place well, the shape of the doorway and its distance from each corner. He was certain that he could easily find it again, either by night or in the daytime, as need might arise. George B. Jashber uttered sounds of satisfaction and quiet triumph; then, stepping backward into the street and lifting his eyes as he did so, became aware of a wooden sign above the globe. Here was a means of identification indeed! Four large letters were painted upon this sign, and, though the light was dim, the tired detective was able to discern them and to comprehend their meaning with absolute certainty. They were:

Y. M. C. A.

Unerringly, George B. had tracked Mr. Dade to his lair in the Young Men's Christian Association building.

CHAPTER LV

HERMAN AND VERMAN ARE ALLOWED TO JOIN

WHEN Penrod got home that evening, Mrs. Schofield was standing at the front gate, looking up and down the street in the darkness. For this reason, Penrod, having seen her before she saw him, quietly entered the yard by climbing over the side fence. Then he sauntered out of obscurity into the faint oblong of light that issued from the open door, thinly illumining his mother's anxious back as she leaned over the gate. He yawned casually, inquiring, "Whatch' doin' out here, Mamma?"

"Penrod!" She jumped, turning upon him sharply. "Where on earth have you been till this time of night?"

"What, Mamma?"

"Where have you been? Do you know it's after ten o'clock?"

"No'm," he said meekly. "I didn't think it was late."

"It's disgraceful, and your father's very angry. Where have you been?"

"Why, I haven't been anywhere, Mamma," he protested plaintively. "I—I haven't lifted my little finger, but you ack like I been doin' sumpthing wrong, and I haven't been doin' anything at all."

"*Where* were you?"

"Just playin'."

"With *whom* were you playing?"

"Why, just around," he responded, his tone aggrieved but reasonable.

"You weren't over at Sam Williams's," said Mrs. Schofield. "We telephoned, and Sam said he hadn't seen you at all."

"Mamma, I didn't say I was at Sam's, did I?" he protested. "I don't see why you got to go and claim, all of a sudden, when I never said I was anywhere *near* Sam's, and go and say I'm telling a l——"

"Penrod, be quiet! I didn't say you were telling an untruth. I only said——"

"Well, it *looked* like it," he insisted accusingly. "I guess I can't lift my little finger around here but I got to go and get accused of sumpthing I never did except just lift my little finger. I expeck there's hardly any other boys around here their mother wouldn't let 'em lift their little finger without scolding 'em just because I lifted my little f——"

"Oh, stop talking about your little finger!" Mrs. Schofield cried, losing patience and conscious of a vague bafflement. "You march into the house and go straight up to bed. I don't know what your father's going to do to you. He's as upset as he can possibly be."

Upon this, Penrod entered the house with some natural hesitation, but was relieved to hear the sound of a shoe dropping upon the floor of his father's bedroom, Mr. Schofield being thus revealed as in process of disrobing for the night, and evidently not so wholly succumbed to agitation as his wife had indicated to their son. In fact, all that Penrod heard from him was a murmured question, a little later, and this came through an open transom over the closed door.

"Where'd he say he'd been?"

"Just playing in the neighbourhood," Mrs. Schofield replied. "But it's dreadful, his staying out till after ten. It's no way for children to be brought up, and you *must* do something. I don't see how you can lie there and go to sleep so calmly when you know how worried I was over it."

Silence was the answer, though probably not intended as one, and, since nothing more was to be gained in that quarter, George B. Jashber, barefooted and in his nightgown, presently stole back to his own room and slid into bed.

In spite of some physical weariness, he did not at once fall asleep, but lay open-eyed, thinking exultantly. Probably a genuine, adult, official plain-clothes man, or detective, tracking a suspected person to residence in a Young Men's Christian Association might have felt rather discouraged, might have abandoned the trail altogether. Not so with the open mind of a boy. For Penrod, it was absolutely as easy to imagine a horse-thief having his lair in the Y. M. C. A. as anywhere else in the world. Why not? And George B. would be hot upon the trail again to-morrow!

The difference between a man's way of thought, in such matters, and a boy's was exemplified at the lunch-table several days later, when Mr. Schofield once more dwelt grumpily upon the subject of Mr. Dade.

"Papa, you're just unreasonable!" Margaret protested, after a discussion that had brought evidence of some emotion into her voice and expression. "*Why* can't I go walking with him?"

"Because we don't know who he is."

"But he goes to everybody's house, and everyone likes him," Margaret said. "Why, he's been here to dinner in your own house, Papa!"

"Well, I didn't ask him," her father retorted.

"Papa, what's the matter with you? Why don't you like him?"

"I've told you."

"Well, what do you *want* to know about him?"

"I'd like to know one thing that I should think even you might consider *fairly* important," Mr. Schofield returned, with satire. "I'd like to know where he lives."

Margaret's eyes glowed sudden triumph. "He lives at the Y. M. C. A."

"What?"

"He lives at the Young Men's Christian Association," she said, laughing lightly.

"How do you know?"

"He told me the other evening that he'd taken rooms there, and he telephoned me from there this morning. I met him at the church bazaar, and he lives at the Young Men's Christian Association, Papa."

Mr. Schofield's expression, after a moment of incredulity, had become one of simple and unmanly disappointment. Margaret's, following an opposite course, now offered a charming contrast of liveliness.

"Is there anything more you want me to find out about him, Papa?"

The defeated man made no reply other than to eat morosely; whereupon his wife laughed aloud. "You can go for that walk, dear," she said to Margaret. "Papa's a funny man when he decides to take prejudices; but it looks as though he'd have to give this one up."

Mr. Schofield said nothing for a time; then he set his napkin beside his plate, rose, and, not looking at his wife or daughter, uttered the reluctant words: "Well, you may be right—for once."

Instantly they broke into peals of laughter, and then, as he left the room, the happy and suffused Margaret pointed across the table at her brother, and shouted: "Look at Penrod!"

Penrod was worth looking at, though he was doing nothing except with his countenance. However, Mrs. Schofield found his action more disquieting than amusing.

"Stop doing that with your face, Penrod!" she exclaimed. "You'll ruin your eyes, and you'll be all wrinkled before you're twenty years old. You *must* get out of that habit; it's awful!"

Penrod, slightly discomfited, relaxed, and, breathing heavily, left the table, followed by continued admonitions from his mother and absurd manifestations of pleasure on the part of Margaret. Disposing of these insulting sounds by closing a door upon them, he went out to the office of George B. Jashber's private detective agency in the carriage-house of the stable, and presently, seated in the wheelbarrow, held an important conversation with an imaginary client. He spoke in a low voice, yet audibly.

"All right, missuz; you say your ole horse got stolen? All right, missuz; I bet I get him back for you in *no* time! Answer one question, please: Who was it stole him? I bet it was ole Dade, wasn't it? I thought so; I thought so! Pray take a seat, missuz. I got to get some o' my men up here." (Penrod used an imaginary telephone.) "Hello! Gimme number Two hundred and eighty-nine. Hello! Is that you, Bill? Bill, send Jim up to my office; I want him. We got a big case goin' on up here now, Bill." (He hung up the receiver, placed the stub of a lead-pencil in the corner of his mouth to serve as a cigar; then, rising, he rapped upon the wall of the harness-closet, listened attentively, rapped again, and returned to the wheelbarrow.) "That's Jim. He's one o' my best men. Come in, Jim. Jim, this lady here's mad at the Dade gang because they stole her horse and everything. We got to help her, Jim. You got your ottomatick with you, Jim? All right. Now, missuz, you go on downtown with Jim to where it says Y. M. C. A. over the door, and you go on around in the alley that's behind there, and keep lookin' and lookin', and when your ole horse comes along, you tell Jim which one it is, and Jim'll grab him and make them give him up. Fifteen dollars, please. Good-day, missuz. Jim, come back here soon's you get the ole horse for her, because we got some more cases about the Dade gang, and I got to——"

Penrod paused abruptly; he started and rose to his feet, staring widely at the thin partition-wall of the harness-closet, while several small but lively chills twittered down his spine. From the invisible emptiness beyond that partition there had come sounds impossible for rats, cats or dogs to make. Unmistakably, these sounds were of human construction; they consisted of muffled gaspings and of profound, irrepressible chokings—and they continued, becoming louder. Penrod stood it for perhaps eight seconds; then he nervously threw an old rake-handle at the wall of the harness-closet, and, uttering one loud cry of alarm, ran out into the yard.

Immediately arming himself with a clothes-prop, he returned as far as the open double doors of the carriage-house. "Hey, you!" he shouted, in a trembling voice. "You get out of our harness-closet, you ole tramp, you! You *better* get out o' there—my father's a policeman!"

The gasping and choking forthwith became a penetrating, silvery African giggle interrupted by sputterings and guffaws; whereupon Penrod, immensely reassured but enraged, entered the carriage-house and poked his clothes-prop savagely into the darkness of the harness-closet.

"You get out o' there, you ole niggers you!" he stormed. "I'll show you who you're laughin' at in there!"

Hysteric calls for mercy preceded the issuing-forth into the light of Herman and Verman. They were weak with laughter and in no condition to resist the clothes-prop.

"Lemme 'lone!" Herman begged, feebly defending himself. "Don' hit me no mo'—*please* don'! We 'uzn't doin' nothin' to you, Penrod. We 'uz dess liss'nun'!"

"Listenin' to what?" Penrod shouted fiercely.

"Liss'nun' to you," said Herman. "Me and Verman, we all time out in our alley hyuh you talk so much to youse'f ev'y time you come out in stable, we say, 'Whut 'at ole boy all time talkin' to hisse'f?' So whiles you in house eatin', we git in closet, an' when you c'mence talkin' so big wif 'iss here missuz an' Bill an' all 'at Dade talk, Verman went an' begin to laugh an' cut up. Couldn' he'p it, 'cause you playin' so funny!"

"Playin'!" Penrod echoed scornfully. "I guess I'll show you that wasn't playin'! I guess if I told you once what it was about, *your* ole eyes wouldn't stick out! *Oh,* no!"

He frowned bitterly as he spoke; but Verman so far lacked in impressionableness as to burst anew into shrill laughter.

"Hay!" he shouted. "Hay hake a heek, mihhuh!"

Penrod correctly interpreted this as "Pray take a seat, missuz", and the mockery was the more unbearable because Verman thought fit to illustrate it by projecting his plaintively insignificant abdomen and patting it pompously.

"Hay hake a heek, mihhuh!" he gurgled, and strutted grotesquely; but his burlesquing ended in a shriek, as the outraged Penrod, unable to bear further insult in patience, swung the clothes-prop in an extensive semicircle that culminated at a point identical with a patch upon Verman's thin trousers.

"Oo hop ak!" Verman remonstrated.

"All right then," said Penrod. "You stop bein' so smart about sumpthing you don't know what it's about, then. I tell you, this is sumpthing perty danger's, and I guess you'd like to have a chance to get sumpthing to do with it if I was to let you, only I wouldn't."

"Whut 'at?" Herman asked. "Whut all 'iss here talk you makin'?"

"You see that?" Penrod demanded, pointing to the sign painted upon the harness-closet; and Herman and Verman examined with some interest the symbols of George B. Jashber's profession and location.

"Who is all 'iss here Jaspuh?" Herman inquired. "Whut all 'iss deteckatuff writin' mean? Whaibouts any Mist' Jawge B. Jaspuh?"

"It's me," said Penrod simply.

"Who?"

"Me."

"Whut you talkin' about, whi' boy? *You* ain't no Mist' Jaspuh. You Penrod."

"I'll show you who I am!" Penrod retorted hotly. "You just looky here once, and I guess you'll see." And throwing back the breast of his jacket, he displayed, pinned near his left armpit, the little metal shield he had bought from Della's Jarge.

This time it was a triumph without any anticlimax whatever; the effect upon Herman and Verman was definite and complete in every way. In their altered attitudes, in their silence, in their almost protuberant eyes, they showed it. To them, such a badge was official; there was no denying such a thing. The contrast between the visible person of Penrod Schofield and their preconceived notions of a detective mattered nothing. This white boy, always a little mysterious, was unquestionably, unsuspectably Number One Hundred and Three. The glittering shield said so. Herman and Verman were overwhelmed.

"I guess you got gumption enough to know who I am now!" said the insufferable Penrod.

"Huccome—huccome all 'iss here?" Herman faltered. "Huccome it?"

"Hi!" Verman murmured faintly.

Penrod's expression at this moment was so profound that his mother could barely have borne it. "Looky here," he said slowly, "I'm shadowin' the Dade gang——"

"Whut 'at shad?" Herman asked.

"Shadowin'," Penrod explained impatiently. "It means followin' 'em around wherever they go, and—my goodness, haven't you ever been to a movie show, Herman?"

"Plenty!"

"Well, the Dade gang are the worst crooks there is, and I'm after 'em. You be Bill, Herman; and Verman, you can be Jim. I'll let you work for me, and I'll tell you all what to do, because you'll be my men. You must always call me 'George', or else 'Number Hunderd and Three'. Well, come ahead, Bill and Jim; we better start downtown, because we——"

" 'Downtown'?" Herman echoed vaguely. "Whu' fo' we got to go on downtown?"

"My goodness! We can't sit around here all day and shadow anybody, can we? I'll tell you what to do while we're walkin', won't I? We'll keep in the alleys all the way down, because we don't want anybody to know who my men are or about me bein' Number Hunderd and Three. Come on, Bill; come on, Jim! I guess we got a perty danger's job on our hands this time, men!"

Herman and Verman had joined, whether they knew it just at that time or not. Penrod and his badge swept them off their feet. And a moment later, the two smallish figures, and the third very small and raggedy one, might have been seen hurrying down the alley. Penrod talked continually in a low, important voice, and Herman and Verman listened with eagerness.

CHAPTER LVI

THE MAN WITH THE FALSE WHISKERS

IT WAS only a few days after this that Mr. Dade commented upon a singular phenomenon he had observed as a characteristic of life in that town. He and Margaret were sitting upon the steps of the verandah, enjoying the evening silence, when a curious hooting, somewhat like an owl's, came from some shrubberies in a corner of the fence. This sound was responded to by a melancholy but wholly undoglike series of barks out of other bushes more remote.

Mr. Dade made a gesture of discomfort. "What *is* that?" he said.

Margaret laughed. "Only Penrod and some boys, playing."

An odd voice issued from the fence corner. "Oh Mihhuh Habe hippum om hump hep!" it cried. "He hippum om hump hep wi mow!"

"What's that?" Mr. Dade asked nervously.

"It's only Verman," Margaret answered, laughing again. "What!"

Margaret spelled the name. "He's a little tongue-tied darky boy," she added. "He lives in our alley."

"Well, that's curious," the visitor observed thoughtfully. "I've stumbled over a hundred coloured boys downtown in the last few days. It seems to me that the coloured boys in this town have an actual habit of getting between people's feet; but the odd thing about it is that if I *have* stumbled over a hundred, at least fifty of 'em were tongue-tied."

As Mr. Dade's significant remark to Margaret amply indicates, Verman—otherwise "Jim" and later, "Number Hunderd and Five"—was of incomparable service to George B. Jashber. His value must be esteemed greater than Herman's, though the latter was both faithful and intelligent, for Verman's impediment of speech made him (to put his virtue in a word) probably the most efficient assistant detective that the world has seen. This defect of his, which he ever regarded less as a misfortune and more as a gift, made it possible for him to give secret information to his associates at any time, in the most public places, and in the loudest and frankest manner.

Thus, Verman called forth upon the night air: "Oh Mihhuh Habe hippum om hump hep! He hippum om hump hep wi mow," which Penrod and Herman, lurking out of sight of the shadowed person, were sufficiently familiar with the Vermanic cipher to interpret: "Ole Mister Dade sittin' on front steps! He sittin' on front steps right now!"

And when Mr. Dade would almost walk over Verman upon the threshold of the Young Men's Christian Association building, Verman, in the very act of extricating himself, would freely and loudly shout, "He hum howp!" or, "He hoe him!" whereupon Herman, posted within hearing, would relay the message to George B. Jashber round an alley corner: "He comin' out!" or, "He goin' in!"

Herman was the only person who understood Verman at all readily, though Penrod, through familiarity, could at times decipher Verman's meanings with fair results. However, George B. Jashber sometimes lost patience with his talented assistant during the ceremony known to George B. and Jim and Bill as "office". Penrod's continuing studies of detectives led direct to this institution. Penrod would sit in the wheelbarrow in the carriage-house, with sheets of paper before him upon a box, and he would frown and take notes while Herman and Verman "reported". Herman's report was usually simple and uninspired; but Verman loved to talk. He found his opportunity upon these occasions, and, with eyes dilating and gestures as unintelligible as his utterance, he would make a report that seldom failed to shatter George B. Jashber's feeble power of endurance. Nor was his volubility checked by a mere, "That's plenty!" or, "Here, f'r heaven's sakes, can't you quit?" Verman would go on, becoming shriller and louder and happier all the while, until George B. Jashber stamped the floor and rudely shouted, "Oh, shut *up!*"

When quiet (save for Verman's giggle) was restored, "What's he been talkin' about, Herman?" Penrod would ask.

"Nuff'm. Dess all time say same fing he done say firs' time he say it."

Nevertheless, Penrod compiled and kept (usually in the sawdust box) something that stood for a record of the movements of Herbert Hamilton Dade; and this document, though fragmentary, must at least have satisfied the typical movie and short-story detective who was its inspiration.

One morning, Penrod showed a recent page of the "report" to Marjorie Jones, and, standing by, watched her in his most sidelong manner as she read it. She read it aloud, of necessity slowly, and a little bit too much in the tone of one conscientious over a task at school.

" 'Office'," she began. " 'George B. Jashber. Report. Report of Bill and Jim. We got to catch this cook——' "

"Crook!"

"What is a crook, Penrod?" Marjorie asked, not profoundly interested.

"You go on readin'. You'll see."

Marjorie proceeded. " 'We got to catch this cook'—crook, I mean—'and keep on the trall'—trail, I guess it means—'trail, night- and daytime. Jim report. The scoddel—scowendel—scondrel—the scondrel went to get his diner—dinner—at a place where it says good meals seventy-five cents. Bill report. The scounderel talk to the crook with the false black whick—whickers——' "

"Whiskers! My goodness, Marjorie, don't you know——"

" 'Whiskers'," Marjorie went on, " 'Whiskers down in the barber stairs. George B. Jashber report. I was with Bill. The crooks said it was cool in the barber and not much news the one with false wh—whiskers said he got his hair cut. End of report.' "

"Hand it back!" Penrod said, and replaced the report in the inner pocket of his jacket.

"What does it mean, Penrod?" Marjorie asked politely, and, except for her politeness, her expression inclined toward a vacancy that piqued George B. Jashber. "Is it something you play all by yourself?"

This more sharply piqued him. " 'Play'!" he echoed morosely. "I guess if you knew sumpthing about it, you wouldn't talk so much! It's a perty danger's biznuss."

"What like?" she inquired mildly.

"Well, you know what I showed you that day?"

"What day?"

Penrod jumped up from the grass where they were sitting in Marjorie's yard. He began to walk toward the gate.

"All right!" she called after him. "If you want to go home mad, 'stead of telling me what it is, I don't care!"

Upon this, Penrod hesitated, halted, then came back and

sat beside her again. "*You* know what I showed you," he said plaintively. "What makes you want to ack as if——"

"Honest, I don't, Penrod!" she assured him earnestly. "I don't remember any——"

"Well, look!" And he threw back his coat, displaying the glittering symbol of his chosen calling. This time, he allowed her a longer inspection.

"It's right pretty, Penrod," she said, and examined the inscription upon the shield with a little curiosity, though its significance was lost upon her, for she read the letters separately. "P, V, D, T, E, T, E, C, A, G, C, Y," she read slowly, and then her face brightened. "Oh, Penrod, I know what it is *now!* It's sumpthing like what they put in schoolbooks that say over it, P, R, E, F, A, C, E, and stands for 'Peter Rice eats fish and catches eels,' if you read it forward; and, if you read it backward, it means 'Eels catches alligators; Frank eats raw potaters'!"

"It don't anything o' the sort mean Peter Rice——"

"Oh, I didn't mean *yours* did!" Marjorie interrupted. "I only meant yours means sumpthing *like* that."

"It does not!"

"Well then, what *does* yours mean, Penrod?"

Penrod breathed hard. "It means sumpthing you wouldn't know what I was talkin' about if I was to tell you," he replied coldly. "I did tell you one thing, and you never hardly noticed."

"What was it?"

"Chasin' these crooks. I told you it was a perty danger's biznuss."

"Penrod, you said you'd tell me what a crook is."

"Well——" He looked cautiously over his shoulder before proceeding. "A crook is—well, crooks are somebody that ought to be arrested. Anybody that's in jail is a crook, like horse-thieves and all. I'm after a gang of crooks now."

Marjorie seemed perplexed. "*You* are?"

"Yes, I am."

"What did they do to you, Penrod?"

"What?"

"What did they do to you to make you after 'em?"

"Well——" He paused. "Well, I'm after 'em all right, and they better look out."

"Who are they, Penrod? Is that little Carlie Chitten one?"

Penrod was becoming exasperated by Marjorie's opacity and her failure to be impressed. "No; 'that little Carlie Chitten' is not one!" he said, bitterly burlesquing her voice. "My goodness! I thought you knew anyways a little about sumpthing!"

"Well, why don't you tell me who these crooks are, then?"

"I'll tell you, all right!" said Penrod. "I guess when I tell you who it is, you won't talk so much about 'little Carlie Chitten' so much!"

"Well then, why don't you go ahead and tell me?"

"Well, I will, if you'd ever give me the chance."

"Well, I'm givin' you the chance now. I won't say a thing till you're through."

"Well, one of 'em's a man that wears false black whiskers."

"You mean a grown-up man, Penrod?"

" 'Course I mean a 'grown-up man'," said the daring boy. "What do you think I'm talkin' about? He hangs around, and every little while he talks to the other one. He's got false black whiskers. There's two of 'em."

"You mean they both have false black whiskers, Penrod?"

"No! I didn't say they had, did I? Who said they both—— My goodness! I said the one with false black whiskers had false black whiskers. I didn't say the other one had. He hasn't got any at all."

"Well, who is this other one, then, Penrod?"

"It's that ole Mr. Dade."

"Who?"

"It's that ole Dade comes to our house and sits around so much."

"Penrod!" Marjorie cried, amazed. "Why, I know him! He comes to see Papa sometimes."

"Well, he's the crook."

Marjorie was utterly skeptical. "He is not!" she cried. "Papa wouldn't let him if he was somebody ought to be in jail. He wouldn't let him in our house. Penrod Schofield, you made all this up, yourself!"

"I did not!" Penrod cried, and he was sincerely indignant. "That's just what crooks do. They go around and get in people's houses, and then they steal sumpthing or else get the people to sign some ole paper and grab everything they got. I don't care if ole Dade does come around and see your father, he's the worst crook there is."

"He is *not!*"

"He is, too! And pretty soon he'll either steal sumpthing or he'll get your father and mother to sign some ole papers, and your father won't have a cent left to his name."

At last he began to make an impression. Marjorie showed signs of alarm. "Penrod!" she cried, her lovely eyes widening, her pink lips parting.

"You'll see!"

"Penrod, do you think he'd steal Papa's money?"

"I don't know," Penrod said modestly, "whether he'd slip it out of his pocket or get him to sign some ole papers, but he'll do *sumpthing* like that. Your father won't have a cent left to his name if he keeps on goin' with that ole Dade or the man with the false black whisk——"

Penrod paused, and his jaw dropped slightly in his amazement, a tribute to one of those supreme coincidences that happen to ordinary people only four or five times in their lives. Marjorie's father, Mr. Paoli Jones, was just entering the front gate, and by his side walked the man with the false black whiskers. Conversing seriously, the two passed along the path from the front gate to the front door —and disappeared within the house.

"My goodness!" Penrod gasped.

"What's the matter?"

"That was *him!*"

"Who?" cried Marjorie. "Where was he?"

"With your father! Marjorie, that was the other crook I and Herm—I and Bill and Jim are after. It's the one with the false black whiskers!"

Marjorie's eyes flashed. "They are not!" she cried. "You ought to be ashamed of yourself, Penrod Schofield, telling such a story! They are not any such a thing false! He had typhoid fever, and when he got well, Mamma coaxed him to let 'em stay on, on account of hiding his chin."

"Do you know who it *is*, Marjorie?"

"I should think maybe I *ought* to know him!" she responded indignantly. "It's my Uncle Montgomery."

CHAPTER LVII

IMPRESSING MARJORIE

I T MAY not be denied that for the moment Penrod was
taken aback. He rubbed his knee in silence, seeming to
find an injury there; then, somewhat feebly, he inquired, "What's his last name?"

"Whose last name?" the offended Marjorie demanded.
"Papa's?"

"No; I mean what's the man with the—I mean what's
your uncle's last name?"

"Jones!" she replied, with an explosiveness beyond her
years.

"Well," Penrod began uncomfortably, "well—all right."

"I guess it is *not* all right, either! You got to take back
all you called my Uncle Montgomery or I'll never speak to
you again."

Penrod felt desperate. He had come, that morning, to overwhelm Marjorie, to leave her almost prostrate with admiration and, conceivably, weeping with anxiety over the dangerous life his position in the world compelled him to lead. Here was a collapse indeed—just as he had begun to diagnose symptoms of success. Vaguely he sought some means to counteract malignant fortune.

"Well, I'll take it all back about your uncle."

"Every last word?"

"I will about *him*."

Marjorie looked at Penrod suspiciously. "Well, what won't you take every last word back about?"

"That ole Dade," Penrod said doggedly. "I won't take back *any* about him, because we're after him, and we're goin' to keep on after him—and he's a crook!"

"I don't believe it! I don't believe a word of it, because look what you just said about my Uncle Mont——"

"Marjorie," the goaded boy burst out, "didn't I just *say* I took it back about your ole Uncle Montgomery? That hasn't got anything to do with the rest of it, has it? I guess *your* eyes wouldn't stick out if I just told you a few things about that ole Dade! Oh, no!"

"Well, what about him, then, you know so much?"

"Well——"

"I won't believe a word of it unless you tell me!"

"Marjorie——"

"You don't know anything any more'n you did about Uncle Montgomery. That's the reason you won't tell."

"You listen here!" the incensed Penrod began. "You just listen to me!"

"Well, I am listening."

"You listen, Marjorie! My father said this ole Dade stole *horses*, and so did my mother, and I heard them say it. I guess you ain't goin' to claim my father and mother don't tell the truth, are you? Anybody that calls my father and mother a liar——"

"Penrod! Did you *honestly* hear your father and mother say that?"

"Yes, I did! And anybody that calls my father and moth——"

"Penrod!" Such passionate defense of his parents' reputation was not needed; they ranked as unquestionable authorities, and Marjorie accepted Mr. Herbert Hamilton Dade's status as that of a horse-thief. "Penrod, it's just terrible!" she cried.

"I know lots worse about him 'n that," he declared.

"Worse than stealing *horses*, Penrod?"

Penrod had carried his point; in spite of everything, he had succeeded in being as impressive as he had hoped to be. Nothing could have been more natural than that he should both protract and intensify the fragrant moment. Marjorie now seemed ready to believe whatever he said, and he more than half believed his ominous projections, himself. He became so mysterious that not only his mother, but a professional oculist, might have warned him to take care.

"Stealing horses isn't much to what *that* gang does—when they get started once," he said.

"Who's the others, Penrod?" Marjorie inquired, and, with gentle urgency, she added, "You took it back about Uncle Montgomery, Penrod."

"Well—he isn't; but they'll proba'ly get him to sign some ole papers or sumpthing."

Marjorie's eyes grew larger than ever. "Would they—would they make Papa sign some, too, Penrod?"

"Well, that's just what I told you, isn't it? That's the way ole crooks do. First, he'll make your father sign the ole papers, and then proba'ly he'll want to get married to you or sumpthing——"

"Why, Penrod!" This was too far beyond Marjorie's horizon; she was not allowed to attend the "movies". "What are you talkin' about?" she exclaimed. "Anyway, I heard Mamma say that Mr Dade wanted to get married to your sister, Margaret."

"Well, I guess he does," Penrod admitted; and then, recovering himself, added scornfully, "I guess I know *that* much, don't I?"

"Well, you just said——"

"*Listen,* can't you, just a minute? Can't you listen just a *minute?* My goodness! If he got all your father's money and his house an' lot, then he could come and marry Margaret, couldn't he?"

"But you——"

"Well, he *could,* couldn't he?"

"*I* didn't say he couldn't, Penrod."

"Well, then, listen a minute, can't you? My good——"

"I *am* listening!" Marjorie felt that there had been a definite inconsistency in Penrod's statement; but, in a moment or two, as he went on, the inconsistency lost its definiteness, became vague, and then she forgot it altogether—and so did Penrod.

"This is the way ole Dade does, Marjorie. First, he gets somebody that drinks, or sumpthing, and gets him to help make some ole father write his name on the ole papers and then he proba'ly gets him arrested and put in jail, or else he takes and kills him——"

"Which one, Penrod? Which one does he kill?"

He deliberated. "Well, gener'ly the one that drinks, and then he takes all the other one's money and his house an' lot. Well, f'r instance, supposin' your Uncle Montgomery is the one that drinks——"

"He does not! He doesn't either drink, and you shan't say——"

"Well, I didn't say he *did,* did I? My goodness, I just said—well, even if he don't drink or anything, I bet ole Dade'll make your father give him all his money and his house an' lot and everything, and *then* where'll you be?"

Marjorie was disturbed, but she had a reassuring thought. "Papa wouldn't do it. He wouldn't give Uncle Montgomery——"

"I didn't say he'd give it to your uncle. He'd haf to give it to ole Dade. My goodness!"

"Why, Papa wouldn't give it to Mr. Dade! If he wouldn't give it to Uncle Montgomery, he wouldn't take and give it to——"

"You'll see!"

"Well, I don't *think* he would, Penrod."

"Listen here, Marjorie," Penrod said argumentatively. "You don't know as much as I do, do you?"

"Well, I know anyway almost as much," Marjorie returned stoutly.

"Well, almost as much isn't as much," said Penrod. "And you don't know *half* what I know about crooks. You don't know anything at all about 'em, and I know 'most everything."

"Well, what of it?"

"Well," said Penrod, "you better look out, that's all; and your father better look out, or, first thing he knows, there'll be—there'll be lots o' trouble around here!"

His manner (that of one knowing much more than circumstances permitted him to tell) had a powerful effect upon Marjorie, who was becoming seriously alarmed. "Why, Papa would go and get that bad man arrested!" she said, but without strong conviction, for it had begun to seem to her that her father was in the toils. However, she had another hopeful thought: "He'd rather have him arrested, any day, than give him his house an' lot."

Penrod had no verbal reply for this; yet he had talked himself into the belief that Mr. Jones was somehow inextricably ensnared by the crook, Dade, and Marjorie's reasonable idea failed to shake him. He made some sounds of derision, and then shook his head portentously.

"Well, he would, wouldn't he?" Marjorie urged. "*Why* wouldn't he?"

"You just wait and see, Marjorie Jones!" said Penrod gloomily.

Marjorie's face fell; again all seemed lost. "Are you *sure*, Penrod?" she quavered.

"You just wait and see."

"Pen——" She paused, interrupted by a call from the house.

"Lunch, Marjorie! Come to the table!"

"I'm coming, Mamma." She took a few steps toward Penrod, who was already moving in the direction of the front gate. "Penrod, do you think——"

"You just wait and see, Marjorie Jones!"

"Oh, Penrod, please——"

In spite of her appealing voice, he continued upon his way; and the summons from the house was repeated.

"Marjorie!"

Thereupon, Marjorie turned obediently and went into the house. Meanwhile, a feeling, undeniably to be diagnosed as one of satisfaction, became part of Penrod's genuinely ominous forebodings on behalf of the Jones family; he was justifiably confident that Marjorie regarded him as an important person not immeasurably unlike an actual George B. Jashber. Still, he had another feeling underneath his satisfaction and his foreboding. This third feeling was less active and feebler than the two others—but it was there. And if he could have seen the excitement in Marjorie's face as she went in to lunch with her family and her Uncle Montgomery, and if he could have read her impulses under that excitement, this relatively insignificant third feeling would certainly have become, upon the instant, the most powerful one of the three.

It consisted of a shimmering disquiet, a foggy sense of having dabbled in vast matters, of having done something —somehow—somewhere—that might bring about results upon the adult plane and far out of his range and class. It did not last long, but while it was present within him Penrod felt a little uncomfortable.

CHAPTER LVIII

THE PURSUIT OF DADE

THAT afternoon Sam Williams returned from a visit
to his uncle's farm where he had happily spent the
fortnight elapsed since the beginning of the summer
vacation. He had heard something there that gave him an
exciting new idea for the future career of Walter-John,
and, taking that still cumbersome pup with him upon a
leash, he sought out his friend Penrod, thus walking
straight into the arms of another of those coincidences that
attend upon the adventures of people engaged in the discovery of crime and the detection of criminals. He came
upon Penrod, Herman and Verman, as the three sat making
up the day's Report in the Jashberian office, though of
course Sam was unaware of what thus preoccupied them,

and even that they were in an office at all. He greeted them cheerfully, and, not realizing that he was intruding, began at once to explain his new idea.

"Look, Penrod!" he said. "Listen! I know sumpthing I bet you don't know, or even Herman and Verman, either. John Carmichael told me out on my uncle's farm where I been, and I bet none of you know anything at all about it."

"Never mind," Penrod said coldly. "We're kind o' busy now, Sam. Maybe I'll tell you sumpthing about it some day; but not now, because Herman and Verman and I got a good deal on our hands to-day. If you want to play some game or sumpthing you better go find Georgie Bassett or Roddy Bitts or——"

"I don't either want to play any ole game or anything," Sam returned, aggrieved. "John Carmichael told me sumpthing out at my uncle's farm, and I'm goin' to train my good ole dog to do it. When I get him trained I guess you won't feel sick you never trained Duke like that or anything! Oh, no! I guess I and John won't make you and Duke look cheap or anything! You won't come around then and say, 'Why didn't you tell me about it so I could train my dog that way, too, Sam?' Oh, no!"

"What way?" Penrod asked scornfully. "What way would I waste all my good time and everything wantin' to train Duke to jump through a hoop or sumpthing you're talkin' so much about. What way?"

"'Jump through a hoop'!" Sam exclaimed derisively. "This dog o' mine isn't goin' to waste any time like that any more'n you would. You wait and see! Some day you'll see me just give John Carmichael, here, one sniff of some ole crook's shoe or his pocket-book or sumpthing, and then —oh, my! Go it, you bloodhound you!"

"What you talkin' about?"

"Listen!" Sam said. "John Carmichael told me that over at the county-seat, near where my uncle's farm is, the sheriff keeps a couple o' bloodhounds. If some ole crook gets out o' jail there or anything, they let the bloodhounds smell sump-

thing that belonged to him, like his shoes or his hat or anything, and then—Whizz! those two bloodhounds go after
him and catch him and pull him down! That's just what
John Carmichael said; they pull him down, John said, and
then they hold him there till the sheriff comes and arrests
him again. John Carmichael said there was proba'ly some
bloodhound in John Carmichael, and anyhow lots of other
kinds o' dogs besides bloodhounds could be trained to go
after crooks just the same as bloodhounds do. So proba'ly
Duke could be trained to do it, 'specially if we trained him
along with John Carmichael. John Carmichael said he was
almost sure John Carmichael had proba'ly a whole lot o'
bloodhound in him, and John Carmichael said John would
learn how without any trouble at all, so if you want to——"

"Hol' on a minute!" It was Herman who interrupted; he
looked interested but puzzled. "Whut is all 'iss here John
Cowmikles? You say John Cowmikles say John Cowmikles
got bloodhoun' in him, an' you go on talk so all mixed up
about how John Cowmikles say John Cowmikles say John
Cowmikles got bloodhoun' in him——"

"It isn't mixed up at all," Sam interrupted crossly.
"John Carmichael works on my uncle's farm, and he's the
man that gave me John Carmichael, and he said I could
train John Carmichael——"

"Hol' on a minute! My goo'niss! John Cowmikles tell
you——"

"There's two of 'em," Sam explained. "What's the matter of you, Herman? Can't you understand anything at all?
Look! This dog is named John Carmichael because I named
him for the other one that gave him to me. The one on the
farm is a man, but this one is a dog, and both their names
are John Carmichael. The man on the farm that's named
John Carmichael is a man; but this dog, here, that's named
John Carmichael is a dog, and he's named for the——"

"Nemmine," Herman interrupted, for Sam seemed to intend to continue his rather laborious explanation indefinitely. "Nemmine; I know whut you mean."

Penrod had become interested in Sam's idea, for the addition of two perfectly trained bloodhounds to the Jashber Agency would of course increase the agency's efficiency—at least dramatically. "Listen here, Sam," he said, "if Walter's got some bloodhound in him, I guess he could be trained that way, and Duke could help train him, because Duke's a full-blooded dog. Anyhow, we were thinkin' about lettin' you be a member after you came home, so I guess you can join. Look, Sam!"

With this simple prelude, he exposed the shield to Sam's surprised gaze, and forthwith explained the organization and purposes of the agency; Sam was given a special name and a number, thus becoming a full member, though of subordinate standing. The training of the bloodhounds then became the next order of business, and Duke was brought into the office to learn the first steps, in company with Walter-John.

"Our good ole bloodhounds got to have some practise," Penrod said. "That's the way we haf to begin, so they can learn what to do when we take 'em out after the Dade gang. This is the way we'll do—— Listen, Sam! Listen, Herman! Listen, Verman! We'll make 'em smell sumpthing that belongs to one of us, then that one'll pretend like he's runnin' away and we'll let the good ole bloodhounds out after him. It wouldn't do for me to be the one, because of course Duke'd follow me anyway, and Sam won't do, because Walter'd follow him."

"It ain' go' be me," Herman announced quickly, as Penrod's eye wandered to him. "Ain' go' be no bloodhoun's pull me down an' hol' me fer no sheriffs!"

"Verman'd be the best one," Penrod said. "The trouble is Verman hasn't got any shoes or hat or even any jacket." He paused in thought, then brightened. "That won't hurt, though. Just to begin with, we can make the good ole bloodhounds smell Verman, himself; then he can begin runnin' away, and we'll sick the good ole bloodhounds on him after he gets a start."

But Verman proved to be unwilling. "Mo!" he said decisively. "Mo!"

"Aw, look here, Verman!" Penrod said. "You don't want to go spoiling everything, do you? This isn't goin' to hurt you any, and you can't ack the cry-baby around here, or else I won't let you be Jim any longer. Come on now, we got to make these bloodhounds smell him good!"

"Mo!" Verman repeated, but with less determination; and, a moment later, as the noses of the two reluctant bloodhounds were forced against his person, he consented to take the part assigned to him in their training, and even giggled when his ribs were rubbed with the nose of Walter-John. " 'Op picka me!" he protested.

Herman giggled, too, "Verman say stop ticklin' him," he interpreted.

"All right," Penrod said. "I guess these good ole bloodhounds have smelled him enough; because they couldn't smell him any more if we kept at it a year, so run, Verman! Run!"

Verman ran out into the yard; the hounds were released and urged to follow the fugitive. "Sick 'im!" Penrod, Sam and Herman shouted. "Sick 'im, you ole bloodhounds you! Go after him! Sick 'im! Sick 'im!"

Thus encouraged, Duke and Walter-John behaved admirably. They ran after Verman, barked at him loudly, frisked round him with the liveliest pleasure in the world; Walter-John frolicsomely seized a loose edge of the largest patch upon Verman's trousers and held to it until a sound of ripping and Verman's aggrieved squealing abashed him into releasing it. Verman returned to the stable loudly complaining and holding the patch in place with his hand; but Sam was delighted and proud. "What did I tell you!" he shouted. "Didn't I tell you John Carmichael said John Carmichael was part bloodhound! C'm on, Verman, we'll make 'em smell you again, and this time I bet good ole John Carmichael'll——"

"Mo!" Verman said, and he remained obdurate, not to be persuaded. Herman declined positively to act as a substi-

tute fugitive, and, as both Penrod and Sam insisted that
they were needed as trainers, it was finally decided to let
the matter rest for the day upon the undoubted success of
the single experiment.

"Anyway," Penrod said, "what we haf to do is to get
some shoes or sumpthing that belong to the Dade gang and
make our good ole bloodhounds smell 'em. Then they'd go
after them the way they just did after Verman. F'r instance,
if we had a pair of their shoes, we could have Verman
wear 'em, and train Duke and Walter to go after Verman as long as he had the shoes on; then when the Dade
gang put these shoes back on again—Whizz! Go it, you
bloodhounds you!"

This idea struck him as so interesting that it recurred to
him at intervals throughout the rest of the afternoon; and
nothing could have been more natural than that it should
recur to him again in the evening, when Mr. Dade, as matters fell out, left a light Panama hat upon the hall table.
Margaret and the young man sat indoors, in the living-
room, the air being chill, and Mr. Dade took his departure
as usual at ten o'clock, a habit of his that had won Mrs.
Schofield's favour and caused her to speak of him as a "well
brought-up young man", which seemed, indeed, to be the
fact. When he left, he did not put on his hat until after he
had descended the verandah steps, Margaret having accompanied him so far; and then, employing it in a courtly gesture of farewell, "Good-night, Princess!" he said, and placed
it upon his head. He experienced a slight surprise; but
rather than spoil the effect of his departing gesture, he
went out of the gate and a little way down the street before
removing the hat and examining it by the light of a street-
lamp. Yes, he was right; there were damp spots inside, upon
the band and upon the fine straw, and there were also some
smudges not there when he had deposited the hat upon the
table. "Curious," he thought. Had water been spilled upon
the table, or had someone else taken the hat temporarily by
mistake?

However, the damage was insignificant, a fact more remarkable than he could have guessed, since Duke and Walter-John had spent whole minutes with their noses held firmly within the hat, and Verman had worn it during several practise excursions as a fugitive in the dusk of the alley. "Curious," Mr. Dade thought again, as he replaced the hat upon his head and resumed his way down the street. Then suddenly, he started nervously and quickened his pace.

A peculiar voice, with which, however, he was now far from unfamiliar, had squealed out of the darkness almost at his heels. "Wam mubbowm!"

Then another voice at a distance seemed to repeat this squealing, though the words it cried came not distinguishably to the ears of Mr. Dade.

Penrod and Sam, farther in the rear, understood this second voice, however. It was that of Herman, interpreting for the small brother. " 'Where 'em bloodhoun's?' Verman say. 'Where 'em bloodhoun's?' "

"Doggone it!" Penrod muttered. For Duke trotted amiably enough by his side, but only looked dejected, or stopped altogether, when urged forward upon the chase; and Sam, a little way behind, was even less successful with Walter-John. Walter-John, indeed, could be kept upon the trail only by means of a leash, and followed Sam in a partly sitting-down attitude, offering the dead weight of a complete, if passive, resistance.

"I expeck he wants to go home," Sam panted, when he and his charge came up with Penrod. "Anyhow he seems to want to sit down all the time. I guess bloodhounds don't like to work at night, Penrod, proba'ly. John Carmichael don't seem to take any interest, like he did this afternoon, and besides, I got to go home, myself, because I'm goin' to get fits for stayin' out this late, anyhow."

They paused for consultation; but stood for a time in silence, and then, from the farther end of the next block, heard faintly another appeal from Verman, and, a moment later, almost as faintly, the faithful brother's interpretation, "Verman say he cain' see no bloodhoun's!"

"Well, what we better do?" Sam inquired, looking down moodily at the bloodhounds. Duke had taken occasion to roll upon his back, and Walter-John was sniffing at him indolently. "We better call to Herman and Verman we're goin' home now, don't you think, Penrod?"

"I don't s'pose we could make 'em hear us," Penrod said. "Not unless we ran after 'em, and I got to go home now, too, Sam. It's better to let them go on shadowin' him, anyway." Then, as the two boys turned, and, followed by the bloodhounds, walked back toward home, he went on: "I guess you're right about our good ole dogs not likin' to go after crooks except in daytime, Sam. We got to teach 'em to trail the Dade gang while it's light, I guess, and I know what'd be the best time for that. Sunday afternoon before last he and my sister went for a walk, and they went last Sunday, too. If they go again next Sunday, why, we can get Herman and Verman and our good ole bloodhounds——"

"Listen!" Sam said.

In the quiet night a far away shrilling in a slender African voice was just audible; then the sound seemed to be repeated like an echo a little louder than the original outcry.

"Could you make out anything he said?" Sam asked.

"No; they're too far down the street. They're mighty good men, that ole Jim and Bill. They'll keep right on the trail until he goes home to bed. It's a good thing for us that Jim and Bill are coloured, I expeck."

Sam was surprised. "Why?" he inquired.

"Well, for one thing, you can't see 'em very well after dark," Penrod answered. "And besides," the observant boy added, a moment later, "coloured people never haf to go home to bed at night, anyhow."

CHAPTER LIX

A SUNDAY STROLL

THE following Sunday morning, Mr. Robert Williams went to church in company with the other members of his own family—that is to say, with his father and his mother and his eleven-year-old brother, Sam. The serious expression of the new Bachelor of Arts was one evidence that going to church with his own family was not one of the summer pleasures he had promised himself in his undergraduate day-dreams, and, during the service, his eyes frequently wandered to another family group of four in a pew across the aisle. On the homeward way, also, his wistful look ran forward, over intervening heads, to where, in this other family group, a frivolous hat affected sedateness for the occasion. No physical force prevented Robert from joining

Miss Schofield; she had no escort or protection except that afforded by her father, mother and brother. Nevertheless, Robert Williams walked with his own family—in peace, it may be, but certainly without jocosity.

In the afternoon, after four o'clock, he came out upon the front verandah of his father's house, sat in a wicker chair and opened a book, but read nothing therein. His gaze was steadfast upon a lawn and gate a little way down the street, and there was in his face an expectancy like that of a person who waits in a dentist's anteroom. It was the look of one who, from previous experience, knows what is going to happen presently but anticipates little to his pleasure.

Nor did his inward prophecies fail of fulfilment—though, as it happened, the facts proved to be an unexpected and fantastic embroidery upon the simple weave of his predictions. From Mr. Schofield's gate, as the disturbed Robert expected, Margaret and Mr. Herbert Hamilton Dade came forth, patently for an afternoon walk; and both were in a mood of gaiety, so far as sight and hearing might disclose their condition to the young man pretending to read a book. The cruel Margaret had looked never more charming.

She and her handsome companion passed along the Williams's fence, and Robert caught the word "Princess" in Mr. Dade's melodious voice, but bent interestedly over his book and did not look up until they had gone by. When he did lift his eyes, it seemed to him that he caught just the end of a swift gesture of Margaret's head; he had the impression that she had glanced back over her shoulder at him.

"Coquette!" he breathed; and then he viciously muttered the word, "Princess!" So she liked *that* awful sort of thing! And Robert remembered a classmate of his who had printed a poem, evidently personal and particular, called "Milady", in a college paper early in the first freshman term, and thus acquired a nickname that had to be carefully explained to the poet's father on class-day, four years later. "Princess!" said Robert. "Oh, *all* right!"

He watched this girl of execrable taste as she sauntered

up the sunshiny pavement beside Mr. Dade, and, though he loathed her romantic tendencies, he could not help feeling that her dress was the prettiest he had ever seen her wear—incomparably prettier than any dress he had ever seen any other girl wear. And she was so graceful! In the light breeze her chiffon overskirt fluttered like sunbeams on a rapid brook. He could have seen it better, he noted with annoyance, if that little darkey boy had not walked so close behind her. The little darkey boy seemed to be intending to pass Margaret and Mr. Dade and walk ahead of them, the gloomy watcher observed, but just at the last moment, when he was close alongside, he always changed his mind and fell back. About ten paces behind him walked another coloured boy, a larger one.

Suddenly, Robert's book fell to the floor of the verandah. Thirty or forty feet behind the second coloured boy walked Sam Williams, Robert's brother, leading the large, reluctant pup, John Carmichael, upon a leash, and, at about the same distance to the rear of Sam came one wearing an imperious—nay, almost satanic—intensity of countenance, evidently in command. This person was he whom Robert may most creditably be represented as defining, mentally, as "that blank Penrod". Penrod was accompanied by Duke, and at times seemed to address him vehemently, though in undertones. The observer's eyes became luminous with wonder and curiosity. Unmistakably, here was some sort of procession!

Robert had no impulse to interfere. If those two small negroes and Sam and Penrod and John Carmichael and Duke found themselves interested in taking a walk, as it were, with Miss Schofield and her dashing admirer, what right had any outsider to intervene? And particularly on the part of a disqualified suitor must any attempt to break up the little parade have appeared an intrusion. However, as it passed up the street, he felt warranted in going as far as the gate to look at it.

Mr. Dade and Margaret had reached the next corner;

but Robert was able to see that Mr. Dade began to be annoyed by the persistent proximity of the smaller negro. In fact, over his shoulder, Mr. Dade seemed to be addressing the little negro harshly, and the latter, to all appearances, was making a voluble and gesticulative but unsatisfactory reply. The other coloured boy, standing aloof, was calling something in the direction of Sam and Penrod, who had each moved aside from the line of vision of Mr. Dade and Margaret—Sam behind a shade-tree, and Penrod behind an ornamental stone upon an open lawn, where he had prostrated himself. The whole proceeding was somewhat conspicuous, and several people across the street had paused to observe it. However, Mr. Dade presently abandoned his argument, and he and Margaret turned the corner, as closely attended by the small negro boy as before. The larger one followed, Penrod rose cautiously, Sam came from behind his tree, and, a moment later, both of them, and their placidly accompanying dogs, disappeared in the same direction.

Robert was profoundly interested; but his dignity did not permit him to add one more to the procession. A grimness that was far cousin to a smile came to his lips, and, as he retired into the house, the least little lightening of his sorrows was perceptible upon his countenance. As the afternoon waned and no sound or sign of a returning Sam indicated that the uninvited strollers had grown disheartened in their mysterious purpose, this alleviation of Robert's increased, so that he appeared at the evening table with a livelier air than his worried mother had seen upon him since the day of his return from college. He even helped Sam in the latter's excuses for being a full ten minutes late, and, after the meal was over, sought that youth's company in the twilight of the backyard. He began by giving Sam a quarter. Sam was sincerely grateful, though hurried.

"I'm cert'nly much obliged," he said, moving toward the back fence. "Well, I guess I got to be goin'."

"Where do you have to go, Sam?"

"Over to Penrod's."

"What for?"

"Oh, nothin'."

"Going to play with Penrod and those two coloured boys?"

"I dunno," said Sam; and, noting a tendency on the part of Robert to detain him with more conversation, he added: "Well, I'm very much obliged, Bob. Well, g'-by!" And he set his hand upon the fence to climb it.

"Wait a minute, can't you? I just wanted to——"

"Honest, I got to go!"

And in confirmation, there came a shout from the alley. It was the voice of Herman. "Hi, Tabber!" it shouted.

"I'm comin', Bill," Sam called in response.

"We goin' begin, Tabber," Herman shouted again. "Ole Jawge, he waitin' on you."

"I'm comin', ain't I?"

But as Sam reached the top of the fence, a detaining hand was laid upon his shoulder. "I only want to talk to you a minute, Sam."

"Honest, Bob, I *got* to go. I got——"

Robert gave Sam another quarter.

"Well, much obliged," said Sam, descending from the fence. "What you want to talk about?"

"Who was it that called you just then?"

"It's Herman; he's a coloured boy."

"What name did he call you?"

"Oh, nothin'. 'Tabber', I guess. We kind of pretend we got other names. Penrod said I'd be Tabber." Sam laughed a little sheepishly. "He made it up, I guess."

"Who's George?"

"It's Penrod." Here Sam laughed again. "He's George —George B. Jashber. Herman's Bill and Verman's Jim and I'm Tabber. They only took me in a few days ago, when I went over there."

"What were you all doing this afternoon, Sam?"

"When?"

"Following Penrod's sister and—and her friend all over town."

Sam at once looked serious. "Well, that part of it isn't playin' at all. It's—it's a perty danger's biznuss."

"So! How is it dangerous?"

Before Sam could reply, the cry came again from the alley. "Hi, Tabber! You *comin'?*"

"Can't you wait a *minute?*" Sam responded impatiently. "Honest, Bob, I *can't* stay any——"

"Oh, yes, you can," said Robert. "For fifty cents."

"Well, where's——"

"I mean the fifty cents I've already given you," Robert explained.

"Oh," Sam said rather blankly, and then, appreciating the justice of his brother's argument, he inquired, "What you want me to do?"

"Tell me what is the dangerous business, and why you and the other boys were following those two this afternoon. First, how long did you follow them?"

"Till they came back," Sam said, with admirable simplicity.

"Well, I always did believe in young people being carefully chaperoned," Robert said thoughtfully. "It seems to me you boys behaved quite properly in this matter, Sam. What did *they* do?"

"You goin' to tell Papa and Mamma?"

"I won't tell anybody at all."

"Well, they got kind of mad, I guess," Sam admitted. "First, they wanted Verman to keep away from 'em, but they couldn't understand anything he said, and I guess they thought he was just goin' the way they were, anyhow; so they went on, way out pretty near to the new park, and when they got out there, they stood around on the new bridge a good while, and then this ole Dade he tried to chase Verman back, but he couldn't catch him. Well, and then he and Margaret went and sat around on a bench. So, after-

*Mr. Dade began to be annoyed by the persistent prox-
imity of the smaller negro.*

while, they got up and started home, and ole Dade he just *wouldn't* let Verman keep anywhere's near 'em. He kep' chasin' him back all the time, and once he chased him pretty near a square—but every time 'course Verman'd come back again, and then he'd chase him again, and Herman, too. He never saw me and Penrod; but sometimes lots of other people did, and they'd kind o' laugh or sumpthing, and ole Dade, 'course he thought it was all Verman's fault—but he never did catch him."

"Thank you, Sam," said Robert, and, to Sam's surprise, his brother's voice was so affable that it was almost tender. "Now, if you'll just tell me what it's all about, I won't keep you any longer. What did you boys do it *for?* What were you up to?"

Sam looked embarrassed, and laughed. "Well—we kind of thought we could train John Carmichael and Duke to be bloodhounds; but I guess we got to give it up. They're awful stubborn about not learning what we want 'em to."

"I see," Robert said. "But what I want to know, Sam, is why you were following Margaret and Mr. Dade."

Sam stepped closer and spoke in a low tone. "Well, Penrod's a detective, now," he said confidentially.

"You mean you boys play he's one."

"No," Sam insisted earnestly. "He *is!* He's a real one. Honest he is, Bob! He's got a badge and everything. He's Number Hunderd and Three. It's the honest truth, and I wouldn't believe him, myself, if he hadn't showed me the badge. He had to pay a whole lot of money for it, honest! He's got a right to shadow anybody he wants to, and he's got a right to tell anybody else to go and shadow 'em, and they got a right to do it. It's the law."

"All right," said Robert. "But what were you doing this afternoon?"

"We were just out shadowin'. We go out shadowin' that ole Dade all the time. Some days we don't all keep after him, because Herman and Verman got to do a lot o' work around their house; but most o' the time they come along, and they keep right up close to him because Verman's tongue-tied."

"I don't see what that's got to do with it."

"Well, listen, Bob," said Sam, obviously believing his explanation ample. "Listen! Verman can understand everything he says; but this ole Dade can't understand a word. Ole Dade tried to kick him four or five times lately; but I don't believe there's anybody in the world can kick Verman. He knows how to get out o' the way when anybody kicks at him better'n any boy I ever knew in my life."

"How does it happen you all like to go out shadowing Mr. Dade, Sam? How'd you decide on him?"

"Why, I told you," said Sam. "Penrod's a detective. He found it all out."

"Found what out?"

"About ole Dade bein' a crook."

"What are you talking about, Sam?"

"Why, he *is* a crook!" Sam exclaimed. "Isn't he, Bob? Don't you think so?"

"Well——" Robert hesitated. "I understood that he was going to organize a new insurance company with Mr. Paoli Jones and his brother Montgomery. I didn't know that was criminal, precisely. What does Penrod say he found out?"

"Penrod says first he found out ole Dade steals horses."

"No! Did he?"

"Don't you believe it?"

"Well, I don't know," said Robert musingly. "Penrod is a very intelligent boy, it seems to me. I *hope* he hasn't made a mistake about this."

"Well, that isn't the worst," Sam continued, becoming eager under the encouragement of his brother's benevolent manner. "He does *lots* worse'n that!"

"What, Sam?"

"Well, you just said yourself he was doin' *sumpthing* to Marjorie Jones's father and her uncle."

"Well——"

"Well, Penrod found out this ole Dade is goin' to get

Marjorie Jones's uncle drunk, and then he's goin' to kill him or sumpthing, and make Marjorie Jones's father sign some ole papers, and take his house an' lot away from him or sumpthing, and get married to Margaret. Penrod says we got to shadow him every minute, because ole Dade's liable to take and do it any day. He's over there now, and that's what I got to go for. We got to keep shadowin' him until we haf to go to bed."

"Run along," said Robert. "I'll ask mother to let you stay out an extra half-hour before she calls you. But here ——" He fumbled in his pocket. "Here's another quarter. It's not for you; it's for Penrod. Tell him it's a secret, though; he mustn't mention that I sent it to him. Penrod's a nice boy, Sam. I'm glad you're such a friend of his."

And as Sam dropped to the other side of the fence, Mr. Robert Williams decided that he liked boys. Wholesome, fine, sensible creatures, he thought them; and, with his hands in his empty pockets, he strolled round the block under the starlight, whistling. But his whistling stopped momentarily as he passed along the Schofields' fence and his ear caught strange, animal-like sounds—not very like. An owl was evidently meant to hoot, and there was a protracted chorus of barking that never would have interested Penrod Schofield's little old dog, Duke.

Robert went on, his renewed whistling loud and cheery.

CHAPTER LX

THE PURSUIT CONTINUES

THE next morning Robert received a letter, written and posted late the previous evening. The girlish handwriting, pretty and appealing, showed signs of jerkiness here and there, seeming to reveal that the writer had been subject to agitation as she wrote. Robert paid a more flattering attention to this phenomenon than to the direct and intentional substance of the missive.

ROBERT:

I really was *so* amused at your pretending to read a book and not even speaking to old friends as they pass your house. I should think if college had done you much good, you would still be polite enough to at least bow to old friends. I suppose you are still cross over what I said that evening. I don't care, because it was just for your own good and didn't have anything to do with what you were nonsensical enough to accuse me of, anyhow. I should *really* like to know what on earth is the matter with you. Just because a girl shows a passing interest in somebody else she may hardly know at all except in the most superficial way, and might even find tiresome or ridiculous if she saw too much of such a person, I think nothing could be sillier than her old friends behaving with *actual rudeness* to her for such an absurd reason. I have always been taught that good manners were just as necessary between old friends as they were anywhere—but, of course, I may be wrong.

Sincerely,
MARGARET PASSLOE SCHOFIELD.

That afternoon, being again in funds, Robert gave Sam a dollar. Sam's amazement fully equalled his gratitude.

"Well, I cert'nly am much obliged!" he gasped.

"I want you to give half of it to Penrod," Robert said affably. "He's a boy the more I think about him the more I *like* to think about him. Ah——" He paused. "There's something more I'd like to ask you about what happened yesterday afternoon, Sam."

"You mean about our havin' to give up training the bloodhounds?"

"No," Robert said. "No, I wasn't thinking of that—not particularly, Sam. Of course it does seem too bad that you've had to give the bloodhounds up, because they certainly did add to the effect, as it were! But what I wanted to ask was whether or not quite a number of people happened to notice the proceedings yesterday afternoon. You told me that some people did notice, and I think you mentioned that they laughed. Is that correct?"

"Yes," Sam informed him casually. "I expeck mostly they were laughin' at Verman as we were goin' along. Sometimes people out on their porches kind of laughed, and a few times people clear on the other side of the street laughed and sort of pointed."

"I see. Did you happen to notice Margaret Schofield, Sam? Ah—did she seem to mind it at all?"

"Well, I kind of expeck so. She was red all the time and walked pretty fast. When ole Dade got so excited and went to chasin' Verman and tryin' to kick him and everything, she was awful red, because that was out at the park where the most people were, and a lot of 'em were laughin' pretty loud, and some of 'em kind of yelled when Verman would dodge. Yes, I guess she was pretty mad, because she stayed red and walked home terrible fast. I expeck it was a good thing for Penrod she never saw him and didn't know he had anything to do with it."

"Yes, I suppose so," Robert assented. "But Penrod's a fine outstanding boy, Sam, and you mustn't forget to give him half of that dollar."

"No, I won't; I'll give it to him right away."

"I suppose you're going on with your game—not 'game', I mean to say——"

"You mean about ole Dade?"

"Yes," said Robert, "that dangerous business you were speaking of last night. Are you boys going on with it to-day?"

"Why, 'course!"

"Don't let me keep you, then," said Robert politely. "Not for a minute!"

Nevertheless, he called Sam back, after the latter had started, and gave him a dime for Herman and one for Verman.

When Sam, bringing these financial encouragements, reached the agency in Penrod's stable, George B. Jashber and Bill and Jim, that is to say, Nos. 103, 104 and 105 (or George B. and his men) felt that they were making real progress. Elated, they went at once to the corner drug store, where each had an afternoon pick-me-up of soda-water thickened by ice-cream and sweet flavouring sirup. Then, carrying with them salted peanuts, salted almonds, cinnamon drops, sticks of licorice, a bag of large, soggy balls of cocoanut-sugar and flour, and a terrible thing almost a foot long, purchased at the grocery and known to them as

a "b'loney sausage", they returned to the stable and performed the rite of the Daily Report. The notes taken by
George B. on this occasion were sketchier than usual, since
the utterance of Bill and Tabber, impeded by mastication,
was not much more intelligible than that of Jim. However,
since these notes covered the shadowing of the previous day,
in which all members of the organization had taken part,
their fragmentary nature was probably of no great detri-
mental importance.

Nor were the chief and his subordinates at all disturbed
by the fact that this report showed nothing more discred-
itable to Mr. Dade than that he had taken a walk with Penrod's sister and had displayed irritation with Verman and,
subsequently, with Herman. Indeed, there was no reason
why the members of the agency should have been more discouraged by this report than by any other in Penrod's collection, for all the others were as innocuous. The trail of
the scondrel, Dade, led sometimes from the Y. M. C. A.
building to Jones Brothers' real-estate office, sometimes to
a barber shop, sometimes to a dairy-lunch or other res-
taurant, sometimes to the post-office—and always, when the
shadowers persisted long enough, back to the Y. M. C. A.
building. There were times when the scondrel had been
tracked to a confectioner's, and twice he had gone to a flor-
ist's; but not once did a report prove him to have entered a
saloon. The truth is that a grown person, examining these
documents, must have judged Mr. Dade to be certainly
harmless and probably exemplary; and, if the young man
had known of their existence, he might well have cited them
in a court of law (supposing such necessity) as proof of his
good habits and testimony to his high character. But whoever surmises that the reports lacked damnatory significance in the eyes of the agency understands little of George
B. Jashber, Bill, Jim and honest Tabber. They had begun
by accepting it as a fact that this ole Dade was guilty;
therefore, whatever he did was suspicious. The nature of his
guilt remained indefinite; sometimes it was one thing, some-

times another. On certain days, he would be spoken and thought of as a man who stole horses; on other days, his habitual crime seemed to be obtaining possession of some ole father's house an' lot through the signing of some ole papers. But never for one moment was there any doubt that he was a criminal. In that capacity, he was securely established—it might be said, indeed, that he had been appointed to the office; he was the official crook of this agency. One noontime, Penrod and Sam shadowed him to a business-men's revival meeting; they even followed him inside, and nothing that he did there shook their constant faith that in selecting him to be the agency's crook Penrod had done well.

And in this—as in other ways of boys, whose ways, fundamentally, are grown people's ways, and of whom nearly all human truth may be learned—in this we see a plain old fact of life prettily confirmed: that once we judge, we no longer possess judgment. That is the reason why grown people who have decided to think of certain other people as enemies, or as bad people, are shocked and troubled (for the moment) when they hear of those enemies or bad people doing something worthy and creditable. The worthy and creditable action is interpreted, in such cases, as the deceptive result of vicious motives. George B. Jashber, Bill, Jim and Tabber merely omitted the pause for being shocked and doing the interpreting. Thus, the report of ole Dade's visit to the revival meeting was written simply:

Report.   Nomber 103 George B. Jashber and Nomber 106 Tabber shad to where lots going on like praying and all such The crook got to senging hims.

Gordon Grant

CHAPTER LXI

TWO RETURN TO PRIVATE LIFE

THE condition of Mr. Herbert Hamilton Dade's nerves may be described—though imperfectly—as shaken. What had first seemed to him merely annoying coincidence had been so persistently repeated that it was folly to think the phenomena could be accounted for by even the most fantastic stretching of the laws of chance. Ordinarily he was not a superstitious young man; nevertheless, his mind had begun to be haunted by uncomfortable, strange ideas. He knew that the days of bewitchment were long since passed; but he had become so sensitive that he was ready to start at the mere sight of coloured children on the street—and that in broad daylight. Then, in the Y. M. C. A. library, early on an evening of rain, he found a book on Voodooism that did little to reassure him; he could not read it without glancing apprehensively over his shoulder from time to time, and after an hour he decided that this work, though learned, was making him morbid. He closed the book abruptly, returned it to its shelf, then went downstairs to the vestibule of the building. Here he paused for some moments of perturbed thought, and his expression was that of a person who debates whether or not to make an experiment that his forebodings warn him will end ominously. Then, with a hand slightly tremulous, he pushed open the outer door. It yielded with reluctance to his touch, as if resisted by something not weighty but unwilling to be dislodged from the step.

"He hum ow!" shouted a querulous voice too well known to him. "He hoohum me how in haim!"

Herman, at the corner of the building, interpreted to Penrod, lurking beyond. "He say ole Dade comin' out. Say he pushin' him out in the rain. I reckon Verman gittin' kine o' mad. We gittin' might tired all 'iss shaddin' an' ev'ything. When we go' git a chance to quit an' do somp'm' else?"

"Well, what's the matter of you?" Penrod demanded crossly, approaching him. "My goodness! I'd like to know what you and Verman *want!*"

"Want to go home an' quit all 'iss shaddin'. Look to me like I nev' git so wet in my days."

"You want to *quit?*" Penrod asked incredulously.

"I sut'ny do!" Herman responded with fervour. " 'Isshere fofe time I be'n wet froo clean to my skin, an' I don' keer whut ole Dade do no mo'. I ain' see no hosses, an' I ain' see no ole papuhs he done sign, an' I ain' liable to see none, 'cause he don' nev' sign none when we 'roun the place. How we go' ketch 'im at it? Look to me like he mus' always sign 'em inside 'isshere buildin', else sometime when we home eatin' meals 'r else in bed. Anyways, I don' keer whut he do no mo'. We be'n goin' on 'iss way an' shaddin', shaddin' all time, shaddin' I dunno how long, an' I'm a-goin' quit!"

"You ain't goin' to quit *now*, are you, Bill?" his chief asked reproachfully.

"Aft' 'iss one night, you kin fill my place," said Herman firmly. "I done got so tired all 'isshere shaddin', shaddin', all time shaddin', I ain' bettin' *no* man I ain' go' drop dead in my tracks."

This was not the first time Penrod had dealt with mutiny of the sort; in fact, if he had not been chief, holding the delightful power to send his men here or there as he chose, and to say, "Do thus", or "Do so", at will, he would have tired long since, himself. But, as things were, he was both grieved and irritated by Herman's complaints.

"My goodness!" he remonstrated. "Haven't you got any *sense*, Herman? I guess you don't remember there's mighty few coloured boys get a *chance* like this."

"Chanst like whut? You gimme chanst fer to walk my feet off, git wet froo to my skin, 'n'en git the hide lammed off o' me when I git back home! 'At's all chanst you gimme!"

"My goodness! I never did hear anybody that liked to talk so much! Now, you kept standin' around here so long talkin', ole Dade's come out——"

"No, he ain'."

"Well, Verman hollered and said——"

"I don' keer what he hollered. He's settin' back scrooged up ag'in' the do', out the rain, like whut he wuz. Ole Dade come out, gone back in ag'in'."

This was accurate, except that Mr. Dade had not come out. At the sound of Verman's voice, he instantly allowed the door to close and withdrew to the interior of the building. His manner was preoccupied, not without perturbation. He declined a game of checkers with a fellow lodger, and, after a few moments of indecision in the reading-room, went upstairs to his own chamber, where he sat upon the edge of his bed and looked long and thoughtfully at his trunk.

The rain beat furiously upon the window of his room; necessarily it was copious upon Penrod and the despondent

Herman, some forty feet beneath that window. Verman was lucky enough to obtain a measure of shelter; but suffered a misfortune, which caused him so greatly to distrust the doorway that he abandoned it definitely. A basket-ball team of hearty young men, all in high spirits and well equipped against the weather, came bursting forth from the building with such sudden gusto and liveliness that Verman, pressed too tightly against the door, found an almost infinitesimal portion of his person, together with a fold of his trousers, caught between the base of the door and the sill and acting as a wedge to prevent the door from opening readily; but, as the full force of the basket-ball team accumulated against this momentary resistance, the door flew open, and Verman, uttering a dolorous shout, sped before it. Seated, he passed to the middle of the splashing sidewalk, and in other postures proceeded as far as the street. Then, having risen, he did not pause, but started at once for home. He went hastily, yet in the attitude of one who nurses himself in affliction, and, upon being joined by Penrod and Herman, kept hurrying on his way, in spite of Penrod's every remonstrance. His attire was damaged, and he had been seriously pinched. With bitterness, he declined to return to his post—and resigned. Herman also resigned.

The next morning, not appearing at the agency, and being summoned (from the alley doors of the carriage-house) for the Report, the brothers came into the stable and resigned again.

"Well, listen, if you ever heard anybody talk like they hadn't got a grain o' sense!" Penrod exclaimed to Sam. Sam, having been detained at home the night before, was still loyal. "Looky here, Herman," the chief went on, turning to the former members, "I guess you got better sense than you act like. What you and Verman want to go and quit now for? Look: Not hardly two weeks ago—didn't you each get a dime, besides all that food Sam and I bought and let you eat as much of as we ate, ourselves?"

"Dime!" said Herman coldly. "We ain' got no mo' dime

now. Yes; an' whut come when we gone et all 'at b'loney sausage an' sody an' ev'y which an' whut? Done h'ist me so bad I ain' sca'cely et nuff'm sense but whut she like to h'ist me ag'in! Me an' Verman froo, I tell you!"

Penrod turned appealingly to Verman. "Well, if ole Herman *has* got to act like he hasn't got a grain o' sense, I bet good ole Verman isn't goin' back on Sam and me. Verman, *you* know what's good for you, don't you, Verman? Verman, *you're* goin' to keep on——"

"Mo!" Verman exclaimed immediately. "*Mo!*"

"Verman, he set on quittin' wuss'n I am," said Herman. "Mammy couldn' sca'cely fix him his pants so's he kin walk roun' nowhere; an' he got sech a pinch' place on him, she say she almos' go' feel sorry to lam' him fer nex' week er two. I don' keer ef ole Mis' Dade steal how many hosses, an' I don' keer ef he tuck an' run away wif fo' millyum house an' lots! I done walk my feet off shaddin', shaddin', all time shaddin', an' I done got soak' froo to my skin an' bones, an' nev' *see* nuff'm' 'mount to nuff'm' nohow. I done walk my feet off fer las' time, I tell you! *No,* suh; me an' Verman *quit!*"

It seemed to be final.

CHAPTER LXII

DISASTER

AFTER lunch, Sam and Penrod sat dispiritedly in the office, lacking heart to take up the chase or even to proceed with the day's Report. Before long, they drifted out into the yard, and thence to the sidewalk, saying little, for they began to feel that the great days of the agency were over, and gloomily they were wondering what they could find to take its place. The conduct of Herman and Verman appeared in a light purely hateful. Just when everything was going so well—and everything——

"Penrod! Penrod Schofield!"

From down the street came the lovely voice of Marjorie Jones, calling. She was running toward them, waving her arms eagerly and crying Penrod's name in excitement. The boys listlessly watched her approach.

"Penrod!" she gasped, as she reached them. She leaned against the fence, trying to recover her breath. "Oh, Penrod! Oh, my!"

"Well, what's the matter of you, Marjorie?"

"Papa!" she panted. "Pup-papa—Papa wants you to come to our house. He wants to see you before he goes back downtown to his office."

"What for?" Penrod asked, surprised.

"About—oh, my, I did run so fast! About—it's about that ole crook, Penrod!"

Penrod stared, incredulous. He felt suddenly uncomfortable, and a vague apprehension stirred within him.

"He wants you to come right away. It's all on account of because I told him all that stuff you told me. I told Papa all that stuff you told me——"

"What—what stuff?"

"About ole Dade, Penrod. I told Papa every bit you said, and what you think. Papa says you haf to come and *tell* him about it!"

"What you talkin' about, Marjorie? What you—what you talkin' so much about?"

"Why, about what you told me about that ole crook," Marjorie informed him cheerfully. "I told Papa all about that shadowin' and everything—and I told him how you found out this ole Dade was such a crook, and how you said he was goin' to get Papa to sign some ole papers and get his house an' lot, and maybe he'd kill Uncle Montgomery or maybe not—because you know you weren't sure about that part, Penrod—and, well, I told Papa everything about it."

"When?" Penrod asked, and a sudden chill played along his spine. "When did you tell him about it?"

"Just a little while ago, while we were having lunch. Papa was saying to Mamma he thought Mr. Dade was such a nice young man, and so they noticed I was makin' a face and asked me what for. Well, Mamma always scolds me for makin' faces, so you see I had to tell why I did it, and then was when I told Papa all about everything you said about ole Dade. When I told him you said your own father and mother told you he stole horses, Papa said they must of been joking or sumpthing, and he would ask your father about that, this evening, maybe; but first he told me to come and bring you over to our house right away, so you could tell him where you had heard all those other things about ole Dade's getting him to sign papers and everything. So hurry and come on, Penrod, 'cause he's waiting. You can come, too, Sam, if you want to."

"Me?" Sam looked at Penrod, who stood staring open-mouthed at Marjorie. "No," Sam said uneasily. "I guess I got to be gettin' along home pretty soon. I expeck I ought to go give John Carmichael a bath or sumpthing, proba'ly."

"Come on, Penrod," Marjorie urged. "Papa said he wanted you to come right away."

But an increasing perturbation had seized upon Penrod. "Right away?" he said, frowning. "I don't believe I ought to—anyhow not right away, Marjorie."

"What!" she cried indignantly. "When my Papa says——"

"Well, I guess I got to ast my mother first," Penrod interrupted, with a heat of conscience never before perceived in him by either of his present companions. "I can't go unless my mother *says* I can, I guess, can I?"

"Well run ast her," said Marjorie, somewhat taken aback but retaining her presence of mind. "I'll wait for you while you run and——"

"She might not be home," Penrod objected. "She might of gone out somewhere. I shouldn't be supprised if she went out to see an ole aunt o' mine that lives 'way out in the country. I guess that must be where she did go."

"She did not!" Marjorie asserted. "I saw her lookin' out of a window at us about two minutes ago. Hurry, Penrod! Run ast her, and I'll wait. Of course she'll let you if you tell her *Papa* wants you."

Penrod seemed to deliberate. "Well, looky here," he said slowly. "This is the best way we better fix it. You go on ahead, because I expeck you better hurry; and I'll go on upstairs and ast Mamma if I can go over to your house, and then if she says I can——"

"Why, of *course* she will!"

"Well, if she does, I'll hurry and run after you and prob-a'ly catch you before you get there. You better start right away, Marjorie."

She looked perplexed and a little troubled. "Well, why don't you go ast your mother—if you're going to, Penrod?"

"Well, I am." He walked toward the front door. "I'm goin' in just as soon as you start."

"Well——" Marjorie said irresolutely; but his suggestion seemed plausible—or perhaps she felt herself ill-equipped for further argument with him. At all events, she began to move toward home, at the same time looking back over her shoulder and making gestures to urge greater haste upon him. "Please, hurry!" she called. "I'll tell Papa you're comin' right away." Then she trotted off down the street obediently, with the sunshine dancing prettily through her undulating amber curls.

But Penrod, gazing after her, as he continued to move at a snail's pace toward the house, found little pleasure in this picture, and the expression of uneasiness upon the countenance of Master Williams had deepened, though, naturally, this uneasiness of Sam's was far less than that of his friend. For the moment, both boys were inarticulate; yet undoubtedly they shared in a common emotion, to which Sam finally gave a certain amount of expression. "Well, anyhow," he said plaintively, "I and Herman and Verman never did a single thing you didn't tell us to, Penrod."

The implications of this bit of self-defense were voluminous, so to speak, and fell upon Penrod heavily. Already, he began to look horrified; it might have been thought that he was not in the best of health. For the thing that a boy most shrinks from—that is, having his private affairs exposed, and himself involved in the mysteries of grown-up jurisprudence, where intentions go for nothing and all is incalculable and ominous—this thing, it seemed, was happening to him.

"Well——" he said, and, swallowing heavily, said nothing more.

"She's motioning to you to go on in and ask your mother," Sam said, still gazing down the street after Marjorie, and he added, with severity, "You better hurry and do it, too, because I guess the sooner you get there the better for you, Penrod!" He turned toward his own home, and, although his uneasiness remained upon him, he contrived to assume the air of a self-righteous person not involved in consequences probably about to descend upon people of questionable conduct. "I can't hang around here any longer," he said, as if in reply to a suggestion that caused him some indignation. "I guess John Carmichael's got a right to have a bath once this summer, anyway! Even a poor dog's got a right to expeck a little good treatment and not to haf to let his fleas eat him up alive!"

Virtuously, Sam quickened his pace to go upon this honourable errand, his attitude, as he went, eloquently expressing the conviction that whoever else might be in grave trouble he wasn't in any whatever, himself, and ought not to be.

Penrod went into the house.

A few minutes later, his mother stood at the foot of the attic stairway. "Penrod!" she called. "Penrod!"

There was silence. She mounted to the top of the stairway and looked about her. "Penrod!" she called again; then, listening intently, followed a very faint noise—the noise made by a button gently rubbing upon a board—and found her son unostentatiously crawling along the floor between some trunks and the wall. "Good gracious!" she cried. "I almost thought there was a burglar up here. What on earth are you doing?"

"I lost sumpthing," he said thickly.

"What was it?"

"Ma'am?"

"What are you looking for?"

"Well—it's a top."

"You couldn't have lost it up here. How absurd! If that isn't just like a boy—to come looking for a lost top in the attic! Get up, Penrod!"

"Ma'am?"

"Get up! You can't play up here; the heat's enough to give you a sunstroke. Get up at once and——" But as he obeyed her, rising to his feet, she uttered a cry of dismay. "Penrod! You're nothing but dust and cobwebs! It'll be a mercy if your clothes aren't ruined! Go down to the bathroom this minute and wash your face and hands in hot water. Then get a whisk-broom and a clothes-brush and come to me, and I'll see what can be done! Run!"

Penrod ran; at least, he made haste. At the bottom of the stairs, he turned in the direction of a bathroom but paused not at its door. Instead, he went down the back stairs, out through the kitchen to the back yard, thence to the woodshed. Hurriedly he climbed the side of the tall saw-dust box and disappeared from the sight of man and the light of day.

Two minutes later, he climbed out again, holding something concealed in his hand. Cautiously peering from the woodshed doorway, he reconnoitred the horizon, then ran to the cistern, near the back porch, removed the iron cover, and dropped within the orifice that small object he had held clenched in his fingers. There was a faint splash, and, sliding down beneath the surface of the brown water, a silvery streak descended—and vanished. It was the shield of Pvt. Detec. No. 103, belonging to Gray Bros. Ag'cy, and thus it disappeared forever—or at least until that cistern should be renovated.

Then the former George B. Jashber, now no more than a small boy pale beneath cobwebs and coatings of dust—

Penrod Schofield, in fact—scurried back to the woodshed and again hastily concealed himself in the sawdust box.

Calamity was upon him. On the instant when Marjorie spoke the words, "I told Papa every bit you said", prophetic fear had seized him. And as she so blithely went on with her artless narrative, she and the whole world became terrible to Penrod. He was sick.

His instinct was for flight; but flight through a town where he might anywhere encounter a policeman was impossible to consider. Therefore, he concealed himself. The sawdust box was his final refuge, and in it—having disposed of the incriminating badge—he burrowed beneath the surface of the sawdust, and heaped it over him as bathers by the sea pile sand upon themselves.

Having become, in the shock of Marjorie's revelation, only Penrod Schofield, with not one whit of George B. Jashber or No. 103 remaining, he had found his situation more desperate than any he had ever been in before. Lovely Marjorie, herself, had become dreadful to him; his inwards shuddered as he thought of her prattling out his imaginings to her father. For the stricken Penrod now saw those imaginings of his in a terrible light; they appeared as inexplicable lies that had brought about deadly results. He was unable to account for his conduct but could only review it fragmentarily and in agonized bewilderment. Only once did any palliating excuse come to his mind, and that but feebly. "Anyway Papa and Mamma both said he was a horse-thief, and I heard 'em say it." But Marjorie's father had said that this must have been spoken in jest, and Penrod now recognized the probable correctness of such an explanation. In fact, he had long since realized within himself the fallibility of the theory that Mr. Dade made any part of his living by stealing horses. After this, no alleviating thought whatever was able to enter his mind.

What would they do to him? He had visions of a frightful Dade, tall as a tree, coming in vengeance, accompanied by Mr. Paoli Jones, Mr. Montgomery Jones and august policemen. He pictured such a group looking over the side of the sawdust box and bellowing at sight of him. He burrowed deeper, squirming.

At a sound from the street, he started violently; and there was sufficient cause, for it was the sound of an automobile gong, recognizable instantly as that of an ambulance—or a police car. It sounded closer, and Penrod was unable to remain in suspense. Trembling all over, he climbed out of the sawdust box and gazed forth from the woodshed door, allowing only his hair, his forehead and his eyes to be visible from outside.

A violently red open car came into sight upon the street, gonging passionately, and he was but little relieved when it passed by and whizzed away into inaudibility without having drawn up at the curb to let Mr. Dade, Mr. Paoli Jones, Mr. Montgomery Jones and the Chief of Police descend to search for him.

He returned to the box and burrowed again. Time elapsed. It was a great hollow time of silence, hot as the Sunday after Judgment Day. Penrod was wet with perspiration, and sawdust was thick inside his collar and down his back, upon his eyelids and in his shoes, and he itched poignantly; but his other troubles were immeasurably greater.

From afar, muffled by the sawdust, came the call of Della: "Penrod! Musther Penrod! Penrod! Come in the house! Yer mother wants you to git washed fer dinner. Musther Penrod!"

Silence.

"You better come, Musther Pen-rod!" The kitchen door slammed; Della gave over.

Then, for another awful, hollow time, there was silence.

CHAPTER LXIII
PROTECTIVE COLORATION

MEANTIME, Samuel Williams sped the gilded hours
of the long summer afternoon by occupying himself in meritorious industry. He began this unusual procedure immediately after his self-defensive aban-
donment of Penrod; he requested a slight loan from his
brother, Robert, in order to make a purchase of "dog-soap"
at the grocery. Robert proved to be amiable in the matter,
produced the sum of money required but offered an oblique
comment.

"I didn't suppose anybody ever washed that sort of a
dog, Sam."

"What? Why, John Carmichael deserves washing just
as much as any dog does, and he needs it terribly. You can't

hardly lead him anywhere, because he spends all his time trying to sit down and scratch behind his ear. He's got so that's almost the only thing he thinks about, and you can't get him to pay attention to anything else. I'm goin' to give him the finest bath any dog ever got in his life!"

This promise appeared to be perhaps a little over-liberal; but later it seemed to Robert that Sam was being as good as his word. The bath lasted two hours, as Robert was able to observe from the library bay-window, which commanded a view of the back yard, and Robert, seated near this window, found his attention frequently wandering from his book to the elaborate ablutions of John Carmichael. Sam bathed John Carmichael first by turning upon him a lively stream from the garden-hose; then he soaped John Carmichael heavily with the "dog-soap" and turned the stream from the garden-hose upon him again, until the soap surely must have disappeared, no matter how strongly it clung. After that, John Carmichael was placed in a wash-tub full of hot water brought from the kitchen in buckets; here, he was lathered again and rinsed pure again. Then the garden-hose was used upon him yet another time; he was soaped, then sprayed, then replaced in the tub, re-soaped, re-rinsed and once more sprayed. Robert began to fear that John Carmichael would be entirely washed away, for the astonished and obviously plaintive pup, in his wetness, looked unnaturally slight; but the drying was as thorough as the bathing. Sam brought forth from the house several torn bath-towels, and, with a protracted vigour of rubbing, restored John to his usual size and a better than normal appearance. The pup's spirits revived brilliantly, and, released, he placed his nose upon the ground between his forepaws, showed the whites of his eyes in wanton mockery, growled jocosely, then, leaping up suddenly, tore round and round the yard in apparently ferocious pursuit of a hundred phantoms.

Robert laughed, observing these high caperings; then, as his eye fell upon what his young brother was doing, his mouth opened and he sat in amazement. Sam, with a conscientious expression, carefully rinsed out the wash-tub, lugged it back into the cellar whence he had brought it, and reappeared with a large mop. With this implement, he soothed away the water from the spot upon the brick walk where the bathing had taken place; but he did not stop there. Evidently he thought that all of this walk needed cleansing, for he followed it, mopping the bricks slowly and carefully until he came near the bay-window, when Robert, addressing him through a fly-screen, interrupted his labours.

"What's the matter, Sam?"

"Matter? Nothin'. Why?"

"All this industry," the older brother explained. "Mopping up the walk when nobody's told you to."

"Well, there's a good deal of dust blows in from the street on this walk, and I'm goin' to give it a good moppin' clear around to the front gate."

"Voluntarily, Sam?" Then Robert had an afterthought as a relief to his sheer incredulity. "I see. Probably somebody did tell you to do it."

"They did not!" Sam returned with indignation, and, in the same tone, he marvellously added, "I guess I like to feel I'm doin' some good in this world, don't I?"

"What!"

"I guess I'd like to be a little use once in a while before I die, wouldn't I?" Sam said, and he renewed his mopping with such honest vigour that he would have passed out of easy conversational distance if the astounded Robert had not again detained him.

"Sam, I've never seen anything like this before. Wait a minute! What have you been doing?"

Sam paused in his work to stare plaintively. "I been givin' my dog a bath and moppin' up our walk. Haven't you got any eyes?"

"Yes; that's what's puzzling me. You aren't looking for any special trouble when father comes home this evening —or anything like that, are you, Sam?"

"No, I am not!"

Robert's perplexity continued to be profound; but he tried a guess at random. "Nothing's gone wrong with that little matter we were talking about a couple of weeks ago, has it, Sam?" he asked, lowering his voice confidentially.

"What little matter?"

"You know. About Penrod Schofield's being a detective, and——"

"Penrod?" Sam interrupted, as if in surprise; but, even as he spoke, he looked away evasively and seemed to be interested in the upper branches of a young maple tree that grew flourishingly not far from the bay-window. "Penrod? I don't know anything much about Penrod and all that stuff you're talkin' about. I got my own business to 'tend to, so I don't know anything much about all that ole stuff."

"What!" his brother exclaimed. "Why Sam, you told me, yourself, that Penrod was *really* a detective!"

Sam continued to be interested in the top of the maple tree. "I b'lieve there's some ole bird or sumpthing got a nest up in the top of this tree," he said.

"Sam! Didn't you tell me that Penrod has a badge, and that——"

Sam allowed his gaze to descend from the supposititious bird's nest, and seemed to become interested in polishing the handle of the mop with a corner of his jacket. "I guess maybe he did have some ole badge or sumpthing; but I don't expeck it amounts to much. Maybe he kind of thought he was a detective—but just pretending, of course."

"But you said——"

"Me? Well, anyhow, if I kind of maybe did think so a little, it was just pretending, mostly, because he isn't one, and I guess he knows that much, himself. Anyhow, I guess he ought to by this time!" Sam spoke with cold severity, thus to detach himself still further from complications involving his friend. Moreover, he could not have explained, even to himself, how it happened that he had previously beiieved (at least to some extent) in the genuineness of Penrod's status as a detective, and now completely disbelieved that his comrade and leader had ever possessed any such official qualification. For Sam as well as for Penrod, Marjorie Jones's innocent communications had been shattering; from the moment when she had told them that her father spoke admiringly of Mr. Dade, and that her own unspeakable indiscretion in placing upon the adult plane George B. Jashber's revelations to her was causing Mr. Jones to begin actual grown-up investigations, the fiction that had seemed almost a reality to both boys instantly and hopelessly lost every vestige of substance. "I guess he hasn't got much sense," Sam added, speaking thus critically of his late chieftain. "But anyhow he ought to have enough to know that much."

To Robert, his small brother's tone seemed highly significant. "Is Penrod in trouble, Sam, about something or other?"

"Penrod? Not that I know.anything about."

"Ah—about that matter, Sam——" Robert hesitated, and his tone became more confidential. "Have you four boys been keeping up the 'shadowing' you told me about?"

"Me?" Sam said reproachfully. "Why, you know, yourself, Mamma wouldn't let me go out on account of the rain yesterday evening. I was right here in the house, and you know it as well as I do."

"Yes; but how about up to last night, Sam? How about when Mr. Dade has been at Mr. Schofield's in the evenings before last night? Haven't you all——"

"He hasn't been there," Sam said, with less caution. "He's only been there once since that Sunday afternoon you saw us and gave me fifty cents, and the next day you gave me a dollar more, but I had to give half of it to Penrod, and two dimes for Herman and Verman. That's about all you ever did give me, too," Sam added unnecessarily, "except on my birthday, maybe, or Christmas or sumpthing."

Robert disregarded this change of subject. "How do you

know?" he asked. "How do you know Mr. Dade only came once after that?"

"Because it was the very next night," Sam informed him. "He and Margaret went in the house; but they left the window open, and she was talkin' kind of cross; but anyway he didn't stay long, and that's the last time he's been there yet, because—because——"

"Because what?" Robert inquired, as Sam hesitated.

But Sam felt that he might betray too much knowledge of Mr. Dade's movements. Robert had proved himself to be sympathetic; nevertheless, Robert was an adult and therefore might at any time suddenly hold inexplicable and punitive views; so reticence became advisable. "I don't know," Sam said, frowning. "I got this walk to clean up, Bob; I can't stand around here talkin' all afternoon."

"Yes; but listen——"

"I got to get this walk cleaned up the right way," Sam said, and applied the mop with earnest industry. "I got too much to do to stand around jibber-jabberin' with everybody day in and day out!"

Rebuffed and full of wonderment, Robert watched his brother's amazing performance of the unbidden task. Sam mopped the walk thoroughly all the way round to the front gate; then, with incredible thoughtfulness, he restored the mop to the cellar, and, emerging, brought the garden-hose to the front yard and began a systematic sprinkling of the lawn. He was thus engaged when his father returned home for the evening, and, after receiving words of surprised commendation from both of his parents, he quietly mentioned the fact that he had given the full length of the brick walk a careful mopping, and added, to their increased mystification, that he liked to feel he was doing some good in this world.

At the dinner-table his expression was dignified and modest, though perhaps a little self-consciously upright; possibly he might have blushed had he been aware how continuously he was the object of his older brother's inquiring, if furtive, scrutiny. Mr. Robert Williams's puzzlement (to which was naturally added some elation) increased with the passing hour, and so did his conviction that mysterious calamity threatened the band of sleuths of which his brother had been a member and Margaret's brother the chief. And when, after dinner, Sam went quietly into the library and sat down meekly with a book he had frequently been urged to read, Robert perceived that the pointed questions he wished to ask would be of little avail; yet he could not forbear some comment.

"I thought you had a prejudice against 'Pilgrim's Progress', Sam."

Sam looked up reproachfully, though it was observable that with the tail of his eye he noted the effect upon his father and mother, who sat near by, looking at him seriously over sections of the evening newspaper. "Did you?" he said gently. "Well, anyhow, I'm reading it. I like to feel——"

"Yes, I know," Robert interrupted. "Of course you like to feel you're doing some good in this world, Sam."

Sam did not like his brother's tone, which seemed to suppress with difficulty emotions of hilarity; but, before an exemplary retort could be devised, the telephone bell rang. The instrument was in another room and Robert went to answer it. Margaret Schofield's voice responded to his "Hello!"

"It's Mr. Williams, isn't it?" Margaret inquired, and Robert replied truthfully yet deceitfully, for he deepened and muffled his voice as he spoke:

"Yes—Mr. Williams."

"Mr. Williams, this is Margaret Schofield. Is Penrod there?"

"No. He hasn't been here."

"He hasn't? Not at all?"

"No, not at all."

"He wasn't there for dinner? We haven't been able to find him and we supposed that he was probably playing with

Sam in the afternoon and stayed to dinner. I'm sorry to trouble you, but would you mind asking Sam if he knows where Penrod is?"

"Just a moment." Robert left the instrument and returned almost immediately to say, "Sam doesn't know. He says he hasn't seen Penrod since just after lunch. He says that Penrod went into the house to ask if he could go somewhere with little Marjorie Jones, and he doesn't know anything more about him."

"Thank you, Mr. Williams. Will you hold the wire just a moment longer, please!" Evidently Margaret engaged in a short conversation with other people near her; Robert heard several voices speaking simultaneously—a little urgently, too, though he could not distinguish what they said. Then she addressed him again: "Mr. Williams?"

"Yes; still here."

"If Sam isn't busy, do you suppose it would be too much trouble to ask him to come over here for a little while?"

"Not at all. I'll bring him, myself."

"Oh, no, you mustn't take all that trouble, Mr. Williams; but if Sam wouldn't mind coming——"

"Not at all. I'll bring him," Robert insisted, and, having clicked this interview to a close before Margaret could further protest, he returned to the library. "Hop up, Sam; they want you at Mr. Schofield's, and I'll go over there with you."

"Where?" Sam inquired sluggishly, not looking up from "Pilgrim's Progress".

"At Mr. Schofield's, I said. Come along!"

"What for?"

"I don't know. Probably because they can't find Penrod and think maybe you could help. Hop!"

Sam showed a strong disinclination to hop; he sank himself a little deeper in the luxurious armchair he occupied and increased his devout concentration upon "Pilgrim's Progress", his lips moving as he read.

"Sam!" Mrs. Williams said a little sharply. "You can

read some more when you get back; we'll be delighted to let you sit up a little later than usual this evening, since you're so interested in a fine book; but if Mr. and Mrs. Schofield want you to help find Penrod it isn't polite to keep them waiting. Go along with Robert immediately."

Upon this, Sam saw that there was no help for it; he must go. He mumbled objections as long as he could, made delays, moved with outrageous deliberation—he consumed actual minutes in restoring "Pilgrim's Progress" to its exactly proper place in the book-case—and finally went so far as to suggest that he ought to wash his face and hands before leaving; but, as he had previously made himself noticeably immaculate, this unprecedented idea aroused serious parental impatience.

"You go with Robert this instant!" his father said.

Sam went; but as he and Robert approached their destination, his reluctance became so extreme that the older brother thought it the part of wisdom to walk with his hand affectionately upon the younger's shoulder. Margaret, looking serious and with a colour already slightly heightened by recent episodes within the house, came to the door to admit them, and the sight of Robert obviously increased her embarrassment.

"Oh," she said blankly. "I thought it was Mr. Williams who——"

"It is," Robert returned with gravity. "I am Mr. Williams."

With that, and no more words upon the matter, he and his diffident charge followed her into the living-room, where sat in conclave apparently serious, Mr. and Mrs. Schofield, Mr. Paoli Jones and Marjorie. Beautiful little Marjorie occupied a sofa all to herself; she sat solemnly in the exact middle of it, and her lovely large eyes remained unmoved by the one side-glance she received from Sam as he came into the room.

CHAPTER LXIV

INQUISITION

THE seriousness of the conclave was not perceptibly
relaxed upon the entrance of the newcomers, although
they were greeted hospitably and the warmness of the
weather was mentioned, as they seated themselves in proffered chairs.

"We thought Sam might be able to help us out in one or
two little matters," Mr. Schofield then explained. "But first
we'd like to hear something more from him about where he
thinks Penrod is. Little Marjorie, here, says she's almost
sure that Sam knows."

Again Marjorie remained unmoved by the inscrutable
side-glance of Master Williams, which remained upon her
for a moment. "I bet he does," the lovely and terrible little

545

girl said, with the utmost coolness. "I bet he knows where Penrod is this very minute and everything about the whole biznuss, besides. You ast him if he doesn't."

"Sam," Mr. Schofield said, "perhaps you didn't take time to think when you sent the message over the telephone that you didn't know where Penrod is. Now that you've had more time, don't you believe you could tell us, if you tried to?"

Sam swallowed painfully and fixed his gaze upon the toe of his right shoe, which moved slowly in a pattern it seemed to be tracing upon the floor. "Sir?" he said inquiringly.

Mr. Schofield looked somewhat annoyed, but repeated his question, adding, "I have an idea that Marjorie's right about it and that if you tried hard you could tell us where he is."

Sam's expression had become vacuous. "You mean where Penrod is, Mr. Schofield?"

"Oh, dear me!" Mr. Schofield said. "Oh, dear me!"

Upon this, Marjorie volunteered a suggestion. "I bet he does know. I bet I know, myself. I bet he's out in that ole sawdust box he goes to."

But Mr. Schofield shook his head. "No. Della said he wasn't there. She climbed up and looked inside and said there wasn't anything there except sawdust. Yet we're positive that he must be somewhere in the neighbourhood; we're not at all uneasy about him, because he's sometimes absented himself like this before, when he's been in—ah—in difficulties, so to speak. He'll turn up after a while, of course; but the point is, we'd like to see him right now. You're sure you don't know anything about him, Sam?"

Here Robert felt that a slight intervention in Sam's behalf might serve to advance matters. "I doubt if Sam's in a position to know much about Penrod's present whereabouts, Mr. Schofield. Sam's been unusually busy at home all afternoon, as I can testify, myself. Perhaps, though," Robert added cheerfully, "there's something else you'd like him to enlighten you about?"

It was Mr. Jones, however, who took up this suggestion.

"Yes," he said. "There is, indeed! As Marjorie has mentioned, Sam probably knows all about it, and in Penrod's absence it might be well for us to obtain the information from him. But as I imagine you're quite in the dark, yourself, Robert, as to what we're talking about, perhaps I'd better explain a little first, so that you'll understand. It concerns a gentleman who came to town before you returned home from college, I think. Perhaps you happened to meet him—a Mr. Herbert Hamilton Dade?"

"Dade?" Robert said inquiringly, and seemed to consider. "Dade. Ah—I think that I may have met him. At least I remember seeing him."

"Then you probably noticed that he was a very nice-looking young man," Mr. Jones said. "In fact, I'd call him quite a fine-looking young man. He came here with the idea that he would possibly settle down and go into business in our city, Robert, and he brought letters of introduction to me and to my brother, Montgomery. Perhaps you don't remember dear old Dr. Behring—he was the pastor of our church for many years but left here to accept a call from a church in Gosport, Illinois, about a decade ago—well, among the letters Mr. Dade brought was one from Dr. Behring. It was a most laudatory letter; Mr. Dade had been the Superintendent of Dr. Behring's Sunday-school for two years before leaving Gosport, and Dr. Behring testified in warm words to the young man's exemplary character. I must say that in every way Mr. Dade seemed to me to live up to the reputation Dr. Behring gave him. It's seldom, indeed, that one sees a young man of such good looks who so thoroughly appears to merit the extreme praise of a man like Dr. Behring, don't you think so, Mrs. Schofield?"

"Yes, indeed," she replied, with a glance at her husband, who looked a little embarrassed. "Go on, Mr. Jones, please, so that Robert will understand."

Mr. Jones obeyed. "I just wanted to be a little emphatic about the testimonial letter and the manner in which Mr. Dade seemed to me to live up to it. He took up his residence at the Y. M. C. A.; he joined our Sunday-school as a teacher, and everywhere, so far as I can learn, made the most excellent impression. As to his business, he had plans for forming a new insurance company and wished to interest my brother, Montgomery, and me in the project. In fact, we were interested and had begun to take the matter up with Mr. Dade quite seriously. Lately, however, both my brother and I noticed that the young man seemed to have grown curiously jumpy and nervous; it was obvious to us that he was becoming upset over something, and he appeared to be losing interest in the insurance business. Once or twice he spoke of possibly moving on to some other city with his project, and only a few days ago he surprised me in the middle of a quiet talk by jumping up and going to my office window in quite an excited way, and then breaking out at me, as if I'd annoyed him, and saying, 'My goodness! I can organize an insurance company in any other town just as well as I can here!' Of course I began to think then that he might decide to leave town; but I must say I didn't anticipate anything quite so abrupt as this." Mr. Jones paused to draw from an inner pocket a letter. "I'll read it to you, Robert, although the others have already heard it. It is simply Mr. Dade's farewell upon leaving town."

"Upon leaving town?" Robert repeated, and, with an effort almost visible, kept his gaze fixed upon Mr. Jones. "You—you mean Mr. Dade has left town—ah—permanently!"

"Permanently," Mr. Jones replied. "He writes as follows: 'I am returning to Gosport upon an early morning train and have concluded to remain there at home, where there will probably be little difficulty in forming the company in which I have endeavoured to interest you and your brother, though of course the field is somewhat smaller. I take this step advisedly, having considered it for some time past. The climate of your city does not agree very well with my constitution, and although I have been most warmly welcomed here in many cordial circles, I believe the social advantages are nevertheless in favour of Gosport, and of course in selecting a permanent residence, such a consideration must be given due weight. Also, my health must naturally receive the first consideration, and in view of this city's unfavourable climatic situation I do not feel that I should defer my departure any longer. Thanking you for many courtesies and your appreciative consideration of the Reverend Doctor Behring's opinion of my character, I remain', etcetera, etcetera." Mr. Jones looked up from the reading. "A very remarkable letter," he observed gravely.

"Is it?" Robert asked, in a deferential tone. "I don't seem to see why—not exactly. He explains that the climate —and—the social conditions——"

"I mean it's remarkable under the circumstances, Robert," Mr. Jones explained. "That's what I've been coming to. At lunch to-day I was speaking regretfully to my wife of Mr. Dade's departure and happened to say what a nice young man he appeared to be, when we noticed that Marjorie was making unpleasant faces, and then, when we reproved her, she told us the most extraordinary story. She said Mr. Dade wasn't nice; he was a bad man—a terribly bad man. When we questioned her she said that Penrod had told her Mr. Dade stole horses. Of course we laughed; but she insisted that Penrod had heard both his mother and father declaring that Mr. Dade stole horses. Well, we've just been talking about that, and Mr. Schofield can't recall any such conversation; but Mrs. Schofield dimly remembers that she and Mr. Schofield made some jocular allusions once upon a time to horse-thieves having good manners in connection with the notably polished manners of Mr. Herbert Hamilton Dade, and she thinks Penrod may possibly have overheard them and taken the allusions literally. But this isn't the gist of the matter; it doesn't explain the rest of it. Penrod told Marjorie he had absolute information that Mr. Dade swindled people by getting them to sign papers; he told her Mr. Dade intended to get my brother,

Montgomery, and me to 'sign papers' which would ruin us. Now, for one thing, in view of the fact that my brother and I would actually have signed quite a number of papers, if we'd concluded to join Mr. Dade in his insurance project, we couldn't help wondering if Penrod had somewhere heard some absurd rumour that ought to be stopped before it went any further."

"I should think that unlikely," Robert said judicially. "At least I haven't, myself, happened to hear of any grown-up rumour or libel attaching to Mr. Dade's undeniably excellent character. I should think it unlikely, sir."

"Yes, possibly," Mr. Jones returned. "But there's something else that has considerably mystified us, and it would be a satisfaction to get at the roots of the whole affair. Here's a sample of what's been happening: one day last week, Montgomery and Mr. Dade were walking along the street together, and Mr. Dade gave a perceptible start and uttered exclamations under his breath. It was broad daylight; the streets were full of people, and my brother naturally asked what was the matter. Mr. Dade was plainly excited and took my brother by the arm. 'Do you see that small, tongue-tied negro boy?' he asked. My brother looked around. 'I see a little negro boy; but I don't know whether he's tongue-tied or not,' he said. 'Well, he is,' Mr. Dade told him, almost angrily. 'He is tongue-tied!' That's all he would say about it; he insisted upon changing the subject, and Montgomery thought the incident very odd, indeed."

"It seems so," Robert said. "Go on, Mr. Jones."

"I will. You see, we seem to have a clue to a possible explanation, and that's what we want to get at. Marjorie says Penrod told her he was 'after' the wicked Mr. Dade and was 'shadowing' him. She tells us that he often plays with two small coloured boys and that one of them is tongue-tied, so you see the suggestion, don't you, that appears to indicate a possible explanation of that bit of nervousness on the part of the young man—perhaps an explanation of more of his nervousness, besides? You see, Robert?"

"Well—in a way," Robert replied slowly. "Yes—in a way."

"It's all quite a mysterious business," Mr. Jones said. "It seems to me we ought to account for it if we can, and, since Penrod is temporarily missing, I thought that Sam, being his most intimate friend and usually mixed up in everything with him, might shed some light."

"I should think that might be entirely possible," Robert agreed. "What about it, Sam?"

Sam was still engaged in making patterns upon the floor with the toe of his shoe. "Me?" he said vaguely. "What about?"

" 'What about'?" Robert returned, with some sharpness. "Why about what Mr. Jones has been talking about!"

"Oh!" Sam said, with the air of a polite person somewhat bored by information in which he has no personal concern. The little company waited; but he said nothing further.

"Now, Sam——" Robert began; but Mrs. Schofield intervened.

"Let me try," she said pleasantly. "Sam, I'm sure you won't mind answering some questions from me, will you?"

"No, ma'am."

"Well, then, you heard everything that Mr. Jones ha⸱ been telling us, and we want you to say just what you knov⸱ about it. You'll surely do that for *me*, won't you, Sam?"

"Yes, ma'am."

"Well, then, what *do* you know about it, Sam?"

"Ma'am?"

"Here, let me!" Mr. Schofield interposed impatiently. "Sam, you heard what Mr. Jones said about a little tongue-tied coloured boy, didn't you?"

"Yes, sir."

"Very good! Now we intend to get at this whole business; but first we want you to tell us what you know about that little tongue-tied coloured boy's making Mr. Dade nervous by following him. Speak up!"

Sam decided that it would be better for him not to say "Sir?" A slight frown appeared upon his brow, as though he engaged himself in thought; then he inquired: "Which little tongue-tied coloured boy do you mean, sir?"

"Good heavens! I mean the one that——" Mr. Schofield began, but paused to pass a handkerchief over his exasperated brow; then he turned to Robert. "Here! He's your brother. Can't you get anything out of him?"

"I think so," Robert said, and, in a sharply business-like tone, took up the investigation. "See here, Sam! This shilly-shallying is only making matters worse and can't do you a particle of good. Everybody here understands that the little tongue-tied coloured boy didn't do whatever he did to poor Mr. Dade of his own volition. That is to say, he didn't invent it, himself. Little Marjorie says that you and Penrod and those two coloured boys from the alley—and we all know that one of them is tongue-tied—she says you were all engaged in an inexcusable performance that became very bothersome to this poor Mr. Dade. Now we all know that, Sam, and, as I said, it isn't doing you any good to evade our questions. You know perfectly well that you and Penrod and the two coloured boys from the alley were pretending that you were detectives and 'shadowing' poor Mr. Dade. There isn't a bit of good in your not admitting it."

"I didn't do anything," Sam returned plaintively. "I didn't have a thing to do with getting it up. I was away at Uncle Henry's farm when a good deal of it happened. I couldn't help what happened while I wasn't even in this ole town, could I?"

"Ah! Now we're getting somewhere!" Robert said, stating a fact that he was shortly to regret; then he increased the severity of his tone. "You admit, Sam, that you four boys were pretending that poor Mr. Dade was a criminal, and that you were——"

But here Robert proved incautious; for the moment, he had forgotten something important, of which he was now reminded, to his far from imperceptible confusion. "*You*

said it was every bit all right," the badgered Sam interrupted suddenly. "You gave us a dollar and seventy cents
for doing it!"

"What!" Three people, Mr. and Mrs. Schofield and Mr.
Jones, uttered the word almost simultaneously, and Mar-
garet leaned forward to ask, "What? What did you say,
Sam?"

"He did!" Sam declared vehemently, roused to active defense by his resentment of Robert's outrageous double-
dealing. "He gave me two quarters, first, to tell him about
it, and after that, he gave me half-a-dollar and half-a-dollar
for Penrod and two dimes for——"

"Never mind, Sam," Robert interrupted hastily; but the
suffusion of colour upon his cheeks made his face almost
painfully conspicuous, as he spoke. With some difficulty he
produced a poor imitation of the conventional murmur of
laughter usually employed to indicate that the matter being mentioned is of negligible importance. "Perhaps I should
explain that at the time Sam is speaking of what the boys
were doing appeared to be merely a little game among
themselves and—ah—perfectly harmless, of course."

"Indeed?" Miss Margaret Schofield inquired, with evident interest. "Perfectly harmless?"

"Ah——" he began; but he neither met her inquiring
gaze nor found anything more to say, and an embarrassing
silence fell upon the room.

Mr. Paoli Jones, however, being a humane person, relieved the tension by coughing, and then by a return to the
previous subject. "Perhaps we might get on a little better
if we followed another lead," he suggested. "I mean if we
could determine conclusively the identity of the little
tongued-tied coloured boy——"

But once more it was proven that coincidences abound at
critical moments in the lives of all who conduct criminal investigations, and a peculiarly striking one took place at
this instant and while Mr. Paoli Jones still had the phrase
"little tongue-tied coloured boy" upon his lips. The windows

were open, and upon the aromatic zephyrs of the July evening was borne an eerie and giggling cry in a unique African voice.

Mrs. Schofield started. "Listen!" she whispered huskily.

From a distance of about forty feet, the strange cry came distinctly. "Oh Mihhuh Habe im air? Wop he boo mow, Pemwob?"

It was unfortunate for Penrod that Verman felt this renewal of interest in the whereabouts and conduct of the official ex-criminal of the dismembered agency. Penrod had emerged to the surface, necessarily, as soon as Della stopped looking over the top of the sawdust box; under cover of darkness he had abandoned that refuge, and, for the past hour, seated upon the ground beneath one of the living-room windows, he had listened anxiously to the conversation within. Verman, with idle time upon his hands, for the first time in many evenings, had gone forth for a stroll, and, glancing over the fence, had happened to espy the dark figure under the window. Then, having nothing better to do, he climbed upon the fence and sat there. Amused, and not being aware that the agency was now wholly obsolete, he had been so ill-inspired as to put the inquiry that had startled the company indoors. his intended words being simply: "Old Mr. Dade in there? What he do now, Penrod?"

Penrod made imperative gestures for him to withdraw, then sprang up and, alarmed by something he heard from within the living-room, would himself have withdrawn; but he was too late. Mr. Schofield, easily recognizing the significance of the vocative, "Pemwob", had dashed out through the front door, turned the corner of the house, and the fugitive was almost instantly seized in a powerful and irritated grasp. One minute later, when, in custody, he was haled into the presence of the conclave, his mother uttered a shrill cry of lamentation. In spite of all his woody immersions, fragments of the attic cobwebs still remained upon him, and he shed a trail of sawdust across the living-room floor, as he was sternly urged forward. What he expected to happen to him, at this juncture, is unknown; his expression was impenetrable; but there is no doubt whatever that the substitution of him as the centre of interest brought grateful relief to both of the brothers Williams.

"Never mind his looks!" Mr. Schofield said sharply to Mrs. Schofield. "That can be attended to later—and so can a few other things!" he added. "Later when I take him upstairs——"

But Mr. Paoli Jones, as he had already proved, was a man of humane impulses, and he could not look at Penrod without having those impulses stirred. "No, no," he said, protesting. "I really didn't mean to get either Sam Williams or Penrod into any trouble; I only wanted to satisfy my own mind a little about what's been happening, and I think that has become rather clear. In fact, it seems to me that what Robert said about it's all having been merely a harmless game was especially significant." Here Mr. Jones laughed and looked genially, not at Robert, but at Margaret Schofield, upon which she straightened and seemed a little indignant. "It appears to be fairly evident," Mr. Jones went on, "that Penrod and Sam and the two coloured boys were merely playing at 'shadowing', and that they felt they had to pick out someone to be 'shadowed', and of course this person had to be supposed to be in the habit of committing crimes. I think I see now that this explanation covers everything Penrod told Marjorie, and that he was only carrying on the game and never dreamed she would repeat what he said as serious information. In fact, I don't believe there's anything serious at all in the whole matter; quite probably Mr. Dade might have gone back to Gosport anyhow; in his letter he speaks of the 'social advantages' Gosport possesses, compared to this city, and in that respect he may have suffered some little disappointment or other here. That's quite possible—quite possible, in spite of the fact of his good looks and excellent conduct. But there is one thing that puzzles me and that I'd like to have solved. In fact, there's a question I'd very much like to have Penrod answer."

"He'll answer it," Mr. Schofield promised grimly. "I'll see to that!"

"Well, then," Mr. Jones said, addressing Penrod, "I'd like to know why it was that when you picked out a person to be 'after', as you told Marjorie, Penrod—that is, when you selected a criminal to 'shadow', how in the world did it happen that you selected a young man of such unexceptional and exemplary character as Mr. Dade?"

"Sir?"

"Why on earth did you select such a good young man as Mr. Dade to be your criminal?"

Penrod swallowed, and moved uneasily, causing a little shower of sawdust to fall upon the floor about him. "Well ——" he mumbled, and stopped.

"You speak up!" his father said, in a tone recognizably ominous. "You answer Mr. Jones's question! What made you pick out Mr. Dade?"

"Yes, Penrod," Mr. Jones urged, rising to go. "Why did you?"

Penrod breathed deeply; he had not an idea in his head. "Well——" he said at last, desperately. "Well—he acted so in love of my sister Margaret, I thought there must be sumpthing wrong with him."

Mr. Jones stared at him strangely, seeming unwilling to trust himself to speak; there was a sound like the sputter of laughter, half-choked and a little hysterical, from the corner to which Robert Williams had modestly retired; then Margaret, after the briefest and coldest glance in that direction, rose and went haughtily out to the verandah.

"I think we must say good-night," Mr. Jones said in a tremulous voice, during this progress. "Come, Marjorie." His face had grown red, and, in passing Mr. Schofield, who likewise had become flushed, he paused to say in a low tone, with a glance toward Penrod, "I hope you won't——"

But it was Mrs. Schofield who replied to this merciful

plea. She, too, displayed a heightened colour, and she spoke indistinctly through a handkerchief held to her mouth. "No," she said, shaking her head, "he won't."

Then, as the departing guests moved on toward the outer door, Mr. and Mrs. Schofield hospitably accompanying them, the little group was passed by Robert Williams on his way to the verandah, and Penrod and Sam were left alone together in the living-room. Somehow, they realized an impending darkness had lightened; a vague doom inexplicably incurred had as inexplicably been avoided. Neither understood what sin he had committed or not committed; neither understood why punishment was commuted. Definitely they had only the sense of a vast escape.

Sam, again making patterns upon the floor, seemed to be preoccupied with the moving toe of his shoe, while Penrod shook down a little more sawdust and stood gazing at it gloomily. They said nothing whatever.

CHAPTER LXV

NEW STARS ARISE

THE midsummer morning was languid with its own warmth; the Schofields' back yard lay aglow in mellow sunshine, and Penrod and Sam stood enthralled, staring at a magnificent creature they had discovered upon the stalk of a lush bush in the fence corner. It might have been a pixie's concertina, painted dusty green and ornamented with brilliant pool balls from a pixie pool-table; but to Penrod and Sam it was known as a "tobacco-worm" —the largest and fattest they had ever seen. The two boys stared in silence for a long time; finally, Penrod spoke in a hushed voice.

"I wonder what he's thinkin' about." And in fact, it was reasonable to suppose the motionless creature lost in reverie.

"Thinkin' about how fat he is, maybe," Sam suggested.

"I bet you don't know which end his head is," said Penrod, his tone somewhat implying that this wagered bit of ignorance was one of Sam's many inferiorities.

"I bet you don't, either."

"Well, whoever said I did?" Penrod retorted crossly.

"Well, did *I* say *I* did?"

"Well, whoever said you did say you did?"

Sam looked annoyed and also somewhat confused. "Well, you said," he began, "you said I didn't know which end his head is, and I——"

"Well, you *don't* know which end his head is."

"Well, you don't, either."

"Well, whoever said I did?"

"Well, *I* didn't say *I*——"

"Well, whoever said you did say you did?"

"Look here——" Sam began; but paused, bewildered by that feeling of having done the same thing before, which inclines people, sometimes, to believe in the theory of reincarnation.

A movement on the part of the green creature distracted the attention of both boys, momentarily, from their incipient feud.

"Look!" Penrod cried. "He's movin'!"

"Climbin' up the bush," Sam observed. "That shows which end his head is on: it's on top."

"It doesn't have to be on top just because he's climbin' up the bush," Penrod returned scornfully. "I guess he could back up, just as well as climb up, couldn't he?"

"Well, he wouldn't," Sam argued. "What would he want to back up for, when he could just as easy climb up? His head's on top of him, and that proves it."

"It doesn't either prove it. Where's his face? The only way you can prove where his head is, is where his face is, isn't it?"

"No, it isn't!" Sam cried hotly. "He hasn't got any face; and, besides, his top end looks just as much like his face as his bottom end. You can't tell the difference. Anyway, anybody with good sense would know his head's on top of him. He wouldn't *want* to have it any place else, would he?"

"How do *you* know what he'd want?" Penrod demanded. "He might want it some place else just as well as not."

"Well, what for?" Sam asked irritably. "What on earth would he want it some place else *for?*"

"What for?" Penrod was sure of a coming triumph in the debate. "You don't know what for?"

"No, I don't, and you don't either!"

"Oh, I don't, don't I?"

"No, you *don't!*" Sam shouted.

Penrod laughed pityingly. "Bet you I can prove it."

"Well, prove it then."

"Well, look here. Suppose sumpthing was *after* him: he'd want to have his face on his bottom end so's he could keep watchin' out to see if it was comin' after him up the stalk, wouldn't he? *That* proves it, I guess!"

It did—so far as Sam Williams was concerned. Sam was overwhelmed; he had nothing to say, and Penrod was not disposed to make his triumph an easy one for the vanquished. "Well," he jeered. "I guess that shows how much you know about *worms!*"

Sam had the grace to admit a fair defeat. "Maybe I don't," he said, with manly humbleness; "—about tobaccoworms. I don't suppose I ever saw more'n five or six in my life." He dug the ground with the toe of his shoe, despondently, then brightened, all at once, with the advent of a recollection. "I bet I know sumpthing about grasshoppers that you don't."

"I bet you don't."

"Well, I can prove it."

"Go ahead and prove it!"

"I bet you don't know grasshoppers chew tobacco."

At this, Penrod yelled in derision.

"They do, too!" Sam asserted indignantly.

Penrod laughed, gesticulated, danced and bellowed. He was outrageous.

"You wait!" Sam began to browse in the grass, searching, while his friend, in order to express a poignant incredulity, threw himself full-length beneath the bush; rolled on his stomach, squealed insults, beat the ground with his hands and wriggled his feet in the air.

"Grasshoppers chew tobacco!" howled Penrod. "Grasshoppers chew tobacco! Grasshop—oh, ho, ho, ho!"

"Here," said Sam, bringing a grasshopper for his inspection. "You watch him, now." He gave the grasshopper a command, squeezed him slightly about the middle, and proved the case absolutely. "Look there!" he cried, flourishing the exhibit upon his thumbnail. "*Now*, say grasshoppers don't chew tobacco!"

Penrod was beside himself but not (as would have been proper) with confusion: ecstasy was his emotion—and there followed a bad quarter-of-an-hour for the grasshoppers in that portion of the yard.

"Pshaw!" said Sam. "I've known grasshoppers chewed tobacco ever since I was five years old."

"You never *said* anything about it!" Penrod exclaimed, marvelling at such reticence. It seemed to him, just now, that he would never know another instant of ennui so long as he lived—at least, not in grasshopper-time.

"I thought pretty near everybody knew grasshoppers chewed tobacco," Sam said modestly. "You told me I didn't know much about worms, and I said I bet I knew sumpthing about grasshoppers you didn't know—but I kind of thought you did, though."

"What else can they do?" Penrod's tone indicated that a sincere deference was no more than Sam's due in all matters concerning grasshoppers.

"Nothin'. That's all they're good for."

"Where d'you s'pose they get their tobacco in the first place? Hop around stores, you guess?"

"Yes; lots of other places."

The experiment had been repeated *ad nauseam* until all the available grasshoppers were in no condition immediately to pursue their bad habits—or their good ones, for that matter—and Penrod paused to seek further knowledge at its recent fountain-head. "Sam, do you know anything else?" he inquired hopefully.

"Yes, I do!" replied Master Williams with justified resentment.

"I mean," Penrod explained, "I mean: Do you know anything else I don't know?"

"Oh!" Sam was mollified at once. "Well, I guess prob-a'ly I do," he said thoughtfully. "Lemme see. Oh, yes! I bet you don't know if you put a black hair from a horse's tail in a bottle and put water in it, and leave it there for three weeks, it'll turn into a snake."

"I do, too!" said Penrod. "I knew *that*, ever since I was little."

"I bet you haven't known it any longer'n I have. I knew it when I was little, too."

"Everybody knows a black hair from a horse's tail will turn into a snake," Penrod declared. "Who doesn't know *that?*"

"Well, I never said they didn't, did I?"

"Well, who said you did say——" Penrod paused, a sudden light in his eyes. "Sam, did you ever *try* it?"

"No," said Sam thoughtfully. "I guess when I heard it we didn't have any horse, and I was too little to get one from any other people's horse—or sumpthing."

Penrod jumped up eagerly. "Well, we aren't too little now!" he shouted.

"*Yay!*" This jubilant outcry from Sam demonstrated what reciprocal fires of enthusiasm were kindled in his bosom on the instant. "Where's a horse?"

Simultaneously their eyes fell upon what they sought. In the side street stood a grocer's wagon, and the grocer had just gone into the kitchen. Attached to the wagon was an elderly bay horse. Attached to the elderly bay horse was a black tail. The prospective snake manufacturers drew near the raw material.

The elderly bay horse switched his black tail at a fly, a gesture unfortunate for Penrod, upon whose eager countenance it culminated. "Oof!" He jumped back, sputtering; and the horse looked round inquiringly; then, seeing boys, assumed an expression of implacable fury.

"Go on," Sam urged. "Pull 'em out. Two's enough."

Penrod rubbed his face and looked thoughtful. "I wonder if they wouldn't do just as well from his mane," he said.

"No, sir! They got to be from his tail. I know *that* much!"

Penrod glanced uneasily at the horse's horizontal ears. "You pull 'em, Sam," he suggested, edging away. "I'll go and be gettin' the bottles ready to put 'em in. I——"

"No, sir!" Sam insisted. "You started to pull 'em and you ought to do it. I didn't start to pull 'em, did I?"

"Now, see here!" Penrod became argumentative. "You don't know where to find any bottles, and——"

"You better quit talkin' so much," Sam interrupted doggedly. "Go ahead and pull those two hairs out of his ole tail or pretty soon the man'll come out and drive him away—and then where'll we be? You started to do it, and so it's your biznuss to. Go ahead and do it, and don't talk so much about it. That's the way to do a thing."

"Well, I am goin' to, ain't I?"

"*Now!*" Sam exclaimed. "He's quit lookin' at us. Quick!"

Seizing this opportunity, Penrod ventured the deed and was rewarded. The elderly horse seemed to have forgotten his animosity; his mood had become one of depression merely; he hung his head, and marked the ravishment by nothing more than a slight shudder. "There!" said Penrod; and, as they went back into the yard, he glanced disdainfully at the gloomy quadruped. "It's easy to get hairs out of a horse's tail for a person that knows the right way to do it. I bet I could of pulled his whole tail out!"

But this was only a thought in passing, and the atten-

tion and energies of both boys were now devoted to the preliminaries of their great experiment. The largest empty bottles obtainable were selected, cleaned and filled with fair
water. Then, with befitting solicitude, the two long black
hairs were lowered into the water, and the bottles were
corked. After that, a label was pasted upon each, exhibiting
the owner's name and address. The fascinating work was not
complete, however; Penrod paid a visit to the kitchen clock,
and, after some severe exercises in computation, the following note was inscribed in precise duplicate upon the labels:

"Hair from Jacop R. Krish and Cos horse tail put in sixteen minutes of evelen oclock July 11 Snake comes sixteen
minutes of evelen oclock July 32."

They set the bottles, side by side, upon an empty box in
the former office of George B. Jashber; stood before them;
gazed upon them.

"Don't you wish they'd turn right now?" Penrod said
yearningly. "I don't see why it's got to be three weeks."

"Well, it has."

"I know that; but I wish it didn't *haf* to be. Well, anyway, three weeks from now we'll be lookin' at our good ole
snakes, all right!"

"Three weeks from now!" Sam echoed, with luscious anticipation. "Yes, sir! *Oh*, oh!"

"What'll we feed 'em?"

"I don't know. Suppose they'll want to come out of the
bottles?"

"You bet they will! I'm goin' to train mine to follow me
all around the yard. When school begins maybe I'll take
him with me in my pocket."

"*Oh*, oh!" cried Sam. "So'll I."

They shouted with joy of the picture.

"I wouldn't take a million dollars for mine!" said Penrod.

"Neither would I!" said Sam. "I wouldn't take two million!"

"Neither would I!"

Then, fascinated, Penrod sat down upon the stable floor close to the box upon which stood the precious bottles, and Sam likewise sat, each gazing earnestly upon his own bottle and its slender occupant. Thus they remained for some time, silently engaged in who can say what paternal speculations; minute bubbles had already appeared upon the submerged hairs, and, to a gaze long fixed, faint stirrings and movements seemed almost perceptible; or, at least, such first tokens of transformation were easily imaginable.

"Sam, I believe mine's begun to breathe already," Penrod whispered.

"Sh!" Sam warned him, and so concentrated was the attention of Master Williams that he did not move when a heavy breath disturbed the short hair on the nape of his slender neck just above the collar. A moment later, however, as the same spot was affectionately caressed by something that felt like a banana peeling that had been dipped in warm water, he decided that too great a liberty was being taken with him. "You go away from here!" he hissed fiercely.

Without resentment, Walter-John returned to the doorway of the stable, which he had just entered, accompanied by a congenial friend, and for some moments the two communed inaudibly through the nose. Then Walter-John yawned inoffensively, although the action was taken in Duke's very face, which was close enough to be almost involved within the cavern; after that, both dogs moved drowsily away from the rhomboid of hot sunshine near the doorway and sought the cooling shade of the interior. Duke stretched himself, then reclined upon his back, and Walter-John, approaching, let himself down awkwardly, and for his heavy head confidingly used the older and much smaller dog's stomach as a pillow. This, Duke found inconvenient, even annoyingly burdensome; he complained crossly, removed himself and lay elsewhere, while Walter-John looked at him reproachfully with one eye, then closed it and slept with his chin upon the floor.

At the sound of Duke's brief vocal complaint, Sam said "Sh!" again, after which the fascinated silence where the miracle worked within the stable obediently became complete; but there were noises outside that grew louder, and before long were too disturbing to be overlooked. In the alley Herman and Verman were playing vociferously with a rubber ball, and, not content with shouting almost continuously, they presently began to throw the ball against the doors of the carriage-house, evidently to catch it upon the rebound.

"My goodness!" Penrod said indignantly. "Haven't they got *any* sense?" And finding the thumping of the ball unendurable, he went to the carriage-house doors, threw them open and shouted angrily: "My goodness! Don't you know anything at *all!*"

Surprised, Herman and Verman came to the doorway. "Whut you mad fer?" Herman inquired mildly. "Whut all goin' on you git so mad, Penrod?"

"Never mind," Penrod said coldly. "We got sumpthing on our hands here we don't want any ole ball bangin' and whangin' up against these doors!"

"Whut all you got goin' on you ack so big, Penrod?"

"Never mind!"

But Verman had already entered the stable, and Herman followed, urged by a natural curiosity, which both Penrod and Sam plainly found annoying. "My goodness!" Sam exclaimed. "What do you haf to come hangin' around here now for, makin' all this noise? Why can't you take your ole ball up the alley and play where we don't haf to listen to you? Haven't you got sense enough to know how to tell when we're busy?"

To be the more impressive, he frowned heavily as he spoke, and the severity of his expression evidently interested Verman. "Wop he mek fafe fo?" the smaller brother inquired of the larger.

"Verman want to know why you makin' faces," Herman

translated, chuckling. "You look so mad Verman think you tryin' to make him laugh."

Upon this, Sam frowned so heavily that Verman did laugh; delighted, he pointed at Sam's face and also at Penrod's, for Penrod was frowning as darkly. Verman squealed hilariously, and then, sobering somewhat, he gave utterance to a thought that deepened the annoyance of the two white boys by its seeming sheer irrelevancy. "Oo dum kef oh Mihhuh Habe yip?"

"He want to know ef you done ketch ole Dade yit," the faithful interpreter explained.

"Oh, my goodness!" Penrod said, and Sam said the same thing almost simultaneously. The two looked at each other, expressing in the glance their mutual hopelessness of so low an intelligence as that just displayed before them. Almost two weeks had elapsed since the hot day spent by Penrod in the sawdust box, principally, and by Sam in laudable, self-imposed tasks; for both of the friends mists of time had intervened, and all the affairs of the agency were dim with remoteness, almost lost over the horizon of the long, long ago. George B. Jashber was as extinct as last year's first day of school. "Oh, my goodness!" Penrod exclaimed again, turning upon Verman. "Don't you know anything at *all?* Why, Mr. Dade doesn't even live in this town any more!"

But Verman received this scornful information without any emotion; he was not interested, for he had observed the two bottles upon the box before which the annoyed Sam still continued to sit. "Wop ap?"

He stretched forth a small brown hand toward Sam's bottle; but, before the shining glass could be violated by this ignorant touch, Sam pushed him away, and said angrily, "You get back! For heavenses' sakes, can't you keep away from here? If you dare to stick your ole hand near this bottle, I'll——"

But Verman was already giggling again, and Herman, too, seemed to be highly amused, so that their united laughter drowned out the sound of Sam's voice. "Makem hake!" Verman squealed, jumping up and down and clapping the pinks of his hands together. "Makem hake! Makem hake!"

"Cert'nly, we're makin' snakes!" Penrod shouted fiercely. "And you quit makin' all that noise in here. You think we want our good ole snakes ruined by everybody comin' in here and yelling and everything? You think our snakes are goin' to begin turnin' with all this noise and——"

"Noise ain' go' hurt no snakes," Herman interrupted, abating his laughter but little. "Ain' go' be no snakes. You cain' make no snakes less'n you put hoss hairs in a bottle an' nev' look at 'em. You put hoss hair in a bottle an' nev' look once fer th'ee weeks you go' to git a snake. You ev' take one peep at hoss hair, snake done spoil'; ain' go' be no snake in nem bottles—nuff'm 'cep' hoss-tail hair."

"What!" Penrod shouted, and his attitude became so threatening that Herman retreated from him, protesting, though with continued laughter. "You get out o' here!" Penrod bellowed. "You get on out o' here! You don't know anything in this world, and you come round here tryin' to ruin these good ole snakes——"

"Lemme 'lone, whi' boy!" Herman begged, sputtering, as he moved toward the alley door. "I ain' done nuff'm to you. All I do, I dess say hoss-tail hair ain' go' turn into no snake ef you look at——"

"You get out o' here!" Penrod shouted, and he seemed to look about him for weapons or something to throw, where-upon, their merriment increasing, both Herman and Ver-man fled lightly with noiseless feet. Their voices, however, could still be heard as they sped down the alley, and the penetrating, silvery giggle of Verman came through the air for some little time longer to four ears reddened by irritation.

Penrod closed the alley doors, returned to the box and again sat down near Sam. "Never did have any sense," he muttered, alluding to the mirthful fugitives, and he added morosely, "Think they know so much!"

"Yes," Sam assented, in like mood. "Why, if I didn't know any more about snakes than Herman does, I'd sell out! I would; I'd sell out my whole biznuss and move away! He just said that to be smart, and because he and Verman haven't got any horse-tail hair, themselves—nor any good bottles to put 'em in, if they did have, proba'ly—and want to behave like they know everything on earth. Nobody that ever lived ever heard anything about not lookin' at 'em, so that proves it." His manner became argumentative. "Because, look here, Penrod—listen, Penrod—just lookin' at anything at all doesn't do anything to it. F'r instance, you could look all day at a tadpole and that wouldn't stop him from changin' into a frog, and you know that as well as I do; but you take Herman and he'd tell you if you had a tadpole and wanted him to change to a frog, you couldn't ever look at him or else he wouldn't."

"Yes, that's exackly what that ole Herman would say," Penrod agreed. "He wouldn't know any more about frogs than he would about snakes, because, listen, Sam: How could you put a horse-tail hair in the bottle, in the first place, without ever lookin' at it? I guess that proves he doesn't know anything he's talkin' about, doesn't it?"

" 'Course it does!" Sam said, well pleased. "Coloured people don't know anything, anyway."

To this prejudiced view of an amiable and interesting race, Penrod, in his present mood, offered no objection; instead, he frowned, pursed his lips and, so far as he was able, assumed an air of maturity and importance. "They don't know anything about anything," he said, in this manner. "I heard my father say, himself, that they're nothing but a mash of stuperstition."

"What?" Sam asked deferentially.

But Penrod felt it better to let well enough alone and not to attempt the phrase again. "I heard Papa say it, myself," he said. "I guess that settles how much Herman knows about snakes, doesn't it?"

"It cert'nly does," Sam agreed, and then for a time they sat in silence, content in the faith that the matter was settled and Herman's unfounded and almost malicious criticism well answered. In the expression of each, as he gazed upon his own bottle's occupant, there was something like tenderness, a hint of the resentful fondness felt by one who has championed, defended and perhaps saved a helpless, loyal dependent. Minutes had elapsed when Sam uttered a muffled but excited exclamation. "Look, Penrod!" he whispered. "There's a new bubble come right at the top end of mine, where his face is goin' to be, because mine's goin' to have his face——"

"Sh!" Penrod interrupted sternly, but without removing his gaze from his own bottle. "Can't you keep still? Sh!"

Duke and Walter-John, disturbed by the arrival of Herman and Verman, had moved out into the yard; but now, returning, they disposed themselves for slumber upon the stable floor at a little distance from their masters, and again Duke, forgetting to what burden he exposed himself, lay partially upon his back. Walter-John almost immediately seized the opportunity to employ the elderly dog's delicate stomach as a pillow, and Duke, too drowsy to move, uttered a few low and threatening complaints, for which he was angrily reproved in a husky whisper.

"You stop that!" Penrod thus commanded over his shoulder. "My goodness!"

Sam also looked round; upon which, Walter-John, without materially altering his posture, thought fit to wag his tail; but it was a tail already of some weight, and its wagging made a thumping upon the stable floor.

"You quit that!" Sam whispered ferociously. "My goodness!"

Walter-John, unreproachful and obedient, at once lay motionless, and Duke, though almost painfully incommoded by the other's naïve selfishness, was now too sleepy either to change his position or to make any further protest. A complete silence fell upon that place. Penrod and Sam, fascinated, sat gazing intently, each at his own hair from the tail of Jacob R. Krish and Company's horse.

From time to time, Duke, not otherwise moving, half opened one eye to let a glance of devotion rest momentarily upon Penrod. Similarly, Walter-John sometimes partly opened an eye to look affectionately at Sam.

CHAPTER LXVI

TWELVE

THIS busy globe that spawns us is as incapable of flattery and as intent upon its own affair, whatever that is, as a gyroscope; it keeps steadily whirling along its lawful track, and, thus far seeming to hold a right of way, spins doggedly on, with no perceptible diminution of speed to mark the most gigantic human events—it did not pause to pant and recuperate even when what seemed to Penrod its principal purpose was accomplished, and an enormous shadow, vanishing westward over its surface, marked the dawn of his twelfth birthday anniversary.

To be twelve is an attainment worth the struggle. A boy, just twelve, is like a Frenchman just elected to the Academy.

Distinction and honour wait upon him. Younger boys show deference to a person of twelve: his experience is guaranteed, his judgment, therefore, mellow; consequently, his influence is profound. Eleven is not quite satisfactory: it is only an approach. Eleven has the disadvantage of six, of nineteen, of forty-four, and of sixty-nine. But, like twelve, seven is an honourable age, and the ambition to attain it is laudable. People look forward to being seven. Similarly, twenty is worthy, and so, arbitrarily, is twenty-one; forty-five has great solidity; seventy is most commendable and each year thereafter an increasing honour. Thirteen is embarrassed by the beginnings of a new colthood; the child becomes a youth. But twelve is the very top of boyhood.

Dressing, that morning, Penrod felt that the world was changed from the world of yesterday. For one thing, he seemed to own more of it; this day was *his* day. And it was a day worth owning; the mid-summer sunshine, pouring gold through his window, came from a cool sky, and a breeze moved pleasantly in his hair as he leaned from the sill to watch the tribe of clattering blackbirds take wing, following their leader from the trees in the yard to the day's work in the open country. The blackbirds were his, as the sunshine and the breeze were his, for they all belonged to the day that was his birthday and therefore most surely his. Pride suffused him: he was twelve!

His father and his mother and Margaret seemed to understand the difference between to-day and yesterday. They were at the table when he descended, and they gave him a greeting that of itself marked the milestone. Habitually, his entrance into a room where his elders sat brought a cloud of apprehension: they were prone to look up in pathetic expectancy, as if their thought was, "What new awfulness is he going to start *now?*" But this morning they laughed; his mother rose and kissed him twelve times, so did Margaret; and his father shouted, "Well, well! How's the *man?*"

Then his mother gave him a Bible and "The Vicar of Wakefield"; Margaret gave him a pair of silver-mounted hair brushes; and his father gave him a "Pocket Atlas" and a small compass.

"And now, Penrod," his mother said, after breakfast, "I'm going to take you out in the country to pay your birthday respects to Aunt Sarah Crim."

Aunt Sarah Crim, Penrod's great-aunt, was his oldest living relative. She was ninety, and when Mrs. Schofield and Penrod alighted from a carriage at her gate they found her using a rake in the garden.

"I'm glad you brought him," she said, desisting from labour. "Jinny's baking a cake I'm going to send for his birthday party. Bring him in the house. I've got something for him."

She led the way to her "sitting-room", which had a pleasant smell, unlike any other smell, and, opening the drawer of a shining old what-not, took therefrom a boy's "slingshot" made of a forked stick, two strips of rubber and a bit of leather.

"This isn't for you," she said, placing it in Penrod's eager hand. "No. It would break all to pieces the first time you tried to shoot it, because it is thirty-five years old. I want to send it back to your father. I think it's time. You give it to him from me, and tell him I say I believe I can trust him with it now. I took it away from him thirty-five years ago, one day after he'd killed my best hen with it, accidentally, and broken a glass pitcher on the back porch with it—accidentally. He doesn't look like a person who's ever done things of that sort, and I suppose he's forgotten it so well that he believes he never *did*, but if you give it to him from me I think he'll remember. You look like him, Penrod. He was anything but a handsome boy."

After this final bit of reminiscence—probably designed to be repeated to Mr. Schofield—she disappeared in the direction of the kitchen, and returned with a pitcher of lemonade and a blue china dish sweetly freighted with flat ginger cookies of a composition that was her own secret. Then, having set this collation before her guests, she presented Pen-

rod with a superb, intricate and very modern machine of
destructive capacities almost limitless. She called it a pocket-
knife.

"I suppose you'll do something horrible with it," she said,
composedly. "I hear you do that with everything, anyhow,
so you might as well do it with this, and have more fun out
of it. They tell me you're the Worst Boy in Town."

"Oh, Aunt Sarah!" Mrs. Schofield lifted a protesting
hand.

"Nonsense!" said Mrs. Crim.

"But on his birthday!"

"That's the time to say it. Penrod, aren't you the Worst
Boy in Town?"

Penrod, gazing fondly upon his knife and eating cookies
rapidly, answered as a matter of course, and absently,
"Yes'm."

"Certainly!" said Mrs. Crim. "Once you accept a thing
about yourself as established and settled, it's all right. Nobody minds. Boys are just like people, really."

"No, no!" Mrs. Schofield cried involuntarily.

"Yes, they are," Aunt Sarah returned. "Only they're not
quite so awful, because they haven't learned to cover themselves all over with little pretenses. When Penrod grows up
he'll be just the same as he is now, except that whenever he
does what he wants to do he'll tell himself and other people
a little story about it to make his reason for doing it seem
creditable."

"No, I won't!" said Penrod suddenly.

"There's one cookie left," Aunt Sarah observed. "Are
you going to eat it?"

"Well," her great-nephew returned, thoughtfully, "I
guess I better."

"Why?" the old lady asked. "Why do you guess you'd
'better'?"

"Well," said Penrod, with a full mouth, "it might get all
dried up if nobody took it, and get thrown out and wasted."

"You're beginning finely," Mrs. Crim remarked. "A year

ago you'd have taken the cookie without this virtuous display of thrift."

"Ma'am?"

"Nothing. I see that you're twelve years old, that's all. There are more cookies, Penrod." She went away, returning with a fresh supply and the prophecy, "Of course, you'll be sick before the day's over; you might as well get a good start."

Mrs. Schofield looked thoughtful. "Aunt Sarah," she ventured, "don't you really think we improve as we get older?"

"Meaning," said the old lady, "that Penrod hasn't much chance to escape the penitentiary if he doesn't? Well, we do learn to restrain ourselves in some things; and there are people who really want some one else to take the last cookie, though they aren't very common. But it's all right, the world seems to be getting on." She gazed whimsically upon her great-nephew and added, "Of course, when you watch a boy and think about him, it doesn't seem to be getting on very fast."

Penrod moved uneasily in his chair; he was conscious that he was her topic but unable to make out whether or not her observations were complimentary; he inclined to think they were not. Mrs. Crim settled the question for him.

"I suppose Penrod is regarded as the neighbourhood curse?"

"Oh, no," Mrs. Schofield cried. "He——"

"I dare say the neighbours are right," the old lady continued placidly. "He's had to repeat the history of the race and go through all the stages from the primordial to barbarism. You don't expect boys to be civilized, do you?"

"Well, I——"

"You might as well expect eggs to crow. No; you've got to take boys as they are, and learn to know them as they are."

"Naturally, Aunt Sarah," Mrs. Schofield said, "I *know* Penrod."

Aunt Sarah laughed heartily. "Do you think his father knows him, too?"

"Of course, men are different," Mrs. Schofield returned, apologetically. "But a mother knows——"

"Penrod," Aunt Sarah said, solemnly, "does your father understand you?"

"Ma'am?"

"About as much as he'd understand Sitting Bull!" she laughed. "And I'll tell you what your mother thinks you are, Penrod. Her real belief is that you're a novice in a convent."

"Ma'am?"

"Aunt Sarah!"

"I know she thinks that, because whenever you don't behave like a novice she's disappointed in you. And your father really believes that you're a decorous, well-trained young business man, and whenever you don't live up to that standard you get on his nerves and he thinks you need a walloping. I'm sure a day very seldom passes without their both saying they don't know what on earth to do with you. Does punishment do you any good, Penrod?"

"Ma'am?"

"Go on and finish the lemonade; there's about a glassful left. Oh, take it, take it; and don't say why! Of *course* you're a little pig."

Penrod laughed gratefully, his eyes fixed upon her over the rim of his uptilted glass.

"Fill yourself up uncomfortably," said the old lady. "You're twelve years old, and you ought to be happy—if you aren't anything else. It's taken over nineteen hundred years of Christianity and some hundreds of thousands of years of other things to produce you, and there you sit!"

"Ma'am?"

"It'll be your turn to muss things up for the betterment of posterity, soon enough," said Aunt Sarah Crim. "Drink your lemonade!"

CHAPTER LXVII

FANCHON

"AUNT SARAH'S a funny old lady," Penrod observed,
on the way back to the town. "What's she want me to
give Papa this old sling for? Last thing she said was
to be sure not to forget to give it to him. *He* don't want it;
and she said, herself, it ain't any good. She's older than
you or Papa, isn't she?"

"About fifty years older," Mrs. Schofield answered, turning upon him a stare of perplexity. "Don't cut into the
leather with your new knife, dear; the livery man might
ask us to pay if—— No, I wouldn't scrape the paint off,
either—nor whittle your shoe with it. *Couldn't* you put it
up until we get home?"

"We goin' straight home?"

"No. We're going to stop at Mrs. Gelbraith's and ask a strange little girl to come to your party this afternoon."

"Who?"

"Her name is Fanchon. She's Mrs. Gelbraith's little niece."

"What makes her so queer?"

"I didn't say she's queer."

"You said——"

"No; I mean that she is a stranger. She lives in New York and has come to visit here."

"What's she live in New York for?"

"Because her parents live there. You must be very nice to her, Penrod; she has been very carefully brought up. Besides, she doesn't know the children here, and you must help to keep her from feeling lonely at your party."

"Yes'm."

When they reached Mrs. Gelbraith's, Penrod sat patiently humped upon a gilt chair during the lengthy exchange of greetings between his mother and Mrs. Gelbraith. That is one of the things a boy must learn to bear: when his mother meets a compeer there is always a long and dreary wait for him, while the two appear to be using strange symbols of speech, talking for the greater part, it seems to him, simultaneously, and employing a wholly incomprehensible system of emphasis at other times not in vogue. Penrod twisted his legs, his cap and his nose.

"Here she is!" Mrs. Gelbraith cried, unexpectedly, and a dark-haired, demure person entered the room wearing a look of gracious social expectancy. In years she was eleven, in manner about sixty-five, and evidently had lived much at court. She performed a curtsey in acknowledgment of Mrs. Schofield's greeting, and bestowed her hand upon Penrod, who had entertained no hope of such an honour, showed his surprise that it should come to him, and was plainly unable to decide what to do about it.

"Fanchon, dear," Mrs. Gelbraith said, "take Penrod out in the yard for a while, and play."

"Let go the little girl's hand, Penrod," Mrs. Schofield laughed, as the children turned toward the door.

Penrod hastily dropped the small hand, and exclaiming, with simple honesty, "Why, *I* don't want it!" followed Fanchon out into the sunshiny yard, where they came to a halt and surveyed each other.

Penrod stared awkardly at Fanchon, no other occupation suggesting itself to him, while Fanchon, with the utmost coolness, made a very thorough visual examination of Penrod, favouring him with an estimating scrutiny that lasted until he literally wiggled. Finally, she spoke.

"Where do you buy your haberdashery?" she asked.

"What?"

"Where do you buy your haberdashery? Papa gets his at Skoone's. You ought to get yours there. I'm sure the tie you're wearing isn't from Skoone's."

"Skoone's?" Penrod repeated. "Skoone's?"

This girl seemed to be talking; but her words were puzzling. It was his first meeting with one of those grown-up little girls produced by the winter apartment and the summer hotel. He began to feel resentful.

"I suppose," she went on, "I'll find everything here fearfully Western. Some nice people called yesterday, though. Do you know the Magsworth Bittses? Auntie says they're charming. Will Roddy be at your party?"

"I guess he will," Penrod returned, finding this intelligible. "The mutt!"

"Really!" Fanchon exclaimed airily. "You *are* an odd child!"

It was too much.

"Oh, Bugs!" said Penrod.

This bit of ruffianism had a curious effect. Fanchon looked upon him with sudden favour.

"I like you, Penrod!" she said, and, whatever else there may have been in her manner, there certainly was no shyness.

"Oh, Bugs!" This repetition may have lacked gallantry;

but it was uttered in no very decided tone. Penrod was shaken.

"Yes, I do!" She stepped closer to him, smiling. "Your hair is ever so pretty."

Sailors' parrots swear like mariners, they say; and gay mothers ought to realize that all children are imitative, for, as the precocious Fanchon leaned toward Penrod, the manner in which she looked into his eyes might have made a thoughtful observer wonder where she had learned her pretty ways.

Penrod was even more confused than he had been by her previous mysteries; but his confusion was pleasant: he wanted more of it. Looking intentionally into another person's eyes is an act unknown to childhood; and Penrod's discovery that it could be done was sensational. He had never thought of looking into the eyes of Marjorie Jones.

Despite all anguish, contumely, tar and Maurice Levy, he still secretly thought of Marjorie, with pathetic constancy, as his "beau"—though that is not how he would have spelled it. Marjorie was beautiful; her curls were long and the colour of amber; her nose was straight and her freckles were honest; she was much prettier than this accomplished visitor. But beauty is not all.

"I do!" breathed Fanchon, softly.

She seemed to him a fairy creature from some rosier world than this. So humble is the human heart, it glorifies and makes glamorous almost any poor thing that says to it: "I like you!"

Penrod was enslaved. He swallowed, coughed, scratched the back of his neck, and said, disjointedly:

"Well—I don't care—if you want to. I just as soon."

"We'll dance together," said Fanchon, "at your party."

"I guess so. I just as soon."

"Don't you want to, Penrod?"

"Well, I'm willin' to."

"No. Say you *want* to!"

"Well——"

He used his toe as a gimlet, boring into the ground; his wide open eyes stared with intense vacancy at a button on his sleeve. His mother appeared upon the porch in departure, calling farewells over her shoulder to Mrs. Gelbraith, who stood in the doorway.

"Say it!" whispered Fanchon.

"Well, I just as *soon*."

She seemed satisfied.

CHAPTER LXVIII

THE BIRTHDAY PARTY

A DANCING floor had been laid upon a platform in the yard, when Mrs. Schofield and her son arrived at their own abode; and a white and scarlet striped canopy was in process of erection overhead, to shelter the dancers from the sun. Workmen were busy everywhere under the direction of Margaret, and the smitten heart of Penrod began to beat rapidly. All this was for him; he was Twelve!

After lunch, he underwent an elaborate toilette and murmured not. For the first time in his life he knew the wish to be sand-papered, waxed and polished to the highest possible degree. And when the operation was over, he stood before the mirror in new bloom, feeling encouraged to hope that his resemblance to his father was not so strong as Aunt Sarah seemed to think.

The white gloves upon his hands had a pleasant smell, he found; and, as he came down the stairs, he had great content in the twinkling of his new dancing slippers. He stepped twice on each step, the better to enjoy their effect and at the same time he deeply inhaled the odour of the gloves. In spite of everything, Penrod had his social capacities. Already it is to be perceived that there were in him the makings of a cotillion leader.

Then came from the yard a sound of tuning instruments, squeak of fiddle, croon of 'cello, a falling triangle ringing and tinkling to the floor; and he turned pale.

Chosen guests began to arrive, while Penrod, suffering from stage-fright and perspiration, stood beside his mother, in the "drawing-room", to receive them. He greeted unfamiliar acquaintances and intimate fellow-criminals with the same frigidity, murmuring: "'M glad to see y'," to all alike, largely increasing the embarrassment that always prevails at the beginning of children's festivities. His unnatural pomp and circumstance had so thoroughly upset him, in truth, that Marjorie Jones received a distinct shock, now to be related. Doctor Thrope, the kind old clergyman who had baptized Penrod, came in for a moment to congratulate the boy, and had just moved away when it was Marjorie's turn, in the line of children, to speak to Penrod. She gave him what she considered a forgiving look, and, because of the occasion, addressed him in a perfectly courteous manner.

"I wish you many happy returns of the day, Penrod."

"Thank you, sir!" he returned, following Dr. Thrope with a glassy stare in which there was absolutely no recognition of Marjorie. Then he greeted Maurice Levy, who was next to Marjorie: "'M glad to see y'!"

Dumfounded, Marjorie turned aside, and stood near, observing Penrod with gravity. It was the first great surprise of her life. Customarily, she had seemed to place his character somewhere between that of the professional rioter and that of the orang-outang: nevertheless, her manner at times just hinted a consciousness that this Caliban was her property. Wherefore, she stared at him incredulously as his head bobbed up and down, in the dancing-school bow, greeting his guests. Then she heard an adult voice, near her, exclaim:

"What an exquisite child!"

Marjorie glanced up—a little consciously, though she was used to it. It was Sam Williams's mother addressing Mrs. Bassett, both being present to help Mrs. Schofield make the festivities festive.

"Exquisite!"

Here was a second surprise for Marjorie: they were not looking at her. They were looking with beaming approval at a girl she had never seen; a dark and modish stranger of singularly composed and yet modest aspect. Her downcast eyes, becoming in one thus entering a crowded room, were all that produced the effect of modesty, counteracting something about her that might have seemed too assured. She was very slender, very dainty, and her apparel was disheartening to the other girls; it was of a knowing picturesqueness wholly unfamiliar to them. There was a delicate trace of powder upon the lobe of Fanchon's left ear, and the outlines of her eyelids, if very closely scrutinized, would have revealed successful experimentation with a burnt match.

Marjorie's lovely eyes dilated: she learned the meaning of hatred at first sight. Observing the stranger with instinctive suspicion, all at once she seemed, to herself, awkward. Poor Marjorie underwent the experience that hearty, healthy, little girls and big girls undergo at one time or another—from heels to head she felt herself, somehow, too *thick*.

Fanchon leaned close to Penrod and whispered in his ear:

"Don't you forget!"

Penrod blushed.

Marjorie saw the blush. Her lovely eyes opened even wider, and in them there began to grow a light. It was the light of indignation;—at least, people whose eyes glow with that light always call it indignation.

Roderick Magsworth Bitts, Junior, approached Fanchon, when she had made her curtsey to Mrs. Schofield. Fanchon whispered in Roderick's ear also.

"Your hair *is* pretty, Roddy! Don't forget what you said yesterday!"

Roderick likewise blushed.

Maurice Levy, captivated by the newcomer's appearance, pressed close to Roderick.

"Give us an intaduction, Roddy?"

Roddy being either reluctant or unable to perform the rite, Fanchon took matters into her own hands, and was presently favourably impressed with Maurice, receiving the information that his tie had been brought to him by his papa from Skoone's, whereupon she privately informed him that she liked wavy hair, and arranged to dance with him. Fanchon also thought sandy hair attractive, Sam Williams discovered, a few minutes later, and so catholic was her taste that a ring of boys encircled her before the musicians in the yard struck up their thrilling march, and Mrs. Schofield brought Penrod to escort the lady from out-of-town to the dancing pavilion.

Headed by this pair, the children sought partners and paraded solemnly out of the front door and round a corner of the house. There they found the gay marquee; the small orchestra seated on the lawn at one side of it, and a punch bowl of lemonade inviting attention, under a tree. Decorously the small couples stepped upon the platform, one after another, and began to dance.

"It's not much like a children's party in our day," Mrs. Williams said to Penrod's mother. "We'd have been playing 'Quaker-meeting', 'Clap-in, Clap-out' or 'Going to Jerusalem', I suppose."

"Yes, or 'Post-office' and 'Drop-the-handkerchief'," said Mrs. Schofield. "Things change so quickly. Imagine asking little Fanchon Gelbraith to play 'London Bridge'! Penrod seems to be dancing with her very nicely, though he wasn't a shining light in the dancing class."

Penrod himself thought he was dancing nicely; that is, he thought so until in the course of his duties as host (duties of which his mother from time to time reminded him) he came to dance with Marjorie Jones. The afternoon was waning; he had conscientiously danced with almost all of the little girls and four or five times with Fanchon. Marjorie accepted his offer expressionlessly; but, after some moments of exercise, she made a little outcry of pain.

"Oh, dear! Why can't you learn to dance like the other boys? You just step on everybody!"

"I don't either!"

"You do too!"

"I don't either!"

"You ought to be ashamed!" she said. "Here it is, just about time to go home and your party nearly all over and you still go around stepping on everybody!" They stopped dancing and stared at each other insultingly. "You ought to be ashamed!"

"I ought not. You ought to be ashamed, yourself! Talking like that!"

"You be quiet!"

"I will not!" Penrod said, so furious that he did not even notice Fanchon and some other little girls, who were trying to make their farewells and tell him they'd had "a wonerfle time" at his party; he had forgotten Fanchon. All he wanted was to make Marjorie ashamed of talking like that. "You be quiet yourself!" he shouted at her, though his departing guests now so pressed upon him that all he could see of her was an amber arc over intervening heads. "You ought to be ashamed, yourself! Talking like that! You ought to be——"

But by this time she was gone entirely, and it was not until the last guest had departed that he recovered his composure. Even then he murmured reminiscently, "Talking like that on my birthday!" as he found himself alone with a remnant of lemonade in the punch bowl, and disposed of it.

CHAPTER LXIX

OVER THE FENCE

PENROD was out in the yard. The sun was on the horizon line, far behind the back fence, and a western window of the house blazed in gold unbearable to the eye: Penrod's birthday was nearly over. He sighed, and took from the inside pocket of his new jacket the "slingshot" Aunt Sarah Crim had given him that morning.

He snapped the rubbers absently. They held fast; and his next impulse was entirely irresistible. He found a shapely stone, fitted it to the leather, and drew back the ancient catapult for a shot. A sparrow hopped upon a branch between him and the house, and he aimed at the sparrow; but the reflection from the dazzling window struck in his eyes as he loosed the leather.

He missed the sparrow, but not the window. There was

a loud crash, and to his horror he caught a glimpse of his father, stricken in mid-shaving, ducking a shower of broken glass, glittering razor flourishing wildly. Words crashed with the glass, stentorian words, fragmentary but colossal.

Penrod stood petrified, a broken sling in his hand. He could hear his parent's booming descent of the back stairs, instant and furious; and then, red-hot above white lather, Mr. Schofield burst out of the kitchen door and hurtled forth upon his son.

"What do you mean?" he demanded, shaking Penrod by the shoulder. "Ten minutes ago I happened to be saying to your mother—almost the first time in my life—that you were a fine, well-behaved boy, and here you go and throw a rock at me through the window when I'm shaving for dinner!"

"I didn't!" Penrod quavered. "I was shooting at a sparrow, and the sun got in my eyes, and the sling broke——"

"What sling?"

"This'n."

"Where'd you get that devilish thing? Don't you know I've forbidden you a thousand times——"

"It ain't mine," said Penrod. "It's yours."

"What?"

"Yes, sir," the boy said meekly. "Aunt Sarah Crim gave it to me this morning and told me to give it back to you. She said she took it away from you thirty-five years ago. You killed her hen, she said. She told me some more to tell you, but I've forgotten."

"Oh!" said Mr. Schofield.

He took the broken sling in his hand, looked at it long and thoughtfully—and he looked longer, and quite as thoughtfully, at Penrod. Then he turned away, and walked toward the house.

"I'm sorry, Papa," said Penrod.

Mr. Schofield coughed, and, as he reached the door, called back, but without turning his head. "Never mind, little boy. A broken window isn't much harm."

When he had gone in, Penrod wandered down the yard to the back fence, climbed upon it, and sat in reverie there.

A slight figure could be seen, likewise upon a fence, beyond two neighbouring yards.

"Yay, Penrod!" called comrade Sam Williams.

"Yay!" Penrod returned mechanically.

"Well, so long!" Sam shouted, dropping from his fence; and the friendly voice came then, more faintly, "Many happy returns of the day, Penrod!"

And now, a plaintive little whine sounded from below Penrod's feet, and, looking down, he saw that Duke, his wistful, old scraggly dog, sat in the grass, gazing seekingly up at him.

The last shaft of sunshine of that day fell graciously and like a blessing upon the boy sitting on the fence. Years afterward, a quiet sunset would recall to him sometimes the gentle evening of his twelfth birthday, and bring him the picture of his boy self, sitting in rosy light upon the fence, gazing pensively down upon his wistful, scraggly, little old dog, Duke. But something else, surpassing, he would remember of that hour, for, in the side street, close by, a pink skirt flickered from behind a shade tree to the shelter of the fence, there was a gleam of amber curls, and Penrod started, as something like a tiny white wing fluttered by his head, and there came to his ears the sound of a light laugh and of light footsteps departing, the laughter tremulous, the footsteps fleet.

In the grass, between Duke's forepaws, there lay a white note, folded in the shape of a cocked hat, and the sun sent forth a final amazing glory as Penrod opened it and read:

"Your my Bow."

THE END